SIX SUSPECTS

Also by Vikas Swarup

Slumdog Millionaire

SIX SUSPECTS

VIKAS SWARUP

Minotaur Books
New York

This is a work of fiction. All of the characters, organizations, and events portrayed in this novel are either products of the author's imagination or are used fictitiously.

A THOMAS DUNNE BOOK FOR MINOTAUR BOOKS.
An imprint of St. Martin's Publishing Group.

Though the author, Vikas Swarup, works for the Indian Government, none of the opinions in this novel are to be construed as reflecting in any way the view of the Government of India or of the author in his official capacity.

www.thomasdunnebooks.com
www.minotaurbooks.com

Library of Congress Cataloging-in-Publication Data

Swarup, Vikas.
Six suspects / Vikas Swarup. — 1st U.S. ed.
p. cm.
ISBN-13: 978-0-312-60503-2
ISBN-10: 0-312-60503-X
1. Rich people—Crimes against—India—Fiction. 2. India—Fiction. I. Title.
PR9499.4.S93S59 2009
823.92—dc22

2009012467

First published in Great Britain by Doubleday, an imprint of Transworld Publishers

First U.S. Edition: July 2009

10 9 8 7 6 5 4 3 2 1

For Aparna

Contents

SOLUTION

CONFESSION

MURDER

'Murder, like all art, generates interpretation and resists explanation.'

Michelle de Kretser, *The Hamilton Case*

The Bare Truth

Arun Advani's column, 25 March

SIX GUNS AND A MURDER

Not all deaths are equal. There's a caste system even in murder. The stabbing of an impoverished rickshaw-puller is nothing more than a statistic, buried in the inside pages of the newspaper. But the murder of a celebrity instantly becomes headline news. Because the rich and famous rarely get murdered. They lead five-star lives and, unless they overdose on cocaine or meet with a freak accident, generally die a five-star death at a nice grey age, having augmented both lineage and lucre.

That is why the murder of Vivek 'Vicky' Rai, the thirty-two-year-old owner of the Rai Group of Industries and son of the Home Minister of Uttar Pradesh, has been dominating the news for the past two days.

In my long and chequered career as an investigative journalist I have carried out many exposés, from corruption in high places to pesticides in cola bottles. My revelations have brought down governments and closed down multinationals. In the process, I have seen human greed, malice and depravity at very close quarters. But nothing has revolted me more than the saga of Vicky Rai. He was the poster boy for sleaze in this country. For over a decade I tracked his life and crimes, like a moth drawn irresistibly to the flame. It was a morbid fascination, akin to watching a horror film. You know something terrible is going to transpire, and so you sit transfixed, holding your breath, waiting for the inevitable to happen. I received dire warnings and death threats. Attempts were made to get me fired from this paper. I survived. Vicky Rai didn't.

By now the facts of his murder are as well known as the latest twists in the soap operas on TV. He was shot dead last Sunday at 12.05 a.m. by an unknown assailant at his farmhouse in Mehrauli, on the outskirts of Delhi. According to the forensic report, he died of a single lacerating wound to his heart made by a bullet fired at point-blank range. The bullet pierced his chest, passed cleanly through his heart, exited from his back and became lodged in the wooden bar. Death is believed to have been instantaneous.

Vicky Rai had enemies, for sure. There were many who hated his arrogance, his playboy lifestyle, his utter contempt for the law. He built an industrial empire from scratch. And no one can build an industrial empire in India without cutting corners. Readers of this column will recall my reports detailing how Vicky Rai engaged in insider trading at the stock market, defrauded investors of their dividends, bribed officials and cheated on his corporate tax. Still, he didn't get caught, always managing to exploit some loophole or other to stay out of reach of the law.

It was an art he had perfected at a very young age. He was only seventeen the first time he was hauled up in court. A friend of his father had given him a swanky new BMW, the five series, on his birthday. He took it out for a spin with three of his buddies. They had a noisy and boisterous celebration at a hip pub. While driving back at three a.m. through thick fog, Vicky Rai mowed down six homeless vagrants who were sleeping on a pavement. He was stopped at a police checkpoint and found to be completely sozzled. A case of rash and negligent driving was lodged against him. But by the time the case came to trial, all family members of the deceased had been purchased. No witnesses could recall seeing a BMW that night. All they could remember was a truck, with Gujarat licence plates. Vicky Rai received a lecture from the judge on the dangers of drink-driving and a full acquittal.

Three years later, he was in court again charged with hunting and killing two black bucks in a wildlife sanctuary in Rajasthan. He professed he didn't know they were a protected species. He thought it funny that a country that could not protect brides from being burnt for dowry and young girls from being picked up for prostitution should prosecute people for killing deer. But the law is the law. So he was arrested and had to stay in jail for two weeks before he managed to obtain bail. We all know what happened next. The only eye witness, Kishore – the forest ranger who was driving the open jeep – died six months later in mysterious circumstances. The case dragged on for a couple of years but ended, predictably, in Vicky Rai's acquittal.

Given these antecedents, it was surely only a matter of time before he graduated to open murder. It happened seven years ago, on a hot summer night, at Mango, the trendy restaurant on the Delhi–Jaipur highway, where he was throwing a big bash to celebrate his twenty-fifth birthday. The party began at nine p.m. and carried on well past midnight. A live band was belting out the latest hits, imported liquor was flowing and Vicky Rai's guests – an assortment of senior government officials, socialites, current and former girlfriends, a few people from the film industry and a couple of sports celebrities – were having a good time. Vicky had a drink too many. At around two a.m. he staggered to the bar and asked for another shot of tequila from the bartender, a pretty young woman dressed in a white T-shirt and denim jeans. She was Ruby Gill, a doctoral student at Delhi University who worked part-time at Mango to support her family.

'I'm sorry, I can't give you another drink, Sir. The bar is now closed,' she told him.

'I know, sweetie.' He flashed his best smile. 'But I want just one last drink and then we can all go home.'

'I am sorry, Sir. The bar is closed. We have to follow regulations,' she said, rather firmly this time.

'F**k your regulations,' Vicky snarled at her. 'Don't you know who I am?'

'No, Sir, and I don't care. The rules are the same for everyone. You will not get another drink.'

Vicky Rai flew into a rage. 'You bloody bitch!' he screamed and whipped out a revolver from his suit pocket. 'This will teach you a lesson!' He fired at her twice, shooting her in the face and the neck, in the presence of at least fifty guests. Ruby Gill dropped dead and Mango descended into bedlam. A friend of Vicky's reportedly grabbed his arm, led him out to his Mercedes and drove him away from the restaurant. Fifteen days later, Vicky Rai was arrested in Lucknow, brought before a magistrate, and managed yet again to obtain bail.

A murder over the mere refusal of a drink shook the conscience of the nation. The combination of Vicky Rai's notoriety and Ruby Gill's beauty ensured that the case stayed in the headlines for weeks to come. Then summer passed into autumn, and we moved on to new stories. When the case finally came to trial, the ballistics report said that the two bullets had been fired from two different guns. The murder weapon had inexplicably 'disappeared' from the police strong-room where it was being stored. Six witnesses, who claimed they had seen Vicky Rai pull the gun, retracted their statements. After a trial lasting five years, Vicky Rai received a full acquittal just over a month ago, on 15 February. To celebrate the verdict he threw a party at his Mehrauli farmhouse. And that is where he met his end.

Some will call this poetic justice. But the police call it an IPC Section 302 crime – culpable homicide amounting to murder – and have launched a nationwide search for the killer. The Police Commissioner is personally supervising the investigation, spurred, no doubt, by anxiety that the promised sinecure of the Lieutenant Governorship of Delhi (reported six weeks ago in this column) will vanish into thin air should he fail to crack this case.

His diligence has yielded good results. My sources tell me that six suspects are being held on suspicion of murdering Vicky Rai. Apparently Sub-Inspector Vijay Yadav was on traffic-control duty at the farmhouse when the killing occurred. He immediately sealed off the premises and ordered the frisking of each and every one of the three-hundred-odd guests, waiters, gate-crashers and hangers-on there at the time. The place was practically bristling with weaponry. During the search, six individuals were discovered to have guns in their possession, and were detained. I am sure they must have protested. After all, simply carrying a gun is not an offence, provided you have an arms licence. But when you take a gun to a party at which the host gets shot, you automatically become a suspect.

The suspects are a motley lot, a curious mélange of the bad, the beautiful and the ugly. There is Mohan Kumar, the former Chief Secretary of Uttar Pradesh, whose reputation for corruption and womanizing is unparalleled in the annals of the Indian Administrative Service. The second is a dim-witted American who claims to be a Hollywood producer. Spicing up the mix is the well-known actress Shabnam Saxena, with whom Vicky Rai was infatuated, if the gossip in the film magazines is to be believed. There is even a jet-black, five-foot-nothing tribal from some dusty village in Jharkhand who is being interrogated at arm's length for fear that he might be one of the dreaded Naxalites who infest that state. Suspect number five is an unemployed graduate named Munna with a lucrative sideline as a mobile-phone thief. And completing the line-up is Mr Jagannath Rai himself, the Home Minister of Uttar Pradesh. Vicky Rai's dad. Could a father stoop any lower?

The six guns recovered are equally assorted. There is a British Webley & Scott, an Austrian Glock, a German Walther

PPK, an Italian Beretta, a Chinese Black Star pistol and a locally made improvised revolver known as a *katta*. The police appear to be convinced that the murder weapon is one of these six and are awaiting the ballistics report to match bullet to gun and pinpoint the culprit.

Barkha Das interviewed me yesterday on her TV show. 'You devoted much of your career to exposing the misdeeds of Vicky Rai and castigating him in your column. What do you plan to do now that he is dead?' she asked me.

'Find his killer,' I replied.

'What for?' she wanted to know. 'Aren't you happy Vicky Rai is dead?'

'No,' I said, 'because my crusade was never against Vicky Rai. It was against the system which permits the rich and powerful to believe that they are above the law. Vicky Rai was only a visible symptom of the malaise that has infected our society. If justice is really blind, then Vicky Rai's killer deserves to be brought to account just as much as Vicky Rai did.'

And I say this again to my readers. I am going to track down Vicky Rai's murderer. A true investigative journalist cannot be swayed by his personal prejudices. He must follow the cold logic of reason till the very end, no matter where and who it leads to. He must remain an impartial professional seeking only the bare truth.

Murder may be messy, but truth is messier. Tying up loose ends will be difficult, I know. The life histories of all six suspects will need to be combed. Motives will have to be established. Evidence will need to be collated. And only then will we discover the real culprit.

Which of these six will it be? The bureaucrat or the bimbo? The foreigner or the tribal? The big fish or the small fry?

All I can tell my readers at this point in time is – watch this space.

SUSPECTS

'The accused are always the most attractive.'

Franz Kafka, *The Trial*

The Bureaucrat

MOHAN KUMAR glances at his watch, disengages himself from the arms of his mistress and rises from the bed.

'It is already three. I have to go,' he says as he hunts for his underwear amidst the tangle of clothes at the foot of the bed.

The air-conditioner behind him stirs into action, expelling a blast of tepid air into the darkened room. Rita Sethi looks crossly at the machine. 'Does this wretched thing ever work? I told you to get the White Westinghouse. These Indian brands can't last the summer.'

The shutters on the windows are down, yet the oppressive heat still manages to seep into the bedroom, making the sheets feel like blankets.

'The imported A-Cs aren't tropicalized,' Mohan Kumar replies. He has half a desire to reach for the bottle of Chivas Regal on the side table but decides against it. 'I'd better get going. There is a board meeting at four.'

Rita stretches her arms, yawns and slumps back on the pillow. 'Why do you still care about work? Have you forgotten you are no longer Chief Secretary, Mr Mohan Kumar?'

He grimaces, as though Rita has scraped a fresh wound. He has still not come to terms with his retirement.

For thirty-seven years he had been in government – manipulating politicians, managing colleagues and making deals. Along the way he had acquired houses in seven cities, a shopping mall in Noida and a Swiss bank account in Zurich. He revelled in being a man of influence. A man who could command the entire machinery of the state with just one phone call, whose friendship opened closed doors, whose anger destroyed careers and companies, whose signature released bonanzas worth millions of rupees. His steady rise through the echelons of bureaucracy had bred complacency. He thought he would go on for ever. But he had been defeated by time, by the inexorably ticking clock which had tolled sixty and ended all his powers in one stroke.

In the eyes of his colleagues, he has managed the transition from government rather well. He is now on the boards of half a dozen private companies belonging to the Rai Group of Industries which together pay him ten times his former salary. He has a company-provided villa in Lutyens' Delhi and a corporate car. But these perks cannot compensate for the loss of patronage. Of power. He feels a lesser man without its aura, a king without his kingdom. In the first couple of months after his retirement he woke up on some nights, sweating and itchy, and reached dimly for his mobile to see if he had missed a call from the Chief Minister. During the day, his eyes would involuntarily turn towards the driveway, searching for the reassuring white Ambassador with the revolving blue light. At times the loss of power has felt like a physical absence to him, akin to the sensation experienced by an amputee in the severed nerve endings of a stump where a leg once used to be. The crisis reached such a point that he was forced to ask his employer for an office. Vicky Rai obliged him with a room in the Rai Group of Industries' corporate headquarters in Bhikaji Cama Place. Now he goes there every day, and stays from nine to five, reading a few project reports but mostly playing Sudoku on his laptop and surfing porn sites. The routine permits him to pretend that he is still gainfully employed, and gives him an excuse to be away from his house, and his wife. It also enables him to slip away for these afternoon assignations with his mistress.

At least I still have Rita, he reasons, as he knots his tie and gazes at her naked body, her black hair spread out like a fan on the pillow.

She is a divorcée, with no children, and a well-paying job which requires her to go to the office only three times a week. There is a gap of twenty-seven years between them, but no difference in their tastes and temperaments. At times, he feels as if she is a mirror image of him, that they are kindred souls separated only by their sex. Still, there are things about her he doesn't like. She is too demanding, nagging him constantly for gifts of diamonds and gold. She complains about everything, from her house to the weather. And she has a ferocious temper, having famously slapped a former boss who was trying to get fresh with her. But she more than makes up for these deficiencies with her performance in bed. He likes to believe that he is an equally good lover. At sixty, he is still virile. With his height, fair skin and full head of hair which he dyes diligently every fortnight, he knows he is not unattractive to women. Still, he wonders how long Rita will stay with him, at what point his occasional gifts of perfume and pearls will prove insufficient to prevent her from falling for a younger, richer, more powerful man. Till that happens, he is content with these stolen afternoons twice a week.

Rita fumbles underneath the pillow and retrieves a pack of Virginia Slims and a lighter. She lights up a cigarette expertly and draws on it, releasing a ring of smoke which is immediately sucked in by the A-C. 'Did you get tickets for Tuesday's show?' she asks.

'Which show?'

'The one in which they will make contact with the spirit of Mahatma Gandhi on his birthday.'

Mohan looks at her curiously. 'Since when did you start believing in this mumbo-jumbo?'

'Séances are not mumbo-jumbo.'

'They are to me. I don't believe in ghosts and spirits.'

'You don't believe in God either.'

'No, I am an atheist. Haven't visited a temple in thirty years.'

'Well, neither have I, but at least I believe in God. And they say Aghori Baba is a great psychic. He can really talk to spirits.'

'Humph!' Mohan Kumar sneers. 'The baba is no psychic. He is just a cheap tantric who probably feasts on human flesh. And Gandhi is no international pop star. He is the Father of the Nation, for heaven's sake. He deserves more respect.'

'What's disrespectful in contacting his spirit? I'm glad an Indian company is doing it, before some foreign corporation trademarks Gandhi, like basmati rice. Let's go on Tuesday, darling.'

He looks her in the eye. 'How will it look for a former Chief Secretary to be seen attending something as outlandish as a séance? I have to think about my reputation.'

Rita sends another ring of smoke spinning towards the ceiling and gives a shrewd laugh. 'Well, if you find nothing wrong in having these afternoon trysts with me, despite having a wife and a grown-up son, I don't see why you cannot come to the show.'

She says it lightly, but it stings him. He knows she wouldn't have said this six months ago when he was still Chief Secretary. And he realizes that his mistress, too, has changed. Even the sex was different now, as if Rita was holding something back, knowing that his power to mould things in her favour had diminished, if not disappeared.

'Look, Rita, I am definitely not going,' he says with injured pride as he puts on his jacket. 'But if you insist on going to the séance, I will get you a pass.'

'Why do you keep calling it a séance? Think of it as just another show. Like a movie premiere. All my friends are going. They say it will be a page-three event. I've even bought a new chiffon sari to wear that evening. Come on, be a sport, darling.' She pouts.

He knows Rita is nothing if not persistent. Once she sets her heart on something, it is difficult to dissuade her, as he discovered to his cost with the Tanzanite pendant she demanded on her thirty-second birthday.

He gives in gracefully. 'OK. I will arrange two passes. But don't blame me if Aghori Baba makes you retch.'

'I won't!' Rita jumps up and kisses him.

*

So it is that at seven twenty-five p.m. on 2 October, Mohan Kumar finds himself alighting reluctantly from his chauffeured Hyundai Sonata at Siri Fort Auditorium.

The venue for the séance resembles a fortress under siege. A large contingent of police in full riot gear are trying their best to control an unruly mob of protestors shouting angry slogans and holding up a variety of placards: 'THE FATHER OF THE NATION IS NOT FOR SALE', 'AGHORI BABA IS A FRAUD', 'BOYCOTT UNITED ENTERTAINMENT', 'GLOBALIZATION IS EVIL'. On the other side of the road, a battery of TV cameras are lined up, filming sombre-looking anchors making breathless live broadcasts.

Mohan Kumar pushes through the mêlée, one hand guarding the wallet in the inside pocket of his off-white linen suit. Rita, looking svelte in a black chiffon sari and corset blouse, follows him in stiletto heels.

He recognizes India's best known TV journalist, Barkha Das, standing directly in front of the wrought-iron entrance gate. 'The most revered name in the pantheon of Indian leaders is that of Mohandas Karamchand Gandhi, or Bapu as he is fondly known to millions of Indians,' she announces into a hand-held mike. 'United Entertainment's plans to make contact with his spirit on the solemn occasion of his birth anniversary have drawn ire across the country. The family of Mahatma Gandhi has termed it a national disgrace. But with the Supreme Court refusing to intervene, it appears that even this most sacred of names will be sacrificed today on the altar of commercial greed. This distasteful séance will take place after all.' She purses her lips and makes a grimace familiar to her prime-time audience.

Mohan Kumar nods his head in silent agreement as he inches closer to the gate. Suddenly the journalist's bulbous mike is thrust in his face. 'Excuse me, Sir, do you believe in spirits?'

A cameraman standing discreetly to the reporter's left immediately swings in his direction, training a Sony Betacam on him.

'Shit!' Mohan Kumar swears under his breath as he flinches instinctively from being filmed on national television. Rita preens by his side, hoping to catch the camera's viewfinder.

'Do you believe in spirits, Sir?' Barkha Das repeats.

'Only of the drinking kind,' he replies wryly, striding past the entrance to join the long queue of ticket-holders snaking through a door-frame metal detector.

'Great answer!' Rita beams and gently squeezes his arm.

Looking at the eager, expectant faces milling around him, Mohan feels vaguely distressed. The inexhaustible capacity of the gullible to be cheated has never ceased to amaze him. He frets at the slow progress of the queue, not having stood in one for the last thirty-seven years.

After an interminable wait, during which he has his ticket scrutinized by three different checkers, his body scanned for guns and metal and his mobile phone confiscated for later return, Mohan Kumar is finally permitted to enter the brightly lit foyer of the auditorium. Liveried waiters hover, serving soft drinks and vegetarian canapés. In the far corner, a group of singers sitting cross-legged on a raised platform sing 'Vaishnav Janato', Mahatma Gandhi's favourite *bhajan*, to the accompaniment of tabla and harmonium. He brightens as he spots several well-known personalities mingling in the crowd – the Auditor General, a Deputy Commissioner of Police, five or six Members of Parliament, an ex-cricketer, the President of the Golf Club and quite a few journalists, businessmen and bureaucrats. Rita breaks away from him to join a group of her socialite friends, who greet each other with little whoops of fake delight and feigned surprise.

The middle-aged owner of a textile mill, from whom Mohan Kumar had once extracted a hefty bribe, walks past him, studiously avoiding eye contact. *Six months ago the man would have fawned on me*, he thinks bitterly.

It is another quarter of an hour before the doors of the auditorium open and an usher directs him to the front. He has obtained the very best seats, right in the centre of the first row, courtesy of an IT company on whose board of directors he is now serving. Rita looks suitably impressed.

The hall fills up quickly with Delhi's glitterati. Mohan glances at the people around him. The ladies look vulgar in their brocaded silks and permed curls, the men faintly ridiculous in their Fabindia *kurtas* and Nagra *jutis*.

'You see, darling, I told you everyone who is anyone would come.' Rita winks at Mohan.

The audience coughs and fidgets and waits for the show to begin, but the velvet curtain draped over the stage refuses to budge.

At eight thirty p.m., an hour behind schedule, the lights begin to dim. Soon the hall is plunged into spooky darkness. Simultaneously, strains of the sitar fill the air and the curtain begins to rise. A single spotlight illuminates the stage, which is bare save for a straw mat on the floor. Arrayed in front of the mat are a number of items – a hand-driven spinning wheel, a pair of spectacles, a walking stick and a bundle of letters. A simple banner at the rear is emblazoned with the blue-and-white logo of United Entertainment.

A familiar baritone booms from the large black speakers on either side of the stage. 'Good evening, ladies and gentlemen. I am your host for the evening, Veer Bedi. Yes, the same Veer Bedi who meets you on the silver screen. You cannot see me in front of you, but you know that I am very much here, behind the scenes. Spirits are similar. You cannot see them, but they are all around us.

'In a few minutes from now, we are going to make contact with the most famous spirit of them all, the man who single-handedly changed the course of the twentieth century. The man of whom Einstein said "Generations to come will scarce believe that such a one as this walked the earth in flesh and blood." Yes, I am talking about none other than Mohandas Karamchand Gandhi, our beloved Bapu, who was born on this very day in the year 1869.

'Bapu attained martyrdom nearly six decades ago, no more than a few kilometres from here, but today he will come alive again. With your own ears you will hear Mahatma Gandhi speak through the medium of Baba Aghori Prasad Mishra, an internationally renowned psychic. Aghori Baba possesses the *siddhi*, the divine energy acquired through yoga which enables one to pierce the veil between this world and the next, and talk to spirits.

'I know there are some sceptics in the audience who think this encounter with Bapu is a hoax. I used to be a non-believer too. But no longer. Let me share something personal with all of you.' Veer Bedi's voice modulates to a conspirational tone. 'Five years ago, I lost my sister in a car accident. We were very close and I missed her terribly. Two months ago, Baba Aghori Prasad Mishra made contact with her. Through him, I spoke to my sister, learnt about her journey to the afterlife. It was the most amazing, transformative experience of my life. And that is why I am here to vouch personally for Aghori Baba. I can guarantee that what you are going to witness today is a once-in-a-lifetime experience, something that will change you for ever.'

There are murmurs of agreement from the audience.

'As you all know, we very much wanted Mahatma Gandhi's family to join us today, but they have chosen to distance themselves from this momentous event. Nevertheless, we have been helped by powerful benefactors who knew the Mahatma intimately. They have lent us items belonging to him which you can see arranged in the centre of the stage. There is the wooden *charkha*, the spinning wheel with which he spun the *khadi* cotton cloth which he always wore. Next to it lies his favourite walking stick. There is his pair of trademark round spectacles, and that bundle contains some letters written personally by the Great Mahatma.

'Before I invite Baba Aghori Prasad Mishra to come on to the stage, let me remind you of the etiquette for the séance. When the spirit enters the medium it is a critical and delicate moment. There should be no noise, no disturbance of any kind. That is why your mobile phones have not been allowed inside. Please maintain absolute silence throughout the show. On behalf of United Entertainment I would also like to thank our sponsors this evening – Solid Toothpaste, for solid white teeth, and Yamachi Motorcycles, way to go! I also thank our media partners, City

Television, who are beaming this event live to millions of viewers in India and across the globe. We'll take a very short commercial break here, but don't go anywhere, because when we return, Baba Aghori Prasad Mishra will be on stage.'

A babble rises in the hall. Someone says loudly, 'I see dead people,' which leads to considerable tittering. The mirth lingers for a while before fading under the weight of nervous anticipation.

Veer Bedi's voice returns after exactly five minutes. 'Welcome back to United Entertainment's *An Encounter with Bapu*. The time has now come, ladies and gentlemen, for which you have been waiting breathlessly. Hold on to your hearts, because you are about to witness the most amazing spectacle in the history of mankind. I am now going to invite on stage Baba Aghori Prasad Mishra.'

A machine sprays dry ice across the stage, adding to the eeriness of the atmosphere. Through the mist appears a shadowy figure, clad in a white *dhoti* and saffron *kurta*. Baba Aghori Prasad Mishra turns out to be slim and of average height. He seems to be in his late forties, with dark knotted hair piled high on top of his head, a dense black beard and piercing brown eyes. He looks like a man who has seen the world, who has conquered his fears.

The baba walks up to the edge of the stage and bows before the audience, holding his hands together in a gesture of salutation. '*Namaste*,' he says. His voice is soft and soothing. 'My name is Aghori Prasad Mishra. I am going to take you on a journey. A journey of spiritual discovery. Let us begin with what our holiest book, the *Gita*, says. There are two entities in this world: the perishable and the imperishable. The physical bodies of all beings are perishable, but the *atma*, the soul, is imperishable. Weapons do not cut this soul, fire does not burn it, water does not make it wet, and the wind does not make it dry. The soul is eternal, all-pervading, unchanging, immovable and immortal.

'But the most important thing about the soul, and I am quoting the *Bhagavad Gita* again, is that just as the air takes the aroma from the flower, the soul takes the six sensory faculties from the physical body it casts off during death. In other words, it continues to have the faculties of hearing, touch, sight, taste, smell and mind. That is what makes it possible to communicate with a soul.

'By the grace of the Almighty, I have had the privilege of interacting with several spirits over the years. But none touched me as deeply as the spirit of Mahatma Gandhi. The term "Mahatma" itself means "Great Soul". Bapu has been guiding my personal spiritual evolution for the last five years. I feel his presence every waking minute. So far this has remained a private dialogue between the Mahatma and me. Today I will share his blessings with the entire world. So it is a vital journey that we will undertake today. The journey of the soul. But also a journey of hope. Because at the end of the journey you will know that death is not the end of life, but the beginning of another life. That we are eternal and immortal.

'I will now commence my meditation. Soon the spirit of Bapu will enter me and speak through me. I request all of you to listen attentively to the message Bapu gives us today. But remember, if the communication is broken midway, immense harm will be done, both to the spirit and to me. So as Veer Bedi sahib has advised you, please, please maintain pin-drop silence.'

The dry-ice machine goes into action once again, and a thick cloud of vapour obscures the Baba momentarily.

When the mist dissipates, the Baba is sitting cross-legged on the mat, chanting incantations in a language which resembles, but is not, Sanskrit. The spotlight changes from white to red. The Baba's chanting subsides gradually and he closes his eyes. A serene calmness descends on his face. He becomes perfectly still, as though in a trance.

All of a sudden there is a burst of light on the stage and a sliver of white smoke sallies forth into the hall. There is a collective intake of breath from the audience.

'Firecracker powder!' Mohan Kumar snorts.

Equally suddenly the spinning wheel whirrs into action. It appears to do so without any external agency, with the Baba sitting a good six feet away from it. The audience watches transfixed as the spinning wheel revolves faster and faster.

'Must be radio controlled, with the remote in Veer Bedi's hands,' mutters Mohan Kumar, but Rita takes no notice. She is bending forward in rapt attention, her fingers gripping the arm rest.

As the spinning wheel continues to rotate, the walking stick and pair of spectacles stir into motion and rise from the floor. They ascend higher and higher towards the ceiling in a synchronized gravity-defying supernatural duet. There are gasps of disbelief from the assembly.

Mohan Kumar feels a prickling sensation in his palms. 'Invisible wires, hooked to the ceiling,' he opines, but his voice lacks conviction. Rita simply gapes.

As suddenly as it had begun, the spinning wheel abruptly grinds to a halt. The walking stick falls down with a clatter. The spectacles hit the floor and shatter.

There is a long pause, and for a moment Mohan thinks the Baba has gone to sleep. Then his body begins to shudder uncontrollably as though in the grip of a violent fever.

'Oh God, I can't see this,' Rita wails. At that very moment comes the sound of a voice unlike anything Mohan Kumar has heard before.

'I wish to tender my humble apology for the long delay in reaching this place,' the voice says. 'And you will readily accept the apology when I tell you that I am not responsible for the delay nor is any human agency responsible for it.'

The voice is grating yet oddly affecting, clear, resonant and so androgynous that it is impossible to tell whether it belongs to a man or a woman. It comes from the lips of Aghori Baba yet does not appear to be his.

A deathly silence falls over the audience. They feel themselves to be in the presence of a superior force, one they can neither see nor fully comprehend.

'Do not regard me as an animal on show. I am one of you. And today I want to talk to you about injustice. Yes, injustice,' the voice continues. 'I have always said that Non-violence and Truth are like my two lungs. But Non-violence should never be used as a shield for cowardice. It is a weapon of the brave. And when the forces of injustice and oppression begin to prevail, it is the duty of the brave to—'

Before the sentence can be completed, the rear door of the auditorium bursts open and a bearded man wearing loose white *kurta* pyjamas storms into the hall. His long black hair is in disarray and his eyes shine with unnatural brightness. He rushes towards the stage, chased by a couple of policemen wielding sticks. Aghori Baba turns silent in the face of this sudden intrusion.

'This is a perversion!' the bearded man cries as he reaches the edge of the stage, standing directly in front of Mohan Kumar. 'How dare you dishonour the memory of Bapu through this commercial spectacle? Bapu is our legacy. You are making him into a brand of toothpaste and shampoo,' he shouts angrily at Aghori Baba.

'Please calm down, Sir. Do not get agitated,' Veer Bedi materializes on stage like a magician's rabbit. 'We'll take a quick commercial break while we deal with this situation,' he announces, to no one in particular.

The protestor takes no notice of him. He inserts a hand inside his *kurta* and produces a black revolver. Gripping it tightly, he points it at Aghori Baba. Veer Bedi swallows hard and hastily retreats into the wings. The policemen appear to be immobilized. The audience is in a stupor.

'You are worse than Nathuram Godse,' the bearded man says to Aghori Baba, whose eyes are still closed, though his chest is heaving up and down in a sign of laboured breathing. 'Godse merely killed Bapu's body. But you are desecrating his soul.' Without further ado, he pumps three bullets into the *sadhu*.

The sound of gunfire crashes through the hall like a giant wave. There is yet another burst of light on the stage and Aghori Baba's head slumps down on his chest, his saffron *kurta* turning crimson.

Pandemonium erupts in the auditorium. Screams cascade down the aisles as people rush frantically towards the exit. 'Help, Mohan!' Rita shrills as she is pushed off her seat by the jostling mob behind her. She tries valiantly to retrieve her handbag, but is sucked into the crowd which surges like an angry river towards the door.

Mohan Kumar, still sitting in his chair feeling dazed and lost, senses something graze his face. It is soft, like a ball of cotton, yet slimy, like the underside of a snake. 'Yes, let's go,' he says abstractedly to Rita, who can no longer be seen. But before his lips have closed, the foreign object has insinuated itself into his mouth at lightning speed. He gulps and senses it sliding down his throat, leaving a bitter residue on his tongue, like the uncomfortable aftertaste of swallowing an insect. He spits a couple of times, trying to get rid of the bitterness in his mouth. There is a mild flutter in his heart, a tremor of protest, and suddenly his body is on fire. A pulsing, throbbing energy crackles through him, from his brain all the way to his feet. Whether it is coming from outside or inside, from above or below, he doesn't know. It has no fixed centre, yet it sweeps everything into a vortex, boring deeper and deeper to the very core of his being. He convulses violently, as though in the grip of a frenzy. And then the pain begins. He experiences a heavy blow on his head, a blunt needle being plunged into his heart, and large hands groping his chest, mangling his guts. The pain is so excruciating, he thinks he will die. He screams in agony and terror, but the sound is washed out by the din in the hall. A blur of motion is all he sees, as people scream and fall, tripping over each other. And then he blacks out.

When he opens his eyes, the hall is silent and empty. Aghori Baba's lifeless body is slumped over the straw mat, looking like a hilly outcrop in a sea of blood. The wooden floor is littered with shoes, sneakers, sandals and high heels, and someone is tapping his shoulder. He turns around to see a policeman with a stick looking at him intently.

'Hey mister, what are you doing here? Haven't you seen what has happened?' the constable barks.

He stares at him blankly.

'Are you dumb? Who are you? What is your name?'

He opens his mouth, but finds it difficult to speak. 'My . . . my . . . my . . . na . . . name . . . is . . .'

'Yes, what is your name? Tell me,' the policeman repeats impatiently.

He wants to say 'Mohan Kumar' but the words refuse to come out. He feels fingers squeezing his larynx, remoulding his vocal cords, shackling his words. They twist inside his gullet, are mashed around and made someone else's. 'My name is Mohan . . . Mohandas Karamchand Gandhi,' he hears himself say.

The constable raises his baton. 'You look like a decent man. This is no time for jokes. I'll ask you once again. What is your name?'

'I told you. I am Mohandas Karamchand Gandhi.' The words come more easily this time, more confident and self-assured.

'Bastard, are you trying to fool me? If you are Mahatma Gandhi, then I am Hitler's father.' The policeman grunts as his stick arcs down and Mohan Kumar's shoulder explodes in pain. The last thing he hears before losing consciousness again is the wail of a police siren.

The Actress

26 March

It's tough being a celluloid goddess. For one, you have to look gorgeous all the time. You cannot fart, you cannot spit and you dare not yawn. Otherwise the next thing you know, your big fat wide-open mouth will be staring at you from the glossy pages of *Maxim* or *Stardust*. Then, you cannot go anywhere without a horde at your heels. But the worst thing about being a famous actress is that you get conned into answering the most incredible questions.

Take, for example, what happened yesterday on the return flight from London. I had just entered the first-class cabin of the Air India 777, wearing my latest bottle-green Versace jacket over denim jeans with a studded belt and dark Dior glasses. I settled down in my seat – 1A, as always – and draped my Louis Vuitton crocodile-skin handbag on the seat next to me – 1B, vacant as usual. Ever since that unfortunate incident on the flight to Dubai with the drunken passenger who tried to paw me, I get my producers to reserve and pay for two first-class seats, one for me and the other for my privacy. I kicked off my Blahniks, took out my iPod, adjusted the ear plugs and relaxed. I have discovered that sitting with my ears plugged is the best way to keep pesky fans and autograph-hunting air hostesses and pilots at bay. The ear plugs allow me to observe my environment, while absolving me of the need to respond to it.

So there I was, immersed in my private digital eco-system, when in walked the air hostess with another woman and a little boy in tow.

'I'm sorry to disturb you, Shabnamji,' the air hostess intoned in the manner they use when they want to coax a favour out of a passenger, like asking him to move to a different seat. 'Mrs Daruwala here has something very important to tell you.'

I glanced at Mrs Daruwala. She looked just like the Parsi ladies in films – large, fair and florid. She was dressed in a fuchsia sari and smelt of talcum powder. Definitely economy class.

'Shabnamji, oh Shabnamji, what an honour it is for us to meet you,' she gushed in a sing-song voice.

I put on my polite but distant expression, the one that is meant to convey, 'I have no interest in you but am tolerating you, so make it quick.'

'This is my son, Sohrab.' She pointed to the boy, who was dressed in an ill-fitting blue suit complete with a bow tie. 'Sohrab is your biggest fan in the whole world. He has seen each and every one of your films.'

I raised my eyebrows. Half the movies I have done carry an Adult certificate. So either the mother was a liar or the boy was a midget.

Mrs Daruwala's face turned grave. 'Unfortunately, my dear Sohrab has got chronic leukaemia. Blood cancer. We were getting him treated at Sloan-Kettering, but the doctors have given up now. They say he has only a few months to live.' Her voice cracked and tears started flowing down her cheeks. I realized that the script had changed and immediately switched my expression to Caring and Solicitous, the one I employ when I do those publicity visits to cancer patients and the AIDS hospice.

'Oh, I am so sorry to hear this.' I pressed Mrs

Daruwala's hand and smiled beatifically at her son. 'Sohrab, would you like to talk to me? Here, why don't you come and sit down next to me.' I removed my handbag from the adjacent seat and placed it at my feet.

Sohrab accepted the offer immediately, plonking himself down on 1B as if he had been travelling first class all his life. 'Mummy, can you leave us alone for a while?' he said peremptorily in the tone of a boss dismissing his secretary.

'Yes, of course, son. But don't trouble Shabnamji.' Mrs Daruwala wiped her tears and beamed at me. 'This is like a dream come true for him. Just give him some precious moments of your time. Sorry, again, eh.' Then she went waddling back to her seat.

I looked at Sohrab, who was gaping at me like an obsessed lover. His intense gaze was a bit unsettling. I wondered what had I got myself into.

'So how old are you, Sohrab?' I asked, trying to put him at ease.

'Twelve.'

'That's a nice age to be. You are learning a lot and also have a lot to look forward to, don't you?'

'I have nothing to look forward to. Because I will never be thirteen. I will be dead in three months' time,' he replied in a completely deadpan manner, without any trace of emotion. Frankenstein couldn't have said it any better.

'Oh, don't say that. I am sure you will be fine,' I said and gently patted his arm.

'I will not be fine,' Sohrab replied. 'But that is not important. What is important is for me to know something before I die.'

'Yes, what is it that you want to know?'

'Promise me that you will reply.'

'Of course. Promise.' I flashed my veneers at him. Things would be simpler now, I thought. I'm a pro at dealing with my little fans. All they want is to know the name of my favourite film, hear about my forthcoming projects and whether I have any plans to star with their favourite actors.

'Go right ahead, Sohrab.' I snapped my fingers. 'I am ready for your question.'

Sohrab leaned towards me. 'Are you a virgin?' he whispered.

It was as clear a confirmation as I could get that sitting next to me was Psycho Junior.

Of course that was the end of my conversation with the little twerp – I sent him packing pronto. The air hostess also received a tongue-lashing from me, which ensured that no more terminally ill passengers interrupted my flight from then on.

Later, when my anger had cooled, I reflected on Sohrab's question. He was crude and rude enough to ask me, but I am sure the twenty million Indians who claim to be in love with me would be no less keen to know the answer.

Men in India classify women into two categories – available and unavailable. The sacred cows are their mothers and sisters. The rest are fodder for their voyeuristic dreams and masturbatory fantasies. Any girl who wears a T-shirt in this country is considered loose. And I am seen most often in figure-hugging costumes, bosom thrusting at the camera, hips bumping and grinding to some catchy beat. No wonder I have been described as the ultimate wet dream. And the more unattainable I seem, the more desirable I become. They write me letters in blood, threatening to immolate themselves if I don't send them an autographed photo. Some send me semen samples, in discoloured patches on tissue paper. Marriage proposals come for me by the thousand, from village idiots and lonely call-centre executives. A men's magazine has made me a standing offer for a nude photo-shoot and sent me a blank cheque. Even women send me *rakhis* proclaiming me as their sister, hoping to enlist my support in keeping their men from straying. Pre-pubescent girls write me flattering letters, asking me to pray for them to become similarly endowed.

38-26-36 is my magic number. In an age of silicone synthetics I represent natural beauty and bounty. I am pure anatomy, and yet my appeal transcends my vital statistics. I exude an orgasmic sweetness which arouses and inflames men. They don't see me. They see only my breasts, get lost in them, become tongue-tied, agree to my every whim and fancy. Call it cynical exploitation of the repressed id, or the unfair prerogative of celebrity, but it has given me all I wanted from life, and then some.

Despite all the changes of appearance, life is indestructibly powerful and pleasurable. So said Friedrich Wilhelm Nietzsche, my Master. I have been extracting every bit of pleasure from life over the last three years, but is it compensation enough for the misery I endured in the nineteen years previously?

31 March

I was invited today as Chief Guest to a function to honour the memory of Meena Kumari, the 'Tragedy Queen', who died this day thirty-five years ago. It was a terribly boring programme, laced with the same unctuous speeches one hears at every award ceremony, and it made me wonder. Is an actor's persona confined only to what is seen on the screen? Cinema is so one-dimensional, just a stream of light, which Jean-Paul Sartre described as 'everything, nothing and everything reduced to nothing'. If I were to be judged solely by my films, history would remember me simply as a vacuous glamour doll. But I am much more than a trifling celluloid dream. And when my diaries are eventually published (with suitable editing, of course), the world will acknowledge this too. I have already thought of an excellent title for the book: *A Woman of Substance: The Shabnam Diaries*.

19 April

Aishwarya Rai got married today. Thank God! She will probably quit films now. That means one less competitor for me. Last year's *Trade Guide*, in its annual top ten heroines in the Indian film industry, placed me at Number Four, just behind Aishwarya, Kareena and Priyanka. Now I'm Number Three.

But in the eyes of my fans I am already Number One. They know that I have got this far in the industry under my own steam, without the benefit of having been Miss Universe or the backing of a *filmi* dynasty behind me.

Be that as it may, my goal for this year is crystal clear:

To become Number One.
To become Number One.
To become Number One.

20 May

A ruckus has been going on in the flat since this morning. A team of six workers in blue overalls has invaded my bedroom and bathroom and is intent on destroying my peace. Supervising them is Bhola, shouting instructions as though he is some PWD engineer. It was his idea to get new lights fitted in the bathroom, the recessed ones in which you cannot see the bulbs. They look really pretty, especially with the dimmer turned down, just like stars in the night sky. In the bedroom, he is having my old Firozabad chandelier replaced by a spanking new Swarovski crystal one and rectifying some faulty wiring.

I must say I have been pleasantly surprised by Bhola. One of the perks of stardom is the discovery of long-lost aunts and uncles, distant cousins and never-before-seen nephews. Bhola is one such distant relative. He turned up at my flat one bright morning, claiming to be my Aunt Jaishree's son from Mainpuri, and beseeched me to get him a role in a film. I took one look at him and burst out laughing. With his slick oiled hair, bulging tummy and rustic manners he seemed more suited to agriculture than culture. But I took pity on his awkwardness and employed him as my assistant secretary cum Man Friday, promising him a role in a film if his performance proved satisfactory. It's been two years since then. I think even he has given up on his dream of becoming an actor, but he has really flowered as a sidekick. Not only is he useful in keeping troublesome fans and autograph-hunters at bay, he is also good with electronics and computers (a technology that still intimidates me). In addition, he has shown wonderful financial acumen. I have gradually started trusting him with my accounts, though I still cannot trust him with my dates. That task continues to be performed by my secretary Rakeshji, whom I share with Rani.

Bhola has no special gift, no real talent. He is utterly mediocre. But then the world is made up of ordinary people. Totally ordinary people, whose only job is to serve the extraordinary, the exceptional, the glorious . . .

31 May

My fingers ache. I have just finished signing nearly nine hundred letters. It is a ritual I have to perform four times a year, another small price for stardom.

The letters are replies to fans who write to me from all corners of the world, from Agra to Zanzibar. Five thousand letters arrive every week, twenty thousand a month. Out of these Rosie Mascarenhas, my publicist, selects approximately a thousand for personal replies, which consist of a standard boilerplate text expressing my happiness at communicating with my admirers, some blah, blah, blah about my forthcoming projects, and closing with best wishes for the health, happiness and prosperity of my fans. The letters are accompanied by a glossy photograph showing a close-up of me – a nice demure one for female fans and children, and a moderately hot one for the adult male fans. Rosie suggested the autopen option to me, in which a machine reproduces my signature on every letter, saving me the hassle of personally signing them, but I overruled her. As it is, I belong to the unreal world of films where everything is fake. I want my signature at least to be real. I think of the glow on my fans' faces when they open my letter and see my picture. There will be screams of surprise and delight. The letter will then be shown to family, friends and relatives. The entire neighbourhood will bask in its halo for a while. It will be talked about for days, discussed, debated, kissed and sobbed over. It may be photocopied, laminated, framed and, quite possibly, even worshipped.

The pain in my fingers disappears.

As a rule Rosie does not open letters marked 'Personal' or 'Confidential'. These come directly to me and have provided me with hours of amusement. India is the most star-struck nation on earth. Every second person wants to become an actor, come to Mumbai and make it big in Bollywood. These wannabees write to me from dusty villages and corner *paan* shops, from malaria-infested swamps and tiny fishing hamlets. They write in broken Hindi and pidgin English, in faltering sentences and floundering syntax, wanting simply to share their dreams with me and asking me for advice, assistance, and sometimes money. Most letters are accompanied by photographs in which they preen and pout, simper and smoulder, and try to compress all their wonderment, longing, commitment and desperation into a freeze frame which they hope will melt a producer's heart. But however hard they try, their rough edges cannot be hidden by the indiscriminating lens of the camera. Their essential crudity and vulgarity spills out of the poses which proclaim not only the silliness of their subjects but also their abject helplessness.

I find the letters from the girls especially disturbing. Some of them are as young as thirteen. They want to run away from their homes, forsake their families, for fifteen minutes of fame. They have no idea what it takes, what it costs, to make it in Mumbai. Even before they made it to the casting couch, they would be lured by some grubby photographer or smooth-talking agent to a steamy massage parlour or sleazy brothel. And their brittle dreams of stardom would crumble against the nightmarish reality of sexual slavery.

But I take a leaf out of my own life story and do not respond to these girls. I have neither the inclination to intervene in their sorry lives, nor the power to alter the trajectories of their doomed destinies. It is the law of the jungle. Only the fittest will survive. The rest are consigned to the dustbin of history. Or the trashcan of society.

16 June

Vicky Rai called again today. He has been pursuing me for the last two years. A real pest. But Rakeshji says I should humour him. He is a producer of sorts, after all, and he does have clout.

'Why won't you talk to me?' Vicky Rai asked.

'Because there is nothing to say,' I replied. 'How did you get my new mobile number?'

'I know you change it every three months. But I have my sources. You have always underestimated my power, Shabnam. There is much that I can do for you.'

'Such as . . . ?'

'Such as getting you a National Award. My dad can pull a few strings in government. Now don't tell me you don't want a National Award. These Filmfare Awards and Hero Honda trophies are OK, but eventually every good actor and actress craves a National Award. It's the ultimate recognition.'

'Well, I am not interested in awards at present.'

'OK, how about if I offer you a part in my next film? It's called *Plan B*. I've already signed Akshay for it. It's going into production next June.'

'I don't have any dates free in June. I will be shooting in Switzerland with Dhawan saab.'

'If you can't spare a month, can you at least spare a night? Just one night?'

'What for?'

'I don't have to spell it out now, do I? Just meet me in Delhi and everything will be taken care of. Or would you prefer me to come to Mumbai?'

'I would prefer you to end this call, and not bother me again, Mr Vicky Rai,' I said firmly and switched off my mobile.

What does the bastard think, that I am a saleable commodity? I hope he gets convicted for the murder of Ruby Gill and rots in jail for the rest of his life.

30 July

Jay Chatterjee is so frustrating; I want to tear my hair out. Arguably the most brilliant director in the industry, he is also the most eccentric. He met me at RK Studios today and said that he had decided to cast me in his new film.

I started trembling with excitement. A Jay Chatterjee film means not only a mega hit, but also plenty of awards. He is the Steven Spielberg of Bollywood.

'What is it going to be about?' I asked, trying to control my palpitations.

'It is about a boy and a girl,' he said.

'What kind of girl?'

'A very beautiful girl, from a very rich family,' he said in his usual dreamy manner, fingers playing an imaginary piano. 'Let us call the girl Chandni. Chandni's parents want her to marry an industrialist's son, but Chandni happens to fall for a mysterious drifter called K.'

'How mysterious!' I chimed.

'Yes. K is of this world and yet not of it. He exudes a power, a hypnotic pull which sweeps Chandni off her feet. She falls under his spell, becomes his slave and only then does she realize that the stranger is actually the Prince of Darkness.'

'Wow, the Devil himself?'

'*Exactement!* My plan is to narrate this story in two voices, those of Chandni and K. It is the interplay of the two stories, the dramatic tension in their relationship, that will power the narrative. So what do you think?'

I let out a deep breath. 'I think it is stupendous. Something never seen before in Indian cinema. It will be another Jay Chatterjee masterpiece.'

'So are you in? Will you be my Chandni?'

'Absolutely! When do we start shooting? I'll commit dates to you straightaway.'

'We begin shooting as soon as I cast K.'

'What do you mean?'

Chatterjee paused and fingered his straggly beard. 'I mean that I want to create a new paradigm for the angry young man. For K. I have been thinking, how long can we continue to give audiences the same bicepped hunks masquerading as action heroes or chocolate-faced nerds pretending to be kings of romance? People want change, they crave something new. I want K to be the harbinger of that change. He will be the ultimate quasi-hero. Someone whose persona combines the qualities of both a hero and a villain. Hard, yet soft. Brutal, yet tender. Someone who has the looks to melt your heart and the anger to chill your blood.'

'Don't you think Salim Ilyasi would be perfect for this part?' I asked.

'My sentiment exactly,' Chatterjee said morosely. 'Trouble is, Salim refuses to work with me.'

'But why?'

'I made the mistake of bad-mouthing his mentor, Ram Mohammad Thomas, in some interview.'

'Then what are you going to do?'

'Try to find another Salim Ilyasi. Till then, the film will just have to wait.'

Have you ever heard anything more ridiculous? A film held up, not for want of a script or a director or finance, but a hero who doesn't even exist. But then, that's Jay Chatterjee. And when he says wait, you wait. So I'll wait.

2 August

The following letter arrived today, marked 'Private':

Respected Shabnam Didi,
Hoping you are fine with God's grace. Myself Ram Dulari respectfully touching your feet. I am being Maithil Brahmin, nineteen years of age, living in Gaurai village of Sonebarsa block of district Sitamarhi and being only girl in village who is Class Six pass.

Myself now in great difficulty. Big floods coming to our village and drowning everything. Our house and cattle being washed away, respected father and mother dying very unfortunately. I am being saved by army boat. First I am staying in very bad camp made of torn tents in Sitamarhi but now myself living in best friend Neelam's house in Patna.

Myself not knowing anything about you because in village there being no big sinema hall like in Patna. But Neelam seeing lots of your fillims and calling me your younger sister. She is taking photu from her camera and asking me to be sending you.

I am being very good cook knowing very many types of recipes including *gulab jamun* and *sooji ka halwa*. Nice sewing also doing and knitting one sweater in only two days. Since myself being Maithil Brahmin, I am cooking food strictly as per rituals, full vegetarian, and all fasts and festivals being observed properly.

Kindly contacting me at above address and helping me out by taking me to Mumbai and giving me shelter and job. God showering you with full blessings.

With feet touching to all elders in family and love to children,

Your younger sister
Ram Dulari.

There was nothing remarkable about the contents of the letter. I receive dozens of such offers from young boys and girls, willing to work as bonded labour in my house, simply for the privilege of sharing space with me. But I was intrigued by Ram Dulari's reference to herself as my younger sister. I immediately thought of my real sister, Sapna, who would also be nineteen. She was probably still in Azamgarh with my parents, though I couldn't be sure as I had had no contact with her, or them, for the past three years. They had erased me from their lives, but I had been unable to erase them from my mind.

So I extracted the pictures from the envelope. They were standard 6 × 4 glossies. I looked at the first one, and almost fell off my chair. Because staring back at me was my own face in close-up. The same large dark eyes, small nose, full lips and rounded chin.

I quickly glanced at the second photo. This one showed Ram Dulari in a cheap green sari, leaning against a tree. Not only her face, even her build was similar to mine. The only visible difference was the hair. She had long, lustrous black tresses, whereas my current hairstyle was a chin-length bob with the latest asymmetrical fringe. But this was an insignificant detail. I knew I was looking at my spitting image. Ram Dulari was my *Doppelgänger*.

What struck me about the photos, beside the uncanny resemblance to me, was the fact that Ram Dulari seemed so unselfconscious. There was no artifice, no pretence, no effort to appear like me. She was just made that way. This was a girl unaware of her own beauty and I immediately felt a sense of kinship with her. Here was I, living in a luxurious five-bedroom penthouse apartment in the best city in India, and there was she, a luckless orphan, barely managing to survive in the heartland of Bihar where marauding gangs roamed free and unchecked. I resolved in that moment to help her, to send Bhola the very next morning to Patna to bring Ram Dulari to Mumbai, and to me.

I don't know what I will do with her. I have enough servants already, even good Brahmin ones. All I know is that I cannot leave the poor girl to her fate. I cannot be a silent spectator to her suffering. So I will intervene in her destiny, alter her fate.

But in so doing, will I be altering my own?

The Tribal

THE CRYING emanated from the middle of the clearing, a long wail punctuated by two short ones, like a funeral dirge. The arc of grief rose to a peak, tapered off, then rose again, mirroring the rhythm of the ocean waves crashing against the jetty a short distance away.

It was the beginning of October. The fury of Kwalakangne, the south-west monsoon, had abated, and the days had started to become hot once again. Stepping out in the scorching sun at noon required constitution and resolution.

Melame and Pemba approached the clearing, where six wooden shacks with corrugated asbestos roofing stood on stilts. A couple of young boys wearing shorts were noisily playing football in front of the huts, oblivious to the wailing in the background. A thin, mangy dog lay flopped on the ground, its tongue hanging out. The smell of chicken shit hung in the air.

Melame paused before the third shack and waited for Pemba to push open the door. The room inside was small and sparsely furnished. It contained a high wooden cot with a mosquito net supported by four bamboo sticks. A clay pot rested on a wooden stool. The walls were adorned with cautionary posters provided by the Welfare Department dispensary, warning against polio, tuberculosis and AIDS. An ancient ceiling fan whirred overhead, bringing some respite from the heat. In the right-hand corner, on the wooden floor, lay the naked body of a man approximately sixty years old. His eyes were closed, but his mouth was incongruously open, gaping in amazement at his own death. There were two people, one on either side of the body, crying in unison. One was a wrinkled old woman, wearing nothing but tassels made of sea shells around her waist, her withered breasts hanging like udders on a cow. The other was a young man wearing a loincloth and sporting a plain clay wash on his face and body, the sign of mourning. He got up as soon as he saw Melame and Pemba.

'Melame is very sad to know that his friend Talai has gone to the great beyond,' Melame said gravely as he embraced the young man. For a couple of minutes they communed in silence, eyes closed, cheek against cheek.

'When is the funeral, Koira?' Pemba asked the young man.

'This evening,' Koira replied.

'I didn't know Talai was sick,' said Melame.

'He wasn't,' said Koira. 'My father just had mild fever yesterday. Mother applied some moro leaves to bring the fever down, but by this morning he was gone. Just like the wind.'

'Look after your mother,' said Melame, gently patting Koira's shoulder. The old woman continued to wail, taking no notice of the visitors. Melame and Pemba said their goodbyes and stepped out of the shack into the sweltering heat once again.

'That's the third death this season,' the older man said, his voice quivering. 'The legions of *eeka* are increasing.'

Pemba nodded grimly. 'When malevolent spirits multiply, things can only get worse. At this rate, our tribe will soon become extinct, like the dugong.'

'Ah, the dugong! I have almost forgotten what it used to taste like,' Melame replied wistfully, smacking his desiccated lips.

'But Pemba still remembers. For my initiation ceremony I actually speared a dugong,' said Pemba.

'You were a great hunter. One of our best,' Melame responded approvingly. 'But look at today's youngsters, celebrating *tanagiru* by drinking beer and coca, that too made by the foreigners!'

'You are right, Chief. Well, what can I say? My Eketi is no better. He roams around the Welfare Office all the time, waiting for handouts. They say he sells honey and ambergris to the welfare officials in exchange for cigarettes. I have caught him several times smoking them. It makes me hang my head in shame,' Pemba replied in a low voice.

They trudged slowly in the direction of the turquoise ocean, wiping the perspiration from their brows. Bordered by casuarinas and coconut palms, the creek looked green, shady and inviting. They could see two white motorboats moored at the jetty. On the other side of the jetty were the cottages of the welfare staff. They passed the powerhouse, where the generator was making a racket as usual, and the dispensary, where Nurse Shakuntala was sitting all alone, fanning herself with a magazine. The next building was a dilapidated old warehouse, which now served as the school. They saw Murthy, the teacher with the slick, oily hair, standing with six tribal kids in the playground. He was distributing paper flags to the children, who wore identical blue shorts and white bush shirts. 'Now look,' they heard him instruct, 'when Minister Sahib arrives on Sunday, you have to stand in line at the helipad just like this and start waving these flags. And I want each one of you to give him a big smile. Now show me smiles, all of you.' He raised his right hand, in which he gripped a wooden ruler. The children gave nervous, toothy grins.

'Looks like another VIP is coming. Now all of us will be ordered to do cleaning and dusting and made to put on those horrid clothes,' Pemba said in irritation.

'Can there be anything more demeaning than parading our children before the *inene*?' Melame asked, his voice bristling with anger.

'No, Chief,' Pemba concurred. 'We have been made slaves in our own land.'

They passed behind the little temple built three years ago by the welfare staff. A square block of concrete with a white dome, it housed a stone image of Hanuman in mid-flight holding up a mountain, the entire thing painted a garish orange. They glimpsed two figures inside the temple, bowing their heads before the monkey god.

'Isn't that Raju and Taleme?' Melame asked incredulously.

'It does look like them,' said Pemba, craning his neck to peer into the semi-darkness of the sanctum sanctorum.

'Now Melame has seen everything.' The chief shook his head slowly. 'Our men have even forsaken our god.'

'That is because our god has forsaken us. Why is Puluga causing all these deaths? You need to do something, Chief, and quickly,' counselled Pemba.

'I think the time has come to consult the *torale*,' replied Melame. 'Today we will all be busy with Talai's funeral. But let us have a full Council meeting tomorrow morning. Spread the word quietly. We will meet inside the forest, at Nokai's hut, where the prying eyes of the welfare staff will not be able to spot us. That welfare officer – what's his name, Ashok – is particularly nosey.'

'Quite right, Chief. He has been taking an unhealthy interest in our tribe. The children have nicknamed him Gwalen – Peeping Tom,' Pemba laughed.

'I think he is more dangerous than a snake. Ensure that he doesn't get wind of our plans.'

'Yes, Chief.' Pemba bowed his head.

The forest was a palette of greens, brushed with patches of pink and white. Climbing orchids burst from branches and clumps of pink lilies poked up here and there like anthills. Triangles of Deodar trees stood like sentinels against the sky. The jungle thrummed with the sounds and scurry of life. Clouds of mosquitoes hummed their monotonous song. Invisible parakeets and parrots cried out from tree branches. Cicadas screeched from shrubs and bushes. Monitor lizards and snakes slithered through the underbrush.

Melame stood in a little clearing under the shade of a lofty *garjan* tree, directly in front of the medicine man's hut, and surveyed his flock. The women were busy as usual, making tassels of nuts and sea shells, gathering firewood or braiding their hair. The men were working on a log with their adzes, trying to fashion a canoe.

Melame breathed in a lungful of fresh air, still redolent with the aroma of morning dew, and looked longingly at the tree-lined vista in front of him. This little stretch of forest was the only surviving patch of green on the island. The settlement in Dugong Creek was littered with tree stumps. Every day ramshackle trucks loaded to the brim with timber rumbled down the Little Andaman Trunk Road, which ran along the island's edge, slowly denuding the island of its forest cover. Virtually every part of the island was now dotted with rice fields and coconut plantations. This was the islanders' last refuge, the only place where they could still hear birdsong and be themselves, naked, free and alive.

'Is the bait ready?' the chief asked Pemba, who nodded and pointed to a large earthen pot lying at his feet. Melame, looking satisfied, tapped on the door of Nokai's conical hut, thatched so low that it could only be entered by crawling.

'Go away,' the *torale* shouted from inside. 'Nokai has been having bad dreams. He cannot step out of his hut.'

Melame sighed. The medicine man was a reclusive, reticent oracle who hardly ever ventured out of the forest and was notoriously difficult to please. But without his powers of medicine and magic, the tribe couldn't survive. He could stop a storm simply by placing crushed leaves under a stone on the shore; he could divine a gathering illness from the lines on a man's face, and advise a carrying woman whether she would give birth to a boy or a girl simply by tapping her belly. The *torale* alone knew how to avoid malicious spirits and propitiate friendly ones, how to protect the clan during a lunar eclipse and what to do to counteract a curse. Melame was convinced that short of bringing a dead man to life, Nokai was capable of working any miracle. So he persisted, holding up the earthen pot.

'See, Wise One, what have we brought. It is turtle meat, absolutely fresh. Pemba caught it just yesterday.' Melame opened the lid, letting the smell of the meat waft into the hut. If Nokai had a weakness, it was for turtle meat.

The bait worked. Presently the door of the hut opened and a wizened hand snaked out, grabbed the pot and dragged it inside.

After a long interval the door opened again and the *torale* gruffly invited them in. Melame and Pemba slithered through the opening.

The hut was quite spacious inside. It contained a single raised sleeping platform in the centre. The ceiling was decorated with all kinds of objects – animal skulls, nautilus shells, bows and arrows and pieces of multi-coloured cloth. There was a wooden pan on the ground full of strips of dried boar and snake meat. A crackling fire burnt in the far corner in another earthen vessel. Nokai sat in the centre of the hut on a majestic tiger-skin rug, believed to have been a gift from the King of Belgium, whom he had once cured of the usually fatal black water fever. The earthen pot was lying in front of him, licked clean.

The medicine man peered at them with his hollow eyes. They glinted like pools of water in the near-darkness of his hut. 'Why have you come to bother me?' he demanded gruffly.

'Our race is in trouble, Wise One,' Melame replied. 'Our wild pigs have disappeared, turtles have become as scarce as the dugong, and our tribe members are dying like flies. Talai was the third one to go. Why are the spirits angry with us?'

'All this is happening because you lost the *ingetayi*,' Nokai said sternly. 'The sea-rock was a gift from our greatest ancestor Tomiti. It was engraved by Tawamoda, the first man. As long as we had the sacred rock, we were protected. Even the deadly tsunami caused no damage to our tribe. On the contrary, we were blessed by a girl child. It is only since the *ingetayi* disappeared that our tribe has fallen on hard times. How could you allow our most sacred relic to be stolen?'

'I really don't know, Wise One,' Melame replied sheepishly. 'We kept the sea-rock hidden deep inside the Black Cave at the far edge of the creek. None of the *inene* ever ventures that far. It is a mystery who could have taken it.'

Nokai gave another burp, groped about amongst the bones, rattles, charms and sea shells scattered across the tiger-skin rug, and came up with a large pearl oyster shell. 'Look at this,' he said. 'Once this was a living body, but today it is just a dead, empty shell. How? Because the spirit which resided in this shell has gone. Puluga resided in the *ingetayi*. When the *ingetayi* left Gaubolambe, Puluga left the island too. Now we are without his protection. The friendly spirits are angry with us for letting our God go. They are the ones causing all this havoc, these deaths. It is the curse of the *onkobowkwe*. Naturally, the person who stole the sacred rock will also be cursed. The spirits will not spare him, but they will not spare us either, for allowing the *ingetayi* to be stolen.'

'So what do we do? How do we save ourselves?' Pemba asked.

'There is only one way. Someone will have to go and recover the sacred rock,' Nokai replied.

'But for that we must first find out who has taken the *ingetayi*, and where it is residing now,' Melame said. 'Only you can help us locate it.'

'Yes, Nokai will help you locate it.' The medicine man nodded. 'But in return I want enough turtle meat to last me the rainy season, a big pot of honey and at least five nice pig skulls.'

'Granted, Wise One. Now just tell us who has the sacred stone.'

Nokai dragged the earthen vessel containing the fire closer to him. He rummaged through the items on the rug again and extracted a large lump of red clay and some brown seeds. He threw the seeds into the fire, where they burst with a bang. He smeared the red clay all over his face and body. He then went to the sleeping platform, raised the thin mattress and brought out four large bones from underneath it. 'These are my most prized possession. The bones of the great Tomiti himself.'

Melame and Pemba kneeled in deference to the great ancestor. Nokai sat down on the rug once again, spreading the four bones around him. Then he put his head between his knees and appeared to go to sleep. Melame and Pemba settled down to wait. They were familiar with the medicine man's routine. He was preparing to visit the spirit world. The brown seeds and the red clay would repel malevolent spirits, the bones of the ancestor would attract benevolent spirits. They would enter the hut, bringing a cold draft in their wake. Being blind, they would feel the *torale*'s body all over, making him shiver with cold. They would then truss him up like a pig, load him on their back, and fly into the sky.

For close to eight hours, Melame and Pemba watched over Nokai's body, as inert as a stationary turtle, while shadows lengthened outside the hut. It was late evening when the *torale* finally woke up with a start. He seemed groggy and disoriented. His eyes were bleary and there were numerous small cuts and bruises all over his body.

'Water, quick, get me some water,' he cried. Pemba had a jug of water handy. The *torale* drank greedily, half the water cascading down his chin. Catching his breath, he announced dramatically, '*Ingetayi a-ti-iebe*. Nokai has seen the sea-rock!'

Weary from his ordeal, Nokai narrated his journey in fragments, with Pemba and Melame having to tease out the details from him. This, he told them, was the longest trip he had ever undertaken. One that took him across the four oceans to the land of the *inene*. Soaring high in the sky, he had passed over snow-covered peaks and long, winding rivers. He had crossed barren sandy deserts and lush green valleys. He had seen metal birds flying in the sky and long iron snakes moving on the ground, smoke billowing from their hoods. The spirit of Tomiti himself had then led him on the trail of the *ingetayi*, crossing dense mangrove swamps, honing in on a vast bustling city teeming with people, where concrete buildings stood taller than the tallest mountains and where the night was lit up by the light of a thousand suns. He had swooped down to a small green-roofed house next to a small pond and that is where the *ingetayi* was, sitting atop a pedestal in a small room, surrounded with images of the *inene*'s gods.

'Tell us who lives in the house, Wise One. He must be the one who stole the sea-rock,' Melame urged.

'I saw only two people in the house. An old woman, wearing a white dress, and a short, bald man, with bushy eyebrows, thin lips and a bulbous nose,' Nokai replied, adding, 'He also wore glasses.'

'Banerjee!' Melame and Pemba exclaimed simultaneously,

recognizing the description of the senior welfare officer who had left the island two months ago in an unseemly hurry.

'Puluga be praised. All our troubles will now be over,' Nokai declared. 'As soon as the sea-rock is returned, the spirits will be propitiated. We will have enough honey and pigs and cicadas and turtles. No one will die and become an *eeka*.'

All three men stepped out of the hut and Melame broke the news to the other members of the Council of Elders, who had been waiting patiently since morning.

'The only issue now is who will undertake this mission? Who will go to the land of the *inene* and recover the sea-rock?' Pemba tossed the question.

The elders looked at each other's faces and looked away. A profound silence fell over the assembly. The wind dropped. Even the children running around with their toy bows and arrows ceased their sport and stood still, nervous and confused. The only sound was that of the distant waves breaking against the reefs. The air became heavy and dark with tension.

Suddenly, an empty bottle of Kingfisher beer dropped from the sky and crashed at Melame's feet, narrowly missing Tumi, who was breastfeeding her baby. Everyone looked up in alarm, wondering what new punishments the spirits sitting up in the heavens were doling out for them. They frowned when they spotted Eketi relaxing up in the *garjan* tree. He waved at them.

'You leg of a chicken. Come down immediately,' Pemba bawled. 'Otherwise I will become the first father to ask Nokai to turn his own son into a dog.'

Reluctantly, Eketi shinned down the tall tree. His movements were quick and nimble, like a monkey's. He jumped to the ground and stood before his father, a sheepish grin on his face. He was tall by the standards of his tribe – a good five feet – and muscularly built. He wore red shorts which were torn in a number of places and a dirty white T-shirt bearing the logo of the Dallas Cowboys. A small plastic bottle containing chewing tobacco dangled from his neck.

'None of you have answered the most important question our

tribe has been asked,' Melame addressed the elders again. 'Who will volunteer to recover the sacred rock?'

The question was met again by a wall of silence.

'What has happened to your people, Chief?' Nokai berated Melame. 'Is there no one prepared to defend the tribe's honour?'

Melame stood like a condemned prisoner, silent and impassive. It was Eketi who finally broke the impasse. 'Eketi will go,' he announced calmly.

Melame looked doubtfully at him. 'Do you think you will be able to handle this task? All day long I see you loitering on the beach, drinking beer and coca, trying to palm money off the foreigners.'

Nokai stepped in. 'Puluga be praised. Eketi is cleverer than you think. For three seasons I taught him my secrets. But he has no interest in becoming a *torale*. He wants to conquer the world. Nokai says give him a chance.'

Melame turned to Pemba. 'You are his father. What do you say?'

Pemba nodded sagely. 'I agree with Nokai. If Eketi stays here, the welfare staff will make him their slave. He will be doing chores for the *inene* all his life. Let this be his initiation ceremony.'

'Yes,' Nokai concurred, 'the ultimate *tanagiru*. It will rejuvenate the entire tribe. And when he returns with the sacred rock we shall give him a hero's welcome, just like our ancestors gave Tomiti when he first brought the rock from Baratang Island.'

Melame turned to Eketi. 'You know it will be a hazardous journey, don't you?'

'It is a risk Eketi is prepared to take,' Eketi replied, sounding more mature than his years. 'It should be a risk the tribe is prepared to take. Our very future depends on it.'

'Don't worry, Nokai will protect you,' the medicine man said reassuringly. 'I will give you tubers which have the protection of the spirits, and pellets which can cure any ailment.' He stepped inside the hut and returned with a decorated jawbone on a black string. 'Once you put this sacred bone around your neck, Puluga himself will become your guardian. No harm will come to you.'

Eketi kneeled before the medicine man and accepted his blessings. Then he took off his T-shirt, ripped the tobacco pouch from his neck, and put on the jawbone which glowed like phosphorescence against his coal-black skin.

Pemba injected a note of caution. 'What if the welfare staff catch my son?' he asked. 'You know the hiding they gave Kora when he tried to get into the speedboat without their permission. That man Ashok is very clever. He can even speak our language.'

Eketi dismissed this with a wave of his hand. 'So what? I can speak English better than him. The welfare staff are fools, Father. They are interested only in making money. They have no interest in me. But how will I go to India? Eketi cannot fly like Nokai.'

'We will make a canoe for you,' said Melame. 'The best boat we have ever made. You will leave at the time of the moon of full dark. No one will spot you. Within a few days I am sure you will be able to reach the land of the *inene*. Then you just have to find that rotten egg Banerjee and recover our stolen rock.'

'And how exactly will Eketi find Banerjee?'

'By finding the green-roofed house.'

'Do you have any idea how big India is?' Eketi cried. 'It is bigger than the sky. Searching for one green-roofed house will be like looking for a grain of salt in the sand. What I need is something called an address. Everyone in India has one. That's what Murthy Sir taught us in school. Now who has got Banerjee's address?'

'Oh, we didn't think of that,' said Melame and scratched his head. The assembly fell silent.

'Puluga be praised. I believe I may be able to help,' a voice rang out. A shadow detached itself from the trees in the background and stepped forward.

The islanders recoiled in shock. It was Ashok, the junior welfare officer.

'*Kujelli!*' exclaimed Pemba, which was the Onge equivalent of 'Oh shit!' though its literal meaning was 'The pig has pissed!'

'I come in peace,' Ashok declared in fluent Onge as he approached the gathering. A clean-shaven man in his early thirties, he was of average height with a thin build and short black hair. 'I will take Eketi to India,' he said. 'I know Banerjee's address in Kolkata. I will help recover your sacred rock. Will you describe it to me?'

He took out a pen from his bush shirt and opened a thin black diary.

The Thief

I WILL BE DEAD in approximately six minutes.

I have consumed a full bottle of Ratkill 30. The powerful poison is making its way through my bloodstream. It takes only three minutes to kill a rat; double that for a human. My body will be paralysed first, then it will slowly start turning blue. My heart-beat will become irregular, then it will stop completely. My twenty-one-year-old life will come to an abrupt end.

This is the time, Mother would say, to remember God. To atone for my sins. But what's the point? Lord Shiva is not going to come down from Mount Kailash to get me out of this jam. He never helps us poor people. He belongs only to the rich. That is why although I live inside the temple, I don't believe in God.

My late friend Lallan would have surmised that I am pretend-ing to commit suicide to impress some chick. But this isn't a drama. And it isn't even suicide. It is murder.

Mr Dinesh Pratap Bhusiya is standing in front of me, pointing a revolver directly at my stomach. An expensive imported piece. He is the one who ordered me to drink the rat poison. Given a choice between dying by bullet and dying by poison, I chose the latter. At least it will be painless, though that watery brown liquid had a terrible taste; it was like swallowing mud.

There is a manic glint in Mr D. P. Bhusiya's eyes as he watches me die. Of all the Bhusiya brothers he is the most dangerous. I saw him the other day, torturing his pet dog, poking him in the eye with a pointed stick. In fact, there is a mad streak in the entire

Bhusiya clan. His elder brother Ramesh is a serial adulterer, trying to bonk every girl in the neighbourhood, from the sweeper to the washerwoman, while his fat wife spends her time at the beauty parlour. And his younger brother Suresh is a serial adulterator, selling impure goods to unsuspecting customers. Everything in his general provision store on Andheria Modh is adulterated. He mixes crushed pebbles in pulses, sand in rice, artificial colours in spices, chalk powder in flour. He sells fake milk, fake sugar, fake medicines, fake cola, even fake bottled water. Come to think of it, it is difficult to figure out which brother is the worst. Partly because they all look like carbon copies of each other. At times even I get confused which of the three brothers I am talking to. Their father, Mr Jai Pratap Bhusiya, also looks exactly like his sons, simply an older model. It is almost as if the Bhusiya women have a factory where they have perfected a mould which makes succeeding generations of Bhusiyas look exactly alike. If you were to meet a member of the family in the street you would be able to say immediately, 'There goes a Bhusiya,' just as you would be able to identify a black buffalo in a herd of cows.

If only the Bhusiya women were as ugly as their men I wouldn't be in this situation. The main reason I began working in this house was because of Pinky Bhusiya, the only sister of the three brothers. She has skin like honey and a body like a BMW. All sleek curves outside and smooth upholstery inside. I saw her in the temple complex one day and foolishly laid a thousand-rupee bet with Jaggu, the flower-seller, that I would start an affair with her within sixty days.

Working as a servant was way beneath the dignity of a university graduate like me, but that was the only way to gain entry into the Bhusiya household. Luckily, the Bhusiyas were in need of a servant. As a matter of fact, every rich family in the capital is in need of one. Good servants are as hard to find these days as spares for the Daewoo Matiz. The fact that I lived on the temple compound was enough to convince the Bhusiyas that I was honest and God-fearing, and they employed me on a salary of three thousand a month.

In hindsight, it was the biggest mistake of my life. A high-flying ex-mobile-phone thief, used to dealing in Nokias and Samsungs, was always going to struggle with Pril dishwasher and Rin soap.

And the Bhusiyas didn't help matters either. They had seemed law-abiding, religious types, who came to the temple every Monday and donated large sums to Lord Shiva. It was only after I started working for them that I discovered they were first-rate crooks and cheats. Uncouth, uncivilized and insensitive, they constantly reprimanded me for some act of omission or commission.

I could have tolerated their boorishness, but what I couldn't stand was the bossiness of the Bhusiya women. They acted as if they owned me. Mr R. P. Bhusiya's wife would send me off to get a DVD from the video parlour and Mr S. P. Bhusiya's wife would demand that I get her dry-cleaning at the same time. Worst of all, Pinky Bhusiya remained completely immune to my charms. I had thought a girl like her would be easy to entice. The way she dressed, she seemed neither too hep nor too staid. Neither too worldly-wise and canny, nor totally timid. I enacted several hero-type roles to attract Pinky's attention, from the sensitive *aashiq* to the dignified servant with a heart of gold. I tried to impress her with my wide knowledge of mobile phones and my deep understanding of national politics, but nothing seemed to work. She treated me just like a servant, angry one day, amiable another, but never seeing me as a man. All she was interested in were her silly girlfriends and her CD player. Even the bathrooms in the house were so constructed that there was no possibility of peeping in. Within a month I realized that it was a waste of time.

I would have quit my job, given Jaggu the thousand rupees and willingly conceded defeat, when a dramatic new development made me stay on. Asha, better known as Mrs Dinesh Pratap Bhusiya, developed the hots for me. One sticky afternoon, as I walked into her bedroom to deliver some toiletries, she caught me by the shirt, closed the door and began kissing me all over. Thus began our affair.

*

Servants are the most under-appreciated class of people in the world. They don't demand the affection or compassion of their employers. They only seek respect. Not for what they do, but for what they know. Just attend a gathering of servants in front of the Mother Dairy booth at six in the morning, and you'll hear more hot gossip and insider info than on Breaking News on TV. That is because servants see everything and hear everything, even though they may pretend to be as ignorant as cows. Their own lives are so tedious, they get their kicks from prying into their masters'. When the family is watching soap operas, the servants are watching the family. They catch little gestures and nuances which escape other members of the clan. They are the first to know that the boss is about to become insolvent, or the boss's daughter is going to need an abortion. They have the low-down on what really happens inside a family: who is bitching about whom, who is plotting against whom.

And beware a servant's revenge. There are so many elderly couples in Delhi whose throats have been slit by their Bihari cooks and Nepali guards. Why? Because the servants were driven to the limit by their employers. I, too, have taken my revenge on the Bhusiyas. Mr S. P. Bhusiya, the adulterator, for instance, has no clue that the chicken curry he has been eating at dinner time is also adulterated. I spit in it liberally before laying it on the table. And the elderly Mr Bhusiya, with his diminished sense of taste and smell, happily drank the vegetable soup which I had garnished with bird droppings, and even asked for a second helping!

But I received the biggest thrill of all from thumbing my nose at Mr D. P. Bhusiya. He pretended to be as tough as a bulldog, but his wife confided in me that in bed he was like a mouse, as useless as a camera without film. *Bole toh*, fully impotent. My affair with his wife lasted two months. The icing on the cake was that she even paid me after every 'performance'. So while Mr D. P. Bhusiya was at his brick kiln in Ghitorni, I would be in his bed with Asha, earning an extra hundred rupees.

I was in his bed this afternoon, when he happened to make an unscheduled visit to the house. It was exactly like they show in films. The husband returning home and opening the bedroom door and his jaw dropping on seeing his wife with another man – worse, his own servant.

'Whore!' he bellowed as I scrambled out of bed and ran into the en-suite bathroom where I had left my clothes. I heard a scuffle and the sound of Asha being slapped. Two minutes later the bathroom door was kicked open and Mr D. P. Bhusiya stepped in with a revolver in one hand and a bottle in the other.

'Now I shall sort *you* out, you bastard,' he hissed, and ordered me at gunpoint to come out.

He took me to the garage on the ground floor, backed me into a corner and forced me to drink the bottle of Ratkill 30. And that is where I now stand, counting the seconds till my death. A murder which will be presented as a suicide.

I look around the large garage, at the empty space marked by grease stains where Mr R. P. Bhusiya's silver Toyota Corolla will be parked this evening, at the stacks of cartons in the corner containing spices and pulses which Mr S. P. Bhusiya will proceed to adulterate, at the steel ladder, the half-empty plastic bottles of coolant and engine oil lying on the wooden shelf. I try not to think of Mother and Champi.

Mr D. P. Bhusiya is looking at his watch with a worried look. It has been twenty minutes since I polished off the bottle. The poison should have done its work by now. But instead of a creeping paralysis, my stomach is experiencing a bubbling effervescence, like you feel after drinking Coca Cola. Something is rising up in my throat. Seconds later, a jet of vomit shoots from my mouth and lands on Mr D. P. Bhusiya's white shirt.

He gets so flustered, the revolver slips from his hand. That is all the opening I need. I kick the gun away and dash out of the garage.

It is amazing what fear of death can do to the human body. I run like an Olympic champion, glancing back from time to time to see if Mr D. P. Bhusiya is following me.

As I near the temple, I marvel at my extraordinary luck. I had stared Death in the face and Death had blinked. But perhaps this is being too dramatic. By now I have figured out that my death would have been a fake one. As fake as the rat poison Mr D. P. Bhusiya must have obtained from his brother's store!

There is nothing fake about the smile on my face as I burst through the temple gates, see Champi sitting at her usual place on the bench beneath the *gulmohar* tree in the back garden and crush her in the biggest bear hug of my life.

'*Arrey*, what's the matter? You are acting as if you have won the lottery,' she laughs.

'You could say that. I have decided two things today, Champi.'

'What?'

'One, that I am never ever going to work as a servant again.'

'And the second?'

'That I am going back to my old profession. Stealing mobile phones. But don't tell Mother.'

There was a time when I actually liked my name. It was a hit with the girls in the locality, who considered it quite cute. And it was a considerable improvement on just plain Munna, which immediately brings to mind some lowly tea-boy or struggling car mechanic. Munna Mobile had a certain ring, a definite charm to it. That was when mobile phones were a high-society item. Now even the bloody washerman has one. What self-respecting youth would like to be called Munna Mobile today? They might as well call me Vodafone or Ericsson.

I acquired the moniker four years ago, after I filched my first mobile phone. I had taken it off a very fat lady who had driven to the temple in a white Opel Astra. She seemed to be in a big rush, the way she wheezed up the steps, as if she had fifty errands to finish that day. It happens. You are very busy. You just want to make a flying visit to God and in your confusion you forget minor details, like locking your car. And leaving your brand-new Sony Ericsson T100 on the driver's seat.

That was the first mobile I had ever touched. Before that I used to steal the shoes and slippers of devotees who were foolish enough to leave them at the bottom of the steps rather than give them for safekeeping to the old lady who charges a mere 50 *paise* per pair.

If truth be told, my exploits as a slipper thief were nothing to write home about. The pickings were slim, though I did manage a couple of pairs of almost brand-new Reeboks and Nikes. Had they not been in sizes nine and ten, I would have kept them for myself instead of selling them to the cobbler at one tenth of their price.

I took the fat lady's mobile to Delite Mobile Mart, the mobile-phone shop just outside the temple. Madan, the owner, gave me two hundred rupees for it, ten times what I received for a used pair of slippers. That first mobile introduced me to a whole new world of SIM cards and PIN numbers. Bata shoes and Action sandals soon gave way to Nokias and Motorolas. That was when I formed a partnership with my best friend Lallan, realizing that stealing mobiles required much greater coordination and planning than stealing shoes. Our favourite targets were cars stopped at red lights with rolled-down windows and mobiles glinting on the dashboards. While Lallan would divert the driver's attention, I would creep up on the other side, snatch the phone from the dashboard and then run like mad through the meandering alleys and side roads that we knew like the back of our hands.

I have kept a record of each and every mobile phone we stole over a three-year period. The total came to ninety-nine. It was good while it lasted. It gave me enough to live a modest life, buy a few decent clothes, have flings with a couple of girls from the locality. The funny thing is, I didn't have to sell the girls any fake story about my being a medical rep or some shit like that. They got their thrills from hearing about my exploits as a mobile-phone thief. And a handset makes a much-sought-after present. A girl will let you touch her breasts for a Motorola C650. She might even open her legs for a Nokia N93.

Not that I am too much into that sort of thing. The *mohalla* girls who work as maids and babysitters are just cheap lays. Dark and coarse, they are good only for fulfilling a physical need. What I really crave are the rich chicks, the memsahibs with their English accents and low-slung jeans. I admire their flawless complexions and fair skin. I gape in amazement at the sleek curve of their waists and the delicate bones of their made-up faces. I inhale the expensive perfume on their bodies, watch the seductive roll of their hips and feel dizzy. But I know they are good only for my dreams. For someone like me, they are almost as unattainable as Shabnam Saxena. Still, I was hopeful of at least ensnaring the middle-class daughter of a chief engineer who was a regular visitor to the temple, when my fledgling career as a mobile-phone thief was abruptly cut short by tragedy.

We had nicked a Samsung from a Mercedes stopped near Qutub Minar. I had managed my getaway with the mobile quite smoothly, but Lallan couldn't disappear fast enough. He was chased by the driver, nabbed and hauled up to the police station, where he was personally interrogated by Sub-Inspector Vijay Singh Yadav, known throughout the area as the Butcher of Mehrauli.

Lallan and I had grown up together. I lived with Mother in the temple premises; he stayed with his family in the sprawling Sanjay Gandhi slum just outside. We played football and cricket on the roadside, went to the same municipal school, which Lallan dropped out of in Class Six while I continued right through to Intermediate. He was my partner in everything, from hustling shoes from the temple to teasing the neighbourhood girls. I called him my best friend, but in reality he was closer than a brother to me. A lesser person would have blurted out the truth when confronted by the Butcher of Mehrauli, but Lallan stuck to his code of loyalty, adamantly refusing to confess.

What happened subsequently in the police lock-up is a dark memory which still gives me nightmares. Lallan was stripped, strung up by a rope, and then kicked, caned and flogged for three consecutive nights while his aged father pleaded and begged and cried and grovelled in front of the police station. But Lallan still refused to squeal on me.

On the fourth day, he disappeared. The police claimed they had released him. We searched for him everywhere, even as far afield as AIIMS and Saket, but found no clue to his whereabouts.

We discovered his bloated, mangled body three days later, lying in a shallow ditch near Andheria Bagh. Flies were buzzing over the sores on his chest and maggots were crawling out of his pus-filled eyes as though he was a common slum dog.

Lallan's death was my wake-up call. It brought home to me the stark fact that I couldn't even take life for granted. So I gave up stealing mobile phones and resolved to make something of myself. But what you make of your life is a function of who you are. If I had a family pedigree and political connections, my university degree would have landed me a cushy job in some air-conditioned office, or at least made me a peon in a government department. But when your mother is a lowly sweeper earning 1,200 rupees per month and you are an ex-thief, your career options are limited. For a brief while I worked as a book-keeper at a grocery store, then as fleet supervisor at a transport company, and finally as a servant for the Bhusiyas. I was a failure in all three. The easy life as a mobile-phone thief had spoiled me. I couldn't see myself counting cartons, sniffing diesel or serving tea for a living.

So I have decided to go back to the only job I do well – stealing mobiles.

Stealing a mobile phone is not as easy as it seems. It really is a fine art. Just as a pickpocket takes your wallet from right under your nose, the mobile thief makes away with your phone. Far from a crude snatch-and-grab operation, it is more like a disappearance trick, a sleight of hand. One moment you have the mobile in front of you and the next moment it is gone. Like magic.

It is also an art which you never lose. A cricketer can be off form, but not a thief. I know it is only a question of time before I nick another mobile and score a century.

Today is 26 January, Republic Day. And I am hiding behind the HP petrol pump on the Mehrauli–Badarpur Road and breathing heavily. I have just stolen my first mobile phone in a year.

I had gone to visit a friend who lives in the tenements behind the Star Multiplex and was walking back to the bus stop. It was late evening and the neon lights of the street lamps were shrouded in the hazy glow of winter. While I was waiting at a red light, rubbing my hands to keep them warm, a red Maruti Esteem pulled up in front of me. The driver was a wiry man with curly hair and a square jaw. What struck me about him was the way he gripped the steering wheel, as if it would come unstuck any minute. In the peak of winter he was sweating like a pig. The man radiated tension like a blower radiates heat. There was a mobile phone on the dashboard and the window was open halfway. Pure habit took over from there. Just as the light changed to green, my hand darted inside with the speed of a bullet. The driver stared ahead unblinkingly, his knuckles turning white. He engaged the gear and the car surged forward, leaving me standing on the pavement with a very stylish mobile phone in my hands. It was a brand-new Nokia E61, so new that the cellophane had not even been removed from the display window. I knew it would fetch me a lot of money on the black market.

I think a woman in a Ford Ikon immediately behind the Esteem saw me take the mobile. She glared at me as she drove past. Before she could raise the alarm, I decamped from the scene, criss-crossing streets for almost two kilometres till I reached the safety of the petrol pump.

As I stand under the grey awning, panting from exertion, the stolen mobile rings. The caller ID says 'Private number'.

I am not sure what to do. Mechanically I press the green 'talk' button.

'Hello, Brijesh? I am going to give you the pick-up location. Are you listening?'

It is a harsh, guttural voice. A voice with authority. A voice which cannot be ignored. Which has to be answered.

'Yes,' I say in an equally guttural voice. A monosyllabic answer which reveals nothing about the person answering.

'Go to the alley next to Goenka Public School on Ramoji Road. The *maal* has been left in a black briefcase inside the municipal dustbin. Collect it within the next half-hour. OK?'

'*Haan*,' I say again.

'Good. We shall talk again after your pick-up. Bye.'

Maal. The word keeps ringing inside my brain like an alarm clock. *Maal* can mean any number of things. Literally, it means 'goods'. In old Hindi films, gangsters used to refer to contraband consignments of drugs and bullion as *maal* which would be offloaded from ships on Mumbai's Versova Beach. A beautiful girl is also *maal,* but unlikely to be packed inside a briefcase. For that matter, even groceries from a provision store can be *maal.* There is only one thing to do. I have to find out what the *maal* is.

I try and get my bearings. Ramoji Road is just a five-minute drive from the petrol pump, twenty minutes on foot. I walk.

The Goenka Public School is one of the premier private schools in Mehrauli. In the morning when the children begin their classes and in the afternoon when they leave, there is a mini traffic jam in the area, caused by all the cars of the rich businessmen whose children study here. However, at eight p.m. it is completely deserted. Only a couple of guards stand in front of its imposing gates, warming their hands over a fire. I pass the school and enter the narrow alley. It is deserted. I find the dustbin almost immediately. It stands unobtrusively at the back of the alley, illuminated by the yellow glare of a lamppost. There is a dog sleeping next to it. 'Shoo!' I say and the dog pricks up his ears and slinks off into the shadows. I push open the lid of the bin to find it brimming with rubbish. I feel around with my hand but my fingers scrape only bulging plastic bags, glass bottles and metal cans. So I begin emptying the bin, removing the plastic bags and stacking them up against the side. The stench of rotting food makes me gag. The dank recesses of the dustbin yield various kinds of rubbish, even a few soiled nappies and a broken transistor. And at the very bottom is a briefcase, wrapped in a white plastic sheet. I have to lean right in to pull it out. It is an expensive black VIP attaché case with a hard top. I rip off the plastic sheet, and press the two side latches. The briefcase clicks open and my eyes are dazzled by stacks of thousand-rupee notes lining the inside. It looks like a lottery advertisement. How could I forget that cash is the ultimate *maal*! I hastily close the briefcase. I do not need to count the wads of notes to know that it contains more money than I have seen in my life.

I take a good look around. Not a soul appears to be in the vicinity. I put all the plastic bags back into the bin. As I am about to leave, the stolen mobile trills again. Its incessant ringing almost paralyses me. With trembling fingers I switch it off and push it deep inside the dustbin. Then, with my heart thumping madly, I pick up the briefcase and hasten towards the main road.

The Politician

'Hello. Is this the Spiritual Meditation Centre in Mathura?'

'Yes.'

'Is Swami Haridas there? Bhaiyyaji wants to speak to him.'

'Bhaiyyaji? Who is Bhaiyyaji?'

'Are you new there? Don't you know that there is only one leader in Uttar Pradesh who is addressed as Bhaiyyaji and that is Home Minister Jagannath Rai.'

'Oh! Home Minister Sahib? But Guruji is in the middle of his discourse. We cannot disturb him.'

'Tell him it is urgent. He never refuses Bhaiyyaji's call.'

'OK. Please hold on. I am going to the lecture hall.'

(*Pause*.)

'I am passing the line to Guruji. Please put Home Minister Sahib on the line.'

Beep. Beep. Beep.

'Namaskar Guruji. This is Jagannath.'

'*Jai Shambhu!* What is the big emergency, Jagannath, that you forced me to interrupt my discourse?'

'Guruji, there has been a disturbing development. I need to consult you urgently.'

'Is it about Vicky? His case is coming up for a verdict, isn't it?'

'No, Guruji. I have managed Vicky's case. I am more worried about the case against me.'

'There are so many cases against you. Which one are you referring to?'

'It is an old murder charge, dating back to 2002.'

'Whom did you kill?'

'It was Mohammad Mustaqeem, a worthless heel who had dared to challenge me. The prosecution case was very weak, based only on circumstantial evidence. Now suddenly a new witness called Pradeep Dubey has come forward, claiming that he saw me shoot Mustaqeem. The court hearing is on the fifth of next month. If the judge convicts me of murder, it could be curtains for my political career. As you know, Guruji, the Chief Minister is already biased against me.'

'According to your horoscope, all this is the result of Saturn sitting in the fifth house. The bad period will last for another four months. After that all your troubles will disappear.'

'So what should I do during this period, Guruji?'

(*Laughs*.) 'You know what to do. After all, the entire police force is under you. But start wearing blue sapphire. It will counteract the influence of the malefic Saturn.'

'When I talk to you, Guruji, I feel at peace. I really believe all my troubles will disappear.'

'That is what gurus are for. Can I also trouble you over a minor matter?'

'Tell me, Guruji, and I will attend to it personally.'

'I bought a small plot in Kanpur, some twenty acres. Now I am told squatters from a nearby slum have erected their huts on part of the land. I am leaving very shortly for a world tour. If they could be evicted before I leave it would—'

'Say no more, Guruji. Tomorrow I will have the bulldozers sent in.'

'Good. Give my regards to Vicky. I hope he is

wearing the coral ring I got specially made for him.'

'Of course, Guruji. Till his case is resolved, he dare not disobey your advice.'

'OK, Jagannath. I have to go now. Richard Gere is here to meet me.'

'Who is he, Guruji? Some car manufacturer?'

(*Laughs.*) 'No, he is an American actor. Bye now. *Jai Shambhu.*'

'*Jai Shambhu, Guruji.*'

*

'Tell me, Mr Tripurari Sharan, are you *my* chief sidekick or am I *your* sidekick?'

'What has prompted such a strange question, Bhaiyyaji? Have I done something wrong?'

'But of course. Since eight o'clock I have been waiting patiently for your call to find out if you managed to speak to the witness, but you did not phone. So I am phoning you.'

'I was going to call you in the morning, Bhaiyyaji. I didn't want you to have a disturbed sleep.'

'So the news is bad, eh? What happened? Was Pradeep Dubey not available?'

'No, I met him. He seems to be an idealistic young man. I offered him a lot of money to keep his mouth shut, even went up to ten lakhs. But he refused to budge. Said he will definitely testify against you. My hunch is that he has been put up by Lakhan Thakur.'

'Hmm . . . (*Long pause.*) So Lakhan is playing games again. He has not heeded my warning.'

'Why should he? He fancies himself as the next Jagannath Rai. Hard to imagine that five years ago he was just a petty gangster. Ever since he won the assembly election, his star has been on the ascendant. It is said he owns half the timber factories in Saharanpur. Now his ambition is to become a minister, like you.'

'That bastard will never succeed as long as I am around.

We'll deal with him at an appropriate time. But first tell me what should we do with this Dubey fellow?'

'Bhaiyyaji, if Dubey squeaks, you are sunk. He has to be prevented from testifying at all cost.'

'Then we'll ensure he doesn't testify. You tell Mukhtar to see me.'

'Don't you know about Mukhtar? He got picked up by the police yesterday in Ghaziabad.'

'What? How could they arrest Mukhtar?'

'I think there is some rape charge. You know Mukhtar, Bhaiyyaji. He cannot keep his pyjama cord tied. Always running after young girls.'

'Who is the police officer who has dared to arrest Mukhtar?'

'There is a new Superintendent in Ghaziabad. Young IPS chap called Navneet Brar. He is a bit over-zealous. Wants to stamp out crime from the State. It appears to be his handiwork.'

'It is actually the handiwork of the stars. They are aligned in an inauspicious manner. That is what Guruji told me. But as long as I have his blessings, I can take on any challenge. You failed with the witness, Tripurari. Now see how I sort out the police officer. Get me his mobile number immediately.'

*

'Hello. Navneet Brar speaking.'

'Navneet, this is Home Minister Jagannath Rai speaking.'

'Well, what I can do for you, Sir?'

'I believe you have arrested a man of mine. Mukhtar Ansari is his name.'

'Yes, Sir. He has been arrested for raping an under-age girl. It is a non-bailable offence, Sir. Section 376, in conjunction with 366. No leniency can be shown.'

'I am not requesting you to show leniency. I am directing you to release him immediately.'

'You cannot issue such an order, Sir. The matter is before

a magistrate. Now Mukhtar can be released only by a court order.'

'How dare you defy the Home Minister of the State!'

'I am sorry, Sir, but I have been tasked with upholding the law.'

'It looks as if you are not too bothered about losing your job.'

'I am more bothered about doing it correctly, Sir.'

'Then do the correct thing. Obey the order of your superior.'

'I regret to say, Sir, that I cannot obey an illegal order.'

'So you refuse to obey me?'

'I refuse to abet a criminal activity.'

'You are a young officer, Brar, and hot-headed. You are making the biggest mistake of your career.'

'I am prepared to face the consequences.'

(*Disconnect.*)

*

'*Jai Hind*. Director General's residence. Constable Ram Avtar speaking.'

'Is the DGP there?'

'Yes. Who is calling?'

'Home Minister Sahib wants to talk to him.'

'It is past midnight. DGP Sahib is sleeping.'

'Wake him up, you ass, otherwise together with the DGP you will lose your job.'

'But DGP Sahib has given strict instructions not to disturb him.'

'It appears you have not experienced Bhaiyyaji's wrath. Ram Avtar, if you don't get me DGP in the next ten seconds, from tomorrow you will be selling bananas in Hazratganj, understand?'

'Yes, Sir. Sorry, Sir. I am putting you through immediately to DGP Sahib's bedroom.'

'OK.'

Beep. Beep. Beep.

'Who is the bastard disturbing me at this time?'

'Jagannath Rai, Home Minister, will speak to you. I am passing the line.'

Beep. Beep. Beep.

'Hello. Maurya?'

'Good evening, Sir. Good evening. Why did you take the trouble of calling at this hour, Sir? I would have come to your house.'

'Maurya, tell me how long have you been Director General of Police?'

'Eight months, Sir.'

'And who made you the DGP?'

'You, Sir.'

'Then why is it that you do things which make me regret my decision?'

'What . . . what, Sir? What has happened?'

'Your police have picked up Mukhtar Ansari from Ghaziabad. I think you know very well that Mukhtar is my right-hand man. How could you allow this to happen?'

'This is the first I have heard about this, Sir. Must have been a local operation.'

'Your SP in Ghaziabad, a chap called Navneet Brar, is the man responsible. Now listen to my instructions. I want Mukhtar released first thing in the morning. And departmental action should be initiated against Brar for insulting the Home Minister.'

'Er . . . if I may make a suggestion, Sir, why don't we just transfer him?'

'OK. Then transfer him to . . . to Bahraich. The good life in Ghaziabad has gone to his head. Let him cool his heels for a while in the boondocks!'

'Sir, your instructions will be carried out immediately. '

'Good. I knew I could count on you, Maurya.'

'If you don't mind, Sir, could I also remind you of your promise to speak to High Command about giving my wife Nirmala the MLA ticket from Badaun?'

'Yes, I have not forgotten. But there are still two years to go before the State elections.'

'Still, Sir, preparations have to begin well in advance. I can assure you Nirmala will be a most loyal party worker. Actually so am I, Sir, it's just that I cannot say so openly, being still in uniform.'

'I know, Maurya. Now go back to sleep.'

'Good night, Sir.'

*

'Mukhtar?'

'Boss? *As-salaam alaykum*. Thanks for getting me out so quickly. Now I am going after that sisterfucker Superintendent of Police.'

'You will do nothing of the sort. I have already had Brar transferred to Bahraich.'

'The bastard! He is lucky to be alive.'

'Who was the girl?'

'Nobody you know, Boss. Just a neighbourhood kid.'

'When will you learn, Mukhtar? If all the girls you have raped delivered babies, half of UP's population will consist of your illegitimate children.'

'Sorry, Boss. I will be more careful next time.'

'Now listen, Mukhtar.'

'Yes, Boss.'

'There is a man called Pradeep Dubey who is threatening to testify against me in the Mustaqeem murder case. He needs to be neutralized. And after you take care of Dubey, you need to take care of his mentor, Lakhan Thakur.'

'Lakhan Thakur? The MLA from Saharanpur?'

'Yes. Why? Is the job too big for you?'

'No, Boss. No job is too big for me. It's just that getting rid of Thakur may be more complicated. He travels with five bodyguards.'

'So get rid of all of them. Come to the house tomorrow and get the cash from Tripurari.'

'I will be there. *Khuda hafiz,* Boss.'

'*Khuda hafiz.*'

*

'Hello.'

'Hello. Can I speak to Prem Kalra?'

'This is Prem Kalra speaking.'

'Then listen carefully, motherfucker. This is Jagannath Rai speaking. And this is my last warning to you. If you publish one more story against me in the *Daily News,* both you and your rag will be history.'

'Such language does not behove the Home Minister of our State.'

'So you think abusing someone is the exclusive preserve of journalists? I have tolerated your nonsense for a long time, but enough is enough.'

'At least tell me what has prompted your ire.'

'Your latest piece, alleging that I had Pradeep Dubey bumped off. When the police have confirmed that he was killed in a road accident, how can you make such a baseless allegation? I can sue you for character assassination.'

'But the allegation was not made by me, Jagannathji. Lakhan Thakur made the allegation on the floor of the Assembly. I have merely reproduced it.'

'And in the process you have become the mouthpiece of the opposition. How much is Lakhan Thakur paying you?'

'I don't do this for money. It is a social service that I render.'

'No one renders greater social service than we politicians. The least we expect in return is some appreciation from the media . . .'

'I cannot promise appreciation, Jagannathji, but I can promise restraint. Goodbye.'

*

'Hello. Home Minister's residence? Chief Minister Sahib wants to talk to Home Minister Sahib.'

'Put him on.'

'No. You put him on. Chief Minister is senior to Home Minister.'

'OK, OK, no need to get angry. I will pass to Bhaiyyaji.' (*Music*.)

'Hello?'

'Hello. Jagannath?'

'Namaskar Chief Minister Sahib.'

'I am under lot of pressure, Jagannath.'

'Now what has happened? The murder case against me has been dismissed.'

'It's about your son. High Command is saying that perhaps you should step down because of Vicky's involvement in the Ruby Gill murder case. If the verdict goes against him, our party's image will suffer greatly.'

'Why? The party's image did not suffer when the High Command made me Home Minister, despite the fact that I have thirty-two criminal cases against me. But have I been sentenced even in one? No, *na*? Then why are you making such a big issue over my son's involvement in just one murder case, when the judgment has not even been delivered?'

'It is no ordinary case, Jagannath. It has become the most high-profile murder case in the country. All the channels are only talking about this case.'

'So will we now be judged by the media? You are a lawyer yourself, Chief Minister Sahib. And the fundamental rule of law is that the accused is innocent till proven guilty. If ministers had to resign simply on the basis of being charged, two-thirds of your Cabinet would be empty. So I say let the case be proven against my son, then we shall see.'

'I have managed to persuade High Command to hold off any action till the local elections. But that journalist Arun Advani continues to cause trouble. Did you read his latest column? He is alleging that you are trying to bribe the judge. It is giving us very bad publicity.'

'Let him write what he wants. The good thing is none of

our voters know English. I was telling the Education Minister that we should ban all English-medium schools in the State. We should teach children only in Hindi. If we take away the bamboo, how will the flute play?'
(*Laughter.*)

'And also Urdu. Don't forget our Muslim voters.'

'Yes, of course, Chief Minister Sahib. Urdu is equally important. In fact, I am brushing up on my Urdu these days. Iqbal Mian has been teaching me Ghalib's poetry. Would you like to listen to a few couplets?'

'No . . . no. I have to go for the inauguration of a primary school. Just remember, Jagannath, I have managed to save you for now, but if Vicky is convicted even I won't be able to do anything for you.'

'Don't worry. That eventuality will not arise.'

'See you at the Cabinet meeting tomorrow.'

'Yes. See you, Chief Minister Sahib.'

*

'Hello. Rukhsana?'

'I am not talking to you, *janaab*. I sent you five hundred text messages. You didn't respond to even one.'

'*Arrey*, what can I do? The whole day I was busy in that wretched State Development Council Meeting which the Chief Minister is so fond of.'

'How can a meeting last a whole day?'

'It can if you have a room full of prize idiot bureaucrats, each one droning for hours about roads and bridges and schools and orphanages. Sometimes I feel it was a mistake to go into politics. When I have to travel hundreds of kilometres every day through dusty villages, when I have to listen patiently to ignorant farmers wanting me to ensure that the monsoon does not fail, when I have to sign endless files about matters that don't concern me remotely, I realize the price one has to pay for being in politics.'

'Then why don't you quit?'

'Easier said than done. Politics is a bitch, but it is like

government. You crib about it but you can't do without it either.'

'And what about me? Can you do without me?'

'*Arrey*, you are my *nasha*, my addiction. Listen to this couplet which I composed in your honour:
*"Although love's pangs may fatal be, there can be no way out
Without love too this heart would grieve, for want of things
to grieve about."*'

'You have become quite a poet. Looks like my love has made you a real Majnu.'

'Indeed . . . *"Love has made me good-for-nothing,
Otherwise a useful man I used to be."*'

'What can I say, *janaab*, today Urdu poetry is flowing from your mouth like bullets from a gun.'

'Don't talk about bullets, darling. This is the story of my life. The moment I try to become romantic somebody brings up the subject of guns and spoils the mood.'

'I am sorry.'

'Forget it. Tell me, how was your day?'

'Good. I went to the beauty parlour. Got full waxing done. Also facial. My body is like silk. You will find out when you touch me.'

'I am dying for that. Sumitra will leave for Farrukhabad on Friday. I will come to you on Saturday and stay the night.'

'Why don't you divorce your wife? She is only causing you grief.'

'My children are no better. I have a son who has had a penchant for getting into trouble ever since he was a kid. And a daughter who adamantly refuses to marry. With great difficulty I have managed to get her engaged to an excellent boy from our own caste, a Thakur belonging to the royal family of Pratapgarh, but she keeps postponing the marriage. Her favourite pastime is to chat with the sons and daughters of the sweepers and washermen who live behind our house. My biggest fear is that one day she will decide to elope with some street loafer and grind our family's nose in the dust.'

'Don't worry about something that might never happen.'

'Guruji says the same. You and Guruji are the only people who understand me.'

'But you don't understand *me*. For months I have been asking you to take me on a foreign trip, but you never oblige.'

'*Arrey*, when there are so many pending issues to be sorted out in this damned place, where is the time to think of going abroad? This is the problem with you. You are never content with what you have.'

(*Sob*.)

'*Jaaneman*, have I upset you? Look, I am giving you a kiss.'

(*Kissing sound*.)

*

'Dad?'

'Yes, Vicky?'

'Is it all set?'

'Yes. But I have asked for judgment to be postponed till 15 February. That is when the inauspicious period will end, according to Guruji.'

'So I need not worry?'

'Not as long as I am around. But have you ever thought how much grief you've given me? How long can I keep bailing you out of trouble?'

'That's what dads are for.'

'You are a real motherfucker; you know that, don't you, Vicky?'

'Well, from a purely technical point of view, that would be you, Dad, wouldn't it?'

'You bas—'

(*Disconnect*.)

The American

TODAY IS the happiest day of my life. Even better than the day Vince Young led Texas on a fifty-six-yard touchdown drive against USC in the game's final minutes to give the Longhorns their greatest ever victory in the Rose Bowl.

I am finally going to India. Land of maharajahs and mutton curry. Home to elephants and kangaroos. And to the most beautiful girl in the whole wide world. Sapna Singh, who will become my wife in two weeks' time.

I really dig Indian weddings. Just rented that flick *Monsoon Wedding* the other night. I love the way Indian girls dance and the wild music simply drives me crazy.

My mother's a great believer in marriage. She's had four already. But she wasn't too keen on my marrying an Indian. 'They're dirty, they're smelly, and they speak bad English!' was her verdict, till I showed her Sapna's pictures. Since then she's been broadcasting all over town that her son is all set to marry Miss Universe.

Me and Mom are closer than ticks on a hound. We've been this way ever since my pa ran off like he did, leaving Mom and me all sad and alone, and so poor we didn't have a pot to piss in. After he disappeared we had to sell the ranch and all the cattle and move to a run-down old trailer, where we lived for six years till Mom married that nice man from the Welfare Office and we moved into his house on Cedar Drive. I really don't think much of my pa. I wouldn't piss on him if he was on fire. But no point getting all worked up. Not on the day I will finally meet Sapna.

How I met my dream girl is one heck of a story. I'm convinced that all marriages are made in heaven. And it's God who decides who will marry whom, and when. So he makes some guys, like my old school mate Randy Earl, who have no trouble at all in scoring with girls. And then he makes some, like me, who, well, have to wait a bit longer, being shy and all. Guess I was just born that way. Not that I am bad looking or ugly, like Johnny Scarface, my foreman. His mom probably had to tie a porkchop around his neck so the dog would play with him. I'm just your ordinary sort of guy. Mr Joe Average. I'm five feet, seven inches tall, and Sandy, my-ten-year-old niece, says that if my face was a little rounder, my nose a bit smaller, my hair a shade darker, and my weight fifty pounds lower, I'd look just like Michael J. Fox! But not to worry, I am working on both my height and weight. I've been using KIMI, the scientifically developed height-increasing device by Dr Kawata which promises to make me three inches taller in just six months, and I'm regularly taking the Chinese Miracle Slimming Powder which I bought off the Home Shopping Network.

Anyway, Mom was getting seriously worried about me turning twenty-eight and still being a bachelor and had begun wondering whether I might be gay, till the folks at International PenPals fixed all that. In return for a nominal membership fee of $39.99 (payable in four instalments of $9.99 each), they gave me the addresses of seven beautiful girls who wanted to become friends with me. Now that's what I call too much of a good thing. I mean, try juggling seven girlfriends all at once. The girls were from all over the world, including places I didn't even know existed. In ABC order, I had Alifa from Afghanistan, Florese from East Timor, Jennifer from Fiji, Laila from Iran, Lolita from Latvia, Raghad from Kosovo and Sapna from India. I wrote to all of them, introducing myself and asking them to reply. And they wrote back, each and every one of them. There was one problem, though. Three of them didn't know good English. I mean it's kind of difficult to carry on a decent conversation when you receive a letter which says, 'Daer Larry, Braenbooking a hello you too. Mares fioggicku. I wanna lioxi plean. Amerika goot place for a leev. Loov you.' Some of the letters were, well, too perplexing. The girls from Afghanistan, East Timor and Iran just talked about the political problems in their countries. And the one from Fiji asked for my credit-card number in the very first letter. Now that I thought was being too upfront. The girl from Latvia was more modest. 'Hello Larry. I'm Lolita,' she wrote. 'I am sixteen years old. I want to be friends with you. Call me on 011-371-7521111.' I thought she was a bit young for me, but you can't tell how deep a well is just by measuring the length of the pump handle. So I called Lolita up. I think she must have a bad case of asthma, because all I got was heavy breathing for, like, five minutes and I freaked out when I got my phone bill and found that the call had cost me $57.49. So that was the end of my friendship with Lolita. Eventually I was left only with the girl from India, Sapna Singh. She wrote me the most wonderful letter, telling me of her brave struggle against cruelty and oppression. She was so poor she didn't even have a telephone. It brought tears to my eyes, made me remember my own struggle to become the best hi-lo driver in Texas. I replied, she replied back. Two months later we exchanged pictures. Till then I had considered Tina Gabaldon, Miss Hooters International 2003, to be the best-looking filly in the field. But one look at Sapna's photo and I knew I had been wrong. She was the most beautiful girl in the universe and I fell head over heels in love with her.

Gathering all the courage I could muster, I proposed to her in June this year. Amazingly, she accepted, making me happier than a rooster in a hen house. I began learning Hindi. She began learning how to make chocolate brownies, my favourite dessert. We fixed a date for the wedding in India. She requested five grand to make the preparations. I was broke as a church mouse, but I begged and scrimped and saved and wired her the money. Three weeks ago she sent me our wedding card. And now I'm off to New Delhi to marry the woman of my dreams.

'Hi y'all! Howdy!' I greeted the two pretty air hostesses who welcomed me on to the United Airlines plane that was taking me to India. The aircraft was huge, almost as big as the Starplex Cinema in Waco. Another tall air hostess directed me to my seat, 116B. It was one of the best seats in the plane, right at the end, and very conveniently located too, bang next to the john.

I put my bag underneath my feet and settled down. Today really seemed to be my lucky day. I was in the middle seat, flanked by a blonde sitting next to the window and a dark, Indian-looking guy wearing a red Hilfiger T-shirt and a Dodgers baseball cap.

The blonde was reading a magazine called *Time*. 'Excuse me, Ma'am.' I doffed my hat and tapped her arm. 'Where are you headed to?'

She shrank away from me like I had the chickenpox and gave me a look which would make a porcupine seem cuddly. I turned to the youth on my left, who seemed more friendly.

'So how's yer momma and them?' I asked him.

He looked at me like a calf at a new gate. 'Excuse me, what did you say?'

Quite clearly the guy wasn't from Texas.

'*Aap kehse hain?*' I asked in my best Hindi.

'I am fine,' he replied in English.

'*Kya aap bhi India jaa rahe hain?*'

'Hey man, why are you talking to me in that strange lingo? I don't speak Hindi.'

'But . . . but you are Indian!' I blurted out.

'Correction, dude. I'm American,' he said and whipped out a blue passport from his front pocket. 'See the bald eagle on the cover? That's American, man.'

'Oh!' I said and fell silent.

Before the plane took off, the air hostess did some hand exercises and made us watch a safety video. I was busy memorizing the instructions given on the card in the seat pocket, but none of the other passengers seemed to be bothered about what would happen to them if the plane fell into the water. And before I knew it, we were flying.

The air hostess returned after a while, trundling a metal buggy loaded with bottles and cans.

'What would you like to drink, Sir?' she asked me sweetly.

'Coke, please,' I told her.

'I am sorry, Sir. We seem to have run out of Coke. Will Pepsi do?'

'Yeah,' I nodded. 'That's Coke too. How much?'

'It's free, Sir,' she said and smiled.

The Indian looked at me curiously. 'Are you flying for the first time?' he asked.

'Yeah,' I replied and extended my hand. 'We've howdied but we ain't shook yet. Hi, I'm Larry Page.'

'Larry Page?' He seemed impressed. 'You know you have the same name as the inventor of Google.'

'Yeah, everyone keeps telling me that. Isn't Google something to do with computers?'

'Correct. It's a search engine for the internet.'

'Johnny Scarface, my foreman, is always on his computer. But I know as much about the internet as a pig knows about playing the piano.'

'Not to worry,' he said and grasped my hand. 'Glad to meet you, Larry. My name's Lalatendu Bidyadhar Prasad Mohapatra, Biddy for short.'

'What do you do, Biddy? You look like a college student.'

'Yeah. I'm a sophomore at the University of Illinois, planning a double major in microelectronics and nanotechnology. And what do you do?'

'I'm your friendly forklift operator at the Walmart Supercenter in Round Rock, Texas. That's the one off I-35, Exit 251. Any time you happen to pass by, stop in and holler at me. I'd appreciate it. Might even get you a five per cent discount.'

That broke the ice between us. Ten seconds later we were talking like old buddies at a school reunion. Biddy began telling me all about some project that he was doing with some stuff called super-cooled conductors. Before I knew it, I was telling him everything about my trip to India and about Sapna.

'Your fiancée sounds like a real nice Indian girl,' he said.

'Would you like to see some of her pictures?' I asked him.

'Yeah. Sure.'

I took out my bag and carefully removed the brown folder full of large colour glossies of Sapna in a whole lot of dresses. I watched Biddy's face as he flipped through the photos. His eyes seemed to pop out, just as I expected.

'This is Sapna Singh, you said?' he asked me after a long time.

'Yeah.'

'And you've actually met her?'

'No. But she'll be waiting for me at New Delhi airport.'

'She took five thousand dollars off you for the wedding?'

'Yeah. It was necessary. She's not from a rich family.'

'And you think you're going to marry this girl?'

'Of course. Two weeks from today, on 15 October. All preparations have been made, including a nice white horse! I tell you, Biddy, I just can't believe my luck.'

He twisted his lips. 'I'm sorry to say, dude, but you've been had.'

'What do you mean?'

'I mean this girl whose glossies you showed me is not Sapna Singh, cannot be Sapna Singh.'

'But why?' I asked, perplexed. 'Do you know her?'

'Every Indian knows her. These photos are of the famous actress Shabnam Saxena. I even have her poster in my dorm.'

'No, no. This is my fiancée. That chick Shabnam probably looks like Sapna.'

Biddy gave me the look Johnny Scarface gives me when I ask for a raise.

'There . . . there must be some mistake,' I tried again.

'There is no mistake,' Biddy said firmly. 'These photos are of Shabnam Saxena. In fact I'm certain that one of the photos is a still from *International Moll*, a big hit starring Shabnam. Don't mind my using one of our Indian proverbs, Larry, but as we say: *Nai na dekhunu langala*. You shouldn't get ready to take a bath before seeing the river.'

The plane suddenly felt like it was diving straight to the ground. I became dizzy and gripped the armrest tightly.

I snatched the folder back from Biddy. 'What you've been telling me is just a bunch of bunk. You're more full of shit than a constipated elephant!' I declared and didn't talk to him for the rest of the flight.

Deep inside me, I felt like crying.

MOTIVES

‘Never judge a man’s actions until you know his motives.’

Anonymous

The Possession of Mohan Kumar

MOHAN KUMAR emerges from Siri Fort Auditorium at eleven p.m. with a sore shoulder and a splitting headache. He steps into the courtyard and blinks in astonishment at his surroundings. The venue for the Gandhi séance resembles a war zone. Wooden desks and chairs lie splintered like firewood. The ground is strewn with clothes, shoes, socks, bags and loops of naked wire. There is an eerie silence all around. The television cameras and protesting hordes have been replaced by police cordons and grim-faced constables, who wave him through the tall iron gates which have themselves been ripped off their hinges.

He walks unsteadily towards the car park, where his silver Hyundai Sonata is the lone private car, surrounded by a phalanx of police jeeps with red and blue beacons.

A thin, gaunt man with a pencil moustache runs towards him. 'Sahib, you have come!' he cries with obvious relief. 'They said a murder has taken place inside. You should have seen the way people were running out. Two died in the stampede. Are you OK, Sahib?'

'Of course I am OK, Brijlal,' Mohan Kumar replies tersely. 'Where is Rita madam?'

'I saw her leaving with another lady in a black Mercedes.'

'That's odd.' He purses his lips. 'She should have waited for me. Anyway, let's go.'

The chauffeur hurriedly opens the left rear door of the car. Mohan Kumar is about to get in when he notices something just below the handle. 'What is this, Brijlal?' he demands. 'How did this big scratch come here?'

Brijlal inspects the door panel with a puzzled look. 'One of the constables must have grazed this with his stick. I am sorry, Sahib. I left the car to look for you. Please excuse me.' He lowers his gaze.

'How many times will I excuse you, Brijlal?' Mohan Kumar asks harshly. 'You are becoming more and more negligent in your work. I should take the cost of repairing the door from your salary – then you might learn your lesson.'

Brijlal does not say anything. He is well acquainted with Sahib's foul temper, which is famous throughout Uttar Pradesh.

He has been with Mohan Kumar for twenty-seven years and treats him with the same mixture of deference and devotion that he accords Lord Hanuman. In his universe, Mohan Kumar is no less than God, a powerful patron who holds the key to his happiness and well-being. It was Sahib, after all, who got him his first job at the State Electricity Board. Sahib then got him upgraded to a permanent job as peon in the State Sugarcane Cooperative. It was Sahib too who had encouraged him to learn to drive, thanks to which he had been employed as a chauffeur in the Secretariat office in Lucknow, a job which carried not only a higher pay-packet but even overtime. For twenty years, he had driven Mohan Kumar's official white Ambassador. When Mohan retired six months ago, Brijlal still had three years of service left, but he, too, took voluntary retirement and joined Mohan Kumar as his personal chauffeur, in the ultimate act of devotion to his Sahib.

In taking premature retirement Brijlal believes he has made a tactical move. He is convinced that there is much Sahib can still do for him and his family. There is one final favour, in particular, he wants from Sahib – a government job for his son Rupesh. Brijlal is of the firm belief that government service, with its security of employment, is the panacea for all the problems of the poor. It is his dream to get Rupesh employed as a driver in the Delhi government. Mohan Kumar has promised to do just that, once Rupesh obtains a driving licence. A government job for Rupesh and a suitable groom for his nineteen-year-old daughter Ranno is all Brijlal wants, the sum total of his dreams and desires. In pursuit of these goals, he will happily suffer insult and abuse from his Sahib.

'Now are you going to just stand there cooling your heels like a fool or will you take me home?' Mohan Kumar demands as he slides into the back seat.

Brijlal closes the rear door and takes his position behind the wheel. Before starting the car, he switches off his mobile phone. He knows how irritated Sahib becomes if it rings while he is driving.

The auditorium blurs in the rear-view mirror as the car moves away. Mohan Kumar has his gaze fixed resolutely outside the window. A ghostly moon hangs in the distance, casting a pale light on the tops of buildings. The traffic has thinned out by now, with even the DTC bus service winding down. They reach the house in just under twenty minutes. As the car enters the wrought-iron gates of 54C Aurangzeb Road, Brijlal's heart fills with pride.

Mohan Kumar's residence is an imposing two-storey neo-colonial villa, with a white marble façade, a covered latticed portico and a magnificent lawn containing a gazebo. It has an out-house with three servant quarters which are occupied by Brijlal and his family, Gopi, the cook, and Bishnu, the gardener. But what thrills Brijlal the most is the rent, rumoured to be in the region of four hundred thousand rupees a month. He gets goosebumps just thinking about this amount. To him, it represents the pinnacle of achievement and forms the practical bedrock of his exhortations to Rupesh. 'Work hard, my son, and you might one day become like Sahib. Then you, too, could have a house whose monthly rent costs what your father took eight years to earn.'

Mohan Kumar's wife, Shanti, is waiting in the portico wearing a red cotton sari. She is a small, middle-aged woman with greying hair which makes her look older than she is. Her normally pleasant face is etched with worry lines. 'Thank God you have come,' she cries as soon as the car draws to a halt. 'Brijlal had me worried sick when he called to say you were inside that hall.'

Mohan casts an angry glance at his driver. 'I have told you repeatedly, Brijlal, not to broadcast my programme to all and sundry. Why did you have to call Shanti?'

'I am sorry, Sahib.' Brijlal lowers his eyes again. 'I was really worried about you. I thought I should let Bibiji know.'

'You do that again and I will take your hide off.' He slams the car door shut and strides into the house. Shanti hurries after him.

'Why did you have to go to that horrible séance?' she asks.

'None of your business,' he replies brusquely.

'It is all the doing of that *chhinar*,' Shanti mutters. 'I don't know how that witch has put you under her spell.'

'Look, Shanti.' He raises his index finger. 'We have had this argument many times. You will get nothing by agonizing over it. Has Gopi put ice and soda in my bedroom?'

'Yes,' she sighs in resigned acceptance of an imperfect marriage. 'If you are determined to finish your liver, what can we do? Go and drink as much as you want.'

'I will,' he says and begins climbing the stairs to the first floor.

Nearly three weeks pass. The incident in the auditorium becomes a distant memory for Mohan Kumar. He immerses himself in his former routine, attending board meetings, examining projects, advising clients. He accepts the offer of yet another consultancy on behalf of a corporate house; puts in a round of golf on Sundays at the Delhi Golf Club and spends two afternoons a week at his mistress's house. He wills himself to believe that everything is normal, but cannot shake off a nagging doubt at the back of his mind. It is like a hazy picture trying to acquire definite shape, a finger of memory attempting to push its way into his consciousness. He tosses and turns at night, finding it difficult to sleep. He wakes up on the floor one morning, in the bathroom on another, without any recollection of how he got there. He pauses in mid-sentence during board meetings, sensing words and phrases fluttering at the tip of his tongue but remaining maddeningly inarticulate. Lying in bed with Rita, he suddenly feels like an old, large animal and loses all desire. He knows something is wrong, but cannot pinpoint what.

He goes to his doctor for a check-up, but Dr Soni, his family physician, is unable to find anything wrong. 'All your vital signs are good, Mohan. The MRI scan is perfectly normal. I believe it is simply a case of Post-Traumatic Stress Disorder.'

'What's that?'

'When someone suffers a traumatic event, like seeing a murder in front of his eyes, the brain tries to cope with the psychological stress. This can lead to symptoms such as nightmares, flashbacks and insomnia. I am going to prescribe some sleeping pills. You should be fine in a week's time.'

Four days later, while Mohan is having his breakfast, Brijlal enters the kitchen where Shanti is busy whipping yoghurt. He touches her feet. 'Bibiji, I need your blessings. A boy came to see my daughter yesterday.'

'Oh, so Ranno is getting married?' Shanti asks in pleasant surprise.

'Yes, Bibiji. The boy is also from Delhi, belongs to our caste and, most importantly, is a class four government employee, working as a peon in the Railway Department. His father is also a peon. I only hope they don't demand too much dowry. I have made them my best offer. Let's see if they accept.'

'I am sure things will work out all right,' says Shanti. Taking a quick peek to see if Mohan is still sitting at the dining table, she whispers to Brijlal, 'Today your Sahib will be visiting that witch Rita, won't he?'

'Yes, Bibiji,' Brijlal replies with a nervous grimace, feeling half guilty himself.

'Just keep a watchful eye on Sahib. See that he eats and drinks properly. I am worried about his health. He has not been himself lately.'

'Yes, Bibiji.' Brijlal nods in agreement. 'Even I find his behaviour rather strange at times.'

'If only he had not met Rita,' Shanti says bitterly. 'Sometimes I feel like going to her house and asking her why is she so intent on destroying my family.'

'Don't demean yourself by talking to her, Bibiji,' Brijlal counsels. 'In God's kingdom, justice may be delayed, but is never denied. You will see, she will be punished eventually.'

'I hope you are right, Brijlal.' Shanti looks briefly towards the ceiling and resumes her whisking.

Mohan's office is a depressingly grey building in Bhikaji Cama Place, a chaotic warren of offices and shops. Finding an empty parking slot is a daily headache for Brijlal. Today he is forced to park in the narrow alley behind the Passport Office. After securing the car, he loiters, chatting with the other drivers, playing a game of rummy, sharing his discontent at rising prices, falling morals. At lunchtime he receives a call on his mobile phone. It is the boy's father, saying that he approves of Ranno, and demanding an extra twenty-five thousand rupees as dowry. 'I accept,' Brijlal says and rushes to a nearby temple.

Mohan comes out of the office promptly at three p.m. for the afternoon tryst with his mistress. As soon as he gets into the car, Brijlal offers him a box of *laddoos*.

'What are the sweets for, Brijlal?' he smiles.

'As a result of your blessings, Sahib, I have managed to get an excellent groom for my daughter Ranno.'

'That's good. Shanti told me that you were looking for a boy.'

'He is a government servant, Sahib. But there is only one problem.'

'Yes?' Mohan responds warily.

'They want an extra thirty thousand as dowry. I was wondering, Sahib, if you could lend the money to me.'

He shakes his head. 'Brijlal, I've already given you fifteen thousand as advance pay. There is no way I can spare any more.'

'God has given you so much, Sahib. I am asking for very little.'

'Giving you any more would be to your own detriment. Why do you people need to spend so much on weddings anyway? There is nothing to eat in your houses, yet you want to ape the rich when it comes to marrying your daughters. Now don't disturb me. I have to read this report.' He opens his briefcase and takes out a ring-bound manila folder. Brijlal's face falls.

Near Vasant Vihar, the car is briefly held up by a small wedding procession crossing the road. A rag-tag band leads the party, tuneless trumpets blaring a *filmi* tune. The twenty-odd guests are dressed rather drably, with some even sporting slippers. An anaemic-looking groom dressed in a gaudy *sherwani* sits astride an equally anaemic-looking horse. Brijlal looks at the procession with the peculiar contempt the poor have for the poorer. His own daughter's wedding will be a lavish affair, he imagines. He will somehow manage to raise the twenty-five thousand and then he will get Sahib to book the Officers' Club on Curzon Road as the marriage venue. There will be a uniformed brass band as well as a live singer. A row of orderlies will carry Petromax lanterns lighting up the night. He can already see the groom's wedding procession walking in through the hallowed gates of the Officers' Club. The hall is glittering like a palace. The melodious sound of *shehnai* pours into the night. Inside, the elegant pavilion is loaded with sweet-smelling jasmine and marigolds. The guests enter the venue and look around in wonderment at the finery and luxury. The groom's father shakes his head. 'Where have you brought us, Brijlal? Is this the right address?' 'Yes,' he says. 'This is the right address. This where my Ranno is getting married to your son. All thanks to the blessings of my Sahib. There he is.' He points out Mohan Kumar, looking regal in a cream *sherwani* suit and a pink turban. As if on cue, the band begins playing a song, but for some reason Sahib is screaming at him: 'Look where you are going, you idiot . . . Stoppppp!' and he finds the big brass trumpet almost blaring in his face, shattering his ear drum and knocking him down.

By the time he wakes up from his reverie, it is too late. His head is lying on the steering wheel and the car is up against a lamppost which is now bent at an impossible angle. There is a small spidery crack in the left corner of the windscreen. His fingers touch something sticky on the steering wheel. He raises his face, looks in the rear-view mirror and discovers blood oozing from the corner of his mouth. He has cut his lip. He shakes his head vigorously, as if to clear it, and steps out of the car to inspect the damage. The front of the Hyundai has taken the brunt of the collision. There is a deep dent in the front fender where the metal has been scrunched up. He suspects the radiator may also have been hit.

Brijlal begins shivering. In twenty years of driving, this is the first time he has made such a mistake. Now he is finished. Sahib will take his hide off. This is the end of his career as a driver, of his dream of getting Ranno married, of a government job for Rupesh.

Then he notices Mohan Kumar on the back seat, eyes closed, looking very still, almost dead. Brijlal's first instinct is to run away, to collect his wife and Rupesh and Ranno and make a dash for the railway station. He will board the Lucknow Mail to his ancestral village, hide out for a few weeks till the matter cools. Then he will settle down in some other city, get another job, look for another groom.

By now the entire wedding party is gathered around the car. The trumpeter touches his arm: '*Kaise hua, bhai?* What happened?' The groom also dismounts from his horse and begins inspecting the car. A perspiring constable arrives, parting the crowd with his stick and cries of 'Move! Move!'

Brijlal edges towards the outer periphery of the circle of onlookers, but cannot tear his eyes from Mohan Kumar. He sees the groom open the rear door and sprinkle a few drops of water on Mohan's face from a mineral-water bottle. Sahib stirs and makes a grimace of pain.

'Where am I?' Mohan asks in a weak voice.

'You are in your car, near Vasant Vihar Police Station,' the constable informs him. 'Your car has had an accident. Do you want me to call an ambulance?'

'Accident?' Mohan asks. He gets to his feet groggily and steps out of the vehicle. It is too much for Brijlal. He cuts through the throng and falls at Mohan's feet. 'I am very sorry, Sahib. Please excuse me, I have caused you grievous harm.' He sobs like a young boy.

Mohan lifts up the driver by the shoulder. Brijlal closes his eyes tightly, expecting a hard slap, but finds Mohan gently wiping his tears with his finger. 'And who are you?'

'I am Brijlal, Sahib. Your driver.'

'Has this fellow lost his memory?' the constable asks the groom.

'No. My memory is perfectly intact,' Mohan replies. He looks at the constable intently. 'Aren't you the one who hit me with a *lathi*?'

'Hit you? Are you out of your mind? This is the first time I have seen you.'

'The use of brute force is not right. Especially from a defender of the law.'

'Has your Sahib gone completely nuts?' The constable looks quizzically at Brijlal.

'It is all my fault,' Brijlal wails.

'It is not your fault, Brijlal,' Mohan says. 'There is a divine purpose behind every physical calamity. Will you now please see if the car is still in working order or whether we should try and look for a taxi.'

Brijlal does not know whether to laugh or cry. 'Yes, of course, Sahib,' he says in between sobs and gets into the driver's seat. With trembling hands, he inserts the ignition key and is surprised to find the engine purring smoothly. He reverses the car, brakes and jumps out. 'It is working, Sahib,' he cries. The onlookers begin to leave, their interest in the car strictly commensurate with the damage sustained by it.

Brijlal holds open the rear door, and Mohan gets in. 'Will you be so kind as to tell me where we were going?'

'To Rita Memsahib's house.'

'And who is she?'

'You will remember everything, Sahib, once you meet her.'

*

Mohan Kumar alights next to Rita's house looking totally lost. Brijlal directs him to the first-floor flat, presses the doorbell, and then, feeling awkward, returns to the car.

Rita opens the door, dressed in a pink nightgown, and Mohan is overpowered by the strong scent of her perfume. 'You are late, darling,' she drawls, and attempts to kiss him on the lips.

Mohan Kumar draws back as though stung by a bee. 'Don't . . . don't. Don't touch me, please.'

'What's wrong with you?' Rita raises her eyebrows.

'And who might you be?'

'Ha,' she laughs. 'Now you pretend you don't even know me.'

'I really don't. My driver has brought me here.'

'I see,' Rita says with exaggerated politeness. 'Well, Mr Kumar, my name is Rita Sethi. I happen to be your mistress and you come to my house twice a week to have sex with me.'

'Sex with a woman! Oh my God!'

'This is getting tiring, Mohan. Come on, cut it out.'

'You see . . . you see, Miss Sethi, I have taken a vow of *brahmacharya* requiring complete celibacy. I cannot have sex with any woman.'

'Have you joined some theatre company?' Rita asks crossly. 'Why are you putting on this act of behaving like Mahatma Gandhi?'

'But I am Gandhi.'

'Gandhi?' Rita bursts out laughing. 'I wouldn't mind being called the mistress of Gandhi.'

'Well, then I should have mentioned this to you a long time ago, but there are seven social sins, Ritaji,' he says, blushing slightly. 'Politics without Principle, Wealth without Work, Knowledge without Character, Commerce without Morality, Science without Humanity, Worship without Sacrifice and Pleasure without Conscience.' He reels them off on his fingers. 'This last one applies to the relationship between a man and his mistress. I hope you understand the import of what I am saying.'

'Yes, I understand very well. It means sex without love. You have simply been using me all this while, without really loving me. Now you have tired of me and want to leave me, hence all this drama,' Rita says bitterly. 'Fine. Leave me. You always were a selfish bastard, concerned only about yourself. I don't know why I wasted my time with a jerk like you. Out.' She points to the open door.

'Before leaving, may I proffer another bit of advice?' he says. 'May I request you to maintain chastity? Chastity is one of the greatest disciplines, without which the mind cannot attain requisite firmness.'

Rita gapes at him, her face darkening. 'You swine,' she hisses and delivers a stinging slap to his left cheek.

Mohan Kumar stumbles backwards, his shoulder crashing into the door frame. 'That was totally unnecessary,' he mutters, nursing his cheek. 'Nevertheless, if it pleases your fancy, you may exercise your violent instincts on my right cheek as well.' He turns his face to the other side.

Rita literally propels him out of the door and on to the staircase. 'Good riddance to you, Mr Mohanbhai Pseudo Gandhi,' she shouts before slamming the door shut.

'Correction, my dear. It is Mohandas Karamchand Gandhi,' she hears him say as he tramps down the stairs.

'What happened, Sahib?' Brijlal asks. 'You have come out very quickly today.'

'We are not coming back here ever again, Brijlal,' he replies.

'Bibiji will be very happy.'

'Who is Bibiji?'

'Your wife.'

'My wife? I have a wife?'

Mohan Kumar wanders through his house like an amnesiac trying to piece together the jigsaw of his past. The first person he meets is Shanti, beaming with the exuberant cheerfulness of a newlywed bride. 'Brijlal tells me you just broke off from that witch Rita. Is it true?'

'Yes. I am not going back to Miss Rita Sethi.'

'Then just give me a minute,' Shanti says and disappears into the small room next to the kitchen which has been converted into a temple. She returns with a small steel plate in her hand. 'Let me do a little *tika*.' With the ball of her middle finger, she rakes his forehead with a pinch of vermilion paste.

Mohan appears mystified. 'What is this for?'

She blushes. 'For starting our married life afresh from today.'

He shrinks back. 'Let me tell you, Shanti, that I have taken a vow of complete celibacy. So please do not have the expectations of a married man from me.'

'You can sleep in your own room,' she says evenly. 'The lifting of that witch's shadow from this house is boon enough for me. In God's court there is some justice, after all.'

He raises his finger like a teacher. 'I will now devote my life to fighting injustice. I will use truth as my anvil and non-violence as my hammer.'

'*Arrey*, what's got into you? You are speaking just like Gandhiji.'

'Then do you mind if I start calling you Ba?'

'You can call me anything. Just don't call that witch ever again.'

Mohan Kumar commences a rigorous new routine, sitting in the temple every morning with Shanti, praying and singing *bhajans*. He gives up his suits and shirts in favour of simple cotton *kurta* pyjamas and develops a penchant for Gandhi caps. He stops dyeing his hair, eats only vegetarian food, becomes a complete teetotaller, substitutes sugar with jaggery and insists on having a litre of goat's milk every day.

He discards his mobile phone, stops going to the office completely and spends his time reading the *Gita* and other religious books, and writing letters to the newspaper on issues such as corruption and immorality, but which are never published because he signs them 'Mohandas Karamchand Gandhi'. His favourite pastime, however, is to collect each and every piece of information on the Ruby Gill murder case, which he pastes diligently into a scrapbook.

'Why this sudden interest in Ruby Gill?' Shanti asks him.

'She was my greatest disciple,' he answers. 'She was doing her doctorate on my teachings before her life was tragically cut short.'

'The entire neighbourhood is talking about Sahib's transformation,' Brijlal confides in Gopi. 'Some people say he has gone mad. He has started imagining himself to be Mahatma Gandhi. Why doesn't Bibiji take him to see a good mental doctor?'

'All rich people are slightly mad, Brijlal. Besides, Bibiji prefers him this way,' the cook replies.

'But madness is a serious illness, Gopi. Today he is calling himself Mahatma Gandhi, tomorrow he might start calling himself Emperor Akbar.'

'*Arrey*, what difference does it make what he calls himself, Brijlal?' Gopi says. 'At least he is doing things which we consider right. Best of all, he does not trouble us any longer.'

'Yes, that is true. So what should I do?'

'Pretend to be Gandhiji's driver, just as Bibiji pretends to be Gandhiji's wife.'

It is Diwali, the Festival of Lights. Mohan Kumar's house is lit up with strings of tiny twinkling bulbs. The night sky is a riot of colour as brilliant pink and green flowers continue to explode with abandon. Every few seconds a rocket goes screaming into the atmosphere. The bursting of crackers reverberates in the air like thunder.

The garden has been taken over by an army of children, clapping and whooping with delight.

Seven-year-old Bunty, the son of the neighbourhood sweeper, is busy lighting a rocket with his eight-year-old friend Ajju, the cobbler's son. The rocket is placed inside an empty coke bottle.

'Ey, Ajju, let's see what will happen if we hold the bottle sideways instead of straight,' Bunty suggests.

'*Arrey*, the rocket will go sideways instead of straight up,' says Ajju.

'Then let's try sending it sideways, into the gate. I will tilt the bottle and you light the rocket.'

'OK.'

Bunty holds the glass bottle in his hand, pointed towards the entrance, while Ajju strikes a match and lights the fuse. With a few little sparks the rocket streaks towards the gate, leaving a cloud of smoke inside the bottle. In mid-flight, however, it reverses its trajectory and heads towards the house. Bunty and Ajju watch in horror as the rocket dives straight through an open window on the first floor.

'Oh my God, Bunty, what have you done?' Ajju asks, cupping his mouth with his palm.

'Shhh!' whispers Bunty. 'Don't tell anyone. Let's grab a couple of cracker packets and run before they catch us.'

A little while later, Shanti steps into the garden with Gopi in tow, holding a tray of lighted clay lamps and a box of sweetmeats. She picks up a *diya* from the tray and places it in the centre of the decorative pattern she has specially drawn on the concrete floor of the gazebo.

A cracker bomb bursts with deafening noise in the western corner of the garden. The cook looks with displeasure at the crowd of children dancing with delight on the grass. 'Look at these idiots, Bibiji,' he tells Shanti. 'They are not bursting crackers, they are burning money. Our money. One bang and a hundred rupees go up in smoke.'

Shanti rubs her eyes, smarting from the noxious fumes of the cracker, and coughs briefly. 'I prefer sparklers, Gopi. These loud crackers are not for old people like me.'

'I don't know why Sahib allowed all these street children into our house and gave them crackers worth five thousand. See how they are trashing our garden. Tomorrow I will have to do the cleaning,' he grumbles.

'*Arrey*, Gopi, have a heart,' Shanti says. 'These poor children have probably never exploded so many crackers in their life. I am glad Mohan invited all of them to celebrate Diwali here. This is the first good thing your Sahib has done in thirty years.'

'Yes, that is true,' Gopi concedes. 'Last year in Lucknow, Sahib spent his entire Diwali gambling. Today he sat in the temple and did Laxmi puja with you, and even maintained a fast for the first time ever. Hard to believe he is the same man.'

'I just hope he remains this way,' Shanti says as she begins distributing the sweetmeats to the children. 'Come, come, take this *prasad*,' she calls out.

Brijlal and his son Rupesh are also in the garden. 'So what is the latest on Ranno's wedding?' Shanti asks the driver.

'With your blessings, Bibiji, Ranno's wedding has been fixed for Sunday, 2 December,' Brijlal beams. 'I hope you and Sahib will grace the occasion with your presence.'

'Of course, Brijlal,' Shanti replies. 'Ranno is like our own daughter.'

'What is that, Bibiji?' Rupesh calls out in alarm, pointing his finger at the first-floor window from which black smoke is billowing out.

Shanti looks up and the box of sweetmeats drops from her hand. '*Hey Ishwar*, that looks like a fire in Mohan's bedroom. And he is sleeping inside. Run, save your Sahib,' she screams as she begins running towards the house.

Gopi, Brijlal, Rupesh and Shanti rush up the stairs to Mohan's bedroom and find it locked from inside. 'Open up, Sahib,' Brijlal hollers, banging at the door, but there is no response from Mohan.

'Oh God, he must already have fainted from the fumes,' Shanti quavers.

'Let's break down the door,' Gopi suggests.

'Get back . . . get back,' Rupesh cries. He rears back and is about to crash his shoulder into the door when it opens suddenly, hitting him with a blast of heat. Mohan Kumar staggers out. His face is bright red and there is black ash on his clothes and hands.

While Gopi, Brijlal and Rupesh run into the bedroom and try to douse the fire, Shanti tends to her husband, who is choking and wheezing.

'Aah . . . aah.' He opens his mouth, taking in gulps of air.

Rupesh emerges from the bedroom with black soot all over his face. 'We managed to put out the fire, Bibiji,' he declares. 'Luckily, it had not spread beyond the curtains.'

'Thank God you woke up in time,' Shanti says to Mohan.

He blinks repeatedly. 'What is happening?'

'There was a fire in your room.'

'Fire? Who could have done that?' He looks around suspiciously.

'Must have been the handiwork of one of the street kids in the garden,' Gopi avers.

'Street kids? What the hell are street kids doing in my house?' Mohan demands.

Gopi and Brijlal look at each other quizzically.

A little while later, Mohan comes down to the dining room in fresh clothes. 'I am hungry. Where is my dinner, Gopi?' he asks the cook.

'It is ready, Sahib, exactly as per your instructions,' says Gopi as he lays a dish on the dining table accompanied by a casserole containing freshly made *rotis*.

Mohan takes a morsel and immediately spits it out. 'This is not meatball curry,' he says, curling his lips in distaste. 'What kind of nonsense food is this?'

'*Lauki kofta,* cooked specially without onions and garlic.'

'Is this some kind of sick joke? You know how much I hate bottle gourd.'

'But now you only eat *saatvik* vegetarian food.'

'You were always without brains, Gopi. Now it appears that you have become hard of hearing as well. Why would I ever ask you to cook this lousy dish? Now either bring me my meat or chicken dish or get ready for immediate sacking.'

Gopi goes out scratching his head and returns with Shanti.

'So you are no longer a vegetarian?' she asks him warily.

'When did I stop being a non-vegetarian?' he sneers.

'Two weeks ago. You told us that you would stop eating meat and drinking alcohol.'

'Ha!' he laughs. 'Only a lunatic would take such a decision.'

'I have already become one, living in this house,' Gopi mutters as he begins clearing the plates from the dining table.

Mohan suddenly looks at Shanti, his brow furrowing. 'What did you say about my drinking? I hope you have not touched my whisky collection?'

'You had all the bottles destroyed a fortnight ago,' Shanti replies evenly.

He gets up from the dining table as if touched by an electric cattle prod and rushes into the pantry which serves as a makeshift cellar. He emerges, ashen-faced, and starts another desperate search through the kitchen, opening each and every cupboard, rifling through the shelves, even checking inside the oven. Finally he slumps down on a chair. 'All my bottles are gone. How could you do that? I had painstakingly acquired those bottles over twenty years. Do you know how much that stock was worth?'

'Well, it was you who gave the order.'

'Now you have really pissed me off,' he hisses, eyes glinting with menace. 'Did I destroy them or did you destroy them behind my back? Come on, out with the truth, woman.'

'Why would I destroy them? I have suffered them for thirty years. It was you,' Shanti says, her face crumbling. 'You are the one who was saying this morning that no one with any wisdom would ever touch alcohol or any intoxicants.'

'Are you mad, woman? No one with any wisdom would ever destroy perfectly good bottles of foreign whisky. Who took them out of the cellar?'

'It was Brijlal.'

'Call that swine.'

Brijlal is summoned and questioned thoroughly. He sticks to the story he has been rehearsing for a fortnight. He had been asked to destroy the bottles by Bibiji. He had taken them to the municipal drain and smashed each and every one of them on the concrete pavement, discarding the glass shards in the rubbish bag which the garbage truck had subsequently carted away.

'Didn't you think of checking with me, first?'

'Well, Sahib, Bibiji said it was your order. Who am I to question Bibiji?'

'This Bibiji is the root cause of trouble in this house,' Mohan says, gnashing his teeth. 'I need a drink right now.'

'Why are you changing the perfectly sensible decision you took to become a teetotaller?' Shanti implores him. 'I maintained a fast all these years only for you to kick this evil habit. When you said you were giving up drinking, I thought God had finally opened your eyes, given you good sense.'

'Good sense is what you need, woman,' he shouts and turns to Brijlal. 'Take me immediately to Khan Market. I cannot sleep without having a drink.'

'But it is Diwali today, Sahib. The market is closed.'

'Then go and steal a bottle from somewhere,' he snaps at the driver, picking up a dinner plate from the counter and throwing it against the wall, where it shatters into pieces.

'Take him, Brijlal,' Shanti cries. 'Take him to some bar before he destroys everything.'

'It is impossible to stay in this house,' Mohan declares and stomps out of the kitchen.

The next morning he asks Brijlal to drive him straight to Modern Liquors in Khan Market. The owner, Mr Aggarwal, greets him warmly. 'Welcome, Kumar Sahib. Do you have some more bottles for us?'

'What do you mean?'

'You sold your vintage collection to us a few weeks ago. I was wondering if there was more. We will pay top price for every bottle.'

'You are mistaken. All my bottles were destroyed.'

'Then someone has cheated you, Sir. I paid twenty-five thousand rupees for your collection.'

'I see.' Kumar strokes his chin and summons Brijlal to the shop. 'Is this the man who sold you the bottles?' he asks Mr Aggarwal.

'Exactly, Sir. He is the man.'

'I think it is time you told me the real story behind the bottles, Brijlal,' Mohan says coldly.

Trembling with fear, the driver blurts out the truth.

'What did you do with all that money?' Mohan demands.

'I used it for Ranno's dowry, Sahib.'

Mohan's rage bubbles over. He raises his hand and slaps the driver. 'You ungrateful dog! You eat my salt and then stab me in the back? Now go and get it back, each and every penny of it. If you don't return my full twenty-five thousand, I will turn you over to the police.'

Brijlal clutches Mohan's feet, tears streaming from his eyes. 'But Sahib, this will ruin my Ranno's wedding. You can deduct it from my salary every month, but please don't ask me to break my daughter's heart.'

'You should have thought of the consequences before you embarked on your little transaction. I want my money by this afternoon. Otherwise get ready to spend the night in jail.'

Brijlal walks into Mohan's study at noon and hands him a brown envelope.

Mohan counts the notes and gives a satisfied grunt. 'Good. Twenty-five thousand. You have now made amends, Brijlal. Let this be a lesson. Another foolish mistake like this and I will have no qualms about dismissing you. Then you won't even have a roof over your head.'

Brijlal says nothing and walks out of the room like a zombie.

A week passes. Mohan Kumar resumes his drinking and meat-eating with such vengeance that his household comes to the conclusion that the brief interlude without alcohol was an aberrant decision, itself taken perhaps under the influence of alcohol. He stops talking to Shanti completely, and looks at her with such revulsion that she avoids crossing his path. Gopi is warned against bringing bottle gourd into the house, let alone cooking it.

Mohan resumes going to the office, and tries to speak to his mistress, but Rita Sethi resolutely refuses to take his calls, which causes him great consternation. And then he gets his bank statement, which leads to an apoplectic fit.

Sister Kamala's face tightens, making her look rather school-matronly. 'Now let me get this straight, Mr Kumar. You are telling me that we have illegally withdrawn the sum of two million rupees from your account with HSBC Bank, right?'

'Damn right,' Mohan Kumar mutters, wiping sweat from his brow with a blue handkerchief. 'I got this statement in today's mail. Look at it.' He thrusts a sheet of paper at her. 'It says cheque number 00765432 for rupees twenty lakhs was credited to the account of the Missionaries of Charity. Well, I never gave you that cheque. So there's obviously some fraud involved here.'

Sister Kamala adjusts the blue sash of her crisp white sari with studied nonchalance. 'In that case we will have to refresh your memory.' She looks at the woman with glasses standing beside her chair wearing a similar dress. 'Sister Vimla, can I have the documents please?'

Sister Vimla pushes the round glasses on her nose a notch higher and places a green ring-binder on the table.

Sister Kamala flips open the binder. 'Would you care to have a look at this, please, Mr Kumar. This is a photocopy of the cheque you gave us ten days ago, on 7 November. Is this your signature or not?' she asks.

Mohan Kumar scans the document with the suspicious air of a probate attorney examining a will. There is a long pause, and then he exhales. 'It does look like my signature. A very good forgery, I must say.' He jabs a finger at Sister Kamala. 'This is a serious matter, you know. You could go to jail.'

'So you say that your signature is forged. Fine.' She flips to the first page. 'Would you have a look at this photograph now? Is this you or has this photo been forged too?'

Mohan Kumar looks at the glossy colour photograph under a plastic sheet. There is a longer pause. 'It . . . it does look like me,' he says weakly.

'Yes, Mr Kumar. It is you. You came to us on a Wednesday. You sat in this very room, on this very chair and gave us the cheque, telling us how much you admired Mother Teresa and her work. You said that possession of inordinate wealth by individuals is a crime against humanity and then you wrote us a cheque for twenty lakhs. Sister Vimla took this photo for our monthly bulletin, to keep a record of the largest single donation this branch has ever received.'

'But . . . but I have no recollection of coming here.'

'But we have full recollection, and full proof,' Sister Kamala says triumphantly.

'Is there no way I can get my money back?' he pleads.

'We have already cashed the cheque. The funds will help us run our hospice for the terminally ill, expand the orphanage and open a small school for children up to Grade Six. Think of what you will earn back in goodwill and blessings from all those who will be helped by your donation.'

'I don't need any goodwill. I just want my money back. I am a very senior IAS officer.'

'And also a very venal one. Sister Vimla did a full background check on you. Aren't you the Chief Secretary who was declared the most corrupt officer in Uttar Pradesh by the Civil Service Association?'

'That's rich. You take my money and also insult me! Now are you returning my money or do I need to go to the police?'

'You don't need to go to the police, Mr Kumar. You need to go to a doctor,' Sister Kamala says. 'And now, if you will excuse us, it is time for our prayer.'

'But . . .' Mohan tries to interject.

Sister Kamala firmly shuts the door and turns to her aide. 'Loco.' She draws circles over her right ear with her index finger. 'Completely loco.'

Dr M. K. Diwan's clinic in Defence Colony is pleasantly furnished with a relaxing couch upholstered in blue, some easy chairs, abstract paintings on the alabaster walls and an artificial silk fig tree in the corner which looks surprisingly real. The décor gives the feel of a drawing room rather than an office. Dr Diwan is a tall man in his late forties, with a brusque manner and a clipped British accent.

'Why don't you kick off your shoes and lie on the couch?' he advises Mohan Kumar, who is standing diffidently next to the wall.

Mohan obeys reluctantly. He lies down, supporting his head with a bolster. Dr Diwan pulls an easy chair next to the couch, and sits down with a black leather-bound diary and a silver pen in his hands.

'Good, now let's hear what's troubling you.'

'Doctor, some unknown force has insinuated itself in my body like a persistent toothache. I have started walking, talking and acting like another person.'

'And who is this other person?'

He pauses. 'You won't believe me.'

'Try me,' the doctor says drily.

'It is Gandhi . . . Mahatma Gandhi.'

He expects Dr Diwan to laugh, but Delhi's best-known clinical psychologist doesn't even raise an eyebrow. 'Hmmm,' he says, fiddling with his pen. 'And who is speaking to me right now?'

'Right now I am Mohan Kumar, IAS, former Chief Secretary of Uttar Pradesh, but at any moment I might start talking like Mohandas Karamchand Gandhi.' He leans towards the doctor. 'It all started with that Gandhi séance I should never have attended. Do you think this could be a case of demonic possession?'

'Demons exist only in films. And films are not real, Mr Kumar.'

'Then am I going mad?'

'No, not at all. Even perfectly sane people can act a bit differently at times.'

'You don't understand, Doctor. The malady is extremely serious. It makes me do crazy things, like wearing *khadi* and that ridiculous Gandhi cap. Like breaking all the bottles in my whisky collection. Like becoming vegetarian and blowing twenty lakhs of my hard-earned money on the Missionaries of Charity.'

'I see. Now when exactly do these episodes happen?'

'I don't really know. I . . . I mean one minute I am myself and the next minute I have become this other person, blabbering some nonsense about God and religion.'

'And you have full memory of what you did as this other person when you revert to your real self?'

'At first I had no recollection. There was simply a gap in my memory. But now, I am slowly beginning to decipher the stupid things I do as Gandhi.'

Dr Diwan interrogates him for another half-hour before making his diagnosis. 'I believe you are suffering from what we call Dissociative Identity Disorder. In films they call this a split personality.'

'You mean my personality has split into two – Mohan Kumar and Mohandas Karamchand Gandhi?'

'More or less. In DID, the usual integrity of the personality breaks down and two or more independent personalities emerge. A person with the illness is consciously aware of one aspect of his personality or self while being totally unaware of, or dissociated from, other aspects of it. Would you mind submitting yourself to a clinical hypnosis session?'

'And what will you do?'

'We will explore your unconscious with a view to understanding whether past events and experiences are associated with your present problem.'

'Will you ask very personal questions?' he asks with a worried look.

'We will have to. The whole idea of hypnosis is to bypass the critical censor of the conscious mind.'

'No. I will not submit to a hypnosis session,' he says firmly.

Dr Diwan sighs. 'You will have to be candid with me, Mr Kumar, if I am to treat you. Tell me, were you abused as a child?'

Mohan Kumar sits up and stares at Dr Diwan irritably. 'Let's cut out all this Freudian bullshit. Just tell me how I can avoid turning into Mahatma Gandhi.'

Dr Diwan smiles. 'There are many individuals in the world, Mr Kumar, who would do anything to turn into Mahatma Gandhi.'

'Then they are stupid, Doctor. You must understand, people didn't like Gandhi, they feared him. He appealed to an instinct they wanted to keep buried. He advised against sex, drink, wealth. I mean what is the fun of living if you cannot have any of these things?'

'There are more important things in life, Mr Kumar.'

'Look, I have not come here for a debate on Gandhian philosophy.' Mohan begins tying his shoelaces. 'But you will have earned your fee if you can tell me what triggers my sudden transition to this Gandhi character.'

'Well, there's no evidence to suggest any biological cause for Dissociative Identity Disorders. In almost all the cases that I have seen, the transition from one personality to another is usually triggered by a stressful event.'

'So if I were to avoid stress, I can prevent the transition?'

'In theory, yes. But I must warn you that the alternate personality can take control of the individual's behaviour at any time. And, what is even more important, over time one personality tends to dominate the others.'

'I assure you, Doctor, I won't let Mahatma Gandhi dominate me.' He stands up. 'Thank you for your time.'

'It was interesting meeting you, Mr Kumar,' Dr Diwan replies. 'Although we didn't quite see eye to eye on the treatment, I hope you now have more clarity about your illness.'

'An eye for an eye ends up making the whole world blind, Doctor,' Kumar says gravely and gently pats the doctor's arm.

'Oh my God!' Dr Diwan exclaims.

Mohan chuckles. 'Just kidding. But that is exactly the kind of thing I say when I switch to Gandhi. That will not happen any more. Good bye, Doc,' he says and saunters out of the clinic.

Dr Diwan watches his receding figure with a puzzled expression.

Immediately after returning from Dr Diwan's clinic, Mohan Kumar becomes more careful than an accountant with tax inspectors on his tail. He tiptoes through the house like a ballet dancer, smooth and light-footed, avoiding collision with doors and walls and keeping clear of the temple room by at least twenty feet. He bans all crackers from the house and issues strict instructions to Brijlal to drive at no more than forty kilometres per hour and to avoid sudden braking. He examines each and every book in his library and incinerates every title which might have even a semblance of a connection to Gandhi, in the process destroying such rare volumes as a first edition of *India of My Dreams* and a biography of Martin Luther King with the tag-line 'American Gandhi'. He increases his alcohol intake to three shots a night and, to ensure that Gandhi doesn't intrude even in his dreams, starts taking Valium tablets just before sleeping.

Shanti accepts Mohan's reversion to his old, difficult self with the robust fortitude of a martyr. Gopi goes back to preparing meat dishes and putting ice and soda in Sahib's room at night.

Mohan is in his bedroom with his second glass of whisky, examining the papers pertaining to Rai Textile Mill, while outside the window an unseasonable thunderstorm rages. The rain comes down in sheets and thunder shakes the roof. He hears the phone ring and picks it up.

'Hello?'

'Hello, Kumar.'

A tiny prick of resentment stabs at his heart every time Vicky Rai addresses him by his surname, but, like a pragmatic bureaucrat, he has learnt to swallow his pride.

'Yes, Sir,' he replies.

'I am just calling to remind you about the board meeting tomorrow.'

'Oh yes, Sir. I received Raha's report today. In fact, I was going over it right now,' he says.

'We will be banking on you to push through the retrenchment proposals. The job cuts are essential, you know, to restructure the textile company.'

'Without doubt, Sir. We need to cut a hundred and fifty jobs at least. Don't worry, I will ensure that the restructuring proposal is passed without any difficulty. Of course, it won't be unanimous. The unions will oppose the lay-offs tooth and nail. Dutta, as usual, will indulge in some theatrics. But what can one union guy do against five from the management? We will steam-roll him into submission.'

'I am sure you can take care of that bastard. Good night, Kumar.'

As Mohan puts the phone down, there is a knock on the door. At first he doesn't hear it, so heavy is the rain outside. But the knock is insistent. With an irritated frown he gets to his feet, puts on his slippers and opens the door.

Brijlal stands in front of him, his eyes bloodshot, his clothes completely drenched.

'What are you doing here?' Mohan demands.

'It is all over . . . It is all over,' Brijlal mumbles, shivering slightly.

Mohan wrinkles his nose. 'You are reeking like a pig. Are you drunk?'

'Yes, Sahib, I am drunk.' The driver gives a hollow laugh. 'What do you expect from country hooch? It will smell. But it gives a kick which your expensive imported whisky can never give.' He lurches into the room.

'Out . . . out,' Mohan gestures, as if reprimanding a dog. 'You are spoiling the carpet.'

Brijlal doesn't heed the instruction and advances towards the bed. 'I am only spoiling your carpet, Sahib, but you have spoilt my life. Do you know what day it is today?' He speaks in a slurred, off-key voice.

'Yes. Today is Sunday, the second of December. What's so special about it?'

'Today my Ranno was to get married. Today I should have been listening to the sound of *shehnai*. My house should have been ringing with laughter and happiness, but instead I have been listening to the sobs of my wife and daughter. All because of you.'

'Me? What did I do?'

'You are the one who had me accosted like a common thief and paraded before the whole of Khan Market. You are the one who demanded the return of the money. So I had to take the dowry back from the groom's family. I have never been more humiliated in my life. And what was my fault? The bottles were going to be destroyed in any case. If I made some money from them, what harm did I cause anyone? You big sahibs cheat your wives and have affairs with other women. You booze and gamble and don't even pay tax. But it is poor people like me who get insulted and arrested.'

'Enough, Brijlal. You have lost your senses,' Mohan says sternly.

The driver continues as if he has not heard him. 'The relationship between master and servant is a very delicate one, separated by a *lakshman rekha*. You crossed the line, Sahib. The groom's family has called off the wedding completely. Now you tell me what should I do? Allow my Ranno to remain a spinster all her life? How can I face my wife, who slaved day and night in preparation for the wedding?'

'I am warning you, Brijlal. You are really exceeding your limit.'

'I know I am exceeding my limit, but you, Sahib, have exceeded all decency. You deserve to be stripped naked, hung upside-down and then lashed with a whip till you feel the pain which I am feeling now.'

'Enough, Brijlal,' he bellows. 'I am ordering you to leave right now.'

'I will go, Sahib, but only after settling the score. You have wealth and power, but I have this.' He inserts his hand into his *kurta* and draws out an old knife. Its dull steel fails to catch the chandelier's light.

Mohan Kumar sees the knife and gasps. Brijlal advances further into the room; Mohan shrinks away till his back collides with the window overlooking the garden. A bolt of lightning rips across the sky, causing the window panes to shudder.

'You are drunk, Brijlal,' he appeals again. 'If you take any foolish action now you might regret it later.'

'I am a desperate man, Sahib. And a desperate man doesn't care for consequences. My wife and daughter, in any case, will commit suicide. My son will find a job somewhere or other. As for me, after I kill you I am going to kill myself.'

The true extent of Brijlal's desperation is slowly becoming evident to Mohan. 'OK . . . OK . . . Brijlal, I will personally ensure that Ranno's wedding takes place,' he blabbers. 'You can take my house, or I can book the ballroom of the Sheraton. And I will give away Ranno myself. After all, she is just like my daughter.' The words gush out of his lips in a torrent.

'Ha,' Brijlal snorts. 'A man confronted with death can make even a donkey his father. No, Sahib, I am not going to fall into your trap again. I am going to die, but first you are going to die.' He grips the knife tightly in his right hand and raises his arm. Mohan shuts his eyes tightly.

The arc of the knife slices through the air and bears down on Mohan's chest, breaking centuries-old barriers, sweeping aside the cobwebs of rank and status. But just as it is about to pierce Mohan's chest, Brijlal falters. He is unable to breach the final frontier of loyalty. The knife slips out of his grip, his hands drop limply to his sides, he sinks to the carpet, throws back his head and lets out a piercing wail, a requiem for his frustrated defiance.

Meanwhile, a slow change is coming over Mohan Kumar. The tension in his face is dissolving, as if a shadow is lifting. He opens his eyes and finds Brijlal at his feet.

'*Arrey*, Brijlal, what are you doing here?' He speaks in a slow, ponderous manner. Then, as if remembering something, he taps his forehead. 'Of course, you must have come to invite me to your daughter's wedding. Ah, Ba is here.'

Shanti bursts into the room. 'What happened?' she asks breathlessly. 'I thought I heard a scream.'

'Scream? What scream? You are imagining things, Ba. I was just talking to Brijlal about his daughter's wedding. Wasn't it supposed to be today?'

Shanti looks at Brijlal, who is still on the carpet, sobbing in short gasps. She wrings her hands. 'I don't know what is wrong with you. One day you are the saint, and the next day you become the devil, then you become a saint again. Are you even aware that Brijlal had to cancel his daughter's wedding?'

'Really? How could that happen, Brijlal? If there has been some mistake from my side I ask your forgiveness with folded hands.' He brings his palms together.

Brijlal falls at Mohan's feet. 'Please don't say this, Sahib. I am the one who should be asking for forgiveness. I came to harm you, yet you have forgiven me. You are not a man, you are God, Sahib.'

Mohan lifts him up. 'No, Brijlal. God is vast and boundless as the ocean, and a man like me is but a tiny drop. And what is all this talk about you trying to harm me? Have you also started imagining things? Oh! What is this knife doing here?'

The board meeting begins promptly at four o'clock inside the premises of Rai Textile Mill in Mehrauli.

The boardroom has the metallic smell of fresh polish. Its large oval table is made of burnished teak with green felt place mats. The walls are decorated with corporate art.

Mohan Kumar enters the room wearing a white *dhoti kurta* and a white Gandhi cap. Vicky Rai, dressed in a blue pinstripe suit, greets him at the door. 'Very clever, Kumar,' he whispers. 'This outfit will fool the unions completely.'

'Where am I sitting?' Mohan Kumar asks him.

'You are my right-hand man, so you sit on my right side.' Vicky Rai winks at him. 'And next to you I have put Dutta.'

Five men and a lone woman take their places around the table. Vicky Rai sits at the head of the table, in front of a projector screen. 'Well, members of the board, for today's meeting there is only one item on the agenda, the restructuring of Rai Textile Mill,' he begins briskly. 'As you all know, we purchased this factory from the government two years ago as a sick unit. Drastic measures are needed to make it healthy.' He gestures to a short, fair man with steel-rimmed glasses sitting on his left. 'I will now ask Mr Praveen Raha, the CEO, to unveil the new corporate strategy for the board's approval.'

Raha adjusts his glasses and pushes keys on a laptop till a Technicolor picture full of charts and graphs is projected on to the white screen behind him. 'Honourable members of the board, let me begin with a stark fact,' he says. 'Last year the company suffered a net loss of rupees thirty-five crores.'

'Total lie.' A slim man sitting next to Mohan in *kurta* pyjamas and thick black-rimmed glasses speaks up in a gravelly voice. 'According to the figures compiled by the workers' union on the production achieved, we believe the company should have made a profit of rupees two crores.'

Raha frowns at him and punches a button on the laptop. A new chart appears on the screen. 'Well, the audit report certified by Messrs R. R. Haldar does not support your contention, Mr Dutta.'

'The audit report is a fraud, like you,' Dutta sneers.

Raha decides to ignore the taunt. 'Anyway, as I was saying, our operating environment continues to remain difficult. The totally illegal strike by workers last May resulted in a loss of thirty-five man days.'

'Please don't blame the strike on the workers,' Dutta intervenes again. 'The management was solely responsible for the strike by unilaterally withdrawing the transport allowance.'

Raha continues as if he has not heard Dutta. 'It is Mr Rai's dream to make this mill one of the biggest players in the textile field in India. Our eventual objective is to modernize the mill in two phases, with the installation of hi-tech state-of-the-art textile machinery. For the restructuring plan to work we are required to bring down non-performing assets and interest-bearing debt. We would need to maximize the use of capital intensive machinery, with the concomitant need to . . . er . . . rightsize some of the other parameters.'

'And what might these other parameters be, Mr Raha?' Dutta asks.

'This will require us to downscale the workforce to an optimum degree.'

'Oh, you mean men will be sacked to make way for machines?'

'Well, Mr Dutta, I wouldn't put it quite so starkly. And, in any case, the restructuring plan will have in-built provisions for matching of competencies and payment of motivational wages and productivity-linked bonuses, together with other incentivization packages which—'

'Stop this charade, Raha.' Dutta pushes back his chair and stands up. 'On behalf of the unions, I totally reject the restructuring plan.'

There is a fizz of silence in the room. All eyes look at Vicky Rai, who drums his fingers on the table, his face inscrutable. 'Well, in that case, I think we should put the proposal to a vote. All those in favour, please say yes.' He stares at a middle-aged man with a long nose on his left. 'Mr Arora?'

'Yes.'

'Mrs Islamia?'

'Yes.'

'Mr Singh?'

'Yes.'

'Mr Billmoria?'

'Yes.'

'Mr Dutta?'

'An emphatic no.'

'Mr Kumar?'

Mohan has an impish smile on his face. 'Well, I must say this has been a most fascinating and thought-provoking discussion. I will make only three submissions. First, that the principle of majority does not work when differences on fundamentals are involved.' He glances at Vicky Rai, whose eyebrows go up a fraction.

'My second submission is that each and every one of you should consider yourself to be a trustee for the welfare of our fellow labourers and not be self-seeking,' he says, emphasizing each word. 'Where there are millions upon millions of units of idle labour, it is no use thinking of labour-saving devices. This company cannot function with greed as its only motive. It has to serve a higher purpose. And this brings me to my third submission.'

Vicky's face is now etched with worry lines. 'What the fuck is Kumar up to? Is he speaking in our favour or against us?' he whispers to Raha.

'My third submission,' Mohan Kumar repeats as he dips his head below the table and brings up a large packet wrapped in brown paper, 'is this.' He tears off the wrapping to reveal a wooden spinning wheel. 'Ladies and Gentlemen,' he announces, pausing for theatrical effect, 'I present to you the *charkha*.'

There are gasps from the board members. 'The spinning wheel was invented in India as a device for spinning yarn from fibres, but somehow got lost to us,' Mohan Kumar continues. 'I had to search in almost fifty shops in Chandni Chowk before I found this one. I claim that in losing the spinning wheel we lost our left lung. I believe that the yarn we spin from this device is capable of mending the broken warp and woof of our lives. The *charkha* is the panacea for all the ills afflicting this company and, indeed, this country. A plea for the spinning wheel is a plea for recognizing the dignity of labour. I am sure our friend from the unions will agree.' He looks pointedly at Dutta, who watches him, mouth agape.

'Yes . . . Yes, of course,' Dutta mumbles. 'Forgive me, Mohan Kumarji. All along we thought of you as a snake, but you are actually our saviour.'

A buzz goes around the boardroom. Hurried consultations are held. Eventually Vicky Rai stands up. 'It appears that we do not quite have unanimity on the restructuring plan. I will ask Mr Raha to further refine the proposal. We shall notify you of the date for the next board meeting. Thank you.'

He gives Mohan Kumar a withering look and leaves the room, slamming the door shut.

Over the next week, Mohan Kumar devotes himself to various causes. He participates in rallies by the Justice for Ruby campaign, sits outside the Supreme Court with activists protesting against the proposed increase in the height of the Sardar Sarovar Dam, attends a candle-light vigil at India Gate for peace between India and Pakistan, and leads a group of angry women picketing country liquor shops. He also replaces his reading spectacles with wire-rimmed, round 'Gandhi' glasses and the media instantly dubs him 'Gandhi Baba'.

On Sunday, while going to a protest march against the creation of Special Economic Zones, Mohan's car gets caught up in heavy traffic in Connaught Place. As it inches towards the red light, his eyes are drawn to the posters adorning a cinema on his left. Full of lurid images of semi-naked women, they bear titles like 'ALL NIGHT LONG', 'A VIRGIN'S TROUBLES' and 'MAN-EATING BEAUTY'. A diagonal strip on the posters proclaims, 'Full of love and sex. Morning show ten a.m. Special Rates.' A tag-line underneath states boldly: 'Sex needs no language.'

'Ram, Ram,' Mohan mutters. 'How has the government allowed such filth in a public place?'

Brijlal sighs knowingly. 'My Rupesh has also been coming to these morning shows. These posters are nothing. I am told in the films they show full naked women.'

'Really? In that case stop the car.'

'What, Sahib, right here?'

'Yes, right here.'

Brijlal manoeuvres the car to the kerb alongside the cinema and Mohan steps out.

The cinema is an old, grey building, with a cloistered, mouldy aura. The paint on the walls is peeling off and the tiles on the floor have been badly defaced. But the frescoes on the ceiling and the Corinthian pillars in the atrium are still intact, decaying reminders of its former grandeur. The morning show is about to start and there is a fair-sized crowd milling around the ticket window. It is a hormonally driven audience, exclusively male, looking for instant gratification. There are even boys in the queue as young as twelve or thirteen. They fidget nervously and puff up their chests in a desperate bid to look older. Mohan Kumar marches straight to the ticket window, oblivious to the protests of those in the queue. The cashier, a middle-aged man with a pencil moustache, sits in a small airless room with wads of pink, light-green and white tickets in front of him. 'Hundred for Dress Circle, seventy-five for Balcony, fifty for Front Stalls. Which ticket do you want?' he asks in a bored voice, without even bothering to look up.

'I want all your tickets.'

'All the tickets?' The cashier raises his head.

'Yes.'

'The special rates for group bookings do not apply to morning shows. Are you bringing a group from some boys' hostel?'

'No, I want all the tickets only for the purpose of destroying them.'

'What?'

'You heard me correctly. I want to destroy your tickets. Aren't you ashamed of yourself, showing such filth, spoiling the morals of the youth of this country?'

'Hey mister, don't talk to me about all this. Go talk to the manager. Next, please.'

'Please call the manager. I refuse to leave till the manager meets me,' Mohan says firmly.

The cashier glowers at him, before getting up from his stool and disappearing through a green door. Presently a short, corpulent man enters the room.

'Yes, what is it? I am the manager.'

'I want to talk to you,' says Mohan.

'Then please come to my office. It is the first room to your right when you come up the stairs.'

The manager's room is larger, with a faded green sofa and a wooden desk which is totally bare except for a black telephone. Framed posters of bygone films adorn the walls.

The manager hears out Mohan Kumar patiently. Then he asks him, 'Do you know who owns this cinema?'

'No,' says Mohan.

'It is Jagdamba Pal, the local MLA. I am sure you don't want to tangle with him.'

'And do you know who I am?'

'No.'

'I am Mohandas Karamchand Gandhi.'

The manager breaks into hysterical fits of laughter. '*Arrey bhai,* that *Munnabhai* film with Gandhi has come and gone. Your dialogues are one year too late.'

'Laugh, Mr Manager, but I would like to see your face when you see your own son entering through the turnstiles. I believe that the reckless indulgence of passions promoted by the films you screen encourages unrestrained licence and corruption amongst our youth. I am afraid I cannot turn a blind eye to this entirely avoidable calamity.'

The manager sighs. 'You are a decent man, but also a foolish one. If you insist on going ahead with your protest, be prepared to face the consequences. Don't blame me if the MLA sets his goons on you.'

'A true *satyagrahi* does not fear danger. From tomorrow I am going to sit outside and fast until you agree to stop showing these filthy films.'

'Be my guest,' the manager says and picks up the phone.

The next morning Mohan Kumar arrives at the theatre clad in his Gandhi dress – a white *dhoti* and *kurta* with a cap on his head. He picks a spot directly in front of the ticket window and sits down on the ground, propping up a simple placard which declares, 'WATCHING THIS FILM IS A SIN'.

The men in the queue look at him curiously. Some bow before him, some drop coins at his feet, but not one drops out of the line. By nine fifty, the ticket window is closed and a 'House Full' board is placed in front of it.

Shanti arrives a little later. 'Why don't you come home now?' she asks anxiously. 'The film has already started.'

He gives her a dry smile. 'Another film will start soon. I am sure someone will listen to me. If I am able to convince even one man that what he is doing is wrong, I will feel that I have succeeded in my mission.'

'But how will you succeed, when no one even knows that you are fasting?'

'My fast is a matter between God and myself, Ba. But you don't worry. I am sure others will join me in this crusade in due course.'

'Then at least drink this juice I brought for you.' Shanti offers him a flask.

'When a man fasts, it is not the gallons of water he drinks that sustains him, but God, Ba. You go home now.'

With a final forlorn look at him, Shanti leaves with Brijlal. Mohan continues to sit on the ground, watching the ebb and flow in Connaught Place, the harried-looking office executives in jackets and ties, the young women with happy glistening faces out for a shopping spree, the hawkers selling belts, sunglasses and pirated books. The roar of traffic is deafening.

When Shanti returns two hours later to check on him, she is amazed to discover Mohan sitting on a wooden platform with another man, their backs resting against foam cushions. A crowd of nearly two hundred people is standing around them, waving placards and shouting slogans: 'PORN IS FILTH', 'GANDHI BABA ZINDABAD', 'DOWN WITH JAGDAMBA PAL'.

Mohan looks smug and content. 'How did this happen?' Shanti wants to know.

Mohan points to the middle-aged man sitting next to him in white *kurta* pyjamas. He has an oval face, a narrow nose, a sharp jawline and shifty eyes. Shanti takes an instant dislike to him. 'This is Mr Awadhesh Bihari. He met me by chance an hour ago and immediately decided to support my cause. It is he who has organized this group and arranged for all the banners and placards.'

'Welcome, Bhabhiji,' Bihari says with the smoothness of a con-artist. 'It is a privilege to meet someone as great as your husband. I was telling him how evil this man Jagdamba Pal is. He owns this sleazy cinema and also several brothels.'

'And what do you do?' Shanti asks him.

'I am a politician belonging to the Moral Regeneration Party. I stood against Jagdamba Pal in the last election. The public was solidly behind me, but he rigged the election and won.' He grimaces.

'So are you doing this just to settle political scores?'

'What are you saying, Bhabhiji?' He appears shocked. 'It is our sacred duty to protect our children from being corrupted. We in the MRP look upon ourselves as custodians of Indian culture. You may remember our protest against that lesbian film *Girlfriends* a few years ago. We tore down all the posters and prevented its screening, despite a court order against us. These sleazy films are an affront to our culture. We are with your husband now, come hell or high water. He will do the fasting; we will provide the back-up.'

'And what if the cinema owner doesn't respond?'

'How will he not respond? We will compel him to respond. But first we need to raise awareness. I have phoned some TV channels to cover our protest.'

Shanti touches her hand to Mohan's forehead, checking to see if he has a fever. 'I am really worried for you. How long can you last without food?'

'We shall both find out,' Mohan smiles. 'Don't worry, Awadhesh here will take care of me.'

In this fashion, bolstered by Shanti's concern and Bihari's assurances, Mohan Kumar passes two days without food. By the third day of the fast, his condition has deteriorated considerably. Doctor Soni checks his pulse and blood pressure and looks concerned. Shanti is beside herself. But there is still no sign of the cinema owner.

That afternoon a van pulls up outside the cinema and a woman dressed in jeans gets out. She has a hard face and cold, calculating eyes. She is trailed by a tall man with a heavy video camera.

Awadhesh Bihari quickly stands up, dusting his *kurta*. The reporter greets the politician. 'So, Awadhesh Bihariji, will there be some action this time? Your last protest was quite tame.'

The politician gives a shrewd smile. 'You just watch, Nikita. This time we have even lined up Gandhi Baba. Jagdamba Pal will be humiliated in his own den.'

The reporter looks at Mohan Kumar lying on the platform and nods at Bihari. 'I like the Gandhi Baba angle. We might cover it in the evening bulletin.' Lowering her voice to a whisper she tells him, 'If he dies, we will make it the lead story.'

Bihari nods.

'Lobo, I want you to start taking shots,' she instructs the cameraman.

'GANDHI BABA CRITICAL' is the headline in all the newspapers the next morning. At ten o'clock the MLA arrives in a Scorpio, flashing a blue beacon. Four commandos with Sten guns accompany him. The MLA is a giant, square-headed man with jet-black hair and mean dark eyes. Sitting down on the platform next to Mohan Kumar, he whispers to him, 'Gandhi Baba Sahib, why are you doing this?'

'To stop this perversion,' Mohan replies, his voice still strong.

'What you call perversion is a natural human drive. However much you may try to hide it, sex will surface in some form or other.'

'I am not protesting against sex. I am protesting against the perversion of sex, this commodification of women.'

'But my films contain nothing objectionable at all. They are cleared by the Censor Board,' he says. 'If you want to see the commodification of women then go five hundred metres to the underground Palika Bazaar. There you can buy all the triple-X films you want for just a hundred rupees each. Go ten kilometres to GB Road and for a hundred rupees you can actually buy a young girl. Why don't you try and stop these evils instead of picketing our hall?'

'A perversion doesn't cease to be a perversion just because it is perverse to a lesser degree. My fast will be a mortal blow against all purveyors of sin in society.'

'Look, Gandhi Baba, we don't want unnecessary trouble. I am a politician. Your protest is damaging my reputation. On behalf of the Distributors Association of North India, I have been authorized to offer you twenty thousand rupees if you call off your protest.'

Mohan Kumar laughs. 'My fight is not for money. You cannot buy me with four pieces of silver.'

'OK, how about twenty-five thousand, then?'

Mohan Kumar shakes his head. 'Mr Pal, once I have taken a vow, no power on earth can stop me from following it.'

The MLA is beginning to lose his temper. 'Who the hell do you think you are? Here I am, speaking to you so politely and you are behaving as if you are really Mahatma Gandhi. Come now, enough of this drama. I want you to vacate this spot immediately or I will have you forcibly removed.'

'A *satyagrahi* has infinite patience, abundant faith in others, and ample hope. According to the code of the *satyagrahi*, there is no such thing as surrender to brute force.'

'You petty bastard.' Jagdamba Pal lunges at Mohan Kumar. A former boxer, he makes unerring contact with Mohan Kumar's face and a fountain of blood gushes from the bureaucrat's nose.

'Hey Ram!' Mohan cries and falls down. Shanti screams in horror. Jagdamba Pal stands for a moment, amazed at what he has done, then scrambles back to his vehicle.

'Gandhi Baba has been hit!' The cry goes through the crowd like bush fire.

'Kill the bastard!' Awadhesh Bihari screams. His followers immediately charge after the MLA, who is already driving away. 'Burn down the cinema!' Awadhesh Bihari shrills and the mob races into the hall.

'Wait . . .wait . . .' Mohan shouts, but his cries fall on deaf ears. Within seconds, the surging crowd has broken down the foyer door and rushed into the hall. Ten minutes later, black smoke is billowing from the cinema, the audience is running out in a panic and the air is reverberating with the sirens of ambulances and fire engines.

A police van screeches to a halt in front of the cinema. Constables spring out like rabbits and train their carbines on Mohan Kumar. An Inspector approaches him, accompanied by the cinema manager. 'Is this the man?' he asks, pointing a finger at Mohan.

'Yes, Sir,' the manager cries. 'This is Gandhi Baba. He is responsible for destroying the cinema.'

The Inspector taps his cane on his palm. 'You are under arrest, Gandhi Baba.'

'Arrest? What for?' Mohan asks, a handkerchief pressed on his nose to stop the flow of blood.

'Section 307: attempt to murder, Section 425: mischief resulting in damage to property, Section 337: endangering personal safety of others, Section 153: provocation to riot. Come on, we have had enough of your antics.'

'But my name is not Gandhi Baba. It is Mohan Kumar. I am an ex-IAS officer,' he says haughtily, drawing himself to his full height.

'Doesn't matter what you call yourself. You are under arrest.' He gestures to his constables. 'Take him away.'

Tihar Jail is a series of seven prison blocks in west Delhi. Originally built for seven thousand inmates, it now houses thirteen thousand prisoners, nine thousand of whom are awaiting trial.

The warden is a fleshy man with heavy jowls and greying hair. Mohan stands before him in his prison uniform, bristling with restrained anger. The warden gives him a greasy smile. 'Welcome, Sir. It is very rare that we have the privilege of hosting senior civil servants.'

'You know that I shouldn't be here at all,' Mohan fumes. 'That magistrate who remanded me to judicial custody for four months deserves to have his head examined. Anyway, I hope you have received a call from my batchmate, the Police Commissioner?'

Yes, Sir,' the warden nods. 'Police Commisssioner Sahib has already instructed us to take good care of you. So I have put you in a high-security cell with Babloo Tiwari.'

'Babloo Tiwari? The notorious gangster?'

The warden nods.

'And how is that a favour?'

'You will see, Sir. In Tihar, nothing is as it seems. Come, let me show you to your cell.'

He escorts Mohan along long narrow corridors, a fat bunch of keys jingling in his hand. The jail seems clean and well maintained, but with a cloying odour, a cross between the astringent smell of a hospital and the bilious smell of a butchery. They pass through a courtyard where prisoners stand in line, doing exercises. 'Here at Tihar, we try our best to reform the prisoners. We have introduced programmes such as vipassana and yoga. We also have an excellent library and reading room,' the warden says proudly.

The cell is located at the southern end of the jail. 'All our cells are seven by ten feet,' the warden says as he unlocks the thick iron grille door. 'This one is the largest, two cells combined into one, actually. And see what it has.' They step inside and Mohan blinks in astonishment. The cell has wall-to-wall beige carpeting, a small colour TV, and even a minibar. There is a bunk bed, with a man in prison uniform sleeping on the lower berth, wrapped in a brown blanket.

'Welcome to jail, VIP style,' the warden grins.

'I should be grateful for small mercies.' Mohan permits himself half a smile. 'But I would have preferred to be alone. Why don't you transfer this fellow Tiwari to another cell?'

'Look, Sir, this is not a hotel where I can allot rooms at my discretion,' the warden says testily. 'Babloo Tiwari is in this cell because he has even better connections than you.' He gently pats the sleeping prisoner's shoulder. 'Tiwariji, please wake up.'

The prisoner sits up, rubbing his eyes. He is a short man, with a round, clean-shaven face and long, straight hair which falls over his forehead. He stretches his arms and yawns. 'What are you doing here, Jailer Sahib?' he asks in a sleepy voice.

'I have come to introduce you to your new cellmate. Meet Mr Mohan Kumar, IAS.'

Babloo Tiwari looks at him curiously. 'Aren't you the guy they are calling Gandhi Baba?'

Mohan remains silent, but the warden nods his head. 'Exactly, Tiwariji. It is our privilege to host such a distinguished personality in our jail.'

'I hope he doesn't start trying to reform me,' Babloo grumbles. 'By the way, Jailer Sahib, did you get me the new SIM card for my mobile?'

'Shhh,' the warden whispers, looking left and right. 'Even walls have ears. I will have it sent tomorrow.'

The iron door clangs shut, creating vibrations which rattle in Mohan's head long after the warden has gone. Babloo Tiwari sniffles and extends his right hand. 'How do you do?' Mohan sees an arm tattooed with anchors and snakes, but he also notices a grid of broken veins and puncture marks on the shrivelled skin. Curling up his lip, he makes no effort to shake the gangster's hand.

'Suit yourself,' Babloo says and takes out a Nokia from his front pocket. He dials a number and, with one leg propped over the other, his free hand scratching his scrotum, begins speaking softly.

Mohan reluctantly climbs up to the top bunk. The sheet is covered in stains and the thin mattress is lumpy. There is dampness in the room which seems to seep in through the walls. A cold draft blows in through the door, forcing him to pull up the blanket. But it is badly frayed and makes him itch. He suppresses an urge to burst into tears.

Lunch is served at noon on a steel plate; it consists of four thick *rotis*, vegetable stew and a bowl of watery *dhal*. Mohan finds the food bland and unappetizing and pushes away the plate after eating just one *roti*. Below him, Babloo Tiwari doesn't even touch the food.

Mohan lies in bed, pretending to read a magazine, while hunger gnaws at his belly. At some point he falls asleep, dreaming of butter chicken and whisky. When he opens his eyes there is a glassful of golden liquid floating before him. A disembodied head materializes alongside the glass. It is Babloo Tiwari, peeking up from below. 'Would you care for a glass of this?'

'What is it?' he condescends to ask.

'Scotch. Twenty-five years old.'

Almost involuntarily, his tongue flicks over his dry lips. 'Well, I wouldn't mind a sip,' he admits, ashamed of his own weakness.

'Cheers, then,' says Babloo. 'You can keep your *gandhigiri* for outside the cell.'

They clink glasses and break the ice.

*

The cell is unlocked again at four p.m. 'Come,' Babloo says. 'Let's go for some fresh air.'

They walk into a courtyard, half the size of a football pitch, where nearly fifty prisoners are milling around. They are of all ages and sizes: some are wizened old men with flowing beards and some look as young as fifteen. There is a group playing volleyball, another gathered around a radio set and a few men just sitting and chatting. The deferential way in which the other prisoners greet Babloo Tiwari clearly establishes him as their leader. Only a group of three men sitting huddled together in a corner takes no notice of him.

'Who are they?' Mohan asks.

'Don't talk to them. Don't even go near them. They are foreigners belonging to the dreaded Lashkar-e-Shahadat who were involved in last year's attempted bombing of the Red Fort.

'Shouldn't they be put in a separate area, if they are high-risk terrorists?'

Babloo smiles. '*Arrey bhai,* even you are now in the high-risk category.'

Mohan nods. His gaze falls on a striking, middle-aged man, sitting alone on the steps. He has Einstein's hair and Hitler's moustache.

'Who is that cartoon?' he nudges Babloo.

'Oh him, he is our chief source of entertainment,' Babloo says. 'Let me show you. Hey, you,' he calls out. 'Come here.'

The man shuffles towards them. He is tall and reed-thin, and has a furtive look about him.

'We have a new visitor. Won't you welcome him?' Babloo asks in Hindi.

'Welcome to the Gulag Archipelago,' the man announces in perfect English, holding both hands together.

'What is your name?'

'My name is Red.'

'What are you in jail for?'

'Atonement.'

'And what do you think will be your punishment?'

'One hundred years of solitude.'

'Who is your best friend here?'

'The boy in the striped pyjamas.'

'Thank you. You can go now.'

'So long, see you tomorrow,' the man says. He tilts his head, stretches his arms and begins running towards the centre of the field like an aeroplane in flight.

Mohan is intrigued. 'Is his name really Red?'

'No,' Babloo grins. 'His name is L. K. Varshney. He used to be a Professor of English Literature at Delhi University. One day he discovered his wife in bed with his best student. So he killed his wife and is now in jail, pending trial. He will probably be sentenced to life. They say he used to be half mad when he was a professor. Tihar has made him completely mad. Now he always speaks in this funny kind of way.'

'And what are you in jail for?'

'For everything. I have committed almost every crime in the Indian Penal Code and all my cases are awaiting trial. But they won't be able to prove anything. I stay in Tihar because I prefer to stay here. It is safer than being outside.'

As Babloo wanders off to chat to a couple of tough-looking inmates, a young boy with a dusty face and short hair comes up to Mohan and touches his feet. He smells of dirt.

'*Arrey*, who are you?' Mohan shrinks back.

'They say you are Gandhi Baba,' the youth says hesitatingly. 'I came to pay my respects and ask for a favour. My name is Guddu.'

'What are you in for?' Mohan asks.

'I stole a loaf of bread from a bakery. Now I have been here five years. They beat me every day, make me clean the toilets. I want to see my mother. I miss her very much. I know only you can get me out,' he says and starts sobbing.

'*Hato. Hato.*' Mohan tries to wave him away. 'Look, there is nothing I can do. I am a prisoner too, like you. I have to get out myself before I can think of others. And don't spread this nonsense about my being Gandhi Baba, OK?'

He moves to the other side of the field and is almost immediately accosted by an old man with an aquiline nose and twinkling grey eyes.

'*Yada yada hi dharmasya glanirbhavati bharata*,' the man intones in Sanskrit, and then translates for Mohan's benefit. 'Whenever there is a fall of righteousness, you arrive to destroy the forces of evil. I bow to you, O great Mahatma. Only you can save this country.'

'And who might you be?' Mohan asks wearily.

'Dr D. K. Tirumurti at your service, Sir. Sanskrit scholar from Madurai.'

'Also professional cheat, you forgot to mention,' Babloo speaks up from behind.

'Let's go, Babloo, I've had enough fresh air.' Mohan tugs at the gangster's sleeve. 'There is one chap who wants me to save him, another who wants me to save the country. Is this a jail or a lunatic asylum?'

Babloo chuckles. 'Actually there is very little difference between the two. Stick with me if you don't want to join the loony brigade.'

The food at dinner time is the same bland fare. But by now Mohan is so famished, he polishes off all four *rotis* and slurps up the cold vegetable stew. Babloo, he notices, eats very little, sniffling most of the time.

'How do you manage on so little food?' he asks the gangster.

Babloo gives a crafty smile. Wiping his runny nose with the sleeve of his *kurta*, he lifts the mattress and brings out a hypodermic syringe. 'My food is this.' He tests the syringe before plunging it into his arm.

Mohan winces. 'So you are a drug addict?'

'No. Not an addict,' Babloo says with sudden vehemence. 'I control the cocaine. The cocaine doesn't control me.' He completes the injection and exhales. 'Ahh . . . this is paradise. I tell you, nothing can beat the rush of crack. Want to try? It will make you forget Scotch.'

'No thank you.'

'I take only one dose at night. And that keeps me going all through the night and all through the next day.'

'Then how do you sleep?'

'I pop some sleeping tablets.'

'Thankfully I don't need sleeping pills to get to sleep,' Mohan says and pulls the blanket over his head.

'Good night, Sir,' Babloo calls out and for no apparent reason bursts into a fit of laughter.

It takes an immense effort on Mohan's part to begin the slow process of adjusting to jail life. He learns to get up at five thirty a.m. for the head-count of prisoners, to sit on the stinking toilet without holding his nose, to tolerate the insipid tea and inedible *rotis*, to attend the prayer assemblies and yoga sessions and even watch the soaps on TV, which most inmates are completely addicted to. He becomes acquainted with Punjabi murderers and Gujarati arsonists, Nigerian drug-pushers and Uzbek counter-feiters, South Indian cheats and North Indian rapists. He begins playing chess and carrom. He borrows three books a week from the jail library and starts maintaining a diary of prison life.

Throughout this period, he is sustained by Babloo's largesse with his Scotch whisky, the punctilious delivery of Shanti's tiffin every Wednesday loaded with mutton curry and chicken biryani, and the soothing assurances of his lawyers that he will be out soon.

He develops an uneasy friendship with Babloo Tiwari. He is revolted by the criminal's crassness, his ignorance of world affairs, but also amazed at the power he wields in jail. Babloo is the uncrowned king of Tihar, each and every official having been bribed or bullied into servicing him. He runs his empire from inside the jail, spending half his time talking to his henchmen in low whispers, arranging abductions and demanding ransoms, receiving contraband consignments of liquor, cocaine and SIM cards, doling out rewards to pliable policemen and bribe-taking bureaucrats. He has a shrewd sense of their weaknesses, knowing whom to lure with a call girl and whom with cash. But he reserves his ultimate display of power for New Year's Eve, when he organizes a 'private concert' for the jail staff and his cohorts.

*

In the reading room, the tables and chairs have been pushed to the corners and a makeshift wooden stage erected next to the wall. The central space is covered with white sheets and scattered with foam cushions. Two bottles of Johnny Walker Black Label are placed in the middle and salted nuts in stainless steel bowls are laid out at strategic intervals.

Babloo Tiwari reclines against a bolster, takes a sip of whisky from the glass tumbler in his hand, pops a cashew nut into his mouth and gazes at the fair young woman on the stage. Dressed in a knee-length *lehnga* and a tight *choli*, she is busy aping the moves of Shabnam Saxena to a taped medley of her film hits.

On Babloo's left sits the warden and on his right is Mohan. Immediately behind them are the other jail staff, and behind them the fifteen inmates granted the privilege of attending the 'show'. The girl thrusts her ample bosom at the men, who leer at her, address her as '*jaaneman*' and 'darling' (Professor Varshney calls her 'Lolita') and make vulgar gestures with their fingers. As the night progresses and the level of inebriation increases, some of the jail staff climb on to the stage and join in the dancing. A constable grinds his hips suggestively while another tries unsuccessfully to catch the girl's flared skirt. Babloo also lurches up to the dancer and showers her with a wad of hundred-rupee notes. The warden looks on benignly, occasionally glancing at the Rolex watch on his wrist which Babloo had given him that morning.

'Fantastic, Babloo Saab! I could never have imagined such a spectacle inside a jail,' Dr Tirumurti compliments the gangster.

'My motto has always been Live and Let Live,' Babloo says smugly and looks at Mohan. 'So Kumar Sahib, what do you think? Is Tihar a bad place to celebrate the New Year?'

'I think you are right,' Mohan agrees. 'Tihar isn't such a bad place after all. Cheers!'

'Tender is the night,' chimes Varshney.

Just before midnight, Mohan feels the urge to take a leak. He leaves the hall, shivering as a gust of cold wind hits him in the face.

It is a chilly night but the sky is alive with the colourful bursts of firecrackers and rockets. As he is crossing the courtyard he hears a faint rustling sound and suddenly a large hand clamps his mouth from behind. He struggles frantically to free himself, but something cold, hard and metallic is thrust into the small of his back. 'One move and the gun will blast your intestines, understand?' Two other shadows materialize out of the darkness, flanking him. He sees their faces and feels his mouth drying. They are the terrorists belonging to the dreaded Lashkar-e-Shahadat. The Army of Martyrdom.

The three men propel him towards the gate. The courtyard is deserted – the sentries are all enjoying the dance programme whose faint sounds can still be heard. There is a lone guard on duty at the main gate. He is watching the fireworks in the sky, his rifle resting against his leg. The leader of the group tiptoes up to the guard. In one swift move, he grabs him by the neck and wrestles him to the ground.

'What . . . what . . . what are you people doing out of your cells?' the flustered sentry asks as he is pinned to the ground.

'Shut up!' the leader barks, while one of his partners picks up the rifle and trains it on the guard. 'Open the gate.'

Shaking with fear, the sentry takes a bunch of keys from his trouser pocket. With trembling fingers he unlocks the padlock and the gate swings open. At that very instant the leader strikes the guard with the butt of the pistol. He topples down soundlessly.

Mohan begins shivering. 'Please don't kill me,' he pleads with his abductors. The leader laughs. It is the last thing Mohan hears before his head explodes in pain and everything turns black.

When he regains consciousness, Professor Varshney is bending over him. 'I'm OK, you're OK?'

'Where am I?' Mohan asks.

'In custody.'

He looks around and finds himself in the prison's dispensary. There is a newspaper on the side table. He picks it up and finds his picture plastered on the front page. 'DARING JAIL BREAK IN

TIHAR – GANDHI BABA INJURED', the headline proclaims. Below it are the details:

> Red-faced officials were hard put to explain what they were doing watching a cabaret in the high-security prison while three dreaded terrorists managed their getaway. How they escaped from their cells and smuggled a pistol into the Tihar complex is still being investigated. Meanwhile, a massive shake-up has been ordered.

The government's retribution is swift. The warden is suspended. Eighteen jail staff are summarily transferred. A tough new jailer is appointed. Babloo Tiwari and Mohan Kumar are shifted from their swanky cell to a narrow dormitory with two new cellmates – Professor Varshney and Dr Tirumurti.

The gangster curses the escapees. 'Bloody bastards, now I will have to suffer like the rest. They have taken away my mobile. Even the radio and TV have been banned. How will I survive in this hell hole?'

'The *Gita* says, give up attachments and dedicate yourself to the service of God and your fellow men,' Mohan intones.

'Who is this Gita?'

'*Gita* is the key to the scriptures of the world. It teaches the secret of non-violence, the secret of realizing self through the physical body.'

'What crap are you talking, Mohan Sahib?'

'True development consists of reducing ourselves to a cipher.'

'Has he gone mad?' Babloo looks at Tirumurti.

'No, Babloo Saab. He is revealing the knowledge that so far he has kept hidden from us. We are witnessing the rebirth of Gandhi Baba.'

'This is very convenient,' Babloo sneers. 'As long as we were in that VIP cell he had no qualms about drinking my whisky. And now that we are in this hell hole, he becomes Gandhi Baba? I tell you, he is nothing but a fraud.'

'Dr Jekyll and Mr Hyde?' Varshney interjects.

'Have you seen this report, Babloo Saab?' Tirumurti points to the newspaper in his hand. 'It says that judgment in Vicky Rai's case has been postponed to 15 February.'

'What difference does it make when they pronounce the verdict? The outcome is already known to everyone.' Babloo waves dismissively.

'Yes, there is no justice in this country,' Tirumurti sighs. 'A man like Gandhi Baba is in jail and a murderer like Vicky Rai is out on bail.'

'We have entered the heart of darkness,' Varshney says gravely.

The mention of Vicky Rai makes Mohan Kumar suddenly alert. His brow furrows and his pupils dilate. 'Vicky Rai . . . Vicky Rai . . . Vicky Rai,' he mumbles, as though someone has raked an old wound.

'I am going to make a wager on this case. I will bet you a million to one that Vicky Rai will walk free,' Babloo declares.

'I agree,' Tirumurti nods his head.

'He will be gone with the wind,' adds Varshney.

'What is this?' Mohan berates them. 'You people are speaking as if the British are still ruling India. In those days, I agree, justice was denied in ninety-nine cases out of a hundred. But now we are our own rulers. I am sure Vicky Rai will get his just desserts. We should have faith in the judiciary.'

'Fine, Gandhi Baba, we shall see who is proved right on 15 February,' says Babloo and shivers slightly.

'Have you got a fever?' Mohan asks with concern.

'No. It is just a passing chill,' Babloo says.

'It is the winter of our discontent,' says Varshney.

Over the next two days, Babloo's behaviour becomes increasingly bizarre. He gets agitated over small things, complains frequently of nausea and blurred vision and has bouts of uncontrollable shaking. Out of the blue he starts suspecting Varshney of being an informer and warns him to keep his distance. He stops eating completely, and refuses to leave the cell. At night he curls himself up and rolls back and forth on the stone floor like a man in terrible pain.

Tirumurti is quick to diagnose the ailment. 'Babloo is having withdrawal symptoms, now that he cannot get his cocaine any longer. We must try and somehow get him his fix, otherwise he will die.'

'I don't agree,' Mohan says firmly. 'A doctor who panders to the vice of his patient degrades himself and his patient. Babloo doesn't need drugs. He needs kindness and companionship.'

'Love in the time of cholera,' opines Varshney.

Mohan's arrival at the prayer meeting the next day causes considerable commotion. He delivers a long and impressive monologue on the dangers of drug addiction, the importance of faith and the benefits of celibacy. He asks for a personal introduction from each prisoner, questioning them in detail about their personal histories and periods of detention. He seems unusually solicitous of people's health, offering several home remedies to a prisoner who has complained of colic pain. He appears to be fascinated by the library, checks out the PA system to determine whether it plays any *bhajans*, and at lunchtime asks the cook for goat's milk.

He starts sleeping on the floor, insists on cleaning the toilet himself and is happy to clean the toilets of others as well. He begins to keep a silent fast once a week, claiming that abstaining from speaking brings him inner peace.

A prison is fertile ground for the emergence of leaders. It contains the dregs of society, willing to cling to any hope to help endure the rigours of prison life. Gandhi Baba quickly attracts a large fan base, his chief disciple being Babloo Tiwari, who is almost cured of his addiction.

'Do you know what is the hardest thing in the world, Gandhi Baba?' he asks Mohan one evening.

'To kill a mockingbird?' Varshney offers hopefully.

'No. To awaken faith in a man who has forsaken religion. I am eternally grateful to you, Gandhi Baba, for opening my eyes to the benevolence of God.'

'So will you sing *Vaishnav Janato* with me at tomorrow's prayer meeting?' Mohan asks with a twinkle in his eye.

'Not only that, I am going to shave off my hair and become a vegetarian.'

'That is wonderful. Now if you would only stop your criminal activities as well . . .'

'Consider it done, Gandhi Baba. Babloo Tiwari the gangster is dead.'

'A farewell to arms,' Varshney quips.

Several other inmates follow Babloo's example and become vegetarian, causing prison officials to revamp the meal plan. Mohan encourages the prisoners to paint and has their paintings sold through a website set up by Tirumurti's brother-in-law. Invited to the women's prison block to deliver a talk, he persuades the women inmates to start producing snacks and savouries which are then marketed under the brand name 'Bapu's Choice'.

Newspapers write editorials on Mohan's reforms. Two British drug-pushers, Mark and Alan, become his disciples and begin collaborating on his biography. Chennai University passes a unanimous resolution recommending Mohan for the Nobel Peace Prize.

As 15 February approaches, there is only one topic of conversation in the jail – the judgment in the Vicky Rai case. The day before the verdict, Mohan is unable to sleep. He paces up and down the cell while the others snore peacefully.

The next day, just before lunch, he leads a procession of inmates to the warden's office.

'What is all this? What are you people doing in my office?' the warden demands.

'We have come to see the circus,' Tirumurti informs him.

'What circus?'

'The trial,' says Varshney.

'Oh, so you people want to see the verdict in Vicky Rai's case? Not a problem. I was going to watch it myself.' The warden presses a button on the remote and a decrepit-looking TV sitting atop a bookcase flickers into life.

Virtually every channel is running live feeds from the courtroom in Delhi. The warden tunes to ITN and Barkha Das fills the screen, dressed in a blue *salwar kameez* with an olive-green photographer's vest on top.

'This will be a landmark day in the history of justice in India,' she says. 'Just as America waited with bated breath for the verdict in the O. J. Simpson case, India is waiting for the verdict in the Vicky Rai case. The courtroom behind me is packed to the rafters, but we have ITN's Shubhranshu Gupta inside, who will give us the latest. Shubhranshu, has the judge delivered his judgment?'

She bends her head and listens to the message being relayed to her ear phone, then looks up and grimaces. 'We've just received word from inside the courtroom. Vicky Rai has been acquitted for the murder of Ruby Gill.'

A hush falls over the gathering. The warden turns off the TV. 'Heard the judgment? Satisfied?' he says gruffly. '*Chalo*, back to your cells now.'

Babloo Tiwari winks at Tirumurti. 'What did I tell you?'

'If he is out, why the hell are we rotting here?' Tirumurti scowls.

'That's because your father is not the Home Minister of Uttar Pradesh,' says Babloo. 'What do you think, Varshney?'

'Things fall apart,' the professor says morosely. 'Cry, the beloved country.'

Mohan feels the ground beneath him shake. He has to grip Babloo's arm to steady himself.

'What do you have to say, Gandhi Baba?' several prisoners ask him at once. He remains silent.

For three days Mohan refuses to eat, refuses to speak, refuses to go out of his cell. He lies in bed all day, staring vacantly at the ceiling.

'Eat something, Gandhi Baba. Ruby Gill will not be avenged by your fasting,' Babloo implores.

'Now there is only one way to avenge Ruby Gill,' he murmurs finally.

'And what is that?'

'Vicky Rai must die,' he says softly.

Babloo inserts a finger in his ear to clear it, thinking something must be wrong with his hearing.

'Vicky Rai must die,' Mohan repeats.

'I find it very strange, hearing this from your lips, Gandhi Baba,' Babloo says.

'But I have always maintained that where there is only a choice between cowardice and violence, I prefer violence. Far better to kill a murderer than allow him to kill again. A person who suffers injustice willingly is as guilty as the person who perpetrates the injustice. So will you do one last job for me?'

'For you I am ready to lay down my life, Gandhi Baba. Just tell me.'

'I want you to kill Vicky Rai.'

'Kill Vicky Rai?' Babloo Tiwari shakes his head slowly. 'There are many causes I am prepared to die for, but none I am prepared to kill for, Gandhi Baba.'

'Don't repeat my own line to me, Babloo.'

'It is not a line. I really believe in it. You have changed me, Bapu.'

'If you can't do it, I will have to do it myself.'

'You cannot be serious.'

'I am deadly serious. Can you teach me how to use a gun?'

'Not a problem. I'll not only teach you, I'll also get you a good gun when you finish your term and get out of Tihar. But won't your anger cool in two months' time?'

'I have no intention of remaining in Tihar till then.'

'What? Don't tell me you are planning to escape. Have you been digging a tunnel at night?'

'No. I don't need tunnels to escape. I will go out through the main gate.'

'So what's your plan, Gandhi Baba?'

'You will see, Babloo, you will see. But first I need you to convene a meeting for me with all the inmates.'

*

Seven days later, a massive non-cooperation movement starts in Tihar. The inmates refuse to cook, to clean, to bathe, demanding better prison conditions, just treatment and an end to extortion by jail officials.

The warden is not amused. 'What is this you have started, Mr Kumar?' he asks Mohan.

'Civil disobedience becomes a sacred duty when the State becomes lawless or corrupt,' Mohan answers.

The warden tries strong-arm tactics but the prisoners refuse to be cowed. The strike enters its tenth day. The garden begins to wilt and the bathrooms stink. Dirt gathers in the courtyard and dust gathers in the classrooms.

Urgent consultations are held between the jail authorities and their superiors. A week later, Mohan Kumar is released from Tihar prematurely. Shanti is waiting for him outside the jail with hundreds of supporters chanting 'Long Live Gandhi Baba!' He is escorted home by a joyous convoy of cars, buses and bicycles, horns blaring, bells tinkling. On reaching his house he delivers a long monologue on the imperative of fighting injustice.

A few days later, a one-eyed man comes to meet him, bearing a parcel. 'Babloo Tiwari has sent me. Can we talk in private?' the stranger asks Mohan.

They go into the garden. The one-eyed man opens the packet and takes out a gleaming pistol. 'It is a Walther PPK .32, top of the line, brand new. Same gun that James Bond uses.'

'How much?'

'Babloo Bhai said I cannot charge you for this. It is a gift from him.'

'And the bullets?'

'The magazine is fully loaded.'

Mohan takes the gun in his right hand and feels its weight. 'Can I try?'

The man looks around. 'Here, in the garden?' he asks doubtfully.

'Why not?' Mohan removes the safety catch and aims at an empty Coke bottle standing on the wooden railing of the gazebo. He presses the trigger and with a deafening blast the glass bottle shatters and disintegrates. He nods his head approvingly, blows at the smoking barrel, and tucks the gun inside his *kurta* pyjamas.

Shanti races screaming into the garden. 'What happened? I heard a gunshot. I thought someone had—'

'Shanti, you imagine too much,' Mohan says calmly. 'Death is blessed at any time, but it is twice blessed for a warrior who dies for his cause – that is, truth.'

That same evening a gilt-edged card arrives bearing a commissioned artwork by M. F. Husain on the cover. '*Vicky Rai invites you to a celebratory dinner on 23 March at Number Six*' it says inside in cursive black letters.

He reads it and his lips curve into a cunning smile.

Love in Mehrauli

THERE ARE only three ways of becoming instantly rich – inheriting a family fortune, robbing a bank or receiving an unexpected windfall. Some receive it in the form of a winning lottery ticket, some as an unbeatable card combination at a poker game. I found mine two days ago in a dustbin.

After retrieving the briefcase from the rubbish bin I caught a bus and headed home to the temple. Mother was in the kitchen and Champi was listening to the TV. I entered my room and tried to find a suitable hiding place for the briefcase. But a small *kholi* does not afford too many locations for concealment. Eventually I had to push the briefcase underneath the mattress, where it formed a rather bulky outcrop.

Later that night, after Mother and Champi had gone to sleep, I took out the briefcase and began counting the money with the help of a torch held between my legs. There were twenty wads of notes in denominations of one thousand and five hundred. The notes were brand new, fresh from a bank. I opened the first wad and began adding up. One thousand . . . two thousand . . . ten thousand . . . fifteen thousand . . . fifty thousand. My head started spinning with all the zeroes I had never used. By the time I reached the twelfth wad, my fingers had begun to ache, the saliva in my mouth had run dry and my eyes were losing focus. To put it crudely, there was more money inside the briefcase than I could count.

A wave of happiness swept over my body, providing me with a more exhilarating rush than high-grade smack. I had more money in my possession than seven generations of my family would have seen. But even as I was rejoicing at my good fortune, the first doubts crept into my mind. What if someone had seen me take the briefcase and reported it to the police? What if a robber came into our hut and stole the briefcase? Desperate men know no bounds. The adjoining Sanjay Gandhi slum has plenty of hired killers willing to slit a man's throat for just five grand. To get their grubby hands on my briefcase, they would stop at nothing. The rich can sleep easy because they have money in the bank and round-the-clock guards and alarms in the house. But how can a poor man protect his stash of cash? I fretted, I sweated, I stayed up all night.

This is the strange thing about money – too much of it can be as problematic as too little.

When I was studying in the government school, we had a teacher called Hari Prasad Saini who liked to play mind games with the students. Once he asked us, 'What would you do if you suddenly got a hundred thousand rupees each?' I remember Lallan said he would buy an entire toyshop. Another boy said he would spend it all on chocolates. I said that I would give the money to my mother. But now, when I actually have much more than a hundred thousand rupees, the last thing I am going to do is tell Mother. She is quite capable of dragging me to a police station and making a public announcement: 'Inspector Sahib, please find out where my son has stolen all this money from!'

I had intended to keep the news of my fortune even from Champi, but within two days I knew that was impossible. I never keep secrets from her, and I have to tell someone. So when Mother goes to the temple for her daily chores, I call Champi to my side of the room.

'I have got money for your operation,' I tell her.

'How much?'

'Much more than we need to pay the doctor.'

'I don't want any operation,' Champi says. 'I am happy as I am.'

I know she is lying. She wouldn't mind the operation, if not for her sake then for Mother, who worries constantly about her marriage. 'Who will marry my Champi, the way she looks?' she frets all the time.

Mother is right. Who will marry Champi? She is a walking disaster. The nicest girl in the world, she is also the ugliest. She has a harelip which makes the lower half of her face a grotesque caricature. Her left arm is completely wasted, and she has pock-marks all over her cheeks. The good thing is she cannot see her ugliness. She is as blind as a bat. Yet she is more famous than any-one in our locality. They often put her picture in magazines and newspapers and she has even been featured on CNN.

Champi is known all over the world as the Face of Bhopal. There was a big industrial disaster in Bhopal more than twenty years ago. Poisonous methyl isocyanate gas leaked out from the Union Carbide plant and all those who inhaled it died, or went blind or became mad. Champi's mother Fatima Bee was living in Bhopal at the time. She too was affected by the gas, although she didn't know it then. She gave birth to Champi five years later. When the doctors saw the newborn baby, they told Fatima Bee that the gas had caused the blindness and all the deformities. It still intrigues me how the gas was locked up in Fatima Bee's body for five years and did nothing to her, yet pounced on poor Champi the moment she was born.

The people affected by the gas were promised some money by the government, but it didn't cover people like Fatima Bee who were affected later. So she joined an organization called Crusaders for Bhopal which has been fighting for compensation. As happens in our country, the case has been dragging on for over twenty years with no resolution in sight. Every three months Fatima Bee would come to Delhi, do the rounds of the Supreme Court, participate in a couple of rallies, and go back to Bhopal. Ten years ago she decided to move to Delhi permanently, along with her husband Anwar Mian and Champi. They lived in the Sanjay Gandhi slum in Mehrauli, which is full of Bangladeshi refugees. Anwar Mian found work in a cement factory in Mahipalpur. I am told he was a grim, taciturn man who drank like a fish, smoked twenty *beedis* a day and hardly ever spoke to anyone. One fine day, he went to work as usual, returned home in the evening as usual, and dropped dead during the night. *Bole toh*, heart failure.

It was a big blow to Fatima Bee, who now had to support Champi all alone. She was forced to start sewing clothes for a living. That is how she came into contact with Mother, who got a couple of my shirts stitched by her. She was a superb tailor. The shirts she made me fitted me more perfectly than anything I have worn since. Unfortunately, Fatima Bee also fought a running battle with illness. Three years ago she passed away of tuberculosis, leaving Champi all alone. That is when the Crusaders for Bhopal people came to the temple. They sought a volunteer family which would be prepared to take care of Champi's upkeep in return for three hundred rupees (subsequently increased to four hundred) per month. There were no takers for their offer, till Mother showed up. She is the queen of all do-gooders, ready to feed even a sick snake. Mother took one look at Champi and embraced her like her own daughter. There was some grumbling from the temple management. The slimy priest, who makes a tidy profit from the daily offerings, objected to a Muslim girl being given refuge inside the precincts of a Hindu temple. But Mother had made up her mind. 'What kind of priest are you? Does humanity have a religion?' she rebuked him, silencing his protest. Since then Champi has lived with Mother and me in our house at the back of the temple. I suppose I could call her a sister of sorts. Crusaders for Bhopal pay Mother the regular monthly stipend and take Champi away for just one day each year – 3 December, which they call Bhopal Action Day. They try to raise awareness of the disaster by going on a huge rally, often with volunteers in outrageous costumes. Last year they had people dressed as skeletons. But the star of the show is always Champi, who doesn't need any make-up to remind people of the horrors of Bhopal.

When Champi first came to live with us, Mother promised her

that we would get her face set right. We even showed her to a plastic surgeon. He told us that the surgery would cost the astronomical sum of three hundred thousand rupees. Since that reality check we stopped having conversations about Champi's face. She accepted our helplessness just as we accepted her grotesqueness.

Now I am trying to rekindle that old hope, but Champi remains adamant.

'I don't want to benefit from gangsters' money,' she declares after I recount the full saga of how I acquired the briefcase.

'How do you know it belongs to gangsters?' I counter.

'Who else would leave it in a dustbin? And what if they trace it to you?'

'They won't. Now this money is mine. And I am bloody well going to enjoy it.'

'Ill-gotten gains can never lead to enjoyment. You have to think of the consequences.'

'Life is too short to worry about the future.'

'It may be for you, but not for me and Mother. She worries about you all the time.'

'You can tell her to stop worrying. From tomorrow she need not even work. I have enough to feed all three of us for a hundred years.'

'Don't let your head swell,' Champi cautions me. 'Better to lie low for a while before making your grand plans.'

Her advice is sound. 'You are right, Champi,' I nod. 'No one must know about this briefcase. I will not touch it for another week. And if no one comes looking for it by then, we can breathe easy, start spending some of the dough, get your operation done.'

'I don't want a penny of your loot,' Champi says firmly. 'But before doing anything, won't you take the blessings of Lord Shiva? Go and bow your head before your God at least today.'

'What did God have to do with that briefcase? I don't need to offer Him any thanks.' I dismiss the suggestion with a wave of my hand.

Champi sighs. 'I shall intercede for you with Allah, the Forgiver of Sin, the Bestower of Favours. *La ilaha illa huwa,* to Him is the final return,' she says with both hands raised to her face.

I shake my head. Considering what has happened to her eyes and face, Champi's faith in God is even more remarkable.

'Don't breathe a word about the briefcase to Mother,' I instruct her and saunter out towards the main gate.

It is a Monday, Lord Shiva's day, and the temple is already filling up with worshippers. By noon there will be a half-kilometre-long queue for the *darshan*.

The Bhole Nath Temple of Mehrauli is a recent construction, no more than twenty years old. It was probably built for the same purpose that most temples in the city are built – to grab land. But its fame spread quickly and it has now become a place of pilgrimage. Devotees believe it has wish-fulfilling properties and they can be seen thronging the massive marble hall at all times of the day, sitting on the floor meditating or chanting. This is also where Mother can be found in the mornings, diligently mopping the floor, scrubbing the tiles, rinsing the side drains of any obstruction.

Several useful activities can be conducted on the temple premises, but the only one which interests me is girl-watching. Because Shiva is considered to be the granter of good spouses, there is a constant stream of unmarried maidens and young brides entering the temple to pray for a suitable husband or a harmonious family life. If only the chicks could be made to realize that an excellent groom is lurking just round the corner, in Kholi Number One!

The temple has been a part of my existence since I was six. I have been a witness to its growth and expansion. I have seen the garden bloom and trees populate the compound. I have grown up watching the increasing prices of flowers and sweets and the widening girths of sweet-makers and priests.

Some of the temple's luck has also rubbed off on us. Before Mother started working here, we lived in the Sanjay Gandhi slum, in a makeshift hut made with corrugated-metal sheets. We had no electricity and no water. Mother cooked with cow-dung patties on a mud hearth which used to fill the entire hut with smoke and make my eyes water. Now we have a pukka one-and-a-half-room house, with a paved brick fireplace, a ceiling fan and even cable TV (which I have siphoned off the temple's connection). Of course, it is still extremely cramped for three people. We have divided the main room into two parts, separated by a wooden partition. I have one side, with my mattress and a small wooden table, and Mother and Champi have the other side. I have decorated the walls on my side with posters of Salim Ilyasi and Shabnam Saxena, though they are mostly obscured by my trousers and shirts draped over the wall-mounted hanger. Mother has some faded old calendars with gods and goddesses on her walls. She also has an aluminium trunk containing some of her clothes. Its top serves as a mantle for a framed black-and-white picture of Father, garlanded with brittle roses. It is Mother's most prized possession. She sees her husband in that photograph, but I see a martyr.

Mother never talks about it, but I have learnt that my father was killed in a road accident. Even though I was only six years old at the time, I still remember Father's dead body lying outside our hut, wrapped in a white sheet, and Mother breaking her bangles and bashing her head repeatedly against the wall. A week later a heavy-set man wearing white *kurta* pyjamas came to meet Mother with folded hands. He shed a few crocodile tears and gave Mother twenty-five thousand rupees. He also got her the job in the temple and this house. Father gave us in death what he couldn't give us in life.

'It has been a month since you quit working for the Bhusiyas. Are you going to look for another job or not?' Mother asks me the moment she returns in the evening. It has become her constant refrain. 'What is the use of all that university education if you are going to remain idle? *Arrey*, if you don't think of your old mother at least think of your sister Champi. How will I get her married if you refuse to earn money? God, why did you make me give birth to a wastrel?'

I smile at her. 'I was waiting to give you the good news. I have just landed a new job – operations manager at the box factory on MG Road. They will pay me ten thousand a month.'

'Ten thousand?' Mother's eyes open wide. She looks at me sternly. 'You are not pulling my leg, are you?'

'I swear on Father, I am telling the truth,' I say solemnly.

'Lord Shiva be praised . . . Lord Shiva be praised.' Mother looks up to the heavens and races out of the house. She will probably start distributing sweets to everyone in the temple complex.

Champi is not amused. 'How can you lie so brazenly? I pity the woman who will marry you.'

'But won't she prefer a millionaire liar to an honest pauper?' I grin.

A young woman wearing denim jeans and a printed *kurti* has come to interview Champi. She is rather pretty, with short hair and brown eyes. Her name is Nandita Mishra and she claims to be a documentary film-maker.

'I am doing a film on the Bhopal Gas Tragedy, and the situation twenty-five years later. I have come to get Champi Bhopali's perspective,' she tells me as she sets up her tripod. Champi quickly goes to the kitchen, scrubs her face with water, puts a flower in her hair and returns to face the video camera. She has become quite adept at giving interviews, peppering her sentences with words like 'contamination', 'conspiracy' and 'compensation'.

After the recording with Champi is over, the woman turns to me.

'Do you know any people in the Sanjay Gandhi slum?'

'Why do you ask? What work could someone like you possibly have there?'

'My next project is a film on slum life. Something along the lines of *Salaam Bombay*, but grittier, edgier. We see slums from afar, sitting in trains and cars, but how many of us have actually ventured into one? My documentary will seek to give viewers an authentic experience of slum life.'

'A slum is not a tourist attraction, Madam,' I scoff. 'To experience slum life, you have to be born in one.'

She looks at me sharply. 'That's quite a good line. Would you mind repeating it for the camera?'

So I, too, prepare to give an interview for the first time in my life, expounding on life in the Sanjay Gandhi slum. It is a subject I know well. The slum has been my playground since the age of three. I have many insights into slum living – how a family of six manages to squeeze itself into an eight-by-eight-foot space. How a girl protects her modesty while bathing underneath a municipal tap in full view of hundreds of people. How a married couple makes clandestine love with furtive eyes watching their every move. How grown men sit in rows and shit like buffaloes at the edge of the railway track. How the poor breed like mosquitoes and live like dogs, while the dogs of the rich sleep on Dunlopillo mattresses in mosquito-free mansions.

I could have said all these things, but face to face with the lens of the camera I falter and become tongue-tied. Nandita Mishra tries to prompt me, but the words have suddenly dried up inside me. She gives up after a while and begins packing up her equipment.

After she has gone I brood upon my failure. Was it because of the camera in my face or the briefcase under my bed? Is it possible that because I now have wealth, I am unable to think like a slum-dweller?

Ten days have passed since I acquired that briefcase and no one has come looking for it. As per plan, inside the temple I will continue my life exactly as before. I will be frugal and abstinent. But outside, I can afford to be an entirely different person. I can start spending some of the money, enjoy the fruits of my good fortune. I decide to begin with a taxi ride.

The taxi stand is two streets down from the temple. There is a yellow-and-black taxi parked on the kerb and the driver is reading a newspaper inside the car. I knock on the window pane. 'Are you free?'

The driver, an old Sikh with an unkempt beard, unrolls the window and spits out something. 'Who needs the taxi?'

'I do.'

He looks at my dirty clothes and dusty face with unconcealed disdain. 'Oy, have you ever taken a taxi in your life? Do you know how much it costs?' he asks tartly.

'I have been riding in taxis all my life, *sardarji*,' I bark, surprised at the arrogance in my voice. I flash a couple of thousand-rupee notes in front of him. 'Now take me to Ansal Plaza. And make it quick.'

'Yes, Sahib.' The driver's demeanour changes immediately. 'Please get in.' He dumps the newspaper and cranks the meter.

I settle down on the back seat of a taxi for the first time in my life, cup my hands behind my head and stretch my legs. The high life has begun.

I shop with a vengeance at the upmarket mall. Everything which my heart has always desired but my wallet couldn't afford, I buy. I purchase a shirt from Marks & Spencer, a leather jacket from Benetton, jeans from Levi, sunglasses from Guess, perfume from Lacoste and shoes from Nike. I compress ten years of window-shopping into an hour of frenzied purchasing, blowing twenty thousand rupees in just these six stores. Then I go into the fancy toilets, wash my face and change, putting on my new jeans, shirt and shoes, with the leather jacket on top. I spray my body with the expensive perfume and stand in front of the full-length mirror. The man who stares back at me is a handsome stranger, tall and lean with a clean-shaven face and curly, tousled hair like actor Salim Ilyasi's. I snap my fingers at the mirror and strike a pose like Michael Jackson. Then I stuff my old clothes and shoes in a shopping bag and swagger out of the toilets in my dark glasses. A hep-looking girl in jeans and T-shirt glances at me appreciatively. Ten minutes ago she wouldn't have noticed me. It makes me realize how much garments can change a man. And I know that there is nothing intrinsically different about the rich. They just wear better clothes.

I feel like breaking into a jig and singing, '*Saala main to sahab ban gaya!*' Munna Mobile has become a gentleman. And now he needs a rich lady friend.

I spend the rest of the evening in South Extension Market, watching the chic girls in their chic clothes. They alight from their expensive cars and enter expensive stores selling designer handbags and brand-name shoes. I follow a group of girls into the Reebok showroom and the guard at the entrance salutes me and holds open the door. The manager inside asks me if I would like a soft drink or a cup of tea. I laugh and chat with the sales girls. They flirt with me. The experience makes me feel all warm and happy inside. Stepping out of the centrally heated showroom, I decide to try the Deluxe Indian Restaurant next door. I have a lavish meal of butter chicken, seekh kebabs and naan bread, costing eight hundred rupees. Back again on the main street, I make a final survey of the stretch of brightly lit emporiums, their plexiglass windows full of dazzling goods. The lurid glitter of the city does not seem alien today. I, too, have become a denizen of its showy world.

My next stop is Infra Red, an exclusive dance club, considered to be the most hip and happening place in the capital after dark. Dinoo, a friend from the slum who worked there briefly as a waiter, had told me that the best-looking girls come to the joint, and 'half naked' too.

The taxi drops me right in front of the club's sparkling neon-lit entrance. It is only nine p.m. but there is already a fairly long queue in front of the carved wooden door, which is blocked off by a velvet rope. Two muscular, bald bouncers in identical black suits stand in front of the door and screen customers. There are a couple of beggars on the pavement who line up hopefully before every car that pulls up. I get in the queue and reach the door after a fifteen-minute wait. One of the bouncers gives me a quick once-over. He nods to his partner, who asks me to fork out three thousand rupees as a 'cover charge for singles'. 'Three thousand rupees? That's outrageous!' I want to shout, but say nothing and strip off three more notes from my wad. I am given a voucher, the velvet rope is unhooked and I am ushered through the door. I go down nearly twenty steps to what seems like a basement. I can hear the distant sound of pumping music. The sound becomes louder as I reach another door. A uniformed doorman checks my voucher and presses a button. The door flips open and I step into a dimly lit hall packed with people. The music is so loud I fear my ear drums will shatter. Immediately to my right is a bar shaped like an island surrounded by small yellow sofas. To my left is the dance floor, a vast space constructed almost entirely of mirrors, with a massive strobe light hanging like a chandelier, flashing green, blue and yellow at regular intervals. The mood is celebratory and the floor is packed with swaying, sweaty bodies dancing with manic energy. The DJ sits some twenty feet above on a projecting balcony made of glass and steel. From time to time white smoke erupts from the middle of the dance floor like a ghostly fountain.

Dinoo wasn't wrong about the club. Every other girl wears a body-hugging dress, halter tops with plunging necklines expose half their breasts, short T-shirts leave midriffs bare and micro mini skirts barely conceal underwear. The dance floor has more skin on display than Fashion TV.

The smoke, the light, the music all contribute to an atmosphere of reckless abandon, as if India has been left behind and we are in some bold new country with its own rules and regulations.

As I become more accustomed to the translucent neon décor and the dim lighting, I recognize some famous faces sitting at the bar. There is Smriti Bakshi, the TV soap star, Simi Takia, the actress, and Chetan Jadeja, the former cricketer. Another familiar-looking man with gelled hair and bulging biceps is chatting to a foreigner. There is a group of girls in designer jeans and stiletto heels, looking like glamour models. Everyone seems important. I feel like I have gatecrashed a party full of movie stars and celebrities.

The bartender, a young man with slick hair and a bow tie, asks me if I would like a drink. 'What do you have?' I ask. 'Everything, Sir.' He points to the array of bottles stacked behind him. I try to eavesdrop on what the models are ordering. They ask for drinks like Long Island Ice Tea, Pina Colada and Strawberry Margarita which I have never heard of and flash their credit cards nonchalantly.

I feel like taking a leak and move to the men's toilets. As soon as I open the door I hear strange sounds. There are a couple of *firang* white girls inside, giggling and snorting cocaine at the wash-basin. They glower at me, making me feel like an intruder. 'Go away,' says one.

I leave hurriedly and head for the dance floor. The DJ, who has been playing English music till now, puts on a remix from the film *Dhoom 2* and a loud cheer goes up. It is a song I know very well, having seen the film no less than twelve times. I have memorized each and every move of Hrithik Roshan's amazing dance routine. And I am not alone. Every slum kid is a Michael Jackson waiting for his moment in the sun. It has always been my secret fantasy to go to a dance club one day where the DJ will put on my favourite number and I will show off the moves perfected over ten years of watching dance shows on TV. I will do the moonwalk and the spot shimmy, I will spin on my head and walk on my hands. The crowds will part and everyone will stand to the side, applauding my every move. But now, when I have the opportunity, I feel strangely nervous and diffident, as if my dancing will expose me as an impostor.

I feel suffocated. The dance floor doesn't seem rocking any more. That is when I notice that behind the dance floor there is another screened-off area. I push my way through the packed, jostling mass of bodies and enter yet another lounge, which is much more informal. Instead of sofas and bar stools it has carpets and cushions. There is a widescreen TV and a few artificial plants. There is also a small bar with a bartender who is yawning. Only a handful of people are in the lounge – a couple sitting in a corner exchanging whispered confidences, a bored-looking girl with an older guy, trying to send a text message from her mobile phone, and a group of foreigners with long hair taking turns smoking a hookah.

I see a girl sitting all alone, with her back towards me, watching the TV, which is tuned to NDTV instead of MTV. She is slender, with long black hair, and is probably the only girl in the entire club wearing a *desi* dress, a blue *salwar kameez*.

I step closer to her. She senses my presence and turns around. I glimpse an oval face, a well-shaped nose, full lips and a pair of dark eyes which look like they will break into tears at any minute. She is one of the most beautiful girls I have seen in my life.

'Hi!' I say, because rich people speak only in English.

She looks at me with a helpless expression and does not respond. I notice she is biting her lip.

Another girl, wearing tight jeans and a studded belt, appears suddenly by her side. She has put on crimson lipstick to match her red-striped T-shirt, whose deep V-neck clearly displays her cleavage. 'Ritu, I hope you are not getting terribly bored, *yaar*,' she says in Hindi. '*Bas*, Tony and I will have a couple more dances and then we'll leave.'

Then she notices me standing behind Ritu. 'Hello, Mister. Aren't you going to buy my friend a drink?' she says in English.

By now I have exhausted all the English I know. 'I prefer to speak Hindi,' I tell her, sounding sheepish.

'Cool,' says the girl and offers her hand. 'My name is Malini. This is my friend Ritu. She also speaks only chaste Hindi.'

As Malini disappears back to the dance floor, I extend my hand and this time Ritu grasps it. Her grip is soft and delicate. I sit down next to her.

'You know my name. What is yours?' she asks in Hindi.

I realize instantly that Munna Mobile will cut no ice in this upmarket club. I need a powerful new name and I need it fast. The most powerful person I know is the Butcher of Mehrauli, Inspector Vijay Singh Yadav, and before I know it, I have blurted out that name. 'Vijay Singh, my name is Vijay Singh.'

She brightens up. 'Are you also a Thakur, like me?'

'Yes,' I nod. 'I am also a Thakur.'

'What do you do, Vijay?'

That's easy. I do what every tin-pot trader does in this city. 'Import-Export.'

'Where do you live?'

That's tougher. I dare not say Kholi Number One. 'Here and there.' I wave my hands. Before she can cross-examine me any further, I launch my own offensive. 'What about you? Where do you live?'

'Oh, I am not from Delhi. I live in Lucknow. I am just visiting.'

That explains her dress and her language. 'What do you do?'

'I am a final-year BA student at Lucknow University. Doing my honours in Home Science. When did you graduate?' she asks.

'A couple of years ago,' I reply.

'Where from?' she persists.

'Delhi University,' I say glibly, conveniently glossing over the fact that it was a correspondence course and that I took four years to pass – and only then with a third-class degree.

We manage to string together a conversation for the next couple of hours, speaking of this and that. She asks me what books I have read and I gently steer her on to the topic of films I have seen. She tells me about Lucknow. I tell her about Delhi. It emerges that we have much in common. We share a distrust of politicians; we decry the arrogance of money and we are both fans of Shabnam Saxena.

Around eleven o'clock, Ritu prepares to leave. 'It was good talking to you, Vijay. I hope we meet again,' she says and passes me a slip of paper. It has her mobile phone number.

I follow Ritu and her friend out of the club. The queue outside the door has become even longer. A black chauffeur-driven BMW draws up and a tall moustachioed black-cat commando carrying an AK-47 opens the door for her. Ritu studiously avoids looking at me as she gets into the back seat with Malini. The car drives away, leaving me standing on the kerb. Throughout the evening Ritu had tactfully evaded answering personal questions about her family, but that uniformed gunman makes me wonder. Who is this mysterious girl and why has she given me her mobile number?

Before I can ponder the question any further I am accosted by a smelly beggar with a bent arm who grips my leg like a leech, a telling reminder that I have stepped back into India. 'I have not eaten for three days. Please give me some money. *Kuch dede baba!*' he implores. I search my pockets and come up with a couple of one-rupee coins. I get rid of him, and then duck into a quiet alley to change into my regular clothes. Vijay Singh has had his fun. Now it is time for Munna Mobile to hit the sack.

I catch a bus back to the temple. Mother is asleep but Champi is still awake. 'You smell different,' she says as soon as I enter, making me freeze. This is the thing about Champi. She may be blind, but she sees more than people with both eyes.

'Yes, I have put on some perfume.'

'Seems expensive. Looks like you have started blowing the money.'

'Well, ten days have passed.'

'Did you meet a girl?'

'What?'

'You are also carrying her smell with you.'

I am left speechless by Champi's powers of intuition.

I wait for her to go to sleep before taking out the briefcase and opening it, both to receive that special thrill again and to count the remaining wads of notes. But once again, the enterprise proves unsuccessful. Not because I cannot count, but because tonight my concentration is broken by another ten-digit number buzzing in my brain. Ritu's mobile.

There is no doubt that I am smitten by her beauty. That old suppressed desire to seduce a rich memsahib rears up in my mind like a coiled snake. I debate when to call her. If I call her tomorrow, I might appear too eager and impatient and it could spoil my chances. On the other hand, if I delay too much she might consider me arrogant and uninterested.

Even as I am thinking what to do, it dawns on me that I don't actually have a mobile phone. So the next morning I go to Delite Phone Mart and purchase a basic Nokia 1110, so as not to rouse any suspicion. It is the same cheap phone that the corner tobacconist and the neighbourhood washerman use. It feels funny paying for a mobile phone for the first time with my own money. Well, it is my money now, isn't it?

*

Try as I might, I cannot resist calling Ritu. Within ten minutes of inserting the SIM card, I am punching in her number. She seems to be expecting my call, picking it up on the first ring.

'Hello, Ritu. Vijay Singh speaking,' I say somewhat lamely.

'Hello, Vijay,' she replies, somewhat coyly.

There is an awkward silence as I think of what to say. I have never had occasion before to chat up a rich girl on the phone. I try to think what girls like her like to do and the only thing that comes to mind is shopping.

'Would you like to go shopping?' I ask.

There is another pause as Ritu ponders what to make of this request. 'Yes. That would be nice. Where do you suggest we go?'

'Where are you staying?'

'Mehrauli,' she answers, surprising me.

'What a coincidence! I live in Mehrauli too! So how about meeting up at the Ambawata Complex? It has all the designer shops.'

'No,' she replies after another pause. 'I would prefer some place which is far from Mehrauli. What do you think of Connaught Place?'

'Yeah, I go there all the time.'

'Good. So should we meet up at three o'clock?'

'Where?'

'The only place I know is the Wimpy. Malini took me there once.'

'Perfect. I know the Wimpy. I'll see you there at three o'clock.'

Even before the call is over, I have figured out Miss Ritu, scoped out the tactics I need to seduce her. It is clear from our conversation that she is a small-town girl looking for cheap thrills in the big bad city, without her parents finding out. I am sure she would be open to a little affair with a fellow Thakur! For a beautiful chick like her, I wouldn't mind blowing even twenty grand. I will take her on a shopping spree, impress her with my extravagance, and then lure her to bed!

*

The first thing I do is buy a new flannel shirt and corduroy trousers from the Metropolitan Shopping Mall. I don't want Ritu to see me in the same clothes as last night. Then, on a whim, I watch an English film in the multiplex. I barely catch any phrases, but a delicious contentment spreads through me as I watch the pale-skinned actors speak non-stop English for one and a half hours. Somehow it makes me feel better equipped to date a rich chick. I leave the cinema, put on my dark glasses and hail an auto-rickshaw.

I reach Connaught Place at quarter to three and wait for Ritu in front of the Wimpy. She arrives a little after three, in a different car this time – a sleek grey Mercedes SLK 350, but there is the same tall moustachioed guard sitting on the front seat with an AK-47.

She steps out of the car, says something to the guard and the car drives away. Today she is wearing off-white *churidar* pyjamas and a matching *kameez*. A red *chunni* is pulled down demurely over her chest. In broad daylight she looks even more beautiful and radiant. I admire the soft contours of her face and the delicate arch of her neck, and marvel at my luck in bagging such a beauty.

She spots me almost immediately and a warm smile spreads on her face. 'Hello, Vijay,' she greets me, as her eyes dart around suspiciously, perhaps looking to see if any of her relatives are snooping around.

I feel it is time I found out about her family. 'Yesterday you came with a gunman too. How come?'

'My father insists that I take one. He is concerned about my security.'

'Is he a big businessman?'

'Sort of,' she says and tries to change the subject. 'So what are you going to buy in Connaught Place? I have never shopped here before.'

'I don't need anything. This is going to be your shopping spree,' I reply and lead her into an air-conditioned boutique selling expensive designer clothes. Ritu browses through the racks, then checks the price tags and rolls her eyes. 'These prices are ridiculous. In Lucknow I can buy ten outfits for what they are charging for one.'

'But this is Delhi. Here you have to pay Delhi rates. Don't worry, today I am paying for your shopping,' I assure her with the brash confidence of a man with a hundred thousand rupees in his trouser pocket.

She looks at me in a funny kind of way. '*Arrey*, why would you spend money on me? Are you my brother or what?'

The word 'brother' jars a bit. I peer into her eyes, which seem transparent and sincere, and wonder if I have made a mistake in reading this girl, a costly error of judgement.

'Let's try this shop.' I indicate the adjacent showroom, which has 'Sale' emblazoned across its window.

Ritu shakes her head. 'These sales are all fake. I think we should go to Palika Bazaar. I am told that the market has much more reasonable rates.'

Why should I quarrel if my seduction budget is going to be reduced by half? So I lead the way to the underground market situated in the middle of the park, full of small shops selling clothes, trinkets and electronic items. The bazaar is teeming with shoppers, mostly middle-class *behenji* types and groups of college students. I am immediately propositioned by shifty-eyed shopkeepers sitting behind rows of computer CDs and DVDs. 'Want blue films? . . . We have Triple X, Sir, very good print,' they whisper as I walk past their cubicles. The stuffy atmosphere of the place suffocates me, but Ritu is entranced by the brightly lit shops. She conducts an impromptu market survey and declares that though Palika Bazaar is marginally more expensive than Aminabad Market in Lucknow, it has more variety. True to her small-town roots, she shows no interest in the shops displaying T-shirts and jeans and heads straight for the corridor vendors selling ladies' suits on open hangers. For half an hour she haggles with a middle-aged shopkeeper over a pair of *salwar* suits. She wants to buy them for three hundred and the shopkeeper wants five hundred. Eventually they settle on three hundred and seventy-five. I offer her a five-hundred-rupee note but Ritu refuses it resolutely. She takes out a worn ladies' wallet from her handbag and pays for the purchase with her own money. Her scrupulousness both impresses and troubles me.

Near gate number three, a gangly youth with a load of belts draped on his back buttonholes me. 'These are imported designer belts, Sahib, one thousand rupees in Connaught Place, only two hundred rupees here,' he says and offers me one with a 'Lee' buckle. I wave him away but he refuses to go. 'Have a look,' he insists. Igniting a lighter, he tries to burn one end of the belt. 'You see, Sahib, genuine leather!'

'Don't fool me,' I laugh. 'These are cheap Rexine belts.'

'No, Sir. It is real leather. And for you I will reduce the price to a hundred rupees.'

'I am not interested,' I declare.

'Please, Sahib. Buy just one,' he pleads. 'I will reduce it further to just fifty rupees.'

'Fifty rupees?' Ritu asks. 'That is quite reasonable.'

'See, Sahib? Even Memsahib wants you to have one. Buy one and God will keep you pair together for ever,' he says with the verve of a professional beggar.

Ritu blushes and the pink glow on her face is the surest sign that she feels more than sisterly concern for me. I grin and take out a fifty-rupee note. 'Here. Take this and keep the belt too. You will also remember this encounter with a rich guy.'

The belt vendor accepts my tip with a surprised look on his face. Ritu taps me on the arm. 'Do you distribute largesse like this to every poor fellow you meet?'

'No,' I say jauntily. 'But I had to respect his appeal to God.'

She blushes again and I feel a shiver of lust run down my spine. I feel I am on the right track now and the shopping expedition will lead to something memorable. As Ritu ducks into another clothes shop, I try to figure out the nearest hotel I can take her to.

I make my move the moment she emerges from the shop. 'How about having coffee?'

She tilts her head at me. 'Coffee? Here?'

'No, in a nearby hotel.'

She hesitates and looks at her watch. 'Oh my God, it is already quarter to five. I promised Ram Singh I would be back by five.'

'Who is this Ram Singh?'

'My bodyguard. I need to return to the Wimpy. That is where he will pick me up. I have to go now, Vijay.'

I realize that Ritu is perhaps not as naive as she pretends to be. The way she has refused to take my bait makes me wonder if she has seen through my dark glasses and glimpsed my true intentions. I try to mask my disappointment behind a show of gallantry. 'No problem at all. Come, I will take you back.'

She looks down at her feet. 'I would prefer it if you let me walk alone.'

'OK,' I nod. 'So when will we meet again?'

'I will call you. I have your number on my mobile. Bye now, Vijay.'

A week passes without any phone call from Ritu. And every time I call her I get a recorded message that the subscriber is not available. Perhaps she has left Delhi and gone back to Lucknow, but I am dying with curiosity about this beautiful girl who travels like a princess and shops like a pauper. So I begin scouring the area around the temple, peeking into the mansions and farmhouses of the rich to see if I can spot either of Ritu's two cars, but most of the houses are screened off by high metal gates and the guards outside rarely allow any loitering.

Just when I am about to give up hope of meeting her again, Ritu calls me. 'Hello, Vijay,' she says in her sweet voice and I go dizzy with delight.

'Where have you been all this time? I went mad trying to contact you.'

'I went to Farrukhabad with my mother. I got back only today.'

'I missed you.'

'I missed you, too. Would you like to meet up for lunch today?'

'Lunch? Yes, certainly.'

'Where would you like to go?' she asks me.

Left to me, I would take her to some nice homely Indian joint like Kake da Dhaba, but I know that pedigree chicks like her prefer to go to fancy restaurants where they eat anything but *dhal roti*. I rack my brains for some suitably exotic eating joint, but the only non-Indian restaurant I know is the corner shop near the temple which serves greasy vegetable chow mein. 'How about Chinese?' I offer tentatively.

'Chinese? Do you like Chinese?'

'It is my all-time favourite.'

'Mine too!' she squeals.

'Then let's go to the best Chinese restaurant in Delhi. In some five-star hotel.'

'Won't it cost a lot?'

'Don't worry about the cost. It will be my treat.'

'Good. Then let's meet at the House of Ming at one.'

'Sure,' I say. 'I'll see you there at one o'clock.'

It takes me half an hour just to figure out where this House of Ming is. A helpful operator at Directory Enquiries finally points me in the right direction. It turns out to be an expensive Chinese restaurant located inside the Taj Hotel on Mansingh Road.

My taxi comes to a stop in the covered portico of the five-star hotel at quarter to one. I alight, wearing a Van Heusen bush shirt and Levi jeans. An impressive-looking guard dressed in a white uniform with brass buttons and a colourful turban on his head salutes me and opens a glass door. I step into a lavishly decorated hall with a marble floor full of intricate designs. Elegantly dressed men and women sit on sofas, talking in low voices. Soft music plays from invisible instruments. A massive chandelier hangs from the ceiling. The lobby even has a small artificial pool containing lotus flowers.

For a few minutes I just stand in the hall, intimidated by the opulence on display. A hostess directs me to the restaurant, which is bustling with customers. Brass lanterns hang from the ceiling, which is made of wood. Flame-spewing golden dragons adorn the walls. The furniture is elegant, rectangular mica-topped tables complemented by black, high-backed chairs.

The waitress, a chinky-eyed girl clad in a long, slinky blue dress with dragon motifs and slits, welcomes me with the effusiveness normally reserved for heavy tippers. She leads me to a quiet corner table and presents me with a thick, leather-bound menu. I take a look at the prices and almost choke.

Ritu arrives promptly at one, trailed by the same gun-toting commando, who sees her to the door of the restaurant before leaving discreetly. She is dressed in a sky-blue *salwar kameez* with delicate embroidery. Lots of eyes turn in her direction and I get envious glances from some office executives sitting at a nearby table.

She sits down opposite me and places her handbag on the side.

The waitress arrives again to take our order. 'What would you like?' Ritu asks.

'Whatever you like.'

'Have you eaten here before?'

'Yes. A couple of times.'

'And which is your favourite dish here?'

For a moment I am stumped, but retrieve the situation with the name of the only Chinese dish I know. 'Maggi noodles!'

'That's so funny!' she laughs and proceeds to order a couple of soups and some strange-sounding dishes.

When the waitress has gone, she turns to me. 'So tell me, Vijay, what is your line of work?'

'I told you, import-export.'

'Yes, but what kind of goods exactly?'

'Boxes.'

'Boxes?'

'Yes. I own a box factory on MG Road.'

'Nice. And where do you live in Mehrauli?'

I am prepared for this question. 'I have a four-bedroom flat on Ramoji Road.'

'And who is there in your family?'

'Just my mother and sister.'

'Is your sister married?'

'No. Not yet. But that is enough about my family. I want to know about yours.'

'What do you want to know?'

'Everything.'

She gazes at me with a half-despairing, half-appealing look. 'Can't we do this some other time?'

'Why not now?'

'Because I don't feel like it. But I promise you, Vijay, once I know you better I will tell you everything.'

'OK,' I shrug. 'If that's what you want.'

Ritu takes my hand and squeezes it. 'Thanks for understanding.'

The waitress arrives with bowls containing a watery concoction with some slimy pouches floating in it. 'Won ton soup,' she announces.

'So tell me, which is your favourite Shabnam Saxena film?' Ritu asks, beginning on her soup.

We have a relaxed meal, talking of many things, joking and laughing, with an undercurrent of flirtatiousness to our banter. The perfectly good afternoon is spoiled by the bill, a full nine thousand rupees, including tip. The costliest lunch of my life. I strip off nine notes from a fresh wad of thousand-rupee notes as Ritu watches appreciatively. I hope she will be worth all this money in bed. But Ritu thwarts me yet again. As soon as I pay the bill, she prepares to leave. 'I have to go now, Vijay, or my family will start getting suspicious.'

'But you haven't told me anything about your family. Friends don't keep secrets from each other,' I remonstrate.

She takes my hand again. 'I promise to tell you everything, Vijay. Soon.'

She does not kiss me, does not even shake my hand, but her departing look is full of longing and promise. My disappointment dissipates. I know it is only a question of time before I succeed in going all the way with her. *Bole toh*, the girl is hooked!

I marvel at how easy it has proved to charm Ritu. These hick country girls are the most gullible. They are just venturing out of their houses, trying to test the limits of parental freedom. These girls view life through rose-tinted glasses. They go to see the matinée of *Love in Canada* and then want to begin their own romance in Mehrauli. And any street Romeo on a Hero Honda, in dark glasses and a leather jacket, can deflower them.

I intend to do just that. At our next meeting.

Today is 16 February and I am in the Sanjay Gandhi slum, where Barkha Das has arrived to do a 'roadshow' for ITN. I have not seen so much excitement since India won the Twenty20 Cricket World Cup. The temple is agog with news of Vicky Rai's acquittal. My friends in the slum are going around with such long faces you'd think the murdered girl Ruby Gill was their adopted sister. The media is also going crazy over the whole affair; every channel is having a panel discussion on the verdict and there are ten TV vans parked outside Vicky Rai's farmhouse. Since yesterday the road to Number Six has been jammed with cars in a victory procession, horns blaring, workers of the People's Welfare Party waving the red-and-green flags of their party and screaming 'Long live Jagannath Rai', 'Long live Vicky Rai.' A giant arch has been put up at the entrance to the farmhouse, bearing posters of Jagannath Rai giving election smiles.

Frankly, I can't understand all this hoopla over Vicky Rai's acquittal. The country is behaving as if he is the first rich guy to get away with murder. But even I cannot resist seeing Barkha Das in person. A crowd of about five hundred is gathered all round her, gawking at the face we see every day on TV. Even Mother has come, drawn by the scent of celebrity. She admires Barkha's flawless complexion and her trademark photographer's vest, worn over black trousers and a white shirt.

Barkha has a fluffy pink mike in her hand. 'So tell me, what do you think of the verdict in the Ruby Gill murder case?' she asks no one in particular and scans the crowd. A swarthy young man with a big bump on his forehead is the first to respond. 'It is very bad. The judgment will send the signal that there is no justice for the poor,' he says in the serious, formal manner people adopt when they appear on TV.

Also in the crowd is a crackpot friend of mine called Shaka, who boasts of being some kind of functionary in the Communist Party. He has long hair and always wears a red bandanna on his forehead. Before Barkha can go to anyone else, he snatches the mike from her hand. 'This country has gone to the dogs. The rich imperialists are breaking the law with impunity. I say shoot them all. Only a revolution can save this country. Only a revolution. *Inquilab Zindabad!*' he declares and pumps his fists in the air.

Barkha Das snatches the mike back from Shaka and glares at him briefly. 'Do you think we need a revolution, *maaji*?' she turns to Mother suddenly.

Mother shrinks back, but Barkha corners her. 'You have to answer, *maaji*.'

'Revolution will not solve our problems, *beti*,' Mother speaks into the mike in her gravelly voice. 'We have to work hard, do good deeds in this life so that our misdeeds in the previous life can be forgiven by God. Only then will we be born rich in the next life.'

I shake my head at Mother. This has always been a sore point between us. She believes in good *karma* and rebirth. I believe only in the accident of birth and the currency of the present. And that idiot Shaka is also wrong. There will be no revolution. The rich can sleep easy. Our revolutions last only until we miss our next meal.

Actually I shouldn't be saying all this. After all, I myself have joined the ranks of the rich imperialists. Thanks to a certain briefcase!

Ritu calls me the next morning, sounding a little upset. 'Vijay, can we meet today? Some place quiet. And far from here.'

'I know just the place. Let's meet in Lodhi Garden. It's on the other side of the city.'

'Yes. I know Lodhi Garden. I'll meet you there at two o'clock.'

I have a gut feeling that today I will finally score with this rich chick. In the salubrious environs of Delhi's most famous park.

I take a taxi to Lodhi Garden and wait for her near the entrance. She arrives fifteen minutes late in an auto-rickshaw, wearing a pink *salwar kameez*. I like her choice of colour. But what

I like even more is the fact that she has ditched the family car and the personal guard. Definitely a good omen.

Lodhi Garden is a wide open green space full of tombs and trees. It is famous for two things: jogging and snogging. In the mornings the park is full of fitness enthusiasts who can be seen running around in soaked T-shirts, and in the afternoons the lovers take over, making out in recessed alcoves of crumbling monuments, kissing behind bushes, groping on strategically situated park benches.

At two o'clock, the park resembles a zoo for lovelorn couples. I can see that Ritu is a bit uncomfortable at the public displays of affection going on all over the park. In small-town Lucknow the necking couples would probably be in jail by now.

'Should we go to another park?' she asks me, glancing around with trepidation.

'You will see the same thing in every other park in Delhi,' I answer and gently guide her to a corner bench which has just been vacated by a couple.

We sit down side by side. Ritu is still jumpy, as though expecting her father to pop up behind the next bush. I try to put her at ease. 'Don't worry. You won't see any of your family members here. At this time of the day the park is reserved only for lovers.'

She blushes and I gently take her hand in mine. She neither resists nor encourages me. I doubt whether she will allow me to kiss her in a public place, but this is the time to find out. I lean over and give her a gentle peck on the cheek, not so much a kiss as a probing gambit. She immediately covers her face with her hands, but I prise them open and discover that she is smiling shyly. I look her in the eye, wink and kiss her again, this time on the lips. She kisses me back. I taste the lipstick on her lips, inhale the perfume of her skin and discover that the rich even kiss differently. The warm, measured kiss from Ritu is quite unlike the slobbering mouth-lock I used to get from the *mohalla* girls. And the delicious tingling sensation it leaves in my mouth spreads all the way to my brain, dissolving all doubt and leaving me only with the heady feeling of success.

'I love you, Ritu,' I say with the earnest expression of a romantic hero.

'I love you too, Vijay,' she whispers, and then and there I feel like standing up and taking a bow. Not because this is the first time in my life that a girl has said these words to me. I've heard plenty of terms of endearment, but they were uttered by the dark, coarse girls from the Sanjay Gandhi slum, who smelt of cheap talcum powder and Boroline. To hear these words from the lips of a fair, svelte beauty who drives in a Mercedes and is protected by a commando is a different experience altogether. I decide to go for broke.

'Come, let us go somewhere more private.' I get up from the bench.

'Where to?' she asks.

'I know a good place.'

She does not demur as I lead her out of Lodhi Garden to a taxi stand. I can easily afford to take her to one of the deluxe five-star hotels, but they ask too many questions which might scare her off. Better to go to one of those cheap, nondescript hotels where the manager is not fussy and rooms are charged by the hour. 'Take us to Paharganj,' I tell the driver.

Decent Hotel is located in one of the narrow alleys of Paharganj, within walking distance of the railway station. A grey, three-storeyed building with fading plaster and a cracked sign-board, I realize soon enough that the only thing which inspires confidence about it is the name. The reception has mildewed walls and an atmosphere of fake cheer. The bellboys appraise Ritu and me from head to toe and go into a huddle. They begin conversing in low whispers, as though hatching some conspiracy against us. The manager leers at me in a knowing way when I ask for a room. 'One hour or one day?' he asks.

'One hour,' I say and he promptly charges me five hundred rupees and hands over a clunky key. 'Room 515, fifth floor. The lift is round the corner.'

I can sense Ritu's increasing discomfort as I usher her into the lift. Room Number 515 turns out to be at the fag end of the corridor and there are cockroaches scurrying across the frayed and dusty red carpet. I am already regretting my decision to come to this dump. But it is too late to backtrack. I open the door and am pleasantly surprised by its neat and efficient orderliness. There is a large double bed with a crisp white sheet and fluffy pillows. The walls are painted a pastel pink, matching Ritu's dress, and adorned with framed pictures of scenes from Delhi. There is even a wall clock, busy ticking the seconds. A small wooden desk and chair are placed near the far wall. The red curtains, made of some kind of rough fabric, look brand new but are not thick enough to keep out the ambient sounds of traffic and trade. The lingering smell of a faint rose perfume enters my nose, either left behind by the previous occupants or sprayed by the management as a romantic touch. But the icing on the cake is the packet of Nirodh condoms left discreetly on the lower shelf of the bedside table.

Locking the door behind me, I take Ritu in my arms. She accepts my embrace willingly but there is a new stiffness in her body. She grimaces slightly as I kiss her again on the lips, more hungrily this time.

My hands get rid of her *chunni* and commence their descent down her back, feeling the heat of her skin through the thin fabric of her *kameez*. She begins shivering as I unbutton her shirt and lift it over her head, uncovering her from the waist up. Only a white lace bra remains and its sight serves only to inflame me further. That is when Ritu does a peculiar thing. She does not try to stop me, does not demurely cover her chest with her hands; she simply starts sobbing. I have been with enough girls to suspect that her tears are not so much a mark of protest as an appeal for caution – this is probably her first time – yet they make me distraught. I know I can ignore this minor hiccup and continue my conquest. But Ritu seems so utterly defenceless, her face so guileless, that my raging desire begins to seem crass and vulgar. Taking advantage of her would be as reprehensible as taking a coin from a blind beggar. So I wipe her tears with my fingers and hand back her *kameez*. Then, fully clothed, we sit down on the bed and simply hold hands. I don't remember for how long we do this, but a curious change begins to come over me. Gradually my eyes lose focus. They don't see the bed and the headboard and the walls and the pictures. My ears stop registering all sounds. They don't hear the honks of the auto-rickshaws, the cries of the fruit-sellers or the screeching of crows. As the clock ticks off the seconds, all I notice is the slight trembling of my skin and the warm beating of my heart. I look into Ritu's moist eyes and feel as if the whole world is contained in their glistening depths.

The spell is broken only by incessant knocking on the door. 'Time is up, Sir. We need the room back,' I hear the manager's voice.

Glancing at the clock, it is a shock to discover that we have been in the room for over an hour. I get up quickly from the bed and unlock the door. The manager seems apologetic but it is the sight of a maid, armed with a fresh sheet, which brings me up short. I hear the sound of the lift opening and a middle-aged couple steps into the corridor, probably the next hourly tenants of the room. The man, dressed like an office clerk, sniggers at me; the woman, heavy set, but fashionably dressed in trousers and shirt, giggles like an adolescent schoolgirl as Ritu and I pass her, her face shining with unrestrained longing.

The encounter with this lusty-eyed couple shames me. But it makes Ritu clutch my hand with a fierce new possessiveness.

When we step back into the street dusk is falling, draping the surroundings in a misty grey light. The quiet murmur of the afternoon has given way to the din of evening traffic, the cacophony of car horns and the revving of bus engines on the main road.

'I am late,' Ritu frets. 'I must return immediately or Ram Singh will come looking for me.'

'When will I see you again?'

'I don't know. I am going back to Lucknow tonight.'

'But how will I live without seeing you?' I cry.

'Love doesn't end just because we don't see each other,' she replies.

'At least give me some idea of when you will return to Delhi.'

'In three weeks. Just in time for my birthday.'

'Your birthday? When is it?'

'On the tenth of March.'

'Then I must get you a present.'

'But you have already given me a present.'

'What are you saying?' I ask, mystified. 'I have not given you anything.'

She smiles. 'You have given me the best possible gift. You have given me respect. See you soon, Vijay.' She gently squeezes my hand in a goodbye gesture and gets into an auto-rickshaw.

As the auto-rickshaw departs, trailing a plume of smoke, a pang of sadness squeezes my heart with such force that I almost cry out. And a new realization dawns on me. I had come to Paharganj a boy, looking for a tawdry thrill. I was leaving it a man, madly in love.

Lying in bed that night I am tormented with dreams of Ritu. She began as an object of desire for me, a seemingly unattainable fantasy, and then somewhere along the way she became real. I am all too painfully aware of the wide gap between us. She is the daughter of an upper-caste, upper-class business tycoon and I am the uncouth son of a temple sweeper. The chasm between us is so wide that it can only be bridged in dreams. But I pinch myself and regain confidence with the knowledge that Ritu returns my love. And, as they say in Hindi film songs, *pyaar* respects no boundaries. Our love will bridge the chasm. With a little bit of help from a black VIP briefcase.

I decide to use the three weeks until Ritu comes back to Delhi to make myself worthy of her. I start going to a private tutor for English lessons. I meet a property agent to discuss renting a four-bedroom flat on Ramoji Road. I visit the box factory on MG Road to familiarize myself with its operation. And then I decide to buy a birthday gift for her. A diamond engagement ring. It seems like the best way to convince her family of my richie-rich credentials and seal our relationship.

I go to a swanky jewellery showroom on Janpath and sit in air-conditioned comfort as a sales girl in a pink top shows me one magnificent ring after another. The glittering diamonds are all shapes and sizes, some as small as a grain of salt and some as big as a thumbtack, but all of them carry indecently large price tags. The cheapest diamond ring in the store costs fifty thousand rupees. What disturbs me is that similar rings, shining just as brilliantly, are available in plenty of roadside shops in Janpath for as little as five hundred rupees. 'Those are not diamonds, Sir,' the sales girl titters. 'They are cubic zirconium pieces, totally fake. Under a microscope you can spot the difference immediately.' For a moment I am tempted to buy a fake diamond ring. It feels silly to be blowing all this money on a piece of rock. And Ritu is not going to examine it under a microscope. But the very next moment I chide myself for thinking like a slum-dweller and select a shiny, one-carat ring costing a whopping 120,000 rupees. I pay cash, have it nicely gift-wrapped, and then call Ritu on her mobile. 'I have a surprise present for you. Can we meet on 10 March?'

'That is the day I arrive in Delhi. My family will not allow me to go out on my birthday.'

'But it is absolutely critical that we meet. How about the Nehru Park at three o'clock?'

'It's going to be very difficult, but I'll do my best to come,' she promises.

On 10 March, I proceed to Nehru Park with the costliest gift of my life in my pocket, my palms clammy with sweat. Ritu arrives on time and alone. We sit down on a secluded bench underneath a shady tree.

I take out the gift-wrapped packet from my breast pocket and place it gently in her palm. 'Open it,' I say. She begins unwrapping the golden paper till the red velvet box is revealed. She slowly raises the lid. I expect her eyes to be dazzled by the glittering diamond and a look of shocked delight to appear on her face, but what I get instead is a pained and pensive expression. 'This looks like an engagement ring,' she says in a shocked voice.

'It is,' I reply. 'Ritu, will you marry me?'

'But I am already engaged,' she whispers.

'What?'

'Yes. My father has got me engaged to Kunwar Inder Singh, the crown prince of Pratapgarh princely State. I have managed to put off the wedding till after my graduation, but I could not prevent the engagement.'

'So you don't really want to marry this fellow?'

'I detest Inder. He troubled me so much in Lucknow that I came away to stay in Delhi with my brother. I love you, Vijay, but I cannot marry you. If I defy my father he will not only kill me, he will also kill you. That is why I cannot accept this ring.' She closes the lid and passes the velvet box back to me.

I purse my lips. 'I think it is time you told me about your family.'

'Yes. I think it is time, too.' She takes a deep breath. 'I am Jagannath Rai's daughter.'

I feel an electric current dart up my backside. '*Arrey baap re!* The Home Minister of Uttar Pradesh? That dreaded mafia don?'

'The same,' she replies in a low voice.

'Then where are you staying? In some government guest-house?'

'No. I am staying with my brother in Mehrauli. At Number Six.'

'You mean you are Vicky Rai's sister?'

'Do you know him?'

'Who doesn't know him? He is all over the news for getting away with the murder of Ruby Gill.'

'I can tolerate the verdict,' she says bitterly. 'What I cannot stand is the gloating that is going on in our house. It sickens me. I feel ashamed to belong to such a family.'

'It looks like you don't get along with your father and brother.'

'I never have. There are two camps in our house. My mother and I are on one side and my father and brother are on the other, and there is perpetual wrestling going on between the two camps. Of course, it is the men who always prevail over the women.' Her head hangs down and a tear trickles out of her eye.

I kiss away her tear. 'Now you can add one more person to your camp. I will be there for you, always.'

'So you still want to be friends with me, Vijay?'

It is my turn now to take a deep breath. In the face of her confession I feel the time has come for full disclosure on my side as well. 'I need to tell you the truth about me, Ritu. Then I will ask whether you want to be friends with *me*.'

'Do not speak in riddles.'

'I won't. Not any longer. So here's the truth. I am not Vijay Singh. My real name is Munna. I am not a Thakur. I don't own a four-bedroom flat. I live in a one-room shack inside the Bhole Nath Temple, where my mother works as a sweeper. Everything I told you before was a lie. But only because I am madly in love with you and didn't want to lose you.'

Ritu crumples in front of me, doubling up in pain as though I have hit her physically. There is a long pause as she digests the information I have given her. Then she turns to face me. 'I am presuming you don't own any factory either. What do you really do, Mr Munna, besides lying and cheating?' she asks accusingly, clenching her fists.

I debate whether to tell Ritu about my career as a mobile-phone thief and decide against it. Love might make one blind, but not stupid. I had to tell her the truth about my family because a man of Jagannath Rai's connections would have seen through my deception instantly. But even Jagannath Rai cannot know about my briefcase. Still, I have the sinking feeling that my love affair is all but over. Even the money in the briefcase will not be enough to restore Ritu's faith in me.

'I am a manager at a box factory,' I say with downcast eyes.

'Then where did you get this diamond ring from? Did you steal it?' Ritu demands.

Having decided not to tell her anything about the briefcase, I am left with just one option. To prove that my love is real, the diamond ring will have to become fake.

'It is not a real diamond ring. It is simply cubic zirconium. This was all I could afford.'

Ritu clenches her fists again and I can sense deep emotion welling up inside her. In Hindi films, this is when the heroine stands up and slaps the deceitful hero. I wince, expecting Ritu to do the same, but what happens next is entirely unexpected. Instead of slapping me, Ritu grasps my hand. 'You sacrificed your hard-earned money for my happiness? And that lunch in the five-star restaurant . . . You must have blown a month's salary just to impress me.'

I nod and her eyes turn tearful again. 'I am glad you told me the truth, Munna,' she says in a broken voice. 'I can tolerate poverty, but I cannot tolerate falsehood.' She looks me in the eye. 'You asked me whether I still want to be friends with you. This is my answer.' She kisses me on the cheek and takes back the ring.

I don't know whether to thank God or Bollywood for this remarkable turnaround. The love affair between the rich girl and the poor boy is staple fare in Hindi films. I wonder whether Ritu Rai is a star-struck scatterbrain, getting her kicks from romancing the poor. Another possibility that crosses my mind is that, like the film-maker Nandita Mishra, she too might be making a documentary on slum life. But when I look into her eyes I don't see any deviousness there, I glimpse only genuine honesty. And a wave of relief sweeps over my body, causing love to gush out of my eyes, drenching the bench and cooling my heart. I kiss Ritu back and clasp her in a fierce embrace as though the two of us are the only living beings left on this planet.

The embrace is broken by someone shaking my shoulder violently. I look up to find a tall man with a thick curled-up moustache glaring at me. It is Ram Singh, Ritu's bodyguard.

'Baby!' he thunders at her with the authority of a trusted retainer. 'Your entire family is waiting at home with your birthday cake and this is where you are spending your time? If Bhaiyyaji were to see you in this condition he wouldn't leave you alive. Now come with me this instant.'

Ritu wrenches herself from me with a terrified cry and gets up from the bench. Ram Singh grabs her arm and begins dragging her towards the car park. She cannot even muster the courage to look back at me.

I am left contemplating the reach of her father. If Ram Singh can inspire so much terror, what will being face to face with Jagannath Rai be like? What kind of nasty things will he do to me once he finds out about the naughty things I have done with his daughter? I can only hope that just as the gangsters whose briefcase I have stolen have no clue to my whereabouts, Jagannath Rai will be unable to trace me.

On returning to the temple, I find Champi sitting in her usual place, chatting to a dark-skinned stranger. This is the first time I have seen her chat with anyone in the temple. I approach the *gulmohar* tree. The man sitting on the bench is the strangest-looking person I have ever seen. He is no more than five feet tall and jet black, like the *habshis* they show in movies dancing with the heroine in a nightclub in their leopard-skin loincloths, chanting some nonsense like '*Hoogo Boogu*' and thrusting their spears in the air.

'Who was that stranger you were talking to?' I ask Champi the next morning.

'He is my friend, and he is staying in the shack next to ours,' says Champi. 'What does he look like, Munna?'

I glance at Champi sharply. There is an expectant look on her face, as though my answer will be a confirmation of what she has already visualized in her mind. I see the same bashful glow on her cheeks as I have seen on Ritu's. With a shock I realize Champi might be falling in love with that tribal. Somehow, because of her ugliness, the possibility has never crossed my mind, and I realize how selfish and insensitive I have been.

'What does he look like?' Champi repeats.

'He is tall and dark and very handsome,' I reply, bringing a smile to Champi's face. No point telling her that her Romeo is a black midget who looks like a clown.

*

The next week is the most agonizing of my life. Ritu does not call me and her mobile appears to be switched off. I am unable to sleep, my mind full of grim portents. And my foreboding seems justified when I get a frantic call on 17 March from Malini, Ritu's friend whom I met in the night club. 'Munna, Ritu needs to see you. With great difficulty I have managed to bring her to my house. Can you come right now to West End?'

I take down the address and rush to her house, a smart villa in a leafy suburb. A distraught Malini receives me and takes me to her room, where I receive the shock of my life. Ritu limps up to me, looking like one of those battered housewives they show on TV. There are bruises on her forehead and chin, welt marks on her cheeks and dark circles under her eyes.

'Who did this to you?' I cry.

'There was a big fight in the house on the day of my birthday. Ram Singh spilled the beans about my affair with you. My father threatened to shoot me. But it was Vicky who actually hit me.'

An incandescent rage begins building inside me. 'How dare he do this to you?' I seethe. 'I will kill him.'

'Now I have been forbidden from leaving the house and my mobile has been confiscated,' Ritu adds. 'Luckily Malini came to meet me today and managed to bring me here. I wanted to warn you to be very careful. Your life could be in danger.'

'But what about *your* life? The butchers in your house are quite capable of killing you.'

'It is a woman's fate to suffer. But I have taken one courageous decision at least. I have told my father that I will not marry Kunwar Inder Singh, even if he kills me. That alliance was arranged by my father only to further his political agenda. I refuse to become a pawn in his dirty game.'

'Then marry me.'

'My family will never allow me to marry you.' Ritu slowly shakes her head. 'But I have made it clear that I shall not marry anyone else either.'

'Then marry me against your family's wishes. We could go to

a temple right now. Once we are legally married, your father won't be able to do a thing. The police will protect us.'

She gives a hollow laugh. 'I have seen how police officers quake on hearing my father's name. They will be the first ones to drag me back to him.'

'Then what are our options, Ritu?'

'None. They say in books that all's fair in love and war. But I have seen with my own eyes, nothing is fair in either, Munna. Our love is a prohibited one.'

'Just because you belong to a high caste and I don't? I do not agree with you,' I challenge her. 'Forty years ago my mother and I were called Untouchables. We wouldn't have been allowed inside the temple. Today she not only works there, she also lives there. And no one dares call us Untouchable.'

'But let her come to our house with your marriage proposal and then see what happens.'

'What will happen? At best your family will say no.'

'Don't be naive, Munna. You know what they did to that poor Muslim boy who dared to marry the daughter of an industrialist in Kolkata. They killed him.'

'But I am not Muslim.'

'Then take a look at this newspaper report.' She produces a crumpled news clipping from her handbag. It is from some Hindi newspaper.

'What does it say?'

'It says that two young lovers were lynched in Uttar Pradesh because they belonged to different castes. Nineteen-year-old Pritam and eighteen-year-old Sonu were hanged one after the other from the roof of a house in their village. He was a high-caste Brahmin, while she was a member of a lower-caste community. Hundreds of people watched as the couple were hanged. What is even more gruesome is the fact that the boy's and the girl's parents not only sanctioned the punishment, but even watched as their children swung from the makeshift gibbet.' She shudders as she reads.

'I don't care if they kill me. I still want to marry you.'

'But I care, Munna, I care. If my brother can do this to me, his own sister, think what he could do to you.'

'You exaggerate unnecessarily.' I wave my hand. 'I am not scared of Vicky Rai.'

At that precise moment my mobile phone trills. This surprises me because the only person other than me who knows this number is Ritu. I press the Talk button and an unknown voice breathes down the line. 'Motherfucker, listen to me carefully. My name is Vicky Rai. And you have dared to raise your eyes to my sister Ritu. Now I will carve you up like a pig, I will break every bone in your body and then I will feed your carcass to my dogs. Get it?'

The line is disconnected and the air inside the room becomes noticeably colder. Ritu doesn't hear the message, but from the expression on my face she guesses the identity of the caller immediately. 'It was my brother, wasn't it?'

'Yes,' I reply, still reeling with shock. 'How did he get my number?'

'He must have taken it from my mobile. What did he say?'

'He threatened to kill me.'

'Oh my God!' she says and buries her face in her hands. There is complete silence in the room for a couple of minutes. Then she raises her head and I see her lips curved into an expression of grim determination. 'Now there is only one option left for us. We have to run away,' she declares.

'I agree,' I say and clutch her hand. 'We must think of our future together.'

'But how will we survive? I don't have any money.'

'I have enough to support both of us.'

'How much?' she asks.

'Much more than you can imagine. I promise that you will not lack anything.'

'Where will we run to?'

'Pick any city you like.'

'I have always wanted to visit Mumbai.'

'So have I. Let's go to the station right now and catch a train.'

'No. If we do that, Malini will be in a lot of trouble.'

'Then when should we go?'

'I know the perfect date. Vicky is having a big party on 23 March to celebrate his acquittal. There will be nearly five hundred people in the house and in that mêlée I will manage to slip out. Wait for me just outside the service entrance of Number Six. It is on the side path perpendicular to the main road. I will come out at exactly eleven p.m. Then we will take a taxi to the railway station and escape to Mumbai.'

'Excellent. I will get two tickets for Mumbai ready.'

Our pact is made and I know that a new phase of my life is about to begin. The future, which was nebulous till now, appears to be acquiring a definite shape. I am looking forward to living in Mumbai. They say it is the city of dreams. It has made people living on pavements film stars and industrialists overnight. Who knows what it might have in store for me.

I am tempted, on returning to the temple, to go to the sanctum sanctorum and prostrate myself before Lord Shiva. This seems like an appropriate occasion to end my tiff with God and seek his blessings. I even climb up the marble steps. In the face of Ritu's love, the songs of Bollywood have begun to seem real to me. I have begun to believe that there might be justice in this world after all. But a tiny voice in my head continues to hold me back. Where was God when those young lovers were being hanged? Was he powerless to stop the murders? Or was he himself a mute spectator to the atrocity?

I go to the railway booking office and purchase two first-class train tickets for Mumbai. The Punjab Mail will leave Delhi at 05:30 on 24 March and take Ritu and me straight to Mumbai Central.

I consider what to do with Champi and Mother. Champi appears to be completely smitten by that tribal. Every day I catch her sitting on the bench, chatting to him animatedly. And for the first time I actually hear her full-throated laugh. I don't grudge her that small happiness. And I feel it is time I informed Mother of my plan.

'Three days from now I am going to Mumbai,' I tell her.

'So suddenly?' she asks. 'Is it because of your work?'

'No. To tell you the truth, I'm getting married.'

'Oh! And who is the girl, if I may ask?'

'Her name is Ritu.'

'And does she live in Mumbai?'

'No, she lives in Delhi. In Mehrauli, in fact.'

'So is she one of the maids from the Sanjay Gandhi slum?'

'They are worthless trash, Mother, that I wouldn't even dream of marrying. Your prospective daughter-in-law belongs to one of the richest and most powerful families in the country.'

'You dream too much, Munna.'

'No, Mother. This is real. Ritu and I are getting married and moving to Mumbai. As soon as we get settled there I will send for both of you. Then Champi can have her operation. And you can finally take some well-deserved rest.'

Mother becomes instantly suspicious. 'Why are you going to Mumbai if the girl is from Delhi? Are you two eloping?'

'Sort of.'

'Look, you had better tell me all about this Ritu. Who is her father? What is her family?'

'Her father is Jagannath Rai, the Home Minister of Uttar Pradesh. Her brother is the industrialist Vicky Rai.'

Mother's hand flies to her mouth. 'No. . . . no . . . no,' she murmurs.

'You always said that we are poor because of our deeds in a previous life. Well, I have managed to escape the fate that the bad karma in my previous life prescribed for me, in this life itself,' I brag, but Mother is not listening to me. She is already in conversation with her gods. 'How could you play such a cruel joke, *Ishvar*?' she addresses the calendars on the wall.

'What joke? What are you saying, Mother?' I demand.

'You don't know, son,' she replies in an anguished voice. 'This Vicky Rai is the one who killed your father. Mowed him down while he was sleeping on the pavement.'

I feel the ground shift beneath my feet. 'What? Are you sure?'

'A wife can never forget her husband's death. Like a film, that scene has been playing in my mind for the past fifteen years.'

'Yet you kept it a secret from me? He was my father, after all.'

'I was sworn to silence by Jagannath Rai. He gave me money for this house, for your education, in return for not implicating Vicky.'

The past has the nasty habit of catching up with you at unexpected moments. I had suspected all along that Father's death had resulted in a pay-off to Mother from the errant driver. But I had been blissfully unaware of the identity of the driver. Or perhaps I had deliberately not tried to probe too deeply into the matter. I had conveniently rationalized that we had to move on with our lives, and Father was not going to come back from the dead. But now he had. And he had detonated a small bomb in my life, throwing everything into disarray. A medley of emotions whirls through my mind, from sadness to anger to bafflement.

'Perhaps this was pre-ordained, Mother,' I say, after brooding for a while.

'What do you mean, Munna?'

'Don't you see, this is God's way of exacting revenge? Many years ago, Vicky Rai snatched something from us. Now we are going to snatch something from him.'

'So you are still going to marry his sister?'

'Ritu hates her family as much as you do. And Ritu and I love each other very much. Even Father would have approved of my decision to marry her.'

'Don't you dare bring your father into this. Or God,' Mother lashes at me. 'I will go to Vicky Rai's house myself and stop this wedding.'

I bar her way. 'You will do nothing of the sort. If Vicky Rai finds out about our plan he will kill Ritu and then he will kill me. Do you want us both dead?'

Mother glares at me for a while and then bursts into tears.

*

An uneasy calm prevails in the house. None of us has dinner that night. Mother sulks in her corner and is comforted by Champi. I lie down in bed and try not to think of anything. Sleep comes much later, and is invaded by multiple dreams. I dream of Father lying in a pool of blood and Vicky Rai grinning over his dead body. I dream of Ritu lying inert on a cold marble floor wrapped in a white shroud. I dream of Lallan being whipped in a police lock-up. I dream of someone pulling my hair, making me scream in pain. I open my eyes and find three men inside the room, surrounding me. I don't know how they managed to raise the latch and enter my room, but I know that this is not a dream.

'Wake up, you bastard,' I hear a voice say as one of the men pulls my hair again with rough hands. I sit up, and someone flicks the light on, dazzling my eyes. I can now take a good look at the three intruders. The first is a bald man with a bulging neck dressed in tight jeans and a white Reebok T-shirt. The second is a very short man in a shimmering cream shirt, and the third man is tall and wiry with curly hair and a square jaw, wearing black trousers and shirt. There is an air of danger about them.

'Is your name Munna Mobile?' the bald man addresses me. He was the one pulling my hair.

'Why do you ask?' I counter-question.

The baldy turns to the tall, wiry man. 'Tell him, Brijesh.'

'You stole the mobile phone from my car.' Brijesh looks at me accusingly and recognition dawns on me slowly. He is indeed the guy from whose Maruti Esteem I took the Nokia. The past has caught up with me again.

The bald man smiles menacingly. 'You have something which belongs to us.'

I try to bluff my way through. 'You are mistaken. What could a poor man like me have?'

The bald man snaps his fingers and his two assistants begin scouring the room. They take in the posters on the wall, the metal torch on the small wooden desk, and their eyes come to rest on the mattress. The little bump where the briefcase lies is plainly visible. 'Get up,' the short man orders. I stand up; he catches the mattress by a corner and lifts it in one movement. The briefcase is revealed, looking like a black island in a sea of dust.

'What do we have here?' the bald man whistles. He reaches down and picks up the briefcase. A pistol appears magically in Brijesh's hand.

At that very moment Mother enters through the wooden partition in her faded yellow sari and maroon blouse.

'Who are you people? What are you doing in my house?' she demands.

In response the bald man shoves her rudely aside. 'Don't ask questions, *budhiya*.'

Mother is not one to give up easily. 'I will teach you ruffians a lesson,' she snaps. She picks up the torch from my desk and whacks the bald man on his buttocks with it, knocking the briefcase out of his hands. Despite his bulk, the man whirls around on the balls of his feet, quick as a cat. In one seamless motion he snatches the torch from Mother's hand and swings his fist at her face, sending her sprawling on the floor. Mother raises her head and whimpers. I can see that she is bleeding from her mouth. She tries to stand up and that is when Brijesh clubs her on the head with the butt of the pistol. I cry out in horror as Mother crashes down, knocked senseless, which is just as well because she wouldn't have been able to bear what happened subsequently.

The bald man regains the briefcase and clicks open the two latches. He raises the lid and examines the contents. 'Hmmm . . . It looks like most of the cash is still here. Only a couple of wads are missing. This might just have saved your life, Munna Mobile. But you will still have to pay the price of stealing from us.'

'What . . . what do you intend to do?' I ask, backing into the wall, my voice sounding hoarse and unnatural.

'Something that will ensure you never steal another mobile phone.' The bald man grins and snaps his fingers again.

Brijesh hands the pistol to the bald man and suddenly grips both my arms. I squirm, try to break free, but he is too strong. The short man raises his hand to hit me when a mobile phone rings in the room. The three ruffians look at one another quizzically before the bald man takes out a Motorola from the pocket of his jeans and checks the display. 'Yes boss?' he says, putting the mobile against his ear and moving off towards the door. I hear snatches of his conversation. 'We found the briefcase . . . looks to be reasonably intact . . . Right now? . . . OK, OK . . . I will leave Brijesh and Natu behind . . . Wait for me. I am coming.'

'That was the boss,' the bald man informs his lieutenants. 'He wants me to come with the briefcase right now. You two finish what you have to. We will meet tomorrow.' He cocks the pistol at me and fires an imaginary bullet, opens the door and steps outside. A little while later I hear a motorcycle being gunned into life.

Brijesh still has me pinioned in a vice-like grip. But it is Natu, the short one, who fills me with dread. 'Have you seen the film *Sholay*?' he asks me, bringing his face close to mine. I can feel his fetid breath on the skin of my neck.

'Yes.'

'Do you remember the scene when Gabbar asks Thakur to give him his hands? Thakur refuses and Gabbar chops off both his hands. I am not going to ask you for your hands, but I will ask for your fingers. All ten of them. Will you give them to me?' He grins, showing uneven teeth stained with betel juice.

I shiver as a chill runs down my back, which by now is completely soaked in sweat. Natu takes hold of my left arm from Brijesh. Then, grabbing my wrist, he lifts up my forefinger and begins arching it backwards. Brijesh hurriedly stuffs a handkerchief into my mouth, smothering my scream. Flesh and bone are stretched to breaking point till the joint pops, accompanied by a sound like that of a hole bursting in a sheet of bubble wrap, and my left index finger droops down. Natu grins and begins to work on my middle finger.

The only good thing about pain is that it empties your mind of everything else. It fills your brain so completely that all feelings of love and hate, envy and jealousy are bleached from it and you are left simply with an excruciating agony filling each and every pore of your body, till even the agony disappears, to be replaced by a dull ache. By the time Natu breaks my left thumb, I have surpassed pain. But that is when the terror begins. Champi wanders into the room, wearing a light-green *salwar kameez* with no *chunni*. 'What is happening, Munna?' she asks in a sleepy voice.

Brijesh looks at Champi and averts his face. I can see that he is revolted by her ugliness. But Natu seems entranced by her. 'Oh ho! Who do we have here?' he whistles wolfishly as Champi tries to feel her way towards me through the altered geography of the room.

'Who is she? Is she your sister?' Brijesh barks at me, pulling the handkerchief out of my mouth.

'Yes. You leave her alone. Your business is with me, not her,' I speak quickly, taking in mouthfuls of air. 'Moreover, she is blind.'

'Blind?' Natu peers at Champi's eyes. 'She doesn't look blind to me.'

'She is, I am telling you,' I say, trying to hide the desperation in my voice.

'OK, let me test,' says Natu and taps her left breast. Champi whimpers in protest and moves her head from side to side, trying to determine the location of her tormentor. Natu claps his hands. 'This is fun. She has solid tits. What do you say, Brijesh, do I have your permission to enjoy a little?'

'Don't you dare touch my sister.' I glare at Natu and strain against Brijesh like a dog on a leash. 'If you touch her I will kill you, motherfucker.'

Natu slaps me across the face with his open palm and Brijesh stuffs the handkerchief back into my mouth. This is all the encouragement the short man needs. He grabs Champi and clamps his hairy palm over her mouth. With his free hand he begins lifting up her shirt as she flails against him like a goat about to be butchered.

Terror, like toothache, cannot be described. It can only be experienced. I stand in Brijesh's grip like a quivering lump of flesh and watch Champi about to be raped.

I wish the earth would open up and swallow me whole, because I know I am directly responsible for the scene unfolding before me. And I have a good inkling of what will happen to Champi after Natu is through with her. She is already blind, now she will become deaf and dumb as well. The whole day she will just sit outside, fanning herself slowly, with a demented look on her face. At night, she will suddenly scream in her sleep. Nightmares will plague her all her life. It is a fate I would not wish on my worst enemy.

For twenty-one years I have lived without faith in God, but at this moment I become a believer. I start praying – to all the gods I know and even those that I don't – making just one appeal, to please, please save my little Champi. I remember all those films in which God responds to prayer and works his magic. But I don't hear the pealing of temple bells; I don't see the floor shake.

Denial is the final refuge of the powerless. Even as Natu is fumbling with the cord of Champi's *salwar*, there is a voice in my head repeating like a stuck record, 'She is not my *sister*, She is *not* my *sister, she is not my sister* . . . She's a worthless Muslim whore.'

All of a sudden, an image flashes through my mind. It is of Lallan strung upside-down in the police lock-up and being tortured by the Butcher of Mehrauli. I had been unable to save him either. But if he was closer than a brother to me, then Champi is closer than a sister. Ties of the mind are stronger than ties of blood.

Like a wounded soldier making his last stand, I muster every ounce of my remaining strength and lash out with my right leg at Natu, catching him at the knee. He is startled into releasing Champi, who tumbles down with a piercing scream. Natu snarls at me and takes out a bicycle chain from his trouser pocket, wraps it around his fist and swings it hard at my face. I try to duck and the metal crashes into the back of my skull. I imagine the door bursting open before I sink into that deep oblivion which is black and fathomless and very, very welcome.

When I come to my senses I find myself in a hospital room. My left hand is in plaster and there is a throbbing pain in the back of my head. I feel it gingerly, expecting to touch sticky blood. But my fingers graze soft fabric. They must have bandaged it. I see Mother lying in the bed next to me, being tended to by Champi, who is wearing a black amulet around her neck.

'What . . . what happened?' I ask Champi groggily.

'A miracle,' she replies cryptically.

A doctor comes in and tells me that I am lucky to be alive. 'You have suffered severe concussion. All five fingers of your left hand are broken. You will need to keep them immobilized in plaster for at least six weeks before they can heal.'

'Is my mother OK?' I ask him.

'She will live,' he says and begins examining a chart attached to the side of the bed.

'How long have I been in hospital?'

'Two days.'

'How much do I need to pay you?'

'Nothing,' he smiles. 'This is a charitable hospital where everything is free, including the MRI scan, the X-rays and the medicines.'

'Thank you,' I say. 'Can I go now?'

I walk back from the Dayawati Hospital to the temple, ignoring the doctor's warnings and the searing pain in my head. My room looks like it has been visited by a hurricane. Even the wooden desk is in pieces. I take the two first-class train tickets from the pocket of my Benetton jacket and proceed to the railway booking office to cancel them. I am not going to Mumbai any longer. Like Delhi, it too is a show-off city, flaunting its Mercedes and mansions. And it belongs only to the rich. There is no place for the poor in our metropolises. Doesn't matter how honestly you earn a living; you can still get accused of thieving and thrown into a cell simply because you are poor and powerless. As long as I had the briefcase full of money I had power. I knew I could take care of Ritu, fulfil my dreams. With the briefcase gone, so have my grand dreams.

Life suddenly seems brittle and pointless. Surprisingly, I don't feel much anger towards my tormentors, the people who took away the briefcase. It wasn't mine to start with. My rage is directed instead at Vicky Rai. The man who dared to hurt Ritu. The man who took my father's life. Love can make you blind, but despair can make you reckless. I decide to buy a gun.

The biggest criminal gang in our area is the one run by Birju Pehelwan. I know several gang members who swagger through the Sanjay Gandhi slum, flaunting their revolvers like fashion accessories. It is Pappu, a recent entrant to the gang, who directs me to Girdhari, an illicit arms-dealer in Mangolpuri.

The arms-dealer does not display his wares in an air-conditioned showroom. I have to go to a smelly alley and climb three flights of stairs to a dim and dingy cubicle, where he sits in front of a massive steel safe. 'I need a cheap gun,' I tell him. He nods and takes out a *desi katta*, a locally made improvised pistol with just one round. 'This costs only eleven hundred rupees,' he grins.

'I want something better,' I tell him.

'How much have you got?' he asks and I produce the 4,200 rupees returned to me by the railway clerk.

He opens the safe and takes out something wrapped in a white cloth. He carefully opens the cloth to reveal a black gun inside. 'This is also a *katta*, but a very good one. Looks just like a Chinese Black Star pistol, but costs only four thousand. Try it.' He hands me the gun, butt first.

I hold the gun in my hand, feel its weight, its raised edges, its long, smooth barrel. It gives me goose bumps. I am fascinated by its promise of violent, instant death. 'I'll take it,' I say.

'Unfortunately I have run out of bullets,' the dealer says regretfully. 'At the moment I have only five cartridges for this gun. Can you come again tomorrow?'

'No, I am happy with five bullets. Actually, I'll need just one.'

10

Operation Checkmate

'Hello?'

'Hello.'

'Is this the residence of the Home Secretary?'

'Yes.'

'Is he there? Home Minister Jagannath Rai will speak to him.'

'One second, Sir. I will pass the line to Home Secretary Sahib.'

(*Music*.)

'Hello. Baglay speaking.'

'One second, Sir. Minister Sahib will come on the line.'

Beep. Beep. Beep.

'Hello. Gopal?'

'Good afternoon, Sir. I am sorry, Sir, I couldn't call you in the morning. My fax wasn't working. But now I have the data. Since yesterday we have had seven cases of murder. Two dacoities have been reported from Hardoi and Moradabad. There have been four rape cases in Azamgarh, Bahra—'

'I am not interested in your daily crime report, Gopal. I am calling you about something much more important. Tell me, have you heard of an American film called *Donchi*?'

'*Donchi?*'

'Maybe *Vinchi . . .Vinchiko*?'

'Do you mean *The Da Vinci Code*, Sir?'

'Yes, yes. That is the film. Have you seen it?'

'Yes, Sir. It's rather good.'

'I want you to immediately ban this film in Uttar Pradesh.'

'Ban it? But, Sir, this film is quite old. It has already completed its run.'

'Doesn't matter. Just ban it. I am told that it has offended the Christian community in the State. It makes all kinds of wild allegations, like Jesus was having an affair with some prostitute. How can we allow such films to be screened?'

'Don't you think you should see the film, Sir, before we ban it?'

'Since when has it become necessary to watch a film before banning it? Don't we ban books all the time without reading them?'

'But Sir, there are other issues, such as freedom of speech. Article 19 of the Constitution—'

'The Constitution be damned, Gopal. Hardly anybody reads in this State. Who has time to read the Constitution? Have *you* read the full Constitution?'

'Er . . . No, Sir. May I ask, Sir, who mentioned this film to you?'

'It was Father Sebastian. He is a good man. I like Christians. They are such nice, docile people. Always dressed immaculately and they speak such wonderful English. He told me that if I ban the film our party will get some Christian votes in the local elections. That can do us no harm. But I don't want to lose other votes into the bargain. So tell me, if we ban this film will the Hindus in the State be unhappy?'

'I don't think so, Sir.'

'Will the Muslims be unhappy?'

'Unlikely, Sir.'

'Will the Sikhs be unhappy?'

'No, Sir.'

'Then there is no problem at all. Just ban the wretched film. It is my order.'

'As you say, Sir. I will have the gazette notification issued today.'

'And Gopal?'

'Yes, Sir.'

'I believe you have still not carried out my instructions regarding that Superintendent of Police Navneet Brar. As long as I am the Home Minister he is not to be given any medals or awards.'

'Sir, I wanted to discuss this with you. Navneet Brar is a very meritorious officer. He has single-handedly liquidated two major Naxalite outfits operating on the India–Nepal border. If we remove his name from the State Republic Day Gallantry Award winners, it might demoralize the police force and—'

'Gopal . . . Gopal . . . Who is the Minister, you or me?'

'You, of course, Sir.'

'And who gives the orders, you or me?'

'You, Sir.'

'Then carry out my order this very minute. Otherwise from tomorrow you will not be Home Secretary but Secretary of the Child Welfare Council. Understood?'

'Yes, Sir.'

*

'Good morning, Bhaiyyaji, this is Alok Agarwal speaking.'

'Good morning. It is my great fortune that a big industrialist like you deigns to remember me once every three to four months.'

'Please don't embarrass me, Sir. I always try to keep in touch with you, but what can I do? Work is such that I have to visit my international associates quite frequently. I got back from Japan just last night.'

'*Arrey*, you businessmen are always jet-setting around

the globe. Japan today, America tomorrow. And people like me, we just sit and rot here in this State.'

'Don't say that, Bhaiyyaji. You are doing so much for the welfare of the people of Uttar Pradesh. I have been following your campaign for the local elections. You seem to be drawing huge crowds everywhere.'

'I am glad you recognize this. The newspapers are always criticizing me. I have now stopped reading them.'

'You cannot say the same about our TV channel Mashaal. I have personally given instructions that it must cover all your rallies.'

'Yes, yes. Mashaal has been doing a terrific job. True to its name, it is a torch. The torch of truth. And you have got a perfect reporter. What's her name, Seema?'

'Seema Bisht? Yes. Seema is quite good. She narrowly missed the Reporter of the Year award.'

'I am sure she deserved it more than anyone else. She is really very pretty. And so fair. Why don't you ask her to interview me one of these days? Just a – what you people say in English – one-to-one.'

'Certainly, Bhaiyyaji. I will ask Seema to make an appointment with your office.'

'That will be nice. But don't involve my office. Tell her to call me directly on my mobile. Now what can I do for you?'

'Well, Bhaiyyaji, you know we have put in a bid for the second power plant near Dadri.'

'Yes. You mentioned it to me last time we spoke. But you know that you are competing with Tatas and Ambanis. And Singhania of the JP Group is there too.'

'I know, Bhaiyyaji, and that is why I need you. You promised me the first power plant in Rewa. I thought we had a deal, but the contract went to the JP Group.'

'Yes. Mohan Kumar, the former Chief Secretary, tried his best, but the Chief Minister double-crossed us at the last minute. Everyone knows he is in Singhania's pocket. Now

Mohan Kumar has retired, so we have to fight that much harder to keep your competitors out.'

'But I hear on the grapevine that Singhania is already acting as if he has got the plant. If this contract also goes to the JP Group I might pull out from Uttar Pradesh completely. '

'*Arrey*, do you think this State is the Chief Minister's fiefdom? He cannot award contracts only to his people. We all have to have an equal share in the spoils. Don't worry, this contract will definitely go to you, on the same terms as we had finalized for the first plant. Agreed?'

'Agreed, Bhaiyyaji. So can I go ahead and tell my international partners to start preparing for the shipment of the machinery?'

'Yes, yes. No problem. Just don't forget about Seema, OK?'

'Not at all, Bhaiyyaji. She will meet you. This week – I will see to it.'

'OK.'

*

'Hello. This is Rukhsana Afsar. Can I speak to the Home Minister?'

'Jagannathji is not at home. He is out addressing an election meeting in Gopiganj. Today is the last day of campaigning for the local elections.'

'Who are you?'

'I am his Private Secretary.'

'Jagannathji is not answering his mobile either. What is wrong? He has not taken my call once in the last two weeks.'

'Madam, don't you know that Bhaiyyaji changes girlfriends faster than you change your hairstyle? (*Laughs*.) You should have got the hint by now . . . Hello? . . . Hello?' (*Disconnect*.)

*

'Dad?'

'Yes, Vicky? You sound worried.'

'I received a letter in the post today. It is from the Maoist Revolutionary Centre, a Naxalite outfit, threatening to kill me if I proceed with the Special Economic Zone project in Jharkhand.'

(*Laughs*.) 'And you have started shitting in your pants? *Arrey*, never forget that you are the son of Jagannath Rai, the most feared name in all of Uttar Pradesh.'

'But my project is in Jharkhand. What if the bloody Naxalites really do something to me?'

'Don't worry. I will get a police battalion posted to your house.'

'Your police force is absolutely third rate, Dad. I am going to write to the Delhi Police Commissioner, requesting commando protection.'

'You are needlessly over-reacting. The Naxalites have not killed a single industrialist so far.'

'I don't want to be the first, Dad. Bye.'

(*Disconnect*.)

*

'Jagannath, have you seen the results of the local elections?'

'Yes, Chief Minister Sahib. They are not as good as we thought they would be.'

'Good? They are a disaster. Our party has lost seventy-one seats. How did this happen? You said everything was going fine.'

'I will do a full investigation. My hunch is that the opposition bribed the election officials. A lot of independents also muddied the waters.'

'Well, my information is that the Muslims deserted us. They cost us at least fifty seats.'

'But why would the Muslims do such a thing? We have done so much for them.'

'Because of the communal riots you instigated in Kanpur. You said it would help us get the Hindu votes. Well, we did not get even one extra Hindu vote and the Muslims deserted us completely.'

'Don't worry, Chief Minister Sahib. I have worked out a new strategy which will help us at the next elections.'

'And what is that?'

'I am going to woo the Christians. I have already taken some steps to ensure that even if we don't get the Muslim vote, we will compensate by getting the Christian vote.'

'Has your brain gone to chew grass, Jagannath? *Arrey*, Muslims are 18 per cent of the population. Christians are less than one per cent.'

'But you should see quality, not quantity. I feel happy from inside whenever I meet Christian people. They are so charming.'

'You do what you want. Just don't interfere in party matters. It was the High Command's biggest mistake to put you in charge of local elections.'

'Don't blame me. If voters didn't vote then it is partly because of you. You are the Chief Minister, after all. Moreover, you never gave me a free hand. If your sidekicks were not countermanding half my decisions, I would have worked wonders.'

'No point talking to you, Jagannath.'

(*Disconnect.*)

*

'Hello. This is Seema Bisht from Mashaal channel. Can I speak to Jagannathji?'

'Let me check.'

Beep. Beep. Beep.

'Hello, Seema. Didn't Alok give you my mobile number?'

'He did, but I thought I shouldn't call you on your mobile before I'd even met you face-to-face.'

'Then let's meet face-to-face.'

'Yes, we will. I also wanted your reaction to the death of MLA Lakhan Thakur.'

'What? Lakhan Thakur is dead?'

'Yes. It is breaking news on our channel. He was shot

dead half an hour ago as he was leaving his house.'

'This is most shocking! Have any arrests been made?'

'No, but the Director General of Police B.P. Maurya has made a statement that the timber mafia appears to be behind the murder. So can we meet?'

'Yes, absolutely. I have a very nice guesthouse in Gomti Nagar. Can you come there tonight, let's say at about ten?'

'Won't that be rather late?'

'It will be a dinner meeting. We have much to talk about.'

'OK, I'll see you there.'

'See you. '

*

Beep. Beep. Beep.

'Bhaiyyaji, Prem Kalra wants to speak to you.

'Who?'

'Prem Kalra. The editor of the *Daily News*.'

'Oh, that swine? OK, put him on.'

Beep. Beep. Beep.

'Hello, Prem. You have remembered me after a long time.'

'I will not take much of your time, Home Minister Sahib. I just wanted to get your comment on the death of Rukhsana Afsar.'

'Yes, it is very sad. She was a loyal party worker.'

'Why do you think she committed suicide?'

'How would I know? You should ask the police.'

'Do you know that she has left behind a suicide note?'

(*Pause*.)

'What does the note say?'

'It says, "Darling Jagannath" and then it has a couplet from Ghalib. A rather good one:

'Hum ne maanaa ke tagaaful na karoge lekin
Khaak ho jaayenge ham tumko khabar hone tak.

I do agree that you won't delay,
But I will die by the time you arrive.'

'A very fine couplet indeed. But what has that got to do with me?'

'It is said that you were having an affair with her and then dumped her.'

'Lies. All lies. I hardly knew her.'

'She has been seen in your company on many occasions.'

'I am a public person. And you know in public life one meets many people, including women. Doesn't mean that I have affairs with all of them. I am a happily married man.'

'There is also a tape.'

(*Longer pause.*)

'What kind of tape?'

'An audio tape.'

'And what is there on this tape?'

'Plenty. It has you talking to her, quoting some rather nice Ghalib couplets. I especially like the part where you tell her your opinion of the Chief Minister.'

'How did you get this tape?'

'It was mailed to me by Rukhsana just before her death. She must have taped you when you were in her bedroom.'

'Do the police know about this tape?'

'No. It is in my custody. Do you want me to play a few snippets?'

(*Pause.*)

'Well, Home Minister Sahib?'

'What do you want, Prem?'

'The truth.'

(*Laughs.*) 'That is the first causality of journalism. Every man has his price. Name yours.'

(*Pause.*)

'Twenty lakhs in cash and one year of government advertisements for my paper. No bargaining.'

'I can do the first, not the second. You need to talk to the Information Minister for the advertisements.'

'Then it will cost you thirty lakhs.'

'Twenty-five.'

'We have a deal.'

*

'Mukhtar?'

'Yes, Boss?'

'An arms consignment has to be picked up from Nepal.'

'Might be tricky, Boss. The border is very heavily policed these days. We don't want the consignment to be intercepted, do we?'

'No problem. Use one of my official cars. The one with the blue beacon. Bring the consignment over the border and take it straight to our godown.'

'That will be perfect, Boss. No one will dare intercept the Home Minister's car.'

*

'Hello. This is Seema.'

'Hello, *jaaneman*. Where have you been? I haven't seen you for a week.'

'I was busy. Had to cover the Awadh Festival. And also the stage show, the biggest ever in Lucknow. The reigning queen of Bollywood was there.'

'*Arrey*, why do you run after these film stars? They have no respect. They are ready to dance like hired eunuchs at a wedding for money.'

'But still half of Lucknow was there to see the performance. I think Shabnam really stole the show.'

'Who is this Shabnam?'

'Shabnam Saxena. She is the hottest actress in India at present.'

'I don't know these new heroines at all. The last film I saw was *Mother India*. What acting Nargis did!'

'You don't know the names of the heroines, but your son is now a big producer.'

'Yes, Vicky fancies that line. I keep miles away from it. And for me, you are better than any film star.'

'Now don't butter me up. Tell me, have you done my work?'

'What work?'

'The liquor contract for my uncle in Phaphamau?'

'Yes, yes, consider it done. But you know it has cost me a packet.'

'How?'

'The liquor tender for Phaphamau is traditionally taken by my man Shakeel. I had to tell him not to bid this time to accommodate your uncle. I will now have to compensate him in other ways.'

'And I will compensate you in bed.'

'Yes, you'd better.'

(*Laughter.*)

*

'Can I speak to Home Minister Jagannath Rai?'

'Speaking. Who is this?'

'This is Superintendent of Police Navneet Brar, Sir. I am calling from Bahraich.'

'Oh, Navneet. How are you? I hope this stint in Bahraich has drilled some sense into your head. So are you calling to apologize for your past mistake?'

'No, Sir. I am calling to inform you that I have just seized your official vehicle. It was returning from Nepal when it was stopped at a checkpoint in my area and discovered to contain a cache of AK-47 rifles. Your driver somehow managed to escape, but I have confiscated the entire consignment and I am in the process of having an arrest warrant issued against you for aiding and abetting a criminal activity.'

'What? You are daring to arrest the Home Minister?'

'I will be arresting a known criminal who has blatantly misused his official position.'

'Navneet, do you know the consequences of tangling with someone like me? Do not be under the illusion that just because you wear a uniform, you are protected. I can have you squished like a fly within minutes.'

'What will you do? Tell that spineless Director General

of Police Maurya to transfer me again? Well, that won't work this time because I have spoken directly to the Chief Minister and he has personally given me authorization to proceed against you. Fortunately, there are still a few principled politicians in our State.'

'Then you do what you want to do. And I will do what I have to do.'

(*Disconnect.*)

*

'Dad?'

'Yes, Vicky?'

'There is just one week left until 15 February. D-Day.'

'Why are you getting so worked up? I got the verdict fixed back in November.'

'I heard that some additional demands have been made.'

'That is part of the game. A lion has to feed the vultures.'

'So I can sleep easy?'

'You can. I wish I could say the same for me.'

'Why? What's been bugging you?'

'A crazy police officer has spoiled my sleep. He had the temerity to issue an arrest warrant against me. It took me two days to convince the Chief Minister that having the Home Minister of the State arrested would not be good for the party's image.'

'You need to do something about this Chief Minister, Dad.'

'I will. But first I have to do something about that police officer. I have put Mukhtar on the job.'

*

'Jagannath?'

'Yes, Chief Minister Sahib.'

'The death of Navneet Brar in the landmine blast has come as a great shock to me.'

'To me as well, Chief Minister Sahib. He was one of our most capable police officers. All his life Brar bravely fought the terrorists, but they ambushed him in the end.'

'Tell me, Jagannath, did you have anything to do with his death?'

'What are you saying? Everyone knows he was killed by the Naxalites operating on the India–Nepal border.'

'But you had a run-in with Brar recently. He impounded your car and was planning to have you arrested.'

'I never took it personally, Chief Minister Sahib. Don't forget, it was I who got Brar posted to Bahraich in the first place. And it wasn't really my car. The arms-smugglers were using fake number plates and an unauthorized beacon. Brar simply did his duty in intercepting the car. That is why I think it would be a very good gesture if we were to give him some posthumous honours.'

'What did you have in mind?'

'Recommendation for the President's Police Medal for Gallantry. An ex-gratia payment of twenty lakhs to the family and a Class One job for his widow.'

'I agree. By the way, are you going to Delhi tomorrow to be present at the verdict in your son's case?'

'No, I will be attending Brar's funeral in Lucknow. That is the least I can do as Home Minister.'

'I must say, that's very decent of you, Jagannath. Best of luck.'

'Thank you, Chief Minister Sahib.'

*

'Dad?'

'Yes, Vicky?'

'Just wanted to say thank you. The acquittal has lifted a massive weight off my mind. There was a time when I actually feared I might be going to jail.'

'Don't thank me, thank Guruji. All this is the result of his blessings. Ever since he asked me to wear blue sapphire, one miracle after another has happened. All my rivals have bitten the dust. He has recently returned from his world tour. I am going to thank him personally.'

'And I am going to party! The acquittal has to be

celebrated. It will be the biggest bash of my life. I have consulted an astrologer and he says the most auspicious date will be 23 March. I will do it at Number Six. You have to come, promise?'

'It is not a good idea, Vicky. There is still too much heat on the case. Let the public outcry die down, then we will see.'

'I am not worried. The judge has given me a clean chit and no amount of chest-beating is going to change that. So put the day in your diary: 23 March. And I promise you, Dad, no one will get shot at this party. (*Laughs.*) OK, I gotta run now. Bye.'

'Bye.'

*

'I am calling from the Chief Minister's office. Chief Minister Sahib needs to speak to the Home Minister.'

'So is your boss also calling to congratulate Bhaiyyaji? He is three days late.'

'How would I know? Just put him on.'

'Why are you always in such a sour mood? I am putting you through to Bhaiyyaji.'

Beep. Beep. Beep.

'*Namaskar*, Chief Minister Sahib.'

'Have you seen the reaction to Vicky's acquittal, Jagannath?'

'Yes. But you know these media people, they are never happy. They only want to present the negative picture. Anyway, they may write whatever they want, it is not going to reverse the verdict. Vicky has been acquitted of the murder charge and that is what counts.'

'But what about public opinion, Jagannath?'

'I don't care about public opinion. I never have.'

'But I do. The party does. The whole country is in uproar, Jagannath. Candlelight vigils are being held from Amritsar to Alleppey in protest at Vicky's acquittal. Protest marches are being organized in eighteen States by NGOs.

Lucknow University students are threatening to immolate themselves. Trade unions have called for an indefinite strike. The TV channels have only one story. Magazines are organizing text-messaging campaigns. Even the *Daily News* has established a Ruby Gill Fund to raise money for the victim's family. No case in India's history has attracted the kind of attention this one has. The judgment has been condemned by one and all. There is even talk of a re-trial. All this has placed us in an untenable position.'

'So what can I do? Should a father disown his own son?'

'Well, when the son is a black sheep, the father has to make some hard choices.'

'I cannot believe that we are having this conversation. My son has been acquitted, not convicted.'

'Doesn't matter. He has lost the battle of public opinion. And for a politician, eventually what matters is public opinion.'

'But Chief Minister Sahib, the media is mad. You know how they trivialize things. They don't show fifty miners trapped inside a coal mine, but all channels will immediately start covering some cat trapped in a well.'

'Yes, I know. But this only goes to show the power of the media. They dictate what we watch, when we watch. They are the ones who make and break public opinion. We will not be able to withstand the public outcry on this issue. It will sweep us out of power unless we do something now.'

'So what do you want me to do?'

'The High Command has taken its decision. You have to choose between Vicky and your Home Ministership. I want your resignation on my desk by tomorrow afternoon. If you prefer, we can say that you resigned on health grounds.'

'Your health may be bad, not mine. I am a fighter. And I will not take this lying down. Let me spell it out for you clearly: if you dismiss me, by tomorrow afternoon your coalition government will be gone.'

(*Laughs.*) 'You may be a mafia don, Jagannath, but in

politics you are a novice. Give in gracefully and you might live to fight another day. In politics, everyone makes a comeback. But if you go against the High Command's dictate, not only will it end your political career, it might force us to end your criminal career as well.'

'Use these threats on the eunuchs in your Cabinet, Chief Minister Sahib. There is no one man enough in the State to challenge me.'

'You are compelling me to dismiss you.'

'And you are compelling me to become a rebel.'

'Fine. Then the battle lines are drawn. Let us see who prevails.'

'Yes, let us see.'

(*Disconnect.*)

*

'Hello?'

'*Pranam*, Guruji.'

'*Jai Shambhu.*'

'When are you returning from Allahabad to Mathura?'

'As soon as the Magh Mela ends. Why?'

'Guruji, I need your blessings.'

'What for?'

'For the greatest battle of my life.'

'I thought you had already won that. Vicky has been acquitted. My coral ring proved to be very potent.'

'Despite that, the Chief Minister is intent on dismissing me. So I have decided to enter the arena. It will be a fight to the finish. Either he will remain standing or I will.'

'You have my blessings, Jagannath. I have recently seen the Chief Minister's horoscope. His stars are in decline and yours are on the way up.'

'Thank you, Guruji. With you on my side, I can take on anyone, even the Chief Minister.'

'*Jai Shambhu*, Jagannath. May victory be yours!'

'*Jai Shambhu*, Guruji.'

*

'Hello, Tripurari. Are you still in Hardoi?'

'Yes, but this is called telepathy, Bhaiyyaji. I was just about to call you to congratulate you on your performance in the Assembly today. The attack on the Chief Minister was marvellous. So subtle. This is called killing with kindness.'

'Now the gloves are off, Tripurari. He wants to dismiss me as Home Minister. Says the High Command is worried about the negative publicity regarding Vicky's acquittal.'

'How dare he? We will dismantle his government brick by brick if he so much as thinks about dismissing you.'

'That is what I need your help for. If by tomorrow I am no longer Home Minister, then by the end of the week the Chief Minister should also lose his chair. We need to plot his downfall. How many MLAs do you think will be willing to come with me?'

'Let's do the arithmetic, Bhaiyyaji. To bring down the government, we need to engineer the defection of only fifteen legislators. We already have a solid bloc of twenty MLAs, all of whom are your followers. We can cut off the Chief Minister's power faster than the State Electricity Corporation's next blackout.'

'It is not that simple, Tripurari. I am playing for very high stakes. It is no longer a question of simply bringing down the Chief Minister. I want to really rub his nose in the dust now. So I have decided to stake my own claim for the post.'

'You mean Chief Minister?'

'Why do you think I have spent fifty-five years of my life in this hell hole? With the money I have I could have gone to Delhi or Mumbai or even America. I stayed behind because I have always wanted the ultimate prize – the Chief Ministership.'

(*Pause.*)

'Then you are playing for very high stakes indeed, Bhaiyyaji.'

'Yes. I have been thinking, who remembers the bloody Home Minister of a State? Ten years from now people will not even know that I was once part of this government. But even in twenty years people will remember who the Chief Minister was. It is like becoming a part of history. And history is never forgotten. Look at Jagdambika Pal. In 1998, he became Chief Minister only for a day, but his name has been entered in the history books for all time to come. I too want that glory. Imagine, a hundred years from now, the history books of the State will still record my name as Chief Minister. Isn't that something worth fighting for?'

'Of course, Bhaiyyaji. But how will we do it?'

'We need to split the party. We already have twenty. We need just five more to make one-third. Then the split becomes legal. Doesn't attract the provisions of the Anti-Defection Act.'

'But how will we form the government?'

'I have already spoken to the leaders of all the opposition parties, especially Tiwariji, who commands the support of at least fifty legislators. They are willing to lend me support from outside. And the Independents are solidly behind me. After all, I helped half of them to win. So what do you think? Can we do it?'

'It is brilliant, Bhaiyyaji. What a strategy!'

'I am going to call it Operation Checkmate. Now you need to execute it.'

'Let's get down to brass tacks. First, we have to isolate our bloc of twenty. Then we have to identify the five that we need to break the party. And lastly we need to get letters of support from all the opposition parties, accepting you as Chief Minister. I will begin work straight away.'

'Good. Do whatever is necessary to achieve success.'

'We will need money as well. Operation Checkmate will cost us plenty. Do you have that much cash handy, Bhaiyyaji?'

'Don't worry about cash.'

'So should I start buying suitcases? At least twenty will be required.'

'Yes, do that. And when I become Chief Minister, I will make you Chairman of the State luggage factory!'

(*Laughter.*)

*

'Hello, can I speak to Alok Agarwal?'

'Who is this?'

'This is Jagannath Rai.'

'*Arrey*, Bhaiyyaji? Sorry, I didn't recognize your voice.'

'What Alok, the moment I cease to be Home Minister, you forget my voice? Is this how a big industrialist like you conducts business?'

'No, it is not that . . . Anyway, tell me, how did you happen to remember me?'

'You know, Alok, I have always considered you my younger brother. Now I am in difficulty and I need your help.'

'What can I do for you?'

'I have decided to stake my claim for Chief Ministership of Uttar Pradesh.'

'That is a big step, Bhaiyyaji.'

'Yes, I know. I have taken this step after considering all options. I am confident that I have the numbers. But to firm up the support of some legislators I need to offer them some inducements. That is where you come in. You know very well how these things are done.'

'I understand. How much are we talking here?'

'At least twelve to thirteen crores.'

(*Pause.*)

'That is a very large amount, Bhaiyyaji.'

'It can't be for a well-established businessman like you. Anyway, consider it just a loan. You will get more than double the money back as soon as I become Chief Minister.'

'I am not worried about that, Bhaiyyaji. It's just that I

don't have that kind of cash lying around. If I had got the Dadri project, things might have been different, but—'

'I know you were disappointed by the outcome in Dadri, but what could I do? Singhania's bid was double yours, so he got it. How much can you spare straight away?'

'Around a couple of crores, at best three.'

'*Bas?* Now don't behave like a stingy money-lender.'

'I am telling you the honest-to-God truth. Business has been poor lately.'

'Is that your final offer?'

'Believe me, Bhaiyyaji. I cannot spare—'

'No need to say any more. It was my mistake that I befriended a third-rater like you. I should have cultivated someone of Singhania's calibre. Now listen to me, motherfucker. Uttar Pradesh is out of bounds for you from today. You can forget about doing any business here. If you so much as step inside my State I will carve you up like a chicken. Understood?'

'Bhaiyyaji. Try and un—'

(*Disconnect.*)

*

'Vicky?'

'Dad, can I call you back? I am in the middle of a very important meeting.'

'Forget your meeting. I need to talk to you right now.'

'Will you guys please excuse me? I'll just step out for a moment . . .Yes, Dad, what is it?'

'Why are you getting irritated?'

'I am not getting irritated. Tell me, I don't have much time.'

'I need ten crores.'

'Oooh! Dad, since when did you start needing money from me?'

'Look, Vicky, I don't have much time either. Can you send me ten by the end of this week?'

'No way, Dad. I am having a big cash-flow problem. We

have ploughed everything into the Special Economic Zone project in Jharkhand. But what do you need all this money for?'

'I'll tell you later.'

'Anyway, I can't help you out, Dad. And please don't call me for the next two hours.'

'Is this the way a son behaves with his father?'

'Look, Dad, I don't—'

'No. You listen to me, Vicky. Just as there are some sons who spend their entire life trying to live up to their father's expectations, there are some fathers who spend their entire lives making up for their sons' mistakes. After this, forget that you have a father who will get you out of trouble.'

'You don't need to get emotional, Dad. Believe me, I would have helped you out if I could. And as for bailing me out of trouble, you needn't bother. I am not killing any more bartenders (*Laughs.*) I'm switching off my mobile now, Dad.'

(*Disconnect.*)

*

'Hello, Seema.'

'Hello.'

'You sound very cold. Have you also forsaken me now that I am no longer Home Minister?'

'No, it is nothing like that.'

'So, *jaaneman*, when do I see you next?'

'I am going to Delhi for a few days. I need to sort a few things out.'

'Such as? Tell me, I will sort them out for you. Are there any other uncles who need liquor contracts?' (*Laughs.*)

'Don't laugh. I need something for myself for a change.'

'What? Name it and it shall be yours.'

'I don't know. It's just that I feel so suffocated at times. Like I've got into a rut. And life is just passing me by.'

'Everyone feels like that from time to time. As Guruji says, the important thing is not to lose your focus.'

'I've always had the feeling that I was meant for higher things. This twopenny TV reporter's job is not what I am meant for. I am good looking, I am young, I won the award for best actress in the University drama competition. Don't you think I can make it in films?'

'*Arrey*, this film line is the worst line possible. Don't touch it with a barge pole.'

'If only you were to speak to Vicky about me. He wouldn't refuse you.'

'No, I can't do that, and Vicky won't listen to me. Don't be difficult now.'

'You are the one being difficult.'

'Look, Seem—'

(*Disconnect.*)

*

'What news, Tripurari?'

'Bhaiyyaji, it was an uphill task. We worked the phones and held meetings all day and learnt a lot about friends and enemies. Nothing like adversity to see the true face of men. Even the twenty that we were banking upon proved tricky. Only eight were willing to side with us. I had to use every trick in the book to persuade them. Finally we managed to get fourteen, leaving a shortfall of six. Add to that the five we needed anyway to break the party, making a total of eleven. Then we did a very careful analysis of the MLAs who could be lured. By working on known weaknesses, we were able to do a good job. The first chap we got was Ramakant Sharma, from Chillupur. He was under High Command's suspicion ever since his wife joined the Opposition, so it was easy to wean him away. Ashok Jaiswal, Prabha Devi, Champaklal Gupta, Madan Vaishya and Ras Bihari were purchased with promises of ministerships in your Cabinet. Ras Bihari has specifically asked for animal-husbandry department. Then we targeted Suresh Singh Baghel. He has not been on speaking terms with the Chief Minister ever since he was divested of the post of Sugarcane

Cooperative Chairperson, and was more than willing to come over. It was he who gave us Rakesh Yadav and Pappu Singh as well. Finally, Iqbal Mian managed to persuade Saleem Mohammad to switch sides. That gives us ten.'

'Good work, Tripurari. But we are still one short.'

'I know, Bhaiyyaji. I have tried everything and I am convinced that there isn't a single MLA left in the party now who can be broken. We are still racking our brains, but that one MLA is proving as elusive as Osama Bin Laden. What should we do now, Bhaiyyaji?'

(*Pause.*)

'Do you know, Tripurari, the difference between a leader and a follower?'

'What is it, Bhaiyyaji?'

'A follower just sticks to the path created by the leader. But a leader creates a new path. The problem with you is that you only see straight. You cannot see round a bend. I see round the next three bends. Tell me, who was the MLA who invited us to Clarks Awadh Hotel last year for his son's birthday party – who was turning three, if I remember correctly.'

'It was a long time ago, Bhaiyyaji. Let me see. It was January last year . . . Yes, I remember now, it was Gopal Mani Tripathi, wasn't it?'

'Yes. That's right. Gopal Mani is the legislator from Bareilly, I think. Did you speak to him?'

'What are you saying, Bhaiyyaji? That fellow is solidly behind the Chief Minister. There are rumours that he might become Forest Minister. How can we even think that he will agree to defect?'

'The love for a son can often be a great motivating factor. (*Pause.*) Anything entering your obtuse brain, Tripurari, or do I have to spell it out?'

(*Pause.*)

'Say no more, Bhaiyyaji. I indeed have a lot to learn from you. Should I ask Mukhtar?'

'Yes, tell him to get cracking. Then you will have your eleven.'

*

'I am calling from Allahabad. Guruji wants to speak to Home Minister Jagannath Rai.'

'Oh, Guruji himself? I will put him through immediately to Bhaiyyaji.'

Beep. Beep. Beep.

'Is that really you, Guruji?'

'Jagannath, I am in a great deal of trouble. I need your help.'

'What happened, Guruji? I was really worried for your safety when I heard about that bomb blast. These terrorists have not even spared the Magh Mela! But Tripurari confirmed to me that you were unhurt.'

'Yes, Jagannath, by the grace of God, the bomb blast did not cause me any harm. But today there has been a raid at my *ashram* in Mathura. The Health Department is claiming that the herbal remedies I have been giving my devotees contain human and animal bones.'

'How is that possible, Guruji? This must be a ploy by the multinational drug companies to malign you.'

'That is exactly what I think, Jagannath. But my troubles don't end there. Three women who claim to be my devotees, whom I have never met in my life, have filed complaints that I have sexually molested them. You know that I am an ascetic and have taken the vow of *brahmacharya*. I cannot even think of doing such an immoral act. Yet your police have issued a warrant and are going to arrest me. I am still in Allahabad and in hiding at a disciple's house. What should I do?'

'It looks to me as if there is a very big conspiracy at work against you, Guruji.'

'I think a rival *akhara* is behind this and my suspicion lies with that swine Swami Brahmdeo, who, you know, is close to the Chief Minister. It must be his doing. Now only you can get me out of this jam.'

'Unfortunately, Guruji, even I no longer have the power to prevent your arrest, as I am no longer the Home Minister. But I can facilitate your escape.'

'Escape?'

'Yes. You must run away to America or Europe immediately, otherwise they will put you in prison for ten to fifteen months. Sexual-molestation charges are taken very seriously because of all the NGOs which have sprouted up in the State.'

'Is that so? Then I must move immediately.'

'I will ask one of my men to contact you within the hour with a getaway vehicle. It will take you to the Nepal border. From there you can go to Kathmandu and catch a flight to wherever you have a visa for.'

'Thank you, Jagannath. I shall remember this favour. Can I ask for one more?'

'Of course, Guruji.'

'My most sacred possession was an ancient *shivling* gifted to me by a devotee from Tamil Nadu. Two days ago, taking advantage of the pandemonium which ensued after the terrorist attack, a thief stole it from my *akhara*, where it was on display. That is why all these troubles have descended upon me. It is imperative that I recover the *shivling*. You told me that the Director General of Police is your trusted man. Will you please ask him to do a proper investigation and try and recover it from the culprit? It might still be in Allahabad. Once it is recovered, he can leave it with you for safe-keeping till I return. Will you do this for me?'

'I would do it gladly, Guruji, but perhaps you don't know that the day I was removed as Home Minister, the Chief Minister also suspended Maurya. I have no influence over the police any longer.'

'*Arrey*, this is very bad. But don't you worry, Lord Shiva will set everything right. Mark my word, this Chief Minister's days are numbered.'

'I hope your prophecy comes true.'

'OK, Jagannath, I shall wait for your man to contact me. *Jai Shambhu*.'

'*Jai Shambhu*, Guruji.'

*

'Bhaiyyaji, I have good news and bad news.'

'Give me the good news first, Tripurari.'

'The good news is that we have all the MLAs we need to break the party and form our own party.'

'Excellent. Shift them immediately to our guesthouse in Badaun and put them under house arrest. Take away their mobile phones. No one must be allowed to contact them. We will trot them out only when the Governor invites me to parade the MLAs in his residence.'

'I have already done that, Bhaiyyaji. A bus has taken them to Badaun. I have also put a minder with them.'

'Then what is the bad news?'

'Tiwariji has conveyed that the Opposition parties have decided not to support your bid for Chief Ministership.'

'What? I spoke to all of them. They did not express any reservations to me. Tiwari himself praised my decision.'

'It has nothing to do with you, Bhaiyyaji. It has to do with Vicky.'

'What do you mean?'

'All this publicity on TV and the daily reports in the media about Vicky's acquittal . . . the public is getting agitated. As a result, the legislators are getting cold feet. They think that if they support your bid to become Chief Minister they might get tainted too.'

'*Arrey*, each of these bastards is already fully painted with corruption. How much more tainted can they get?'

'I know, Bhaiyyaji, but this is not just an excuse. They really think you should cool it for a while, disappear from the public view, let this whole case die down. Tiwari says he will support your reinstatement as Home Minister, but not your becoming Chief Minister at this juncture. Some of the

Independents I spoke to also share this view. Vicky has become your biggest liability.'

'So what do we do now?'

'Tiwari says he will go as your emissary to the Chief Minister. He will help hammer out a compromise. In return he has asked for one crore.'

'This is ridiculous. Why should I pay him to get back a position which is rightfully mine? After all, I have not been convicted.'

'Bhaiyyaji, sometimes the sins of the son are visited on the father. Without the Home Ministership we will become vulnerable. And the Chief Minister can always tell the police to start needling us. Now we don't even have the protection of the Director General of Police. I say we should accept Tiwari's offer.'

'OK, but tell him the pay-off will take some time.'

'That is fine, Bhaiyyaji. Your word is good enough.'

*

'*Jaaneman*, are you still in Delhi?'

'Yes. It is such a refreshing change from Lucknow. Compared to the vibrant life in this city, Lucknow is like a cemetery.'

'Don't say that, Seema. After all, I am here. I am missing you terribly. Even Guruji has gone away to some place called Featherland.'

'Netherlands, *mantriji*, Netherlands.'

'Whether it is feather or nether, what is it to me? I care only for you. When are you coming back?'

'Not in a hurry.'

'Then should I come to Delhi too? We could meet in some nice hotel.'

'No, no. I will contact you as soon as my work is over.'

'OK, *jaaneman*. Now give me a kiss.'

(*Kissing sound.*)

*

'Tripurari here, Bhaiyyaji. Tiwari has delivered. A compromise has been worked out. The High Command will reinstate you as Home Minister, provided you do not stake a claim to the Chief Ministership and issue a public statement of support for the Chief Minister.'

'I'll be damned if I agree to do that.'

'But what options do we have, Bhaiyyaji? We have already seen that while you have the power to bring down the Chief Minister, you don't have enough steam to become CM yourself. Please agree to this minor condition. I will draft something which doesn't compromise your dignity.'

'I wish I hadn't lived to see this day. '

'If only you didn't have a son like Vicky, Bhaiyyaji. Today you would have been sitting in the CM's chair. Who knows, you might even have become PM one day. But for now, we will have to curb our ambition.'

'So the Chief Minister has won round one.'

'Not really. I would say it is one-all. Operation Checkmate has resulted in stalemate.'

'I never accept defeat, Tripurari. Eventually this will end in a checkmate, you'll see.'

*

'Congrats, Dad, on getting back your Home Ministership. With you out, I was seriously worried about how I was going to drive my new Lamborghini at 180 miles per hour in Noida.' (*Laughs.*)

'Vicky, you have no idea how much harm you have caused me. But for you, I would have been – forget it. So are you still going ahead with your party on 23 March?'

'Of course, Dad. Cards are going out as we speak. But my idiot secretary has made a big blunder. She used an old mailing list and, as a result, invitations have gone to people like Mohan Kumar and Singhania. Should I call them up and disinvite them?'

'The problem with you, Vicky, is that you hire secretaries for their beauty rather than their brains. But an invitation, once given, cannot be withdrawn. It is against our culture.'

'But Mohan Kumar has gone completely mad, and Singhania is now my business rival.'

'You know the old adage – Keep your friends close and your enemies closer. Besides, Kumar may provide us good entertainment in his new role as Gandhi Baba.'

'Talking of Gandhi reminds me, Dad, do I need to worry about all this talk of a possible re-trial?'

'It will fizzle out, Vicky. Eventually, everything does, even a son's love for his father.'

'Are you still upset that I couldn't send you the money?'

'No, Vicky. I never linger over the past.'

'By the way, Dad, do you know a girl called Seema Bisht?'

'Yes. I know her very well. She is a reporter for a third-rate channel called Mashaal. How do you know her?'

'She came to my farmhouse last night, gave me your reference.'

'Yes, she told me she was going to Delhi. Did she interview you?'

'She did much more than an interview. She was angling for a role in my next film.'

'So what did you do?'

'What do you expect? (*Laughs*.) She seemed like a good lay. And was more than willing.'

(*Long pause*.)

'Dad?'

(*Disconnect*.)

*

'Hi. Seema here. I have been trying to reach you for two days. Congratulations, Mr Home Minister.'

'Don't you dare talk to me, you cheap whore!'

(*Disconnect*.)

*

'Hello? Hello?'

'Thank you for calling the Novotel Hotel. How may I help?'

'Is this 00 31 20 5411123?'

'Yes it is, Sir. How may I help?'

'Please give me room number 567.'

'One moment, Sir. Your call is going through now.'

Beep. Beep. Beep.

'Hello. Who is this?'

'Hello, can I speak to Guruji?'

'Guruji is busy right now. He does not want to be disturbed.'

'I know. Just tell him that Jagannath Rai is calling from Lucknow. It is very urgent.'

(*Whispered.*) 'Guruji, someone called Jagannath Rai is calling. Says he wants to speak to you urgently.'

'Give me the phone, and you go into the bathroom. (*Pause.*) Hello, Jagannath. So you have tracked me down even in Amsterdam? (*Laughs.*) *Jai Shambhu.*'

'*Jai Shambhu*, Guruji. Who is this woman who picked up the phone?'

'She is . . . Sister Reena. She coordinates my European operations. But tell me about yourself. How have you been?'

'I have been having very bad thoughts for the last few days.'

'There is nothing unusual in that. Those who have not grasped the fundamental truths of existence are bound to suffer from negative energy.'

'I feel I have been deluded and only you can show me the true path. Just as Arjuna came to Krishna on the battlefield of Kurukshetra to get his divine guidance, I have come to your refuge, Guruji, even though you are thousands of miles away.'

'Reasoning is destroyed when the mind is bewildered, Jagannath. The mind is bewildered by delusion. And delusion arises from anger. Are you angry about something?'

'I am angry about many things, Guruji. I know you always counsel me not to become tense, but what can I do? Politics means tension.'

'Tell me, how is your campaign for the Chief Ministership going? I read in the *Times of India* that you have got the support of a large number of MLAs. '

'That is old news, Guruji. For now I have become Home Minister once again.'

'Oh, that is excellent news. So can I return to India now? Will you be able to get the arrest warrant cancelled?'

'Not immediately, Guruji. I am still facing some difficulties. But I have a plan by which I will become Chief Minister soon.'

'Good. Then I shall return only after you have become Chief Minister. So what is your plan?'

'I don't want to go into that, Guruji. I want you to tell me something much more vital and fundamental. I want to know the real truth about existence, about life.'

(*Laughs*.) 'Don't we all want to know that?'

'Guruji, you have known me for a long time, long before I joined politics. Tell me, is killing someone the worst thing anyone can do?'

(*Laughs*.) 'Killing what? This body? But Jagannath, as I have repeatedly told you, this body, like the universe is *mithya*, just a false notion, like the horn of a rabbit, or the water in a mirage. It has only a temporary existence. It has to die, in any case.'

'But then why do we lament over the dead?'

'The wise grieve neither for the living nor for the dead. Because death is certain for the one who is born, and birth is certain for the one who dies. Therefore, only fools lament over the inevitable.'

'And even if the body dies, the soul never dies?'

'Yes. That is correct. The soul is unborn, eternal, permanent and primeval. The *atma* is not destroyed when the body is destroyed.'

'So if someone is killed, he doesn't really die. He merely acquires another body, doesn't he?'

'Exactly. A person who knows that the *atma* is

indestructible, eternal, unborn and imperishable, neither kills anyone nor causes anyone to be killed.'

'Even if the person being killed is a close relative?'

'There is no such thing as a relative. The essence of a true *yogi* is detachment. He is detached from his son, his wife, his family and his home. He is a person whose mind is unperturbed by sorrow.'

'You have cleared my doubts, Guruji. You have lightened my mind.'

'Remember what Krishna told Arjuna: "Grieve not, for I shall liberate you from all sins."'

'You have indeed liberated me, Guruji.'

'I have to go now, Jagannath, to deliver a talk. Please try and do something about that warrant. I cannot remain abroad indefinitely. Even my Schengen visa will run out in two months. I am told that bastard Brahmdeo gave an interview on the Devotion Channel in which he made all sorts of allegations against me. So my suspicion was true.'

'Don't worry, Guruji. The day I become Chief Minister, that very day Swami Brahmdeo will have an arrest warrant against his name. *Jai Shambhu*.'

'*Jai Shambhu*.'

*

'Mukhtar?'

'Yes, Boss?'

'Are you in Lucknow?'

'Yes, Boss.'

'Tell me, Mukhtar, are you a devout Muslim?'

'Not really, Boss. But I try to attend the *namaz* at least every Friday.'

'Still, you must be familiar with the concept of sacrifice. Have you heard of Abraham?'

'Every Muslim has. He was a great man who was prepared to sacrifice his son to please Allah.'

'It must have been very difficult for him. And the job I

am going to give you now is equally difficult for me.'

'*Hukum*. I am ready. Just tell me what the job is.'

'I cannot talk on phone. Can you come to the house right now?'

'I am in coming, Boss. *Khuda hafiz*.'

'*Khuda hafiz*.'

11

Mail-Order Bride

THE UNITED AIRLINES plane touched down at New Delhi Airport bang on time at three ten p.m. All the other passengers seemed to be in a mad rush to get out, as though free candies were being distributed outside. I took my time stuffing the nice airline magazine and the card about all the safety precautions into my bag, even using the toilet when the other passengers had gone.

There was a long queue at the passport counter when I arrived and the man at my desk was slower than a three-legged turtle. Every ten minutes or so he would push off to have a cup of tea or chat with his friends. I was chomping at the bit by the time my turn came.

'Good day, Sir,' he said, flipping open my passport. He looked at me and checked my photo in the passport, then looked at me again. 'Is this your passport?'

'Yeah,' I said.

'Well, you look different from your photo.'

'That's coz Mom said send in your best picture. So I sent in my best picture. And that happens to be when I was in High School.'

'Please wait here,' the officer said and went out to consult with his foreman. He came back after ten minutes. 'Sorry, we cannot allow you to enter India. We suspect you have a forged passport. You will have to be deported back to the United States.' He handed the passport back to me and pointed to a corner. 'Just sit down on that bench.'

'What?' I cried. 'No, you can't be serious. Are you pulling my leg? I got a wedding to attend here.'

He shook his head. 'There's nothing I can do.'

'Please don't say that. I've come all the way from Waco just to meet my fiancée. I am sure you can pull some strings for me,' I pleaded.

'Well . . .' He looked around to see if anyone else was listening. 'I might be able to help you, if you can help me.'

'I'll do anything you say.'

'I collect foreign-currency notes,' he whispered. 'I have all the notes from America except the hundred-dollar bill. Can you give me a hundred-dollar note? Just put it inside your passport and slide it over.'

I thanked the Lord that he didn't have a thousand-dollar bill missing from his collection, coz I hadn't seen one either, and immediately peeled off a hundred-dollar note from my wallet. I put it inside my passport and handed it to the officer, who quickly stamped the passport and returned it to me. 'Have a nice stay, Mr Page,' he smiled at me. I opened the passport. The greenback had disappeared.

It took me twenty minutes to get my Delsey from the baggage merry-go-round and another ten to convert some dollars into Indian rupees. Then, nervous as a long-tailed cat in a room full of rocking chairs, I walked out of the terminal building.

India welcomed me with a blast of warm air. It was hotter than a well-digger's ass in August. There was a whole bunch of people shouting and waving; car horns were blaring, uniformed chauffeurs were running around with placards, and brown-shirted men were asking everyone, 'Taxi? Taxi?'

I began hunting for Sapna in the crowd. Although there were plenty of girls at the airport, no one looked like her.

I waited for three hours at the kerb, but my bride-to-be didn't arrive. All the other passengers left. The airport became half-empty. I wandered out towards the taxi stand, wondering if she was waiting outside, and that's when I saw her. She stood in a red sari, her hands folded in namaste, her neck loaded with jewellery, a big smile plastered on her face. Next to her picture, the huge billboard said in big blue letters, 'WELCOME TO INDIA.'

I'm not a weepy sort of guy. The last time I really cried was way back in 1998 when Mankind (a.k.a. Mick Foley) lost to the Undertaker in the famous Hell in a Cell match on WWF. But at that moment I felt all choked up. I just wanted to rush into Mom's lap and cry my heart out. I wished the officer had sent me back on that plane. I wished I had never come to India. But when you make your bed, you got to lie in it. It was getting dark now and I needed a place to stay. Slowly, I walked towards a yellow-and-black taxi.

The taxi-driver was a turbaned fellow with a thick black moustache and beard. 'Can you take me to some cheap hotel?' I asked the gentleman.

'Of course, Sir. I am knowing just the right place for you. Which country are you coming from?'

'America,' I said.

'I like Americans.' He nodded his head. 'Half my village is living in New Jersey. First time in New Delhi?'

'Very first time in India,' I replied.

'Then get in, Sir.' He opened the rear door for me and put my suitcase and bag in the trunk.

The taxi had torn seats and a strange, greasy kind of smell. The dashboard was decorated with pictures of old people with long white beards. The driver pushed down the meter and started the car.

New Delhi seemed bigger than Waco and the traffic was quite amazing. Apart from cars, there were buses, cycles, motorcycles, scooters, and strange contraptions which the driver said were called auto-rickshaws, all moving together side by side without crashing into each other or killing the people walking on the road. Suddenly I saw a huge grey elephant lumbering towards us from the opposite direction.

'Hey, has this fellow escaped from the zoo?' I asked in astonishment.

'No, Sir,' the driver laughed. 'Here we don't need zoos. You can see all the animals you are wanting in the city itself. There,' he pointed in the distance, 'you can see some nice buffaloes and cows, too.'

We drove like crazy for almost two hours. At one point it seemed to me that we had returned to the airport. I started getting worried, but the driver laughed. 'The city is being very far from the airport, almost one hundred miles, Sir. But not to be worrying, we will get there. In India you must be learning to be patient.'

Eventually, he took me into a market lit up with yellow light bulbs and white tube lights. I saw narrow lanes teeming with people and cows. Dusty men pulled wooden carts loaded to the brim with sacks of stuff. Fat ladies rode in rickety rickshaws. Auto-rickshaws zipped around like toy cars. Cyclists weaved in and out, tinkling their tinny bells. The market was full of small shops selling fruit, groceries, televisions and books. Signboards were plastered on every space – advertising everything from ceiling fans to perfume oils. Tilted at various angles, they seemed like any minute they would crash down on the people below.

The driver stopped in front of a crumbling yellow building which bore the sign 'Ruby Guest House, Paharganj'. Below that it said, 'Decent Laxury Higenic backpaker accomodation.'

'This is your hotel, Sir. Very good and very reasonable,' the driver said, and charged me a thousand rupees.

As I was about to step into the hotel, a big fat cow stopped right in front of me.

'Shoo,' I told the animal, but it shook its head at me. I pushed my bag at her and the next thing I knew I was flying in the air. I landed with a thud, crashing headlong into a parked cycle. The cow was on me again, snorting and digging its heels into the ground. I looked around for help, but the people around me simply laughed. I got up slowly, dusting my pants, and made another attempt to enter the hotel, but the cow refused to let me pass. It had taken to me like a buzzard takes to guts.

I was saved by a hawker selling bananas in a cart. The cow mooed and made a beeline for him. I quickly stepped into the building.

The guesthouse reception had a tattered green sofa, a dusty red carpet and dying plants. The manager was an oily young man with slick black hair. 'Welcome, Sir, to our five-star guesthouse,' he greeted me. He asked me to pay two thousand rupees as a week's rent deposit and allotted me room number 411 on the second floor without any fuss. A young boy in dirty underpants picked up my suitcase and took me to the room up a creaky staircase.

My room was nothing to write home about. Only a little bigger than a cubby-hole, it had a single bed, a cupboard and a small desk and chair. The walls were painted grey and the floor was covered with a cheap carpet. There was an attached john with a smelly WC, a tap, a bucket and a mug.

'Breakfast from seven to seven thirty in TV lounge,' the boy announced as he placed my suitcase on top of the desk. 'Can I get you anything? Food? Girl? Coke? Smoke?'

I thought about the choices. 'I wouldn't mind a Coke,' I said.

'Five hundred rupees, please,' he demanded. That was more than ten dollars for a can of Coke! I couldn't cotton on to these Indian price tags. Reluctantly, I parted with the money.

After the boy left, I opened the dark-green curtains at the window to check out the view. A tangled mass of cables greeted my eye, stretching from one building to another like a roof above the street. There was enough dodgy wiring here to electrocute the whole of Texas. Some kind of black smog hung in the air. Two people were arguing loudly on a roof below me. A radio was playing a Hindi song. I wondered how I would sleep with this racket going on.

The bell boy returned in ten minutes and handed me a little plastic packet containing some white powder.

'What the hell's this?' I said. 'I asked for a Coke.'

'This is coke. High grade. Top class,' he said and scampered out of the room.

'Hey, wait!' I shouted, but the boy had already disappeared. I sniffed at the powder. It didn't smell like Coke at all. I was wondering whether I needed to mix it with water when the door was kicked open and a fat policeman barged in. 'Hold it right there, Mister,' he announced in a stern voice. 'What is this in your hand?'

'I dunno. I asked for a Coke and I got this,' I said, spreading my hands.

'Aha! So you admit you asked for cocaine.'

'Cocaine? What do you mean?'

'Don't act the innocent. In Paharganj, when a foreigner asks for a smoke, he means marijuana. And when he asks for coke, he means cocaine. But possession of cocaine is a very serious criminal offence in our country. Now you will go to jail for ten years.'

Jail for ten years? For ordering a Coke? I almost puked.

'Come on, I am taking you to the police station,' the cop announced and took out a pair of handcuffs from his hip pocket.

I flipped on seeing the cuffs, and that's when I remembered what had happened at the airport. In a flash I took out a hundred-dollar bill from my wallet and waved it at the cop. 'Would you like a little something for your dollar collection?'

The cop's eyes began shining. He grunted and snatched the note. 'I am forgiving you this time. Don't do drugs in India,' he warned me, pocketed the plastic packet and left, tapping his stick on the staircase.

I slumped down on the bed, just plumb tuckered out from all that had happened in a day. I had taken my first foreign trip, been stood up by the girl I'd fallen in love with, almost been sent back from the airport, been head-butted by a cow and nearly arrested by a cop.

I opened the brown folder and took out the pictures I had been sent. I looked into the eyes of this woman – Sapna or Shabnam – and tried to ask her, Why did you do this to me?

The next morning I was woken up by a fluttering sound. I opened my eyes and found two pigeons making out next to my bed. I shooed them out the window, and leaned out to see the morning view. The sun had not yet come out, but the day had already begun for the people on the street. There were little girls in frocks busy filling a whole heap of plastic bottles from a tap. A man was taking a bath on the pavement. He soaped himself, standing in striped underpants next to a plastic bucket, and then rinsed off with a mug of water.

A little later, I, too, stripped off and entered the bathroom. Standing under the tap, I turned it on full blast. A small trickle of lukewarm water came out. Five minutes later even the trickle stopped, leaving me only half-showered. I now knew why water was more precious than gold in this city.

After breakfast I headed for Reception.

'Where can I make a call to America from?' I asked the manager.

'You should go to a PCO, Sir,' he told me.

'What's that?'

'Public Call Office. There are plenty in the neighbourhood. Best place to make international calls. And they are open twenty-four hours.'

So I stepped into the street and found every second shop to be a PCO. There were more phone booths in Paharganj than strip clubs in Houston. I entered the booth closest to the guesthouse and dialled Mom's number. I sure was glad to hear her voice.

'Larry, when are you bringing my beautiful daughter-in-law home?' she asked, all excited. 'And don't forget to send me the wedding photos.'

I had called to tell her there wouldn't be no wedding, but suddenly I didn't have the heart to tell her the truth. 'I won't forget, Mom. Everything is fine,' I mumbled and hung up.

As soon as the market opened, I looked for a travel agent to book my return flight. Luckily, Lucky Travel and Tours was just across the road, in an office complex full of tiny shops. The owner was a friendly man who examined my ticket carefully and spent a lot of time punching keys on his computer screen. 'Sorry, Mr Page,' he shook his head, 'your ticket is of the cheapest category and there is no seat available on any flight. As you know, this is peak tourist season. The earliest I can get you a confirmed seat to Chicago is 24 November.'

'But that's a long way off,' I cried. 'I want to return right now, today if possible.'

'In that case you will have to buy a new one-way ticket. I can arrange one for you immediately. We have a special offer on Tajikistan Airways. Delhi–Dushanbe–New York will cost you just thirty thousand rupees.'

I checked my wallet. 'I've only got thirteen grand.'

'Sorry, then you will have to wait for 24 November. Till then enjoy our country.'

I stepped out of the travel agency feeling madder than a hornet. That's when I came across a nameplate which said 'Shylock Detective Agency. Specialists in matrimonials.' My eyes lit up. A PI was just the man I needed.

I knocked on the door and the sign almost fell off. I tried to tack it back and the door creaked open.

I stepped into a room which looked like it had been hit by a twister. There were cardboard boxes lying around and various things scattered on the floor – some framed pictures, file boxes, a big pile of newspapers, even a hammer and a couple of screwdrivers. The walls looked like they hadn't been painted in years and the room smelt like someone had been pissing in it.

There was a cloud of smoke in the room and for a moment I feared it was on fire. 'Come in, come in, my friend,' a voice announced.

I approached the voice. The clouds parted and I discovered an oldish-looking Indian guy in a tweed jacket and a brown cap sitting behind a wooden desk. With one hand he was busy trying to take dirt out of his ear and with the other he was smoking a pipe.

As soon as he saw me, he dumped the cotton bud, dusted his jacket and stood up. 'Welcome to the Sherlock Detective Agency. I am K. P. Gupta, the owner. What can I do for you?'

'Can you find someone for me?' I asked.

'Elementary, my dear Watson,' he said and puffed on his pipe.

'Page.'

'What?'

'The name's not Watson. It is Larry Page.'

'Oh yes, of course.' He took another puff on his pipe. 'Well, who is this person you want me to find, Mr Larry?'

'Are you moving from here?' I pointed at the stack of boxes.

'Well, this place isn't exactly Baker Street. And the idiots here don't know enough English even to write the name of my agency correctly. But don't worry, I'm not going anywhere. We are merely redecorating. Why don't you take a seat?'

I sat down on a stringy chair which looked so weak I was worried it might collapse at any minute.

'I was wondering if you could find the girl who sent me these pictures,' I said and handed him the brown folder.

He did a quick scan and frowned. 'But this is our famous actress Shabnam Saxena. Why do you need to find her?'

So I explained the whole story of my friendship with Sapna Singh and the reason for my trip to India.

'Tch-tch,' he said, shaking his head. 'This girl Sapna has really duped you, Mr Larry. What do you want me to do?'

'I want you to find her. Before returning to the States I want to meet her just once. Can you locate her for me?'

'Of course. I can even locate Osama bin Laden if the government asks me. Do you have any letters written by this girl?'

'Yes.' I took out a fat bunch of letters from my bag. 'I can give you her address, but I'm afraid I cannot show the letters to you. They are kind of private.'

'And I am a private investigator.' He grinned and snatched them from my hand. 'Hmmm,' he said as he read the first few letters. 'A Delhi PO box has been used. Very clever. But not cleverer than me. Mr Larry, consider your work done. Within a few days I shall have the full details of this girl. Of course, it will cost you.'

'How much?'

'My normal rate is ten thousand rupees, but given that you are a guest in our country, I'll give you a fifty per cent discount. So let's say five thousand rupees. I need half in advance and half when I finish the investigation.'

I took out my wallet and counted out 2,500 rupees.

'Good,' he nodded, and sent another cloud of smoke out of his mouth. 'Come back on Monday 8 October.'

I returned to the guesthouse, first checking to see if that nasty cow was around. Today she was sitting in the middle of the road like a traffic island, with a garland of fresh marigolds draped around her neck. Cars and scooters honked at her, cyclists cursed her, but she sat there like a queen, chewing a plastic bag. I shook my head in despair at this country where cows were treated like goddesses. Back home she'd already have become steak.

Once inside the guesthouse, I headed for the TV lounge. There was only one other guy in the room, sitting in an armchair, with a cushion in his lap. He was fair, with brown eyes and a wispy beard.

The TV set was tuned to CNN. The screen showed rubble in some street and then people lying in hospital all covered in blood and bandages.

'What happened?' I asked the guy.

'Another suicide bombing in Baghdad. Seventy people killed,' he replied tersely. 'You are Larry Page from America, aren't you?'

'Yeah,' I nodded. 'How did you know?'

'I saw your name in the hotel register.'

'And who might you be?'

'I am Bilal Beg, from Kashmir.'

I had no idea where Kashmir was, but I nodded my head again.

'Tell me, Mr Page, why doesn't your country just quit Iraq?' Bilal demanded suddenly.

'I dunno. Isn't it because we need to get that guy Saddam or something?'

'But Saddam has already been hanged!'

'Oh really? Sorry, I haven't watched CNN for, like, a year.'

He looked at me as if I had stolen his wallet and walked out of the room.

That evening I made the mistake of eating out at a roadside restaurant. The food was mind-blowingly hot, some kind of flat-bread filled with potatoes and pickle that went to work on my stomach straight away. As soon as I returned to the guesthouse, I had to rush to the john.

The whole of Friday and Saturday I spent in my room, with the worst stomach ache of my life. I felt like ten pounds of shit in a five-pound bag. The only person who came to look me up was Bilal. He even gave me some kind of green syrup which helped me recover. By Sunday morning, I was raring to go out, having been cooped up with the runs for the last two days.

The streets of Paharganj were quieter on Sunday. Even the rickshaw-wallahs who normally started plying their glorified cycles by seven a.m. seemed to be taking a break. Two of them were sleeping with their feet propped up on the handlebars. The girls were out again, busy filling their plastic bottles and buckets from the municipal tap.

Most of the shops were closed today, but the little roadside restaurants were open. One sold fried omelettes wrapped in two slices of bread. Another was making pretzel-shaped Indian sweets which were fried in a vast vat of boiling oil, then dumped into another pot containing a sugary syrup. People huddled around stoves which were furiously boiling tea.

For some reason, Indians preferred doing things out in the open. I saw open-air hair-cutting saloons, where barbers lathered and scraped customers in full public view, and tailoring shops, consisting of a tailor sitting on the pavement busy working his sewing machine. There were even people who cleaned your ears on the side of the road. I saw an old man in dirty clothes busy poking inside a customer's ear with a long, pointy thing. It was enough to give me an earache.

There was a man selling DVDs on a cart. I picked up some fabulous bargains from him – *Spiderman 3*, *Batman 4* and *Rocky 5* for the equivalent of fifty cents a piece!

Wandering further south, I reached a busy fruit market. Women sat on tattered burlap mats with mounds of tomatoes and onions, lemons and ladies' fingers, and tried to out-shout each other. 'Tomatoes twenty rupees a kilo! . . . Lemons five for two!

. . . My potatoes are the best!' They weighed the vegetables in deformed copper scales with black iron kilogram weights and put the money under the burlap mats. Suddenly, something flicked my face. I turned around and saw that nasty cow staring at me. Before she could make her move, I began to run. Ten minutes later, I found myself near New Delhi railway station.

The station was another world. The poverty of India hit me like a hammer. I saw entire families living on pavements inside makeshift tents made of plastic sheeting. And there were some who didn't even have that. One man lay stretched out in the middle of the road, like a drunk outside a bar. Another sat on the pavement, naked as a jay bird, his body caked in mud, scratching his chest with his nails.

A haggard-looking woman approached me, wearing a green sari with a yellow blouse. She was as thin as a bar of soap after a hard day's washing and her hair looked like she had combed it with an egg beater. She held up a skinny little boy who looked like he hadn't eaten in a year, all bones and hollow eyes. The woman didn't say anything, just cupped her hands and made a motion from her stomach to her mouth. It was enough for me to take out my wallet and give her five hundred rupees.

No sooner had I done this than I was surrounded by an army of beggars. They zeroed in on me like those dead guys in *Night of the Zombies*. There were limbless beggars and eyeless ones, beggars who pushed themselves on skateboards and those who walked on their hands. Like the fruit vendors displaying oranges and apples, they showed me their open wounds and pus-filled sores, their mangled limbs and deformed backs, and held out tin begging bowls as crooked as their bodies. It was impossible to proceed any further. I ran back to the hotel, locked myself in my room and buried my face in the pillow.

In just three days, Delhi had broken my heart, blown my mind, and blasted my intestines.

The PI was waiting for me on Monday, dressed in exactly the same clothes, but today he'd ditched the pipe. Most of the boxes had been removed, making the room seem as empty as a church on Monday morning.

'True to my promise, I have found the girl who sent you the letters,' Mr Gupta announced as soon as I sat down.

'Who is it?' I asked eagerly.

'It will come as a surprise to you, but those letters were written by none other than Shabnam Saxena.'

'You mean that actress?'

'Exactly.'

'How do you know? Can you be sure?'

'Haven't you noticed how she uses her initials – S and S – in her fake name too?'

'I'll be dipped! It never struck me.'

'But to a trained investigator like me, the pattern was apparent immediately. Nevertheless, to be doubly sure I also compared her handwriting with the handwriting in the letters you were sent. It's a perfect match.'

'But how did you get hold of her handwriting?'

He laughed. 'We Indians are very advanced. We have built atom bombs which your CIA couldn't even find. So we have very superior databases, including the handwriting of each and every Indian who knows how to read and write. I am assuring you, Mr Larry, the author of these letters is Shabnam Saxena.'

'Then why didn't she come to meet me at the airport?'

'Now that is a more difficult question. I think it is best that you ask her yourself.'

'But—'

'I know what you are thinking. You are wondering why would a famous actress want to be friends with an ordinary American. Right?'

'Yeah. Why?'

'Because love conquers all, Mr Larry. You will understand this when I tell you Shabnam's story. She was a small-town girl with big-city ambitions. She was born and brought up in Azamgarh, a small town in north India famous for its gangsters. Her upbringing was strictly middle class. Her father was a bank clerk, her mother a primary-school teacher. She was the middle one amongst three sisters, and the prettiest. The constant refrain she heard from her parents was weeping over their misfortune to be saddled with three girls. They fretted about how to marry off their daughters. Where to get the money for their dowries from. Shabnam studied till Grade 12 in the local girls' college and then went to Lucknow University for her graduation in Philosophy honours.

'When she returned to Azamgarh after her BA she found the town sordid and dirty. Her parents wanted to get her married, but the only marriage proposals seemed to come from the local dons. A particularly violent gangster, who flitted between Azamgarh and Dubai, began making unwelcome advances. She resisted and her parents started receiving death threats. She knew if she stayed in Azamgarh her destiny would inevitably become that of a gangster's moll, at best his wife. So one dark night, she took money from her father's purse and ran away to Mumbai to try her luck in the film industry. She struggled for a bit, but eventually got a break from producer Deepak Hirani. Now she has made it, but she does not want to acknowledge her roots. Her parents have disowned her. She maintains no contact with any of her relatives. She lives all alone in a Mumbai flat. What does this tell you?'

'What?'

'That she is hungry for love. L-O-V-E. That is why she wrote to you. She wants you to be her friend.'

'But then why didn't she use her real name? She must be filthy rich. Why did she take money from me?'

'Because she wants to test you. If you knew that she is a famous actress, you too might have ended up treating her like Indians do. Men lust after her. But she wants you to love and respect her, Mr Larry.'

'Yeah,' I nodded. 'It's starting to make sense.'

'And for all you know, she might be trying to give you a message. Maybe things are not fine with her. Maybe some mafia types are after her again. Therefore she is forced to use a fake identity. She is asking you for help.'

'Well sock my jaw! You may have struck upon something. So should I try to contact her myself?'

'Why not? Maybe that's what she is waiting for. Now tell me, do you have a mobile?'

'No. I haven't bought one so far.'

'Then do so, because as a special favour for you, I've got you Shabnam Saxena's phone number. This is her very own personal mobile number which she doesn't give to anyone.' He dropped his voice to a whisper. 'People would kill for this information.'

'Really?'

'Yes. But this is extra. It will cost you another 2,500 rupees. So if you take it, you will need to pay me a total of five thousand now.'

It took me less than a minute to decide I wanted that number. I forked out five grand from my wallet. The PI counted the notes and put them in his coat pocket.

'Write it down,' he said, reading from a piece of paper. 'It is 98333 81234. Got it? I have got this number with great difficulty. So please use it with discretion.'

'Can I try it right now from a PCO?'

'You can, but you won't get her. I've found out that Shabnam has gone to Cape Town to shoot a film. The mobile will start working only when she returns to India. You can try the number after a week or so.' He knotted his hands. 'Will that be all?'

'Yeah. Thanks for all your help.' I got up.

'Let me wish you the very best, Mr Larry,' the PI said and shook my hand vigorously. 'Your girlfriend is every Indian's dream girl. I feel very envious of you. Very envious indeed.'

I stepped out of his office, happy as a pig in manure. For the first time, things seemed to be looking up.

I bought an expensive Nokia that very afternoon, together with a pre-paid card. Then, sitting in my room, I dialled the number with shaking fingers. The call went through, but no one picked up the phone. After a while a recorded voice told me, 'The subscriber you have dialled is presently not available. Please try again later.'

Disappointed, I hung up. The PI was right. I would have to try later. A whole week later.

I carefully put the little slip of paper with Shabnam's number in my wallet, and that's when I discovered that the wallet was almost empty. I had only got a thousand rupees and two hundred dollars left. And I had to survive another forty days in this city. So that evening I turned to Bilal in the TV lounge.

'Is there anyone here who might require the services of a fork-lift driver, you reckon? I need to make some quick cash.'

'You don't need to drive forklifts in India. You can do much better as an English teacher here,' he said. 'Let's find you a job.' He picked up a newspaper from the centre table and flipped through it. 'Here, this might be just the job for you.' He pointed out an advert in the 'Job Openings' section:

> Wanted: Voice & Accent Trainers for a leading BPO. Job Requirement: Conduct refresher training on Phonetics, Grammar & Culture as and when needed. Complete daily tracking, including end-of-day course evaluations and trainee assessments. Qualifications: No prior experience or specialization needed. Good command of American English the only pre-requisite. Apply with resumé and references for immediate position.

The advertisement was as clear as mud to me. 'What the hell's a BPO?' I asked.

'Business Process Outsourcing. A fancy name for a call centre,' said Bilal. 'You should get the job easily. All you need to do is speak like an American.' He told me not to worry about the resumé and references, but just to go for the interview.

I spent the rest of the week waiting for the week to end. Every day I tried Shabnam's number no less than fifty times and every time I got the same recorded message. I finally lost my patience when I got the recorded message even after ten days. So I marched back to the Shylock Detective Agency and found the office locked and all boarded up. There was a printed notice fluttering on the door. It said 'Prime Office Space. For immediate rent/sale – Contact Navneet Properties 98333 45371.' I called up the number and was told that Mr Gupta had vacated his rented office and gone somewhere without any forwarding address.

For the first time, the thought entered my mind that the PI might have been as crooked as a dog's hind leg. And that he may have given me a bum steer. But the Lord never closes one door without opening another one. As I was returning, I spotted a magazine called *Filmfare* at a bookstand with Shabnam's picture on the cover, and bought it.

Mizz Henrietta Loretta, our Third Grade teacher, taught us about a crazy dude called Archie-something who lived long, long ago in some country called Grease. The fellow dived into a bath-tub and was the first to discover that water starts overflowing from a tub when you fill it too much. He got so excited he jumped out of the tub, naked as a jay bird, shouting 'Eureka! Eureka!' That's exactly what I felt like doing on reading the article about Shabnam Saxena. Coz what I discovered in that magazine was nothing short of a gold mine. It gave the whole life story of the actress and was word for word exactly the same as the story told me by that PI. My respect for Mr Gupta went up a couple of notches. The guy was right on the money. But the magazine had two additional pieces of info Mr Gupta hadn't given me. It had Shabnam's address in Mumbai and even her birthday – 17 March, which happened to be exactly the same as the birthday given to me by Sapna Singh. That was the clincher which convinced me that Sapna and Shabnam were one and the same. I felt so happy, I guzzled down four cans of Coke!

That night I sat down at the desk in my room, took out a piece of paper and began composing a letter to Shabnam. 'My dearest darling Shabnam,' I began. 'I reckon a love like ours is as scarce as hen's teeth,' and before I knew it, I'd filled twenty pages. I put them all in an envelope, marked it 'Highly Confidential', wrote Shabnam's address and posted it first thing in the morning.

The next day, I wrote another letter to Shabnam. And then it became as easy as shooting fish in a barrel. In a week's time, I'd spent more cash on postage than on food and I was down to borrowing money from Bilal.

'You better get that BPO job,' he warned me.

So on 25 October I landed up in Connaught Place for the interview in my best clothes. I was shown into a swanky office with glitzy paintings, plush leather seats and a pretty receptionist.

The person conducting the interviews was a balding guy in his forties called Bill Bakshi. He sat behind a polished steel table dressed in denim jeans, a Buffalo Bills sweatshirt and a Yankees baseball cap. He looked at me with a puzzled expression. 'Mr Larry Page . . . I thought you would be an Indian Christian from Goa. But you look American. Is that right?' He spoke like one of those damn Yankees from New York.

'Yeah. I'm American. Always have been. Is that a problem?'

'No . . . no . . . not at all,' he said quickly. 'In fact, what could be better for us than having an American to teach the American accent? I am assuming you are a true blue American, someone who has actually lived in the US?'

'Yeah. I'm just visiting India. I live in Waco in Texas.'

He smiled, stretched his legs and put his hands behind his head. 'I am a Buffalo Bills fan, as you can see. How about you, Larry? Are you into American football?'

'You telling me! Being from the great State of Texas, I support America's team, the Dallas Cowboys – only team in NFL history to have won three Super Bowls in four years.'

'And what about the Houston Texans?'

'Sorry to say, but they are a shit team.'

'Why do you say that?'

'Coz they lose all their games. They had their chances in the 2004 season but the 22–14 loss to the Cleveland Browns sealed their fate. Since then the team's been pretty much in self-destruct mode. I mean the whole decision to draft Mario Williams as the number-one pick in preference to Reggie Bush or Vince Young was probably the biggest mistake in NFL draft history. The guy can't hit the broadside of a barn!'

'Wow, you seem to know the history of the NFL by heart. Do you have any previous industry experience?'

'Well, this ain't my first rodeo. I've been working with Walmart for nearly five years now.'

'Walmart? Mr Larry Page, you are hired. Welcome aboard.' He got up to shake my hand.

'Gee, thanks. But what am I supposed to do? I mean, can you tell me a little bit about your company?'

'Of course. Rai IT Solutions is a BPO company. We do many things for our overseas clients. We sell telephone services, handle consumer complaints, conduct market research, make airline bookings, compute income tax and process insurance claims. But our biggest operation is in geographic information systems. Our largest client is the ARA – American Roadside Assistance. You've heard of them?'

'Yeah. But our company vehicles have contracts with the Triple A.'

'Well, the ARA is very similar to the AAA. Now imagine yourself to be a customer of the ARA. Suppose your car breaks down or your subscription expires or you are lost on the highway.'

'Whereabouts on the highway?'

'Doesn't really matter. You can be lost in Alaska or Hawaii, for that matter. We've got all the road atlases. So what do you do when you get lost? You call a 1-800 number. That call comes to us, to our call centre in Gurgaon. And it is our customer-support associates who help out the American customer. The trick is not to let on that we are answering the call in India. The customer should think the call is being answered in America by Americans. That's where you come in.'

'Gee, to be honest, I'm not all that good at giving directions. I mean I get lost myself all the time on the I-35. Once I took just one wrong exit and ended up in New Mexico.'

'No, Larry. We are not asking you to work as a customer-support associate. We want you to be their accent trainer only. You need to teach our new call-centre employees everything about America – how Americans talk, what they play, what they eat, what they watch, so that when Deepak from Moradabad says he is Derek from Milwaukee, the caller in the US should not doubt him. Do you think you can help us do that?'

'You bet. Sounds like a piece of cake.'

'Perfect. Now see, an Indian would never use an expression like "piece of cake".' He slapped his thighs. 'A white American as our accent trainer . . . We've hit the bloody jackpot!' He leaned towards me. 'I hope you know that call centres in India work the graveyard shift – from eight p.m. to eight a.m. Will that be a problem?'

'Nah. I'll just sleep during the day. By the way, how much moolah will I be making on this job?'

'Well, we pay our Indian accent trainers twenty thousand rupees per month. For you we can go up to thirty thousand. Is that acceptable?'

Thirty grand! That meant I'd have enough money to go home in a month.

'When do I start?' I asked.

I began working for Rai IT Solutions the very next day, in their office complex in Gurgaon. A company van picked me up daily from Paharganj at seven p.m. and took me on an hour's drive, past the international airport, to a bustling city full of shopping malls and high-rise buildings. Gurgaon looked more like Dallas than Delhi.

The office complex was pretty impressive too. All tinted glass and marble. Inside, the call centre was just like a Walmart shop floor, a huge air-conditioned space with row upon row of cubicles with computers. There were hundreds of young Indians sitting on swivel chairs in front of the computer screens with telephone headsets on. The place hummed like a giant beehive and looked busier than a strip joint on buck night.

My job involved teaching a bunch of smart young boys and gals to speak like Americans. I started off with the brass tacks. 'There are three kinds of students,' I told the class. 'One, those that learn by reading. Two, those that learn by observing. The rest have to pee on the electric fence by themselves.'

A pretty young thing in a tight little T-shirt put up her hand. 'Excuse me, Professor Page, what does peeing on an electric fence mean?'

Professor Page? My head got all swole up just hearing that word. I wished Mom could have been here to see her son being called Professor. 'It means, there ain't nothing in life worth your while that don't come hard, you understand? So you keep practising and quick as a hiccup you are gonna start to talk like me. OK folks, time to paint your butts white and run with the antelope.'

It was as easy as that. Quickest thirty grand I've ever made in my life. The rest of my job involved sitting in an office on the mezzanine floor with a headset over my ears, watching the activity in the shop floor, listening in on the chatter, marking crosses against those 'customer-support associates' whose English and manners were not up to speed.

The whole call-centre thing amazed me. Here were Indian boys and gals with perfectly good Indian names who were becoming Robert and Susan and Jason and Jane during the night. In fact there were strict rules that they had to call each other by their American names even during the tea and dinner breaks.

'That's the problem,' a supervisor by the name of Mr Devdutt told me. He was a short guy in his fifties, with a crew-cut and wire-rimmed spectacles. 'These kids think they've really become Americans. Not only do they talk and dress like Americans, they are now even going out on dates like Americans. I work in the call-centre industry, Mr Page, but I will never allow my daughter to join it.'

'Why not?'

'Because call centres have become dens of vice and corruption. You don't know what I have to deal with every day. How can I enforce discipline when I have girls coming in dressed like prostitutes? They wear low-cut tops showing their breasts. One came wearing jeans so low, I could see her underwear. I have conducted random searches of girls' handbags and found condoms in there with their lipsticks. I have a strong suspicion that some of the associates are having sex in the toilets during the dinner break.'

'That's nothing,' I told him. 'Back home, I've seen boys and gals making out in the classrooms of Richfield High.'

'Hah! That may be tolerated in your morally corrupt America, but I cannot allow activities which go totally against Indian culture and traditions.' He pointed proudly to a poster stuck on his wall. 'No sex please, we're Indian,' it said.

I shook my head at the guy. He was so narrow-minded he could have peeped through a keyhole with both eyes.

'So what are you gonna do?' I asked him.

He smiled like a cunning fox. 'I'm having video cameras installed in the toilets. This way we shall close the barn door before the horses bolt.'

'Yeah. But be careful. You own barn door's open.'

'What?'

'Your fly's unzipped,' I said.

He looked down and went all red in the face.

Before I knew it, four weeks had passed. My life fell into a nice routine. I would work at the call centre all night and then return to the guesthouse in the morning and sleep most of the day. In the evening, like clockwork, I would write a letter to Shabnam and try her mobile. I didn't get a reply to either, but I continued to hope.

I learnt plenty of jargon at the call centre and made many friends among the associates. These were young kids, fresh out of college, on their first jobs. They wanted to party, to shop, to have a good time. There was Vincent (a.k.a. Venkat), who was such a smooth-talker he could sell a drowning man a glass of water. There was AJ (Ajay), who was always a day late and a dollar short. Penelope (Priya) had the best stats in the business, meeting her weekly targets faster than anyone, and Gina (Geeta) had half the guys drooling over her. Reggie (Raghvendra) was so short, he'd have to stand on a brick to kick a duck in the ass! And Kelly's (Kamala's) *sambar vada* was the best food I ever wrapped my lips around.

I learnt to watch a game called cricket with the guys, which was about as exciting as watching grass grow, but bursting crackers on Diwali was way more fun than the fourth of July. The girls shared their tiffin and their secrets with me. The unmarried ones talked about the guys they liked and the married ones cribbed about their mothers-in-law. All of them were constantly match-making for me, without realizing it was like going to a goat's house for wool.

Before I knew it, 23 November arrived. I had a booking to fly to America the next day. And that's when it hit me – I didn't want to leave. It was crazy. Suddenly this crowded, congested city where cows roamed the streets and beggars slept naked seemed to be the most exciting place on earth. The mosquito-infested, crummy guesthouse had begun to feel like home. The call-centre job felt like a million dollars. India had started doing funny things to me. I had taken to dipping biscuits in tea before nibbling them. I had begun eating *masala dosa* with my hands. I enjoyed taking a bath with a bucket. I felt no shame in getting a haircut from the barber shop on the pavement. Sometimes I even stepped out into the streets of Paharganj in my pyjamas, which I wouldn't be caught dead in back home. India had become an extended holiday. No bills to pay, no driving on I-35, no cooking to do, no tiffs with Johnny Scarface. And it wasn't as if I had plenty of friends waiting for me back home. Even Mom, the last time I spoke with her, seemed more excited about her fourth divorce than my first marriage. But the real reason I didn't want to return was Shabnam. There was a little voice in my heart which kept saying maybe she's still shooting in that town in the Cape. Maybe she didn't get my letters. So I decided to give myself another fortnight and made a new booking for Wednesday 5 December. If I didn't hear from her by then, I would say goodbye to her, chuck her out of my life, and go home.

Truth be told, I didn't hear a squeak out of Shabnam even in the next ten days. But I couldn't take the flight on 5 December. That's coz a very weird thing happened on 3 December. I was heading to the bank to convert my rupees into dollars. Leaving my wallet in the guesthouse, I had put all my cash, my mobile and my passport in a money belt around my waist and was just about to cross the street when I saw a huge crowd of people marching towards me. The procession was led by the most frightening girl I'd ever seen. She had a face as ugly as a mud fence. To top it all, she was blind as a bat and walked with the help of a stick. Following her were three people all wrapped in white, looking like ghosts. Behind them was a guy in an all-black skeleton costume. And behind this party was a whole group of young people, dressed like students. They held up placards with the title 'CRUSADERS FOR BHOPAL' and chanted slogans like 'We demand compensation' and 'Do or die'.

The procession stopped very close to where I was standing. The people in white lay down in the middle of the road, pretending to be dead, while the skeleton guy danced around them.

'Are you guys celebrating Hallowe'en?' I asked a young lady in jeans and slippers with a cloth bag hanging from her left shoulder and a big red dot on her forehead.

She looked at me like I was some kind of vermin. 'Excuse me?'

'I said is this the Indian version of Hallowe'en? Back home we celebrate it on 31 October. But why do you folks need to ask for compensation like this? Don't they give you chocolates and sweets here?'

She went wild. 'You think our protest against the worst industrial accident in the world is funny?'

'Hey, hey, hey, don't get your knickers in a twist!' I tried to calm her.

'Are you insulting me, you swine? You must be on the payroll of Dow Chemicals!' she screamed at me.

'Look lady, I don't know what you're talking about. I've never heard of this Dow dude. You're barking up the wrong tree.' I threw up my hands.

Another student, a young guy with a goatee, tapped me on the shoulder. 'What did you just say? Did you call my colleague a dog?'

A third guy, with a weird hairdo, who looked meaner than a striped snake, snapped his fingers at me. 'Aren't you American?' he asked.

'Yeah, I'm American,' I replied.

'Hey! Looks like we've got the son of bloody Warren Anderson here,' he shouted, and caught me by the scruff of my sweater.

'Come on, give us our money,' a man in dirty *kurta* pyjamas demanded.

'Yes, we are not going to wait any longer,' the guy with the goatee snarled at me.

'No, guys.' I shook my head. 'I'm not going to give any money. This is not how you should be trick-or-treating.'

'The bastard won't part with his money. Let's teach the bloody American a lesson!' the weird-hairdo guy shouted and the crowd pounced on me like dogs on fresh meat. The men started beating me up. The women began tearing off my clothes. I tried to fight them off, but I was like a gnat in a hailstorm. Before I knew it, they'd taken off my sweater. Two minutes later, my shirt was shredded, my vest was in tatters, one of my sneakers was gone and I was wrestling with a fat girl in pigtails who was trying desperately to take my jeans off. I managed somehow to ward her off. And that's when I discovered that my money-belt had disappeared.

Mizz Henrietta Loretta had taught us about the weird customs of foreign tribes. I remember she told us about the Aztec tribe in Argentina, which ate human skulls, and the Maoris of Mexico, who sold their daughters. But I didn't know that Indians also had peculiar customs, like beating up Americans if they didn't give chocolates on Hallowe'en.

I trudged back to the guesthouse looking like Shawn Michaels after the Undertaker had pummelled him in the famous 1997 Hell in a Cell match on WWF.

'What happened to you?' Bilal cried.

'I got beaten up by a bunch of loonies. All my money is gone. And so is my passport. What the hell do I do now?'

'You need to visit the American Embassy to get a new passport,' advised Bilal.

The American Embassy in Chanakyapuri was a nice building. It had a huge lawn with fountains, overlooked by a massive golden eagle. The Marines at the gate didn't seem too happy to see a fellow American. They told me to go round the corner to another building which handled passport and visa stuff.

There were two queues, one for Indians and one for Americans. The Indian queue was a mile long. Whole communities appeared to be living in front of the Embassy with their suitcases and slippers. There was a Sikh family saying their prayers. A harassed-looking mother was feeding her children. A couple of men were playing cards in the shade. Luckily there were no Americans needing visas and I managed to enter through the gate in just ten minutes.

I was frisked like a new inmate in jail. After four security checks, I finally walked into a reception area.

'I'm Larry Page and I've lost my passport,' I announced to the Reception lady.

'Please have a seat!' the lady said and called someone on her phone. In three minutes flat, a glass door opened and a tall blonde in black high heels came in to greet me. Dressed in a grey skirt and matching top with golden buttons, she looked hot as a firecracker.

'Welcome, Mr Page,' she said with a big smile and shook my hand warmly. 'We knew you were coming to India for the Nasscom Conference. It's a great honour for us to have you visit the Embassy. I am a huge fan of your work. Please come this way.'

She led me along the corridors, hips swinging like two cats fighting in a bag. Her office was at the far end of the building. She unlocked the door with a swipe card and asked me to enter.

I sat down on a beige sofa and took a look around. The room was quite large and very well furnished. There were all kinds of maps on the walls and the desk was full of gadgets with long pointy aerials.

The blonde sat down next to me. 'My name is Elizabeth

Brookner,' she said, crossing her long legs. 'I'm the Head of the Consular Section in the Embassy. It's very unfortunate that you have lost your passport, Mr Page, but we'll try to get you a new one within a day.'

'That'll be real nice,' I replied. 'I gotta catch a flight tomorrow.'

'Aw, come on,' she said, patting my arm. 'People who travel in their private 767s don't have to worry about flight schedules.'

I had no idea what a 767 was, so I kept quiet.

'So what's Sergey Brin up to these days?'

I'd never heard of Sergey Brin, so I said nothing.

'You don't speak much, do you, Mr Page?'

'Well, Mom always said, don't let your mouth overload your tail.'

She looked at me again in a funny kind of way. 'Fancy me having Larry Page in my office. You know, I've been using Google for, like, ages. In fact, I even own a few shares from the IPO in 2004 . . . Isn't it a bit hot in here?' she said and undid the top two buttons of her jacket. 'So where are you staying, Mr Page? At the Sheraton?' She batted her eyes at me and gave me a coy smile.

'Look Ma'am, I'm not—'

'My friends call me Lizzie. And here, let me give you my mobile number. You can reach me any time, day or night.' She scribbled a number on a piece of paper and passed it to me. I put it in my wallet, which was as empty as Jesus's tomb on Easter morning.

'Yes, so you were telling me about where you are staying. And didn't you recently win an award for Best Innovator of the Year?'

'No, Ma'am. The only award I've ever come close to winning was last year's Forklift Rodeo over in Cisco. With my Hyster H130F, I was tops in loading and unloading the trailer and stacking and shelving pallets, but I didn't do too well in the written exam coz they had trick questions like "If a forklift travelling at 10 mph takes 22 feet to come to a full stop on a dry surface, how long will a forklift travelling at 20 mph take?" I wrote the answer as 22 × 2 = 44 feet, but they said the correct answer was the forklift has no business travelling at that speed.'

'You really have a terrific sense of humour, Mr Page – or can I call you Larry? How come you know so much about forklifts?'

'That's coz I am a forklift operator at the Walmart store in Round Rock, Texas. You know, the one on the I-35, exit 251?'

'You mean you are not the Larry Page of Google fame?'

'That's what I've been trying to tell you. My name's Larry Page, but I'm not that Google guy. I was just visiting India, but now I can't go back coz I've lost my passport.'

'Oh!' she said and quickly buttoned up her jacket. She stood up from the sofa and her face became like Johnny Scarface's when he's about to pull up a worker. 'Well, Mr Page, I am sorry for the misunderstanding. You are required to complete forms DS-11 and DS-64, available at the counter. Then you need to submit a copy of the police report, show us proof of your citizenship, pay ninety-seven dollars and schedule an appointment with one of the consular section staff.'

'But I'll still get a new passport tomorrow, won't I?'

'No, Mr Page. That expedited service is available only for distinguished Americans, which you obviously are not. My secretary will show you out.'

I stepped out of the Embassy cursing my luck. I wish I hadn't opened my stupid mouth. Lesson learnt. If people want to think I'm Mr Google, I should let them.

I went to Lucky Travel and Tours and made yet another booking. The earliest seat available this time was for 15 January. I had no option but to stay in India for another forty days.

I didn't stop writing to Shabnam, but seeing that she wasn't replying, my letters became shorter and shorter. I continued to try her mobile from the PCO, but didn't strike lucky there either. The only good news came from the call centre, where they dismissed Mr Devdutt on 15 December. He was caught with a whole bunch of pictures of naked girls on his computer. And it was discovered that for two years he had been using the office telephone line to speak to some lady by the name of Sexy Sam in Las Vegas.

The days passed quickly and before I knew it, 31 December arrived. I had plenty of offers to attend New Year parties from Vincent, Reggie and Gina, all of whom had taken leave. But after all that had happened, I just didn't feel like celebrating. That's when I received an offer from the management. They wanted volunteers to man the call centre on New Year's Eve and were offering triple pay. Since I had nothing else to do, I volunteered for the night shift and sat down like an associate in what Priya called the 'hot seat' for the first time in my life.

Handling calls in a call centre is not as easy as it looks. In fact, it's a pretty stressful job. As Vincent used to say, it's just a huge crap shoot. You never know what kind of callers you're going to get. There was not much traffic that night, and it was two hours before I got my first call. It was a gentleman by the name of Mr Jim Bolton.

I adjusted the headset and followed the script taped to the screen. 'Thank you for calling American Roadside Assistance. My name is Larry Page. How may I assist you?'

'Thanks, son. We're from San Francisco. We were visiting friends in New York. From there we were going to Philadelphia for a New Year's party, but we got caught in a blizzard. We've lost our bearings a bit. It seems we have crossed Dallas and we are now in White Haven on the I-476. Can you tell us how to get to Philly from here? And please make it quick, the battery on my mobile is running out.'

'Yes, of course, Sir. From Dallas I can give you directions even to the moon. Can I have your ARA customer number, please?'

The guy gave me his subscription number and I pulled up directions from Dallas, Texas to Philadelphia, New York on the computer. The guy appeared to be nearly fifteen hundred miles off course. What was worse, I was unable to locate White Heaven on the map. I punched in all the other colours, even 'Black Hell', but the result was the same. Zip. Zilch. Nada. The place just didn't exist and I was as confused as a cow on Astroturf.

All associates are expected to complete a call in no more than three minutes, but even after ten minutes I was unable to find Mr Bolton's location. He was getting more and more impatient.

'I can't seem to find directions for Philadelphia, Sir. Would you like to travel to Waco?' I asked hopefully.

The guy blew his top. 'Listen, you bastard,' he shouted. 'For the last half-hour you've been giving me the run around. Why don't you just confess that you know shit all about the roads of the United States? You're not really Larry Page. You are some arsehole Indian sitting in some shit-hole office in goddamn Bangalore trying to fleece unsuspecting Americans, aren't you? Come on, admit it, and I might still excuse you.'

'No, Sir. My name is Larry Page and I am an American, just like you,' I replied.

'So you persist in calling yourself American, eh? You think you can fool me? I know all about how your teeny-weeny call centres operate in India. I'll expose your lie in a sec. Tell me, Mr Page, what is the population of the United States?'

'I dunno. Is it one billion?'

'Wrong. Name the ten amendments to the US Constitution.'

'Aw, shucks, that's harder than Chinese arithmetic. By the way, what's a Constitution?'

'You've not heard of the Bill of Rights? I suppose it is pointless asking you who wrote our national anthem?'

'Can I take a guess?'

'Go ahead.'

'Is it Stevie Wonder?'

'Wrong again. Can you at least recite "The Star-Spangled Banner"?'

'Gee, I used to sing it in school, but that's a long time ago. All I remember is it had something about rockets bursting in the air and bombs entering the home of the brave.'

'That does it. I can't take it any longer. You are an insult to the American nation.'

'I am sorry, Sir. But then I haven't gone to any of those fancy universities like you have.'

'You don't need an education, son. What you need is a hole in the head. Now tell me, what's your real name?'

'I told you, Sir. It's Larry Page.'

'Look, it's no use pretending any longer. I've already proved that you are not American. So what's your real Indian name? Is it Sitaram? Or is it Venkatswamy?'

'Well, Sir, you can put your boots in the oven, but that doesn't make them biscuits. I told you, I'm Larry Page and I'm an American from the great State of Texas.'

'I am asking you for the last time, what is your *real* name? Your Indian name, goddamnit.'

'And I'm telling you for the last time, it's Larry Page and I am not Indian, I'm American.'

'You motherfucking Indians are taking jobs away from here and you have the cheek to call yourselves American? Shame on you.'

'Well shame on you, too, Sir, using such language. Mom says, pretty is as pretty does.'

'Listen, arsehole, it's time you crawled back to your black Indian Mama. This is the last time you are going to sit in that Indian shit-hole of yours and waste precious American time. Who is your supervisor? I need to have a word with him.'

'You've done with preaching and gone to meddling now,' I told him.

'I'll tell you what meddling is, arsehole. I belong to the Teamsters. I'm the head of Local 70, and I'm going to pull the plug on you. And if your company doesn't fire you, I'm going to pull the plug on your shitty company. I demand to speak to your supervisor right now. And let me make—'

The call was cut off abruptly. Looked like his battery had died on him. I passed a hand over my face, relieved to be rid of such a nasty caller, when a message started flashing on my computer screen. 'Please see me immediately – MK.'

Madhavan Kutty was the supervisor of supervisors, a no-nonsense guy with snow-white hair and a foul temper. When I entered his room on the mezzanine floor, he was standing near his desk and there was another guy sitting in his chair. The stranger was dressed flashily in a black leather jacket and pointy white shoes. I wondered if he was blind coz he was wearing shades at one a.m. His face was pretty, but spoiled by a long scar running from his left eye to his cheek. He looked as shifty as a used-car salesman.

Madhavan looked like the cheese had fallen off his cracker. 'This is Mr Vicky Rai, the owner of our company. He was passing by and decided to check in on how we were doing. He monitored just one call at random and that was yours, Larry. You have set a new benchmark for how not to handle a call.'

'Listen, I can explain. That guy was a loony. Even a blind man on a galloping horse could see it,' I began, but the flashy guy cut me short.

'No need to argue with this idiot, MK. Larry Page, you're fired,' he said and walked out, his spanking white shoes tapping on the tiled floor.

Two days later I was kicking a can aimlessly on the road in front of the guesthouse when Bilal came to me. 'Listen, Larry, now that you are no longer working in the call centre, would you like to come with me to Kashmir for a few days? I am going back today with a couple of friends.'

I had nothing better to do and a fortnight to kill. 'Yeah,' I said and sent the can spinning into the gutter.

We arrived in Srinagar the next night. When I got off the bus the wind was blowing like a tornado in a trailer park and it was cold enough to freeze the balls off a brass monkey. A blast of icy air struck me so hard, I almost fainted. Bilal quickly brought me a blanket and rushed me to a nearby house, where I fell asleep instantly.

The next day, we set out for a spot of sightseeing. It was a very cold day but Bilal had just the right outfit for me – a long, loose gown with upturned sleeves called a *phiran*, inside which I clutched a small fire-pot – my own private oven. I was as snug as a bug in a rug.

Srinagar was pretty as a picture and the people on the streets seemed very friendly. Children in brightly coloured shawls waved at me, flocks of bright-eyed schoolgirls, their heads covered, giggled shyly, women loaded with silver jewellery looked up from their houses and men wearing gowns and black hats murmured greetings to Bilal. Everyone smiled.

Our first stop was Dal Lake, which was the most awesome lake I have ever seen. It was lined with tall trees and was full of little houses on boats called – what else? – houseboats, with fabulous carved railings. The lake was dotted with lotus flowers and choked with weeds. Dazzling birds kept darting over its surface. A number of small boats paddled in between the lotus plants. As the fog lifted, I saw snow-covered mountains even taller than Mount Livermore.

On the other side of the lake was a white-domed mosque called the Hazratbal Shrine, which blasted the call for prayer from loudspeakers. Bilal said the shrine was very holy and housed a hair of the Prophet Muhammad. Even the beggars were nice here. They offered me a flower before asking for money.

Our next stop was the Jama Masjid mosque at Nowhatta, in the heart of the old city. Bilal said prayers while I browsed round the bustling old bazaar just outside.

For lunch, Bilal took me to Lal Chowk, which was like Main Street, and we had larrupin' Kashmiri food in a small roadside restaurant.

In the evening, however, there was a bomb blast at the bus station and a curfew was declared from eleven p.m., which didn't really matter because in any case the whole city closed down and went to sleep just after six.

In the middle of the night, Bilal suddenly shook me awake. 'Get up, Larry, there's going to be a raid. We need to go.'

'What happened?' I asked.

'Someone has reported you as a suspicious character. The army may come to arrest you. We need to go to a safe house.'

Bleary eyed, I got up and padded out of the house in my *phiran*. The street was quiet as a graveyard. Litter burned here and there and a couple of men were gathered in a corner warming their hands over a coal brazier. A few stray dogs howled. Bilal knew the city like the back of his hand. He took me through a maze of alleyways, crossing several streets, skirting a bridge, evading a sentry post, to a small, dilapidated house with a green door.

Inside the house were three of the queerest men I've ever met. The leader was a heavy-set guy with a flowing black beard and a black turban. He had a craggy face with a strange dark mark on his forehead. The second guy was younger and wore a woollen jacket over trousers and shirt. He was the same height as me, but so bucktoothed he could have eaten corn through a picket fence. Standing next to him was a tall, fair, wiry dude with long hair and a handsome, scruffy face. He was clad in baggy cream pyjama bottoms and a long black shirt.

Bilal seemed to be in a hurry to leave. '*Bas*, my job was only up to here. These are my friends. They will take you to a safe place. I have to go now, Larry. All the best,' he said, and before I could stop him he rushed out like the dogs were after him.

The three guys in the room looked at me like Mike 'Mad Dog' Benson, the security chief at Walmart, looks at shoplifters. Bilal had said they were his friends. To me they seemed just about as friendly as fire ants.

'Take off your *phiran*,' the turbaned guy ordered.

'Why?' I asked.

'We want to check you're not carrying a weapon.'

'Whatever floats your boat,' I said and took off the gown.

The bucktoothed guy patted my sweatshirt and jeans. 'He's clean,' he announced. The tension in the air cooled a little.

'Howdy!' I said and extended my hand. 'I'm Larry Page.'

The bucktoothed guy brightened up. 'Bilal told us your name, but I didn't believe him. Are you really the Larry Page who invented Google?'

I cursed pa for naming me Larry (Mom said it was his idea). But if the Indian army was after me and my only chance of escaping was these three jokers, I thought it best to play along. Mr Bucktooth obviously didn't know baby shit from butterscotch, and if he thought I was the Google guy, I had no problem with that. No problem at all.

'Why? You think I can't invent an engine?'

His eyes widened. 'You mean you are the real Larry Page?'

'Is a frog's ass waterproof?'

'Meaning?'

'Meaning yes. I am the guy who invented Google.'

Bucktooth looked like he would faint. 'My name is Rizvan, Mr Page, but everybody calls me Abu Teknikal. It is a great honour to meet you. I am a great fan of Google. I use it all the time,' he gushed.

'Yeah,' I nodded. 'People tell me it's the best thing since sliced bread. But why are you called Teknikal?'

'That's because he is a computer,' said the pyjama guy. 'He knows everything about everything.'

'Really?'

'Show him, Teknikal,' the pyjama guy said.

'Mr Page, I probably know more about you than any other man alive,' Teknikal boasted.

'You're kidding.'

'Yes. I can prove it. You were born on 26 March 1973 in Lansing, Michigan to Dr Carl Victor Page and Gloria Page. While a student on the Ph.D. programme in Computer Science at Stanford University, you met Sergey Brin and together you developed the Google search engine in 1998. The World Economic Forum named you a Global Leader for Tomorrow. You are currently the President of Products at Google Inc. with an estimated net worth of 16.6 billion dollars, making you the twenty-sixth-richest person on Earth. How's that?'

The twenty-sixth-richest person on Earth! The guy was off his rocker. Mom always said it is better to keep your mouth shut and let people think you are an idiot than to open it and remove all doubt. But I pretended he was the cat's whiskers. 'Well, sock my jaw, that's pretty impressive!'

'What has fascinated me, Mr Page, is your Page Rank technology. How on earth did you get the idea to use an iterative algorithm which corresponds to the principal eigenvector of the normalized link matrix of the web to determine the ranking of an individual site?'

I didn't have a clue what he was blabbering about, but I said 'Yeah . . . Yeah,' and nodded my head a couple of times. 'Page

Rank. Now that was a terrific idea, wasn't it? Third best thing to come along since sliced bread.'

The guy was persistent. 'What exactly was your tipping point, Mr Page?'

'You mean the point when it tipped over?'

'I mean the point when you and Sergey knew that you had a winner.'

'That was in April, I would say. Yeah. In April we knew we had a winner.'

That shut him up.

'Won't you introduce me to your friends?' I asked.

'Oh yes, sorry, Mr Page. This is Abu Khaled,' he said, referring to the turbaned guy. 'He's our emir, our leader, our *zimmedar*.'

'What about him?' I pointed to the pyjama dude.

'That is Abu Omar.'

'So are you guys brothers or what? All of you are called Abu.'

'We are brothers in arms, Mr Page,' he smiled. 'But we're not related to each other. In fact we don't even speak the same language. I'm from Pakistan, from Rawalpindi. Abu Khaled is from Egypt and Abu Omar is from Afghanistan. I speak Urdu, Abu Khaled speaks Arabic and Abu Omar speaks Pashto. So we talk to each other only in English.'

'Good for me. But what are you folks doing in Kashmir?'

'We are helping our friends like Bilal in their fight against the infidels. I am glad you sympathize with our point of view, Mr Page. It is wonderful to have the support of someone as influential as you.'

'Glad to be of assistance, but when do you think I can get back to Delhi? I got a plane to catch, you know – my private 767.' I winked.

'Soon, Mr Page, very soon. But first we need to take you to a safe place. You need to rest now because tomorrow we will go on a very long journey.'

We slept in a small room which was not half as cosy as the one in Bilal's house. What was worse, I had Abu Teknikal on my left and

Abu Omar on my right for company. And they kept pestering me with questions half the night.

'You know what,' Teknikal told me. 'Ever since I was seven, it has been a dream of mine to visit America, abode of the internet and the Xbox 360. Home of the Blue Gene and the BigDog. I actually cried when I saw a picture of the Cray X-MP in my school. But your achievements dwarf even those of Vinton Cerf and Robert Kahn. If the internet is heaven, then Google is God. Do you know what that makes you, Mr Page?'

'What?'

'The Godfather,' he said and grinned.

Abu Omar had other interests. 'So how many girls have you banged, Mr Page?' he asked me.

'Excuse me?'

'I mean how many girls have you had sex with? Abu Khaled tells us in America girls start having sex when they are only ten and eleven. Is that true?'

'I dunno. I'd need to ask my niece Sandy. She's ten and she's a girl.'

'I know it is forbidden in Islam, but I keep having these immoral thoughts. All because of this Indian actress.'

'And who would that be?'

'Her name is Shabnam Saxena. The bitch is so hot, I become crazy with desire.'

I felt like walloping the pervert, but restrained myself. 'Have you seen any of her movies?' I asked.

'I can't. Films are un-Islamic.'

'Good for you,' I murmured and laid a protective hand on my wallet, which contained a picture of Shabnam as well as her number.

'Don't tell the *zimmedar*,' Omar whispered, 'but I once saw an American film at a video parlour in Kabul. It was called *Debbie Does Dallas*. Have you seen it?'

'Never heard of it. Is it about the tourist places in Dallas? I hope it showed the ballpark in Arlington and the—'

'No, no, Mr Page, the film was full of naked women. Thank

God the Taliban closed down that video parlour or else I would have gone blind.'

The guy was hornier than a two-peckered billy goat.

'They say in America you can get these kinds of films even at grocery shops. Is it true?' he continued.

'I dunno. I only buy milk and bread at Quik-Pak,' I said and turned my back on him.

Teknikal was waiting on the other side to pounce on me. 'What is your view on anonymous peer-to-peer networks, Mr Page? *PC Mag* says that the proliferation of such networks increases the risk of a devastating attack on the networked information infrastructure. Do you agree?'

The guy had diarrhoea of words and constipation of thoughts.

'With due respect to Mr Mag, if brains were gasoline, he wouldn't have enough to run a piss ant's go-kart around the inside of a donut!' I said, and before he could figure that one out, I pulled the blanket over my head. 'If y'all excuse me, I'm now gonna get some shut-eye!'

I was sandwiched between two top-notch loonies. The rocks in Teknikal's head would fit the holes in Omar's. I don't remember when I finally fell asleep, dreaming of Shabnam in a valley full of snow.

The next day we left the house around nine a.m. A few minutes later I found myself in a street full of tumbled-down houses and charred temples.

'What the hell happened here?' I asked.

'We kicked out the Hindu Pandits from here,' grinned Teknikal.

These guys obviously knew the area pretty well. Like Bilal, they evaded all the sentry posts, and after an hour of hotfooting it across the city I found myself at a fruit-and-veg market.

They made me travel in a grain truck, hidden among sacks of wheat with a blue tarpaulin over my head. The truck took us to a Podunk town surrounded by mountains and dense forests.

We spent the night in a quaint little cottage, outside which a mad dog kept howling. Luckily, they put me in a room with Abu

Khaled this time. He didn't speak a word to me, but I still couldn't sleep coz he kept getting up either to go to the toilet or to pray. The guy got up to pray even at four in the morning.

'Which prayer is this?' I asked him, rubbing my eyes.

'It is called Tahajjud. This prayer is not obligatory for Muslims. But the truly devout do not miss it.' He kneeled and touched his forehead to the ground.

I now knew how he got that dark mark on his forehead. It was from all this praying.

The next morning we took off in an open jeep which Teknikal had arranged from somewhere. From both sides, dense forests seemed to rush in like giant waves at our jeep. The clouds were so low, it felt as if I could reach out and touch them. Thankfully the wind wasn't blowing, otherwise even my warm *phiran* would have been as useless as a windshield wiper on a goat's ass.

The only trouble was the roads. They were so bad, even buzzards couldn't fly over them, and so crooked you could see your own tail light. Many a time the jeep narrowly avoided going into a pothole or over the edge, and I had to shut my eyes on the hairpin bends and just hang on for dear life.

We came across very little traffic, just the odd farmer tilling his land or a shepherd grazing his cattle. The jeep stopped abruptly near a mosque, and I was ordered by Khaled to get out. Teknikal said there was a big army camp just a short distance away and travelling by jeep would attract attention. So for the next couple of hours we made our way on foot up a steep mountain pathway, with Omar leading the way.

We finally neared a place called Trehgam. As we reached the top of a hill, Omar took me aside and pointed to the village in the distance. I saw a cluster of houses with corrugated-iron roofs. 'See that roof painted green on that single-storey house? That is the house of my *zerrgay*, my love. She lives there with her mother,' Omar said.

'Then why don't you go down and meet her? I'm sure she will be very happy to see you.'

'Are you out of your mind? The army has its brigade headquarters in Trehgam and keeps a close watch on that house. The moment they see me I will be arrested. I am not afraid of capture, I am ready to die, but I don't want to be tortured.'

We didn't stay in Trehgam village. Khaled made us climb yet another mountain. I was about to faint from exhaustion when suddenly we reached a clearing.

Under a few *chinar* trees was a hideout. It was a slum hut, inside the ground instead of above it. A rectangular pit had been dug, six feet deep into the ground. Two tree trunks had been planted at two corners, supporting a corrugated sheet which served as the roof. The roof had been covered with branches, leaves and shrubs, so that to a visitor coming up the mountain the foxhole would look like a little bush. There was only one entrance and exit. I descended into the foxhole and discovered there were four men already inside it. They were all young and bearded. One was bent over what seemed like a wireless set, another was reading a book, and two were cooking something. The foxhole was well equipped with provisions, a gas stove and even a pressure cooker. The mud walls were lined with blankets on all sides. There were plenty of guns and rifles lying around, together with magazines and boxes of cartridges. I reckoned the foxhole had enough ammo to take the Fidelity Bank of Texas.

'Make yourself at home, Mr Page,' Teknikal told me. 'This is where you will be staying with us for a while.'

The space inside the hideout was barely big enough to sleep six people, and there were eight of us. I'd rather have jumped barefoot into a bucketful of porcupines than stayed in that dump. In two shakes of a goat's tail, I was out of that foxhole.

'I'm sorry, folks, but I don't think this is such a good idea.'

'But there is no other place to stay,' Teknikal protested.

'I'm fixin' to go over yonder to that village. I'm sure they'll have a hotel there.'

'But the army will catch you if you go to Trehgam.'

I looked Teknikal in the eye. 'Something doesn't seem right to me. I've been thinking, why would the Indian army be after me? I've done nothing wrong.'

There was a long pause.

'You're right.' Teknikal nodded his head. 'Actually the army is not after you. It's after us.'

'Why?'

'Oh, we've done a couple of things. Like blowing up the Srinagar bus station, a market in Delhi, a temple in Akshardham, the stock exchange in Mumbai. We escaped recently from Tihar Jail.'

'Well sock my jaw! You guys are terrorists! In that case, I want nothing to do with you folks. And here I was, thinking you were my friends.'

Abu Khaled, standing by my side, laid a hand on my shoulder. 'You moron, we're not your friends. We're your kidnappers.'

'Kidnappers?'

'Yes. You've been kidnapped.'

I laughed. 'You guys are jokers. That's about as funny as a fart in a church.'

'No, Mr Page. We're dead serious. You've been kidnapped. Now we are going to demand a ransom of three billion dollars for your release. We're going to get George Bush to vacate Iraq. We'll get him to force Israel to vacate Palestine. We'll force him to quit meddling in Somalia. We'll ask him to remove the un-Islamic regime in Saudi Arabia. We'll compel him to make reparations to—'

'Whoa, whoa, whoa, just hold your horses for a minute,' I interjected. It was time to set the record straight before these crazies started asking the President to send a man to the moon. 'You folks have got the wrong guy. I am not *that* Larry Page.'

'What?'

'Yeah. You heard right. I am not that Larry Page. I've got nothing to do with that Google guy. I ain't loaded. So if you were expecting me to eat spinach and shit greenbacks, you'd better think again.' I laughed.

That went down like a lead balloon.

'Come again,' said Teknikal.

'I said I am not rich. I was fooling you guys. If it took a nickle to go around the world, I couldn't cross the street.' I looked at Abu Khaled. 'You catch my drift?'

The big guy moved like greased lightning. Without any warning, he swung his fist at me. I didn't see the blow coming and caught it in the mouth. I staggered back against a tree and collapsed like a pole-axed lap-dancer. When I got up there was blood in my mouth and a ringing in my left ear. I touched my face and felt the cut on my lips burning under my fingers.

Abu Khaled was still glowering at me like a mean rattlesnake.

'Er . . . do you guys take Visa?' I asked hesitatingly.

Teknikal was plumb weak north of his ears, but he finally saw the light. 'So you really are not the Larry Page of Google fame? I had my doubts from the beginning. Who the fuck are you?'

'I am a forklift operator in Walmart.'

'A goddamn hi-lo driver! This guy probably makes less than four-fifty a week. And we thought he was a billionaire! Not only that, we even paid that crook Bilal a million rupees to bring him to us.' Teknikal started laughing like a hyena on helium.

Abu Khaled looked at him sternly. 'Abu Teknikal, behave yourself! And make sure this infidel doesn't escape.'

I knew two things now. One, that Bilal was nothing but a low-down, no-good varmint. And two, that I was up shit creek without a paddle.

My hands and feet were tied and I was dumped in a corner of the foxhole like an old sack of clothes. The youths looked at me curiously, then picked up their guns and went out of the hut. I heard them reciting some prayers and running around like they were in boot camp.

It was close to evening when Teknikal and Abu Khaled returned. Teknikal daubed the cut on my lip with some kind of ointment.

'So who exactly are you guys?' I asked them.

'I am Abu Al-Khaled Al-Hamza,' the big guy replied. 'I am

number four in the hierarchy of Lashkar-e-Shahadat. The Army of Martyrdom. We are a part of Al Qaeda. Our commander is Abu Abdullah Osama bin Muhammad bin Ladin. You've heard of him, haven't you?'

'Yeah. Isn't he the guy who is supposed to have blown up those towers down in New York City?'

'Correct.'

'And wasn't the President going to smoke him out of some place called Kabool?'

'You mean Afghanistan. Quite right, except we're the ones who've won the war. Your countries are burning with terror and fear and panic, and we are still going strong. Abu Teknikal, tell this infidel how much reward his President has put on my head.'

'A full fifteen million dollars!' announced Teknikal.

Fifteen million my ass, I thought. If bullshit were music, this guy would have a brass band!

'So what do you guys do?'

'We are fighting for a revolution – the creation of an Islamic Caliphate, the Nizam-i-Islami,' Abu Khaled said. 'Our kingdom will be governed by Sharia law, based upon the Holy Koran and the Sunnah. We are responding to the calls of Allah and his Prophet for jihad in the cause of Allah.'

'And who exactly is Mr Allah?'

Khaled hit me across my face. 'Don't ever talk about our God like that.'

I rubbed my cheek. 'So what do you folks want from me?'

'We need you to tell that evil Bush to convert all Americans to Islam. He should abolish your usurious banks. He must jail all those homosexual swine. He needs to stop women from degrading themselves by appearing in filthy magazines. He needs to preserve the environment. He needs to—'

'I get your drift, Mr Khaled. And I can tell you, I'll do my darndest to get the President to agree to your demands. But I can't do this sitting here in bumfuck Egypt.'

Khaled stepped forward and slapped me twice this time.

'What's that for?'

'One for interrupting me and the other for abusing my country.'

'But what will you folks do with me?'

'We'll still use you for ransom,' said Khaled. 'You may not be a billionaire, but you are still American. Teknikal, draft a press release for CNN. We will send it out tomorrow with a video. Let's teach Mr George Bush a lesson he won't forget.'

I turned to Teknikal. 'Listen, Teknikal. I'm of no use to you guys. The President won't listen to me. Why don't you let me go? I promise you, I won't tell a soul about you folks. It'll remain between you and me and the fencepost.'

'No. Now listen carefully, Mr Page.' He stared at me with eyes shining like light bulbs. 'We are the Army of Martyrdom. We are prepared to die. And we are also prepared to kill.' He traced his fingers over my neck. 'So don't entertain any thoughts of escaping.'

I knew at that moment that Teknikal was as dangerous as Abu Khaled. They were like two peas in a pod. Still I couldn't resist asking him, 'But I thought you liked America.'

'I do,' he answered. 'I just hate Americans.'

That shut me up.

By evening the hideout had become darker than a cow's belly and I was so hungry my belly button was getting awful acquainted with my backbone. One of the boys lit a lantern. In its yellow glow I had my first good look at the other occupants of the foxhole. The youths were named Altaf, Rashid, Sikandar and Munir. They were slim and lanky and aged between sixteen and twenty-two. Altaf told me he was from Naupura in Kashmir, while the other three were from Gujranwala in Pakistan. To me they seemed just like the boys at the call centre, fresh-faced and eager, except they dealt in guns and grenades instead of computers and phones.

The foxhole was warm, but sleeping in it was very uncomfortable. Since space was so limited, you had to sleep in just one position. This time I was sandwiched between Sikandar and

Munir, which was a relief, coz I would have had difficulty looking Teknikal in the eye after what he'd done to me.

They took me to the meadow outside the next day, put a black blindfold over my eyes, made me kneel and told me to fold my hands. 'Now beg for your life, pig,' Abu Khaled barked, as Teknikal trained a video camera on me.

'I've been kidnapped by these Al Qaeda dudes. Creek's rising and I'm up to my ass in alligators! Mom, get me outta here,' I said and was rewarded with a kick in my backside.

'This video is going to your president, not to your mother, cretin,' Khaled yelled at me.

I stayed in the foxhole for close to fifty days. It was as boring as watching paint dry. I relished any opportunity of going out into the open – hearing birds chirping every morning and watching the mist rise slowly towards the clouds made me forget for a moment that I was a hostage. But they always had a man to watch over me, even when I was taking a shit.

The food they gave me was pretty horrible, just plain *roti*, *dhal*, rice and vegetables cooked by one of the boys. The one saving grace was the clabber milk, which was finger-lickin' good. Sometimes Omar would get a cow or buffalo from one of the shepherds and then we would have a feast.

Every day, Teknikal and Omar would train the four young recruits on using guns and ammo. After the evening prayer, Abu Khaled would give a lecture, sitting under the trees.

'God compensates the martyr for sacrificing his life for his land,' he would say, stroking his beard. 'If you become a martyr, God will give you seventy-two virgins, eighty thousand servants and everlasting happiness.'

'I am ready to become a martyr for Allah,' Sikandar shouted. 'I will make my body a bomb that will cause havoc among the infidels.'

Rashid was not to be outdone. 'I will blast the bodies of these sons of pigs and monkeys and cause them more pain than they have ever known.'

Listening to these young boys talking about killing themselves made my hair stand on end, but Abu Khaled nodded approvingly. 'Your pictures will be posted in schools and mosques,' he said. 'The moment you lose your life, your next life will start in heaven – a life that you have waited so long for. A life of everlasting happiness. May the virgins give you pleasure.'

'Allahu Akbar,' the rest of the class shouted in response. 'God is Great.'

Only Omar didn't look too happy. 'I too, want to die as a martyr, but the *zimmedar* has chosen Sikandar and Rashid for the job.'

'What job?'

'I cannot talk about it.'

'But why do you want to kill yourself?'

'So I can get seventy-two virgins in heaven. As a martyr I will also be able to recommend seventy relatives for heaven.'

'But how do you know that there *is* a heaven?'

'That is what the wise men have always told us.'

'But have the wise men been to heaven themselves?'

'No, because first you have to die.'

'Well, I wouldn't take that chance. I'm not so sure that heaven is such a rocking place.'

'But they say Las Vegas is. A cousin told me that you can get more than seventy-two girls at the Chicken Ranch in Nevada. Have you ever been to Las Vegas?' he asked eagerly.

I'd not stepped within a thousand miles of Vegas, but I wanted to spite him. 'Yes, I have,' I said. 'I've also been to the Chicken Ranch. They even have special-offer days with discounts. You can get six girls for the price of two.'

Omar's face became a turd of misery and mine broke into a grin.

Teknikal didn't show much interest either in virgins or Vegas.

'How the hell did you get mixed up with a guy like Abu Khaled?' I asked him one day when he seemed to be in a good mood.

'I used to be an honours student at the College of Electrical and Mechanical Engineering in Pindi, Mr Page,' he replied. 'But your country took away my father. He is in detention in Guantanamo Bay. He is not a terrorist. But America has made me one.'

I had no reply to that.

As the days passed, my worry grew, because Teknikal told me there was still no response from the President. No newspaper had reported me missing. No TV channel had announced my capture. I had just disappeared off the face of the earth.

This upset Abu Khaled quite a lot. 'What kind of government do you have?' he shouted at me. 'They don't even care about you. Forget about responding to our threats, they have not even acknowledged our message. But come 21 February we will show the world what we are capable of.'

'Why?' I asked. 'What's so special about 21 February?'

'It is a major Hindu festival. And it is also the day when we launch our most spectacular attack against the infidels.'

'What will you do?'

'You will find out soon enough.'

I thought long and hard about their plan, but couldn't figure out what they were up to. It was Sikandar who eventually tipped me off. A week before 21 February I saw him trying on a big leather belt, just like the type the WWF wrestlers win in championship fights.

'Hey, that's cool,' I said. 'Where did you get it from?'

'Abu Teknikal made it for me,' said Sikandar.

'Wow! So is there going to be a RAW title match?' I asked, all excited. 'Is Randy Orton coming?'

Sikandar didn't have a clue who Randy Orton was, so I decided to teach him a few moves. Snatching the belt from him I draped it around my waist. As I was about to clip the buckle, Sikandar pulled it off me. 'You fool,' he screamed. 'You would have killed us all.'

'Killed you all? How?' I asked, mystified.

'Because this is not a belt, idiot. It is an IED, an Improvised Explosive Device,' Teknikal chipped in. 'Enough to kill fifty people, the moment the detonator – which is this buckle – is pressed.'

In a flash I understood the job Sikandar and Rashid had been entrusted with. They would wear the belts, go into town and challenge the Indians to a tag team fight. Then the heels would press the button and blast themselves and God knows how many other innocent people to smithereens.

That night, as Sikandar lay in bed next to me, I leaned towards him. 'Do you like killing people?'

'I don't kill people, the bomb does,' he replied in a flat voice.

'But you are the one who will be pressing the switch.'

'I am a soldier and this is a war. Soldiers need to kill other people. Otherwise they kill you.'

'Don't you have a family? A mother? Have you thought what will happen to her when she finds out you're gone?'

'I left my mother's house a long time ago.'

'Have you forgotten it completely?'

'I remember it had square windows through which sunlight used to stream in. A small doorway opened out on to the street. A narrow staircase led to a room with a photo of my grandfather. That's all I remember.'

These were Sikandar's memories of his lost home and in a few days they would be buried with him. I shuddered when I looked into his eyes. They were frozen. I wondered if his heart was as cold as his eyes.

I couldn't sleep that night. There were wars going on in this world about which I knew nothing. People were dying, kids still wet behind the ears were getting ready to blow themselves up and I didn't even know what they were fighting for. It was as scary as it was real.

Sikandar and Rashid left the foxhole the next day with plenty of provisions. It seemed they were going on a very long journey. 'Now we just wait,' said Khaled and rubbed his hands.

21 February came and my kidnappers sat glued to the satellite phone. Around midday came the news they had been waiting for. Sikandar and Rashid had blown themselves up and thirty infidels.

There was a massive feast that evening. A whole cow was carved up by Munir and Altaf. I didn't eat a morsel. I couldn't, after having seen into Sikandar's eyes. That night, the foxhole seemed colder than hell.

We abandoned the hideout immediately after Abu Khaled's four o'clock prayer. Teknikal explained the reason for the sudden move. 'The army will conduct a cordon-and-search operation before sunrise. We need to leave right now.'

Khaled, Teknikal, Omar and I struck out towards the north side of the escarpment. Munir and Altaf were left behind to wipe out all trace of the hideout. Teknikal had the satellite phone. Khaled and Omar carried AK-47s.

It was a difficult journey. We crossed mountains so steep you could look up the chimney to see the cows come home. But gradually the route flattened out and the mountains lost their sharp ridges. By late evening we reached a quiet valley. An empty wood-framed house was our abode for the night. Omar was sent out to get some provisions and didn't return. Teknikal and Khaled spent a restless night wondering if he had been caught by the army. 'You shouldn't have sent Omar,' I told Abu Khaled. 'He's so stupid, he'd foul up a two-car funeral.'

Omar finally returned at dawn, drunk as a billy goat. He swayed into the house and vomited all over the bed.

It took him a couple of hours to sober up. 'I've done it, Larry,' he grinned. 'I'm a real man now.'

Unfortunately for him, Abu Khaled overheard him. There was the mother of all rows between Omar and the *zimmedar*. Teknikal told me later that Omar had had sex with a shepherd girl who was barely thirteen, and would now be punished with thirty days of *roza*. That meant no food for him from morning till evening.

Trouble was, for some reason Khaled figured I was in cahoots with Omar. So my food and drink was cut off as well.

The next day we began another journey, easily the most dangerous journey of my life, crossing from Indian Kashmir into Pakistani Kashmir. We travelled only by night and hid during the day. Teknikal guided us, wearing night-vision goggles. We followed him blindly across mountains and meadows, hills and trenches, freezing rivers and slick snow. We had to evade Indian mines, tracer flares and Indian border patrols. Mercifully, they had equipped me with Wellington boots, a waterproof jacket and even some woollen cloth to wrap around my calves as protection from frostbite.

A week later I found myself in a large green meadow in the middle of nowhere. Across the pasture stood an old two-storey wood-framed house with a black chimney. The paint was peeling, the beams looked cracked, but it was a whole lot better than that foxhole.

'This is our new home,' said Abu Khaled. 'We've reached Pakistan. Now there is no need to hide. No need to worry.'

But I had plenty of cause for worry. There was still no response to my kidnapping from the President and these guys were getting angrier and impatient. 'Let's give the Americans an ultimatum,' Khalid told Teknikal. 'Come on, pick a date.'

'How about 20 March, which is Milad al-Nabi?' Omar said.

'Too late,' said Khaled. 'I want something sooner.'

Teknikal looked at me. 'Why don't *you* pick a date, Mr Page?'

'March 17,' I said instantly.

'Any particular reason for choosing this date?'

'It's the birthday of someone very special.'

'Even that's too late. I pick 12 March,' said Khaled.

'Why?'

'That is my birthday.'

Pakistani Kashmir was exactly the same as Indian Kashmir – the same nomadic shepherds, the same wooden houses, the same food, the same weather. I spent the days waiting for some news from the President, and dreaming of Shabnam.

Before I knew it, it was 10 March. I asked Omar about the ultimatum. 'So what happens if you guys don't hear from my folks in the next two days?'

'Simple,' Omar said. 'We kill you.'

The guy was as subtle as a horse turd in the cream pitcher.

I couldn't sleep for the next two nights. Every time I tried to concentrate on something, a hooded gentleman with a scythe would come into my view. And I would begin shaking like a jackhammer.

To make matters worse, a blue norther arrived on 11 March, bringing with it screaming winds and more rain in one day than I had seen in the last five months. It was a real gulley-washer, with thunder and lightning. As sheets of rain struck the house, I thought of Mom. I thought of Mizz Henrietta Loretta. I thought about the Undertaker. About that freak April snow in Waco. I even thought of pa. But most of all I thought of a woman I had never even seen.

I woke up on 12 March and was told by Teknikal that there was still no word from the President. I was given a nice breakfast which I didn't touch, and then I was taken to Abu Khaled.

'Mr Page, looks like your people have decided to sacrifice you. Now you know why I call the Americans heartless. You better say your prayers.'

'Let me kill him, Boss,' Omar said, full of piss and vinegar. Ever since he bonked that girl he had become queer as a three-dollar bill.

'No, Chief, I will do it,' Teknikal said quietly.

I was ushered out of the house and taken to an open field which was slicker than owl shit with all that rain. Omar handed me a shovel. 'Come on, dig your grave, American pig,' he barked.

For half an hour I slaved over that trench, shovelling soil out of the hole in the ground that would be my final resting place. Finally, the grave was ready. The sun was halfway into the sky by then. A few birds chirped in the sunshine. It didn't look at all like someone was going to die.

Teknikal took out a black piece of cloth from his trousers. 'Would you like to be blindfolded?'

'No. I want to see what you guys are doing,' I said.

'Very brave, just like Saddam,' he mumbled. His AK-47 brushed against my leg. I was pretending to be brave, but inside I was shaking like a leaf.

They say when you're about to die your whole life flashes before your eyes. Well, that's not true, coz the only thing that flashed before my eyes was a crow, and an ugly one at that.

'Come on, just do it, Abu Teknikal,' Omar urged, looking at me through a video camera.

Abu Khaled recited a prayer in Arabic. For himself, or for me, I didn't know.

'Any last wish?' Teknikal asked me in a low voice. I knew he had grown fond of me, just as a family grows fond of a pet dog. But even pet dogs are put down when the time comes.

'Any last wish?' Teknikal repeated.

I thought about it. They wouldn't have any chocolate brownies in this hick town. That's when I noticed Teknikal had the sat-phone in his pocket. 'Can I make one phone call?' I asked.

'Who will you speak to?'

I first thought of calling Mom, but she would worry the warts off a frog and I didn't want to spoil her supper.

'There is only one person I would like to speak to before dying. The woman I love.'

'And who is she?'

'Her name is Shabnam Saxena.'

'Shabnam Saxena? The actress?' Omar suddenly became interested.

'Yeah. She is my fiancée. We were going to get married.'

'The bastard is lying, Abu Teknikal,' Omar shouted. 'There is no way he can know Shabnam Saxena.'

'I have her picture in my wallet, and also her mobile phone number,' I said.

'Let me check the bastard's wallet.' Omar ran to me and took out the wallet from my hip pocket.

I heard him whistle. 'The bastard wasn't lying. He does have Shabnam's picture.'

'Show me, show me,' Teknikal said and snatched the picture from Omar.

He whistled too. 'Oh my God! She is the most beautiful woman I have seen in my life.'

'Abu Teknikal, can I talk to her one last time?' I interjected.

Omar turned to Abu Khaled. 'Boss, the bitch wears very few clothes in her films. Very un-Islamic. Can I be in charge of the operation to kidnap her?'

'I want nothing to do with this woman.' Abu Khaled shook his head.

'Give me her number,' Teknikal said. 'I've got the Thuraya and I've put it on speakerphone.'

'No, I'll speak with her,' Omar said, and snatched the phone from Teknikal. He extracted a slip of paper from my wallet. 'I've got the bitch's number.'

He dialled the number and the call went through.

I was expecting the recorded voice to come on as usual when suddenly someone picked up the phone.

'Who is this?' I heard a woman's voice say. My heartbeat quickened.

'Do you know who you are talking to, bitch? This is Commander Abu Omar. Number five in Lashkar-e-Shahadat.'

'Excuse me?'

'You better watch out, bitch. You are doing obscene films and wearing skimpy clothes. We are going to kidnap you. Then we will torture you and kill you.'

'Is this some kind of joke?'

'No, Shabbo, this is not a joke.'

'Shabbo? You've got the wrong number.'

'Wrong number? You are not Shabnam Saxena? Then who are you?'

'This is Elizabeth Brookner, US Embassy.'

'Elizabeth Brookner?' asked Omar.

'Elizabeth Brookner?' asked Khaled. 'Who's she?'

'Chief, Elizabeth Brookner has been the CIA Station Chief in India since 2006,' Teknikal replied. 'A Summa Cum Laude from Stanford University, she joined the CIA in 1988 and has served in Ukraine, Jordan and Kuwait. She is an expert on Al Qaeda. Fuck!'

'This means this bastard has double-crossed us.' Khaled wagged a finger at me.

'Kill him. Just kill him!' Omar screamed.

'No, first we have to find out his connection to the CIA,' said Khaled.

So, for the next ten minutes, I had to explain how I happened to have Elizabeth Brookner's mobile number in my wallet. Then Khaled gave a signal and Teknikal put the AK-47 to my head. He was hiding his eyes, trying not to look at me. 'Don't worry,' he whispered. 'There will be no pain at all. It will be over in a second.'

Suddenly there came the sound of a giant flapping, a rat-a-tat-a-tat-a-tat-a.

'What in Allah's name is that?' asked Abu Khaled, pointing to a strange-looking object which appeared over the hill like a rising cloud.

'That, Chief, looks suspiciously like an MQ-1 Predator drone – that is, a medium-altitude, long-endurance unmanned aerial vehicle system, and what is worse, it is equipped with two laser-guided AGM-114 Hellfire missiles,' croaked Teknikal. 'The Brookner bitch has triangulated us. And even as I speak, the missiles have been fir—'

There was a flash of fire and a big explosion. The earth shook, something sharp hit my leg and I toppled into the trench. All the soil I had dug out fell in after me, almost burying me.

It took me nearly fifteen minutes to fight my way out of the grave. I came out choking and wheezing. There was mud in my ears, mud in my eyes, mud in my mouth. My left leg felt as if a chainsaw had run through it. There was a raw wound, an inch deep, just below my knee, from which blood was still dripping.

The area looked like it had been visited by the Terminator. The ground had been ploughed up, leaving craters the size of a bathroom.

Abu Khaled and Abu Omar had been blown to pieces. I saw a mangled hand here, a crumpled leg there.

Teknikal lay bleeding on the other side of the trench. I dragged myself to him and cradled his head in my lap. His chest was heaving and he was struggling for breath.

He looked up at me. 'Do you think they have broadband in heaven, Mr Page?' he asked, and his head lolled down and his eyes closed. He looked kind of dead to me.

I ran from the scene as fast as my one good leg could carry me. The wind whirled around, groaning and moaning like a woman in labour. I ran past mud houses and startled villagers. I scattered herds of goats and flocks of pigeons. I charged down a hill, came to a river and jumped in. On the other side of the river I found a gravel road. I was making progress. The road ended at what looked like some kind of warehouse. A rusted sign at the entrance said 'Hafiz Timber Exports, Keran'. I pushed open the metal doors of the warehouse. They were unlocked and I entered to find stacks of lumber, but not a soul around. 'Hello! Is anyone home?' I shouted, but only heard the echo of my voice. I ventured further and discovered chainsaws and machetes, axes and choppers. The floor was covered with dried grease and oil stains. I followed a trail of oil and came upon an extraordinary sight. A forklift stood in a corner of the warehouse. It was a Nissan Nomad AF30 and looked like it had diesel in the tank. I cranked the engine, and it worked! My spirits rose like a corncob in a cistern. Two minutes later I was driving down the gravel road, shouting 'Hee-haw!' and breaking every forklift speed record in the book. Those idiots at the Cisco Rodeo should have seen me go. I'd have shown them how a forklift with a maximum speed of 10.6 mph could do twenty without blowing the engine.

My leg was still bleeding, but in my excitement I had forgotten all about it. I just kept driving that forklift till I hit a T-junction. I had to decide whether to go left or right. I chose right, and just five minutes later ran into an army picket. Fifty Pakistani soldiers swarmed all over the forklift, cocked their rifles at me and told me to get down.

'Whoa, hold your horses, fellas, I surrender.' I put up my hands, stepped down from the hi-lo and fainted on the road.

I learnt later that I was taken to a town called Muzaffarabad and put in a military hospital. It took me a week to recover. In the meantime Mom called and blabbered something about the President having called her up, though she was more excited about being able to wear all the shoes she wanted for free coz she had just got married to Mr Hinson who owns the Fabulous Shoe Store in downtown Waco.

An officer called John Smith from the American Embassy over in Islamabad came to meet me, wearing a dark suit and dark shades. 'We know all about you, Mr Page,' he said. 'We've been trying to track you down for the past two months.'

'Well, here I am,' I said. 'What you gonna do? Put me in jail?'

'No, Sir, we are going to send you to New Delhi in a USAF plane. Your case officer is Miss Elizabeth Brookner. She will de-brief you.'

'Holy cow! You mean she'll take off my underwear?' I cried.

'No, Sir, that's just company slang for extracting humint,' John Smith said, making me even more confused.

Two days later, on 22 March, I was back at New Delhi airport.

It was a chilly morning, but Mizz Brookner was waiting for me, together with a stretch limo, right on the tarmac.

'It's an honour to welcome you back to New Delhi, Mr Page,' she said. 'You look different.' She was damned right. I had lost sixty pounds of fat since she last saw me. I looked leaner, trimmer and fitter.

'You sound different, too,' I replied.

'I have some good news and some bad news. Which do you want first?'

'I've had enough of bad news. Out with the good first.'

'Well, in recognition of your sterling role in the elimination of three dangerous terrorists, including one on our most-wanted list, on the recommendation of the Secretary of State and the Attorney General, you have been awarded fifteen million dollars under the Rewards for Justice programme. The cash is waiting for you at the Embassy. And it's all tax-free. Congratulations!'

It took me a minute to digest this info. 'Fifteen million dollars!' I couldn't believe my mouth. That jerk Abu Khaled wasn't boasting. 'Then what's the bad news?'

'An inter-agency process has determined that there may be continuing danger to your life from Al Qaeda and other terrorist elements. You are therefore required to accept our Witness Protection Programme and agree to relocation.'

'You mean just like in that flick *Eraser*?'

'Kind of. You will have to assume a new identity, a new name – even a new face, if you so wish.'

'I got no problem with that. To be honest, I never liked my name all that much. Can I look like Arnie Schwarzenegger?'

She smiled. 'That might take some doing. But do you have any ideas with regard to a new career? This is your chance to do what you've always wanted. With fifteen million, you can even retire on a ranch in Texas if you want.'

'Tell you what, I've always been fascinated by the Fibi guys.'

'Fibi? Oh, you mean FBI?'

'Yeah. I was there outside Mount Carmel in '93, when the Fibi guys were doing their siege of the loonies at the ranch.'

'Oh, the Branch Davidians? What were you doing there?'

'Mom thought my pa may have joined that Koresh dude, but he wasn't there.'

'So you want to be an FBI agent?'

'Yeah.'

'I'm sorry, Mr Page, but that's out of the question. To become an FBI agent you need a bachelor's degree and at least three years of related full-time work experience.'

'Do I also need a degree to become a Hollywood producer?'

'A Hollywood producer?'

'Yeah. Those guys who make movies.'

'I don't think so.'

'Then can I become one?'

Lizzie thought about it. 'That should be possible, I reckon. We could probably set you up within a week.'

'That would be just great. Then I can meet Arnie Schwarzenegger and Harrison Ford and—'

Lizzie cut me short. 'We'll talk about that when you come in for your de-brief. I've scheduled it for 15:00 hours at the Grinder.'

'Grinder? What's that?'

'That's company jargon for a secure room. Sensitive Compartmented Information Facility. Now get into the limo.'

Later that day I went to the Embassy and received my fifteen million dollars in a spanking new Samsonite suitcase, together with a thank-you letter from the President. I thought he lived in Washington, but he actually lived in a place called White House.

'Your wish has been granted, Larry,' Lizzie told me. 'Under the Witness Protection Programme, you will be relocated to Los Angeles, California. A production company called Sizzling Films has been registered in your name. A bucket squad of two undercover FBI agents will provide you round-the-clock surveillance and protection.'

'Well I'll be dipped! So when do I start meeting Brad Pitt and Julia Roberts?'

'Actually you won't.'

'I won't? Why?'

'Because Julia Roberts and Brad Pitt charge twenty million dollars per movie. So with fifteen million dollars you can forget about producing Hollywood blockbusters. We are therefore setting you up as a producer of, er . . . adult films.'

'You mean films with only adult actors?'

'No, it's a polite word for porn.'

'Oh no! What if my mom finds out?'

'She won't. We are giving you a completely new identity. Now tell me, how familiar are you with the adult film industry?'

'I don't know a thing. Mom would have killed me if she caught me watching that filth.'

'I thought so. That's why I got you their latest directory. It's the most comprehensive database of all actors and actresses working in the US porn industry. Study it, or you'll blow your cover.' Lizzie handed me a thick red book.

I flipped through the first few pages and suddenly stopped. Sandwiched between Busty Dusty and Honey Bunny was a handsome man wearing nothing but a cowboy hat. 'Oh my God!' I said.

Lizzie peered at the photo. 'It says he is called Big Dick Harry and he has been in the business since 1989. Do you know him?'

'Yeah,' I said, squirming like a worm in hot ashes. 'That's my pa!'

'Are you certain?'

'Well, he sure looks like my pa, only slightly older.'

'I'll put Langley on the job right away. We'll have positive ID within forty-eight hours. And here's your new passport.' Lizzie handed me an envelope.

I opened it and discovered that the passport belonged to a gentleman by the name of Mr Rick Myers. 'Hey, you got me the wrong passport,' I cried.

'No. That's your new name, Rick Myers,' said Lizzie. 'A private jet is standing by to fly you to the States. Is there anything you want to do before you leave India?'

'Well, there was one other thing . . .' I hesitated.

'Just tell me, and it will be done, Mr Myers.'

'I was wondering if I could meet the actress Shabnam Saxena just once before I go back.'

'That can be arranged.'

'She lives in Mumbai.'

'Well, tomorrow she'll be in Delhi.'

'How do you know that?'

'You are forgetting, Mr Myers, you're talking to the CIA Station Chief. It's my job to know. But the honest answer is that I've just been invited by an industrialist friend, Vicky Rai, to a party at his farmhouse in Mehrauli tomorrow night, and I am told this actress will be there. I have no interest in Bollywood and I was not planning on attending the party, but I can arrange for you to go.'

'Wow, that'll be great.'

'Good. But I want you to be very careful. Al Qaeda also has India in its sights. And as long as you're in India, you are my responsibility. I don't want to lose my jock-strap medals just because you fail to CYA – that's company code for Cover Your Ass. So here, take this gun.' She opened a drawer and drew out something long and mean. 'It's a Glock 23 with an Abraxas titanium suppressor. Standard supply to all FBI officers. A real hush puppy. Keep it with you at all times, even when you are sleeping.' She passed it to me, butt first. 'I presume, being from Texas, you know how to handle guns?'

'Oh yeah.' I waved my hand. 'I've been handling guns since I was seven.'

Lizzie was about to say something when her mobile rang. She listened and then swore. 'Shit!'

'What happened?' I asked.

'It's ears-only information. We inserted an indigenous for an over-the-fence op in Tibet. Now the plumbing's come unstuck and I have to arrange a nine-millimetre pension plan for the joker.'

'What kind of plan is that?'

'That's one plan you don't need in a hurry,' Lizzie laughed. 'It's Agency code for termination with extreme prejudice. Look, I have to leave right away. I'll get someone to escort you out.'

Lizzie took off faster than a prom dress, but no one came to take me. I waited for half an hour before walking out of the secure room on my own. I found myself in a beautiful garden. There was not a soul in sight. With fifteen million dollars in one hand and a gun in the other, I was a pig in clover. I'd been handling toy cowboy guns since I was seven, but this was the first time I had held a real gun in my hand. It was a mighty fancy piece, with a barrel as long as a dog's tail. I was fumbling with the magazine when suddenly there was a click and the dadgum gun recoiled in my hand like a startled mongoose. Little wisps of smoke were curling from the barrel. It seemed to have a mind of its own, so I locked it inside the Samsonite and strolled towards the exit.

There was a big black limo parked near the steps and a dude with white hair wearing a blue suit was lying face-down on the ground. The marines were all over him like flies on shit.

'What's the matter with him?' I asked a marine who was bending over the old guy.

'A sniper just tried to kill the Ambassador!' the marine screamed. 'Get down, get down!'

I hurried to the main gate, where a guard took back my visitor's badge and waved me through.

Once out on the road, I patted the Samsonite. If there were crazies roaming the city shooting people, I sure was glad to have some protection of my own. With Lizzie's gun, I'd tell the Al Qaeda dudes to KMRA – that's Page family jargon for Kiss My Royal American!

The Curse of the *Onkobowkwe*

THE TRIBAL from Little Andaman sat on tram number thirty plying between Kalighat and Howrah Bridge and felt the breeze caress his face.

It was nine thirty a.m. on 19 October. The air was pleasantly warm, the early-morning smog had lifted and the sky was without a cloud – a seamless expanse of blue broken only by the jagged pinnacles of the high-rises. The tepid sunlight tickled Eketi's skin. He inhaled the heavy, acrid smell of the city, spread his arms wide, threw back his head and revelled in the dazzling delight of being alive. As if on cue, two grey pigeons fluttered over his head in synchronized unison, sharing in the day's jubilation.

He was in Esplanade, the teeming heart of the metropolis, and everywhere he looked he saw people and more people. Children pointed at him excitedly, men simply gawked, and women drew their breath sharply and covered their mouths with their hands; he smiled and waved at them. All around the tram was a vortex of traffic – cars, taxis, rickshaws, scooters, cycles. Horns blared, honked, buzzed and screeched. Swarms of battered private buses hurtled along the road, with uniformed conductors hanging out from the side shouting destinations at the top of their voices. Garish advertisements for toothpaste and shampoo screamed for attention from huge billboards. The tall decadent buildings on either side of the road loomed like a range of ancient hills.

Eketi felt as if he was floating through a magnificent dream.

It was just over a fortnight since that fateful day when he had volunteered to recover the sacred rock stolen by Banerjee. The Elders had been taken by surprise by Ashok Rajput, the junior welfare officer, who had eavesdropped on their deliberations. They had been even more surprised by his willingness to take Eketi to India by ship and help recover the *ingetayi*. Under duress, they had grudgingly accepted his offer. Not only had he discovered their plans, he was the only one who knew Banerjee's address. But they had cautioned Eketi to be wary of him. The welfare officer was to be used to reach the sacred rock and then discarded like a pesky fly.

The preparations for the trip had taken more than a week. Ashok had to obtain leave from the Welfare Department. And Nokai, the medicine man, took his time putting together Eketi's 'survival kit' – tubers and strips of dried boar for eating, medicinal pellets for healing, lumps of red and white clay for body-painting, a pouch of pig fat for mixing the clay, and the pièce de résistance, the *chauga-ta*, a charm to ward off disease, made of the bones of the great Tomiti himself. Eketi had hidden all these in a black canvas bag – a fake Adidas he had picked up from Hut Bay – and covered them up with a few old clothes. Following a night of feasting and festivity, he had received a hero's send-off. The next day he had left Little Andaman with Ashok for Port Blair in a government speedboat. That same night he had been smuggled aboard *MV Jahangir*, a large passenger ship which sailed three times a month to Kolkata and whose captain was known to Ashok. The welfare officer had taken a deluxe cabin while Eketi had been dumped in a third-class bunk, to stay hidden from prying eyes in a cramped closet close to the engine room.

'Now remember,' Ashok had instructed Eketi, 'no one must find out that you are an Onge from Little Andaman. So you must keep your hair covered at all times with your cap and ensure that the jawbone around your neck is hidden underneath your T-shirt. If anyone asks, you should say that you are an *adivasi*, a tribal called Jiba Korwa from Jharkhand. Jharkhand is an Indian State which has many primitive tribes like yours. Understood? Now repeat your new name.'

'Eketi is Jiba Koba from Jakhan.'

'Idiot!' Ashok knocked him on the head. 'You need to say, "I am Jiba Korwa from Jharkhand." Now put on your cap and repeat after me twenty times.'

So Eketi had put on his red Gap cap and repeated his new name till he had memorized it.

The ship had completed its 1,255-kilometre journey in three days, arriving at the Kidderpore Dock in Kolkata the evening before. They had waited for all the passengers to leave and for night to fall. Then they had disembarked and taken a taxi.

No sooner had the taxi left the docks than the night sky had come alive with a brilliant display of fireworks. The ground shook with the sounds of exploding crackers. 'Are they welcoming me?' Eketi asked excitedly, but Ashok shushed him and tapped the driver's shoulder. 'How come you guys are celebrating Diwali twenty days before it is due?'

The driver laughed. 'What, you don't even know that you have arrived in Kolkata at the time of our biggest festival? Today is *Saptami*, tomorrow is *Mahashtami*.'

'Oh shit,' Ashok swore under his breath. 'I didn't realize we were landing here bang in the middle of *Durga Puja*.'

The city was indeed in the grip of *puja* fervour. There were magnificent *pandals* at virtually every street corner, glittering in the night like lighted palaces. Eketi sat in the front seat and gaped at the temporary temples of cloth and bamboo, each competing with the other in raucous gaudiness. Some had domes, some had minarets. One called to mind a South Indian temple tower, while another harked back to a Tibetan pagoda. There was one shaped like a Grecian amphitheatre and another which resembled an Italian palazzo. The approach to these *pandals* was lined with red carpets and lit with a series of illuminated panels.

The streets were full of people, more than Eketi had seen in his life, and the city was slick with sound. Loudspeakers boomed from every *pandal*. Drum beats reverberated from every corner, a primal call for the tribe to gather. And they gathered in their millions, in their starched saris and immaculately ironed shirts and trousers, converting the city into one giant carnival. The taxi was forced to take several detours as entire streets were blocked off by the police, who blared out cautionary instructions to pedestrians from their megaphones.

An hour and ten minutes later, the taxi stopped in Sudder Street, the backpacker ghetto full of mildewed hotels and decrepit shops selling food, souvenirs and internet access. Ashok checked into Milton Hotel, which had a strange atmosphere of gloomy decay. The manager looked suspiciously at Eketi and asked to see his passport. Ashok had to produce his government ID card to prevent further questioning.

They went through dimly lit corridors to a room on the first floor which was very basic, just two beds separated by a small table. In the harsh glare of the strip light, Eketi noticed damp patches on the walls and cobwebs in every corner. A dripping sound came from the adjoining toilet.

'Eketi doesn't like this hotel.' He curled up his nose.

Anger flared up on Ashok's face. 'What did you expect, darkie? That I'd put you up at the Oberoi? Even this dump is much better than your lousy huts. Now shut up and lie down on the floor.'

As Eketi looked on sullenly, the welfare officer enjoyed a meal of chicken curry and naan bread ordered from room service. Then he took out his lighter and lit up a cigarette.

The tribal eyed the open packet. 'Can Eketi also have one?'

Ashok raised his eyebrows. 'I thought you had vowed not to touch tobacco till you got the *ingetayi*?'

'Yes. But this is not my island. Here I can do as I please.'

'No, blackie,' Ashok sneered. 'Here you do as I please. Now go to sleep.'

Eketi lay down on the cold floor with the canvas bag as his pillow and chewed on a strip of dried boar. Soon he could hear Ashok's loud snores, but he found it difficult to sleep. The drumbeats appeared to be coming closer, making the wooden floor tremble. He got up and sat by the open window, watching the glow of a *pandal* in the far distance, observing the junkies and the dogs sheltering under the awnings in the street, breathing in the air of this vast and mysterious city, feeling a frisson of guilty pleasure.

The next morning he tagged along with Ashok, who was going for a walking tour of the area around the hotel. In the next two hours, he saw the white-domed Birla Planetarium, the impregnable brick-and-mortar octagon of Fort William, and the verdant green Maidan, full of gardens, fountains and memorials. He saw men exercising with huge weights, running, skipping, and walking with dogs. He smiled when he came across a group which was standing in a circle and simply laughing, and fell silent upon seeing the grandiose baroque of the Victoria Memorial, its white marble shading pink under the nascent sun. It was the biggest building he had seen in his life and the most beautiful. He shivered with the thrill of discovery.

They continued to walk, passing the tall Shaheed Minar column tower at the northern end of the Maidan, and ended up in Esplanade. The relentless bustle of thousands on the move, the high-rise buildings, the cacophony of sounds thrilled and amazed Eketi. He was especially fascinated by the sonorous trams, moving at a leisurely pace in the middle of the road. 'Can Eketi ride one?' He tugged at Ashok's sleeve and the welfare officer grudgingly relented. They boarded the next tram that came along. It was moderately crowded and they managed to squeeze themselves in. But at the very next stop a throng of commuters charged on and the tram became choked to the gills. Eketi got separated from Ashok and found himself trapped between two executives with briefcases in their hands. The crush of people was unbearable. Eketi began to feel suffocated. Fighting for breath, he dropped down and began burrowing through the legs of passengers, inching towards the rear exit. Managing eventually to reach the door, he swung himself out through the metal railing, used the open window as a ledge and nimbly hoisted himself over the top. Now he sat on the roof of the tram, just below the overhead electricity cable, with his black canvas bag beside him, and felt the liberating rush of a bird released from its cage.

The tram moved into Dalhousie Square, now known as BBD Bagh, the administrative epicentre of the city, and that is where his journey ended. A traffic constable on duty gaped at him in amazement, then ran in front of the tram and brought it to a jerky halt.

Inside the crowded tram Ashok Rajput had finally managed to find a seat. He wiped the sweat and grime from his forehead, looked distastefully at the seething mass of humanity swirling around him and wondered whether this would be his last journey by public transport. Kolkata, he had concluded, did not suit him. There was something about the air of the city – it congealed at the back of the throat like phlegm. And the snarling traffic, the sickly beggars, the filthy streets did not help matters. By this evening, if all went well, he would have the sacred rock in his hands.

He had done considerable research on the *ingetayi*. It was reputed to be a piece of black sandstone, approximately thirty inches tall, shaped like a phallus and carved with indecipherable hieroglyphics, dating back at least seventy thousand years. He would get Eketi to steal it from Banerjee. Then he would get an exact replica made from a sculptor he knew in Jaisalmer. Eketi would then be quietly sent back with the replica to his hell hole on Little Andaman, and he would sell the original to Khosla Antiques, who had already agreed to pay him eighteen lakh rupees for the oldest engraved *shivling* in the world.

Ashok Rajput thought of all the things he would do once he got the money. First of all, he would go to see Gulabo. He had taken up the demeaning job of junior welfare officer on that far-away island, cut off from civilization, only to spite her for turning him down. He had not visited her in five years, though he had continued to send her money orders for two thousand rupees a month to pay for Rahul's education. But he had been unable to forget her. Gulabo called out to him over the expanse of all those thousands of kilometres of land and sea separating Rajasthan from the Andamans, invaded his dreams, still made him hot and furious with longing.

Now he would go to Jaisalmer, shower her with wads of thousand-rupee notes and taunt her, 'You always called me a good for nothing. Well, what do you say now?' And then he would propose to her again. He was quietly confident she would accept him this time. Without any preconditions. He would give up his third-rate job dealing with wretched tribals in the middle of nowhere and settle down in Rajasthan. The *ingetayi* was the ultimate good-luck charm and it would change his life for ever.

He was jolted out of his reverie by the tram suddenly screeching to a halt.

'*Korchen ta ki?*' the cop barked, pointing a finger at Eketi and gesturing him to get down. '*Namun dada namun.*'

As soon as Eketi descended from the roof, the tram conductor confronted him. 'Did you want to commit suicide? *Ticket kothai?*'

The passengers craned their necks out of the windows to stare at him.

'*Nam ki?*' the constable demanded.

Eketi simply shook his head.

'This fellow is not Indian,' the conductor declared. 'See how black he is. He looks African to me. Let's check inside his bag. He must be a drug-dealer.' He tried to pull the canvas bag from Eketi's shoulder.

'No!' Eketi cried and pushed the conductor away.

The constable caught his ear and twisted it. 'Do you have a ticket?'

'Yes,' Eketi replied.

'Then where is it?'

'With Ashok Sahib.'

'And where is this Ashok?'

Eketi pointed towards the tram.

'I don't see any Ashok,' the constable said as he caught Eketi by the scruff of his neck. 'You'd better come with me to the police station, where we shall check what you have in your bag.'

He was about to drag Eketi over to the other side of the road when Ashok finally managed to extricate himself from the tram and came running towards the cop. 'Excuse me, Officer,' the welfare officer wheezed. 'This fellow is with me. I have his ticket.' He produced two tickets from his breast pocket.

The constable snatched the tickets and scrutinized them. With great reluctance, he let go of Eketi.

The moment they were out of earshot of the constable, Ashok delivered a stinging slap on the tribal's cheek. 'Now listen, you black swine,' he fumed. 'You pull another stunt like this and I'll let you rot in jail for the rest of your life. This is India, not your jungle where you can do as you please.'

Eketi glared at him and said nothing.

They returned to the hotel and had a light lunch. At around six p.m. Ashok decided to check out Banerjee's house.

They hailed an auto-rickshaw and Ashok gave the driver the address from a slip of paper in his wallet. 'Take us to Tollygunge. At the corner of Indrani Park and JM Road.'

The auto-rickshaw took them through quiet back lanes to avoid the mad rush of shoppers on the main streets. They alighted at the corner of Indrani Park and discovered the pond they were looking for almost immediately. It was little more than a depression in the ground, full of dirty monsoon water and edged with decaying reeds. But it was ringed by five houses, and the one on the extreme right had a bright-green roof.

'Banerjee's house!' Eketi exclaimed.

It was a typical middle-class residence, modest and undistinguished. Made of brick, it had a small garden surrounded by a wooden fence. The nameplate on the rickety gate said 'S. K. Banerjee'.

'Should Eketi go in and get the *ingetayi*?' the tribal asked.

'Do you think you can just enter the house and ask Banerjee for the sea-rock?' Ashok scoffed. 'He stole it from you, now you will have to steal it from him.'

'How will Eketi do that?'

'That is something I will have to figure out.'

For the next hour, they cautiously surveyed the house from all possible angles, looking for an open window or back door. Ashok couldn't find any obvious vulnerability.

'Eketi knows how to go inside,' the tribal declared suddenly.

'How?'

'Through that.' Eketi pointed to a blackish-green chimney on the roof.

'Don't be foolish. You'll never be able to climb that roof, let alone get inside that narrow chimney.'

'Eketi will,' he declared confidently. 'I can show you right now.' He was about to jump over the fence when Ashok caught his shoulder. 'No, no, you idiot. You cannot break into someone's house in broad daylight. You have to wait for Banerjee and his neighbours to go to sleep.'

They killed time by browsing at the many roadside market stalls which had sprouted in Tollygunge during the *puja* season. After a late dinner of appetizing fish curry and rice, they returned to Banerjee's house.

The area around the pond was quiet. The lights in the neighbouring houses had been switched off, but a single striplight still glowed inside Banerjee's house.

They waited under the awning of a milk booth till the striplight was extinguished just after midnight. Eketi instantly zipped open his bag and took out lumps of red and white clay, together with the pouch of pig fat. He removed his cap and began stripping off his clothes. 'What are you doing?' Ashok asked in alarm.

'Eketi is preparing for taking the *ingetayi*. Onge have to show it proper respect.'

He disappeared behind the booth and emerged half an hour later wearing only a genital pouch and the jawbone around his neck. There were horizontal stripes of red and white across his face and a delicate white herringbone design along the middle of his chest and abdomen. He looked like a trick of the night.

'I hope no one sees you like this. Even I am getting the jitters.'

Ashok pretended to shiver and squinted at his watch. 'It is almost one o'clock now. Time for you to climb that roof.'

Without a word, Eketi loped off towards Banerjee's house.

He jumped over the wooden railing around the house effortlessly and clambered on to the roof with the nimbleness of a monkey, his bare feet making no sound. The chimney was quite narrow, but by twisting his body he managed to lower himself inside it, black soot coming off on his hands like powder. Through the strategic placement of hands and legs, the tribal climbed down the chimney and landed on the kitchen counter with a little thud.

It took him only a few seconds to get used to the pitch darkness. He opened the kitchen door and stepped into a gallery. There were three doors to his left. He entered the first one. It was an empty bathroom and there was no sign of the sacred rock in it. He tiptoed out and tried the second door. It was unlocked, but the moment he stepped inside a switch flicked on and his eyes were dazzled with light. He saw a bespectacled old man sitting on the bed, wearing light-blue pyjamas.

'Come in, I've been expecting you,' Banerjee said in Onge, his voice deadpan.

'Where is our *ingetayi*?' Eketi demanded.

'I will tell you. But first tell me who you are. I know you people can travel out of your bodies. Are you real or are you just a shadow?'

'What difference does it make?'

'You are right,' he said morosely. 'Even dreams can kill. So are you going to kill me for stealing your sacred rock?'

'Onge people are not like Jarawas. Eketi has come only for the stone. Where is it?'

'It is no longer with me. I got rid of it ten days ago.'

'*Onerta*? Why?'

'Because it is cursed, isn't it? I should have known. It took away my son, my only son.' Banerjee's voice broke.

'What happened?'

'He was studying in America. Two weeks ago, he died in a freak road accident. I know I am to blame. If only I had not taken your *ingetayi*, Ananda would have been alive,' Banerjee sobbed.

'Who has it now?'

'I will tell you, but on one condition.'

'What?'

'You have to tell me how to bring a dead person back to life.'

Eketi shook his head. 'Even Nokai cannot do that. No one can challenge the will of Puluga.'

'Please, I beg you. My wife is going insane grieving over our son. I cannot continue like this any more,' Banerjee cried with folded hands.

'It is the curse of the *onkobowkwe*. You have invited it upon yourself,' Eketi shrugged. 'Now tell me who has the *ingetayi*.'

'No,' Banerjee said with sudden fierceness. 'If you cannot bring my son back to life, then you are not getting your *ingetayi* either.' With the speed of a cat, he jumped off the bed, darted out of the door and locked himself inside the bathroom.

'Open up.' Eketi banged at the door, but Banerjee refused to open it. Seething with frustration, the tribal made a thorough search of all the other rooms in the house, damaging a couple of cupboards and breaking some porcelain idols in the process, but did not find the sacred rock. In Banerjee's bedroom, however, he discovered a black leather wallet lying on the bedside table. He grabbed it, walked to the front door, undid the latch and let himself out into the garden.

Two minutes later he was back at the milk booth.

'What happened? I saw a light come on. Is everything all right?' Ashok asked breathlessly.

'Yes.'

'But where is the sacred rock?'

'It is not in the house.'

'Not in the house? That means Banerjee must have sold it. Did he give any clue?'

'No. But I brought you this.' Eketi handed over the leather wallet. Ashok flipped it open. There was very little cash inside, but he whistled as he extracted a business card. 'Calcutta Antique Traders,' it said. 'Prop. Sanjeev Kaul. 18B, Park Street, Kolkata 700016.'

'I bet you Banerjee has sold the *ingetayi* to this dealer,' Ashok declared.

'So how do we get it from him?'

'I will pay him a visit tomorrow.'

'But how do we go back to the hotel? Will we find a taxi now?'

No sooner had the tribal said this than an auto-rickshaw spluttered to life in a nearby alley. They ran towards it. 'Will you take us to Sudder Street?' Ashok asked the driver, a middle-aged man who reeked of alcohol.

The driver looked at him with large eyes, then looked at Eketi, and ran screaming from his vehicle.

Park Street was a modern, upmarket shopping area, full of designer clothes shops and trendy boutiques. Calcutta Antiques turned out to be a fairly big establishment next to a fancy Continental restaurant. Ashok Rajput entered through an ornate brass door to find extensive repair work being done inside the shop. The ceiling was blackened with soot and there was a strong smell of charring. A tall, fair man with an overly long nose looked at him enquiringly.

'What happened here?' Ashok asked.

'We had a devastating fire three days ago. Half our shop burned down. We lost a lot of antiques, but luckily no one was injured.'

'Are you Mr Sanjeev Kaul?'

'Yes. What can I do for you?'

'My name is Ashok Rajput. I am with the Tribal Welfare Agency in the Andamans,' he declared in an officious tone and produced his laminated ID card. 'I am here in connection with the theft of an ancient stone artefact belonging to the Onge tribe. Did Mr S. K. Banerjee sell a *shivling* to you?'

'Yes. About ten days ago.'

'Do you realize, Mr Kaul, that you are in violation of the Antiquities and Art Treasures Act 1972?'

'Banerjee did not tell me that it was an antiquity from the Andamans.' Kaul frowned. 'Look, I was not aware I was breaking any law. I thought it was just an old rock .'

'I would like to see it.'

'I am sorry, it is no longer with me. Last Monday I sold it to a client of mine from Chennai.'

'Chennai?'

'Yes.'

'Oh no!' said Ashok and balled his hands into fists. 'I want full details of this person to whom you sold the stone.'

Ten minutes later he emerged from the showroom with a slip of paper bearing yet another address. When he returned to the hotel room, Eketi was still sleeping.

'Get up, you bastard, and start packing,' he said.

'Where are we going now?'

'To Chennai,' Ashok replied. 'To meet one Mr S. P. Rajagopal.'

'And how will we go?'

'By train.'

Howrah station was busier than usual because of the festive season. Eketi gazed at the chaos on the platforms, the rows of passengers sprawled on the cold floor, the shrill vendors selling magazines and sodas, and especially the porters in red, their heads loaded with suitcases and boxes. He observed the sweat pouring down their faces and turned to Ashok. 'Why do you people work so hard?'

'Because we don't get free meals like your tribe,' Ashok said scornfully. 'Do you know how much these tickets to Chennai have cost me? This trip is becoming a nightmare.'

'But Eketi is loving it!'

As the train came hurtling towards the platform, Eketi tightened up in alarm. He cowered behind Ashok for a few moments before gingerly stepping inside the sleeper compartment. Women shrank back as soon as he entered, and clutched their handbags nervously. Children looked at him in fear and receded into their fathers. Eketi smiled. A dazzling, pearl-white smile. The train relaxed.

He grabbed a seat next to the window and didn't budge from it throughout the twenty-seven-hour journey, feeling the sun in his eyes, the wind in his face, watching the changing kaleidoscope of colours as dull brown cornfields gave way to lush green rice fields, marvelling at the vastness of this country where you could travel for hours, passing village after village, and still not reach your destination. As day dimmed to night, the relentless rhythm of the train became a lullaby which gently rocked him to sleep.

Everything was different about Chennai. The weather was hotter than Kolkata and more humid. The men were swarthier and wore moustaches. The women were dressed in colourful saris and had flowers in their hair. No one spoke Hindi.

As soon as they left the brick-red Gothic structure of Chennai Central, the tribal sniffed the air. The north-east monsoon was still active and the aroma of rain hung in the air like a moist perfume. 'Does this place have a sea?'

'Yes. How do you know?' asked Ashok.

'Eketi can smell it.'

They boarded one of the ubiquitous yellow-and-black auto-rickshaws and Ashok told the driver to take them straight to Rajagopal's residence on Sterling Road in Nungambakkam. As they entered the swirl of traffic outside the station, Eketi looked in wide-eyed wonderment at the imposing buildings and elegant showrooms lining the crowded boulevard. The city was full of hoardings, advertising the latest Tamil blockbusters, but what fascinated him most were the giant plywood images of politicians and film stars dotting the streets, some as tall as two-storey buildings. Chennai was a cut-out city. A giant smiling woman in a sari competed for votes with an old man in dark glasses. Lusty-eyed heroines and moustachioed heroes with exaggerated hair-dos towered over the traffic like colossi.

Sterling Road was a busy thoroughfare, full of commercial establishments, banks and offices, interspersed with large houses. The auto-rickshaw dropped them off directly in front of Rajagopal's residence, which was an elegant green-and-yellow-painted villa. Two uniformed guards stood impassively on duty on either side of the high metal gates, which for some reason were open.

'Have you come for the prayer meeting?' a guard asked Ashok.

The welfare officer nodded blankly.

'Please go inside. It is in the main drawing room.'

'You wait here,' Ashok instructed Eketi, and entered the gate. He went along a curved driveway with well-kept lawns on both sides. The house had a solid teak door which was also open, and he stepped into a large drawing room from which all furniture had been removed. There were white sheets on the floor on which approximately fifty people were seated, mostly wearing light-coloured clothes. Men sat on one side and women on the other. At the far end was a large framed picture of a young man with a crew-cut and a thick moustache, which was decorated with a garland of red roses. Incense sticks burnt in front of the picture, the smoke curling upwards in thin wisps. A good-looking, slightly overweight woman in her early thirties sat beside the picture. Clad in a plain white cotton sari with no frills and no ornaments, she looked every inch the grieving widow.

Ashok sat down in the last row of the men's section and put on a suitably solemn expression. Through discreet questioning of the other mourners he learnt that this was a condolence meeting for the industrialist Selvam Palani Rajagopal – known to friends as SP – who had died of a heart attack two days ago, caused by a sudden and unexpected business loss.

Ashok waited two hours for the assembly to be over. After the last of the mourners had left, he went up to the widow and folded his hands. 'My name is Amit Arora. So sorry to hear about SP's death, Bhabhiji, so sorry,' he mumbled. 'It is hard to imagine that a man of thirty-five can suffer a heart attack. I met him just ten days ago in Kolkata.'

'Yes. My husband had a lot of business in Kolkata,' she replied. 'How did you know Raja?' There was a strangled quality to her voice which he found oddly erotic.

'He was my senior in IIT Madras.'

'Oh, so you are also an alumni of IIT-M? It's strange Raja never mentioned you.'

'We sort of lost touch after graduation. You know how these things happen.' He spread his hands and fell silent. Somewhere inside the house a pressure cooker whistled.

'So are you also living in Chennai?' Mrs Rajagopal enquired. 'There are not too many North Indians here.'

'No. I now live in Kolkata. I left Chennai soon after graduating.'

A maid brought him tea in a bone-china cup.

'If you don't mind, there is one thing I wanted to ask you, Bhabhiji,' Ashok said in the oily tone of someone bringing up a delicate subject.

'Yes?' she responded warily.

'SP told me he had bought a *shivling* from an antique dealer in Kolkata. Can I see it?'

'Oh, that *shivling*? *Adu Poyiduthu!* It's gone. It is now with Guruji.'

'Guruji? Who is he?'

'Swami Haridas. Raja was his disciple for the past six years. Guruji came for the funeral yesterday. He saw the *shivling* and asked if he could have it. So I gave it to him. Now that Raja is gone, what would I have done with it?'

'Can you tell me where Guruji lives? Is it close by?'

'He lives in Mathura.'

'Mathura? You mean Mathura in Uttar Pradesh?'

'Yes. That is where he has an ashram. But he has branches all over India.'

Ashok slumped back. 'So now I will have to travel all the way to Uttar Pradesh!'

'Why? What is your interest in that *shivling*?'

'It is rather complicated . . . Can you give me Swamiji's telephone number in Mathura?'

'Actually Guruji is not in Mathura now.'

'Then where is he?'

'He has gone on a world tour. Yesterday he left Madras

for Singapore. From there he will go to America, then Europe.'

'So when will he return to Mathura?'

'He will only return after two to three months.'

'Two to three months?'

'Yes. Your best chance of finding him will be at the Magh Mela in Allahabad in January next year. He told me he would be going there for discourses.'

'Thank you, Bhabhiji. Take care. I shall be in touch,' Ashok said, trying to mask the disappointment in his voice, and took his leave.

Eketi was still sitting on the kerb outside the entrance when Ashok emerged from the gates. 'What took you so long?' He looked quizzically at Ashok.

'The sea-rock has eluded us once again. Worse, it has left the country,' Ashok said dejectedly. 'It will come back only after three months. So I am taking you back to the island.'

'Back to the island?' Eketi sprang up in alarm. 'But you promised that we would return with the *ingetayi*.'

'I know. But what will I do with you for three months? I don't want to get into trouble with the Welfare Department.'

'But Eketi doesn't want to return to the island.'

Ashok looked at him sharply. 'Are you out of your bloody mind? Why don't you want to return?'

'What is there to return to? Eketi was trapped on that island, suffocated by it,' the Onge cried. 'I would look at the pictures of India in the book they gave us in school and dream about them. I observed the big ships crossing the ocean and wondered where they went to. I used to see the foreigners arrive with their cameras to gawk at us, and my mind used to go crazy. I felt like jumping into their boats and just going somewhere. Anywhere. That is why I came here. To escape from the island. And Eketi is not going back.'

'Is that why you volunteered to recover that rock?'

'Yes. Eketi wanted to come to India.'

'And you have no concern about what will happen to your tribe if they don't get that sacred rock back?'

'Eketi will help you recover the *ingetayi*. Then you can take it back, and Eketi will remain behind in your wonderful country.'

'So this was all part of a devious plan, eh? And have you thought of what you will do here?'

'Eketi will get married. Back home, old people marry all the young girls. I had no hope of finding a wife if I stayed on the island. Here I can have a new life. Get a wife.'

'This takes the biscuit.' The welfare officer gave a sardonic laugh. 'You really think that a worthless idiot like you will get a wife here? Have you taken a look at yourself in the mirror? Who will marry a black midget like you?'

'Leave that to Puluga,' Eketi said petulantly.

Ashok's demeanour suddenly changed. 'Look, you bastard. This is not a tourist excursion I brought you on. You came to get the *ingetayi*. We didn't find it. So you must go back to Little Andaman. Tomorrow the *Nancowry* will sail for Port Blair from here, and you will be on that ship with me. I've had enough of your nonsense. Now come with me, we have to find a hotel for the night.'

Ashok flagged down an auto-rickshaw, but the tribal refused to board it. 'Eketi will not go,' he said adamantly.

'Don't force me to hit you, blackie.' Ashok raised his hand.

'Eketi will not go even if you hit him.'

'Then should I call the police? Do you know that any tribal caught outside his reserve can be jailed immediately?'

Eketi's eyes flickered with fear, and Ashok pressed home his advantage. 'Now get in, you bastard,' he said through clenched teeth and pushed the tribal into the auto-rickshaw.

'Take us to Egmore,' he instructed the driver.

As they drove through the mid-afternoon traffic, the tribal sat in tense anticipation, like a sprinter crouching at the start line. His pulse quickened when the auto-rickshaw approached a busy intersection. The moment it stopped at the traffic light, he leapt out with his black canvas bag. Ashok could only watch, flabbergasted and helpless, as he dashed through the maze of cars, buses, scooters and rickshaws, and soon disappeared from the welfare officer's view.

He ran for a long time, dodging carts and cows, darting through empty playgrounds and passing jam-packed cinema halls. Finally he stopped to catch his breath in front of a cycle repair shop. Stooped on his haunches, he drew in a lungful of air and then took a good look at his surroundings. The cycle shop was situated in the middle of a bustling market. In the distance he could see a traffic island with a big statue in the centre. For a long time he stood at the edge of the road, inhaling the noxious fumes from passing trucks and cars, listening to the din that radiated from the crossing, feeling increasingly like a lost boy in a crowd of strangers. He was also beginning to feel hungry. That is when he noticed a tall man standing on the opposite side of the road, wearing fashionable dark glasses, a loose white linen shirt and grey trousers. He was leaning casually against the metal railing of a bus shelter and smoking a cigarette. Like him, the stranger also had small knots of closely coiled hair. But what drew him to the man was the colour of his skin, almost as jet black as his.

Eketi crossed the road and moved towards the bus shelter. The stranger noticed him almost immediately and quickly crushed the cigarette under the heel of his shoe.

'Who do we have here? An African brother!' he exclaimed.

Eketi gave him a nervous smile.

'And where might you be from, my brother? Senegal? Togo? *Parlez-vous français?*'

Eketi shrugged his shoulders and the stranger tried again. 'Then you must be from Kenya. *Ninaweza kusema Kiswahili.*'

Eketi shook his head. 'Myself called Jiba Korwa from Jharkhand,' he said.

'Oh! So you are Indian? How wonderful.' The stranger clapped his hands. 'Do you speak Hindi?'

Eketi nodded.

'I speak eight languages, and your language is one of them,' he said in perfect Hindi. 'I studied in Patna University,' he added by way of explanation.

'What is your name?' Eketi asked.

'Michael Busari at your service, from the great city of Abuja in Nigeria. My friends call me Mike.'

At that very moment a policeman rode past on his motorcycle and Eketi instinctively ducked behind the bus shelter. He continued to skulk even after the cop had crossed the intersection.

Mike patted him on the shoulder. 'I can see that you are in some sort of trouble, brother. The world is not a good place, especially for black people. But fear not, now I shall protect you.'

There was something deeply reassuring about the Nigerian's manner, which appealed immediately to Eketi. 'Do you know this city well?' he asked.

'Not really, brother. I've lived mostly in North India. But I know enough about Chennai to guide you.'

'I am hungry,' Eketi said. 'Can you give me something to eat?'

'I was going to have lunch myself. What would you like to eat?'

'Do they have pig meat here?'

'Pork, eh? I can arrange that for dinner. But for lunch let's go to McDonald's.'

'What's that?'

'You've never tasted a Big Mac? Then come, brother, allow me to introduce you to the wonderful world of junk food.'

Mike led the way to a nearby McDonald's where he bought Eketi a full-size meal and an ice-cream cone. As the tribal polished off a juicy burger, Mike draped his arm across Eketi's shoulder. 'Now tell me, my friend, what have you done? Have you killed someone?'

'No,' said Eketi, munching on his French fries.

'Then you must have robbed someone?'

'No,' said Eketi and slurped his Coke. 'I have only run away from Ashok.'

'Ashok? Now who is this Ashok?'

'*Kujelli!*' said Eketi and bit his lip. 'He is a bad man who was troubling me.'

'Oh, so he was your employer? And you got fed up of him and ran away from your village?'

'Yes, yes,' Eketi nodded eagerly, beginning on the ice cream.

'But how did you land up in Chennai, brother? That's a long way from Jharkhand.'

'Ashok brought me here for some work. I don't know what,' said Eketi and gave a satisfied burp.

'If you are on the run, I'm presuming you don't have a place to stay. Is that right?' Mike asked.

'Yes. I don't have a house here.'

'No problem. I shall take care of that as well. Come, let me take you to my pad.'

They boarded a garish green MTC bus for T. Nagar, where the Nigerian rented a modest two-room house. Mike took Eketi inside and pointed to an oversized sofa in the drawing room. 'You can sleep on that. Now get some rest while I nip across to buy provisions for dinner.'

Mike had taken off his dark glasses and for the first time Eketi saw the Nigerian's eyes. They were cold and emotionless, but the tribal was reassured by his smile, which was full of warmth and friendship. Mike was also an excellent cook and his dinner of lentil soup and spicy pork sausages had Eketi licking his fingers.

Lying on the sofa that night, feeling sated and safe, the Onge thanked Puluga for the kindness of strangers. And the tastiness of pork.

Michael Busari loved to talk. And even though he addressed Eketi while he was speaking, the tribal felt he was talking to himself. Through these monologues, Eketi learnt that Mike had been living in India for the past seven years. He said he was a businessman with several ventures and had come to Chennai a week ago to conclude a transaction with a jewellery merchant by the name of J. D. Munusamy. 'This is where I might need your help, brother.' He patted Eketi on the knee.

'What kind of help?'

'I have persuaded Mr Munusamy to make a major investment in the Nigerian oil industry. It is a venture which will bring him a very hefty profit. As the middleman, I am entitled to my commission. Munusamy was to have transferred one hundred thousand dollars to my bank account, but at the last minute he said he would give me cash. I want you to collect that cash on my behalf from his house. Can you do this little job for your brother?'

'For you I can even give my life,' Eketi said and hugged Mike.

'Good. Then you shall have an appointment with Mr Munusamy at nine p.m. on 26 October – that's two days from now. Till then relax, enjoy, eat, drink.'

Eketi took that advice to heart, spending the rest of the day lazing in the house, watching television and gorging on pork sausages. In the evening he requested Mike to take him to the beach, and the Nigerian obliged.

They went through the clogged artery of Mount Road with its gleaming skyscrapers and neon-lit shopping plazas. Eketi became delirious as the MTC bus entered the narrow alleys of Triplicane, full of old houses and ancient temples, and the heavy smell of salt entered his nostrils. He craned his neck to catch a glimpse of the sea, and lost all interest in the impressive statues and imposing memorials lining the promenade.

He was the first passenger to jump out of the bus the moment it stopped at Marina Beach. Even at this time of night the beach was quite crowded. Several families relaxed on the sand, eating their dinner. Children rode horseback, squealing with delight, while their mothers shopped for trinkets in lantern-lit shops. The swirling beam of a lighthouse sent glitter across the ocean's surface. The lights of a distant ship twinkled in the night as the foamy waves rolled gently on to the shore. Eketi inhaled the tangy air of the ocean, redolent of salt and fish, and from that single smell a whole island rose in his memory. He waved at Mike, still a good hundred metres behind him, and began wading into the water fully clothed.

'Jiba! Jiba! Come back!' Mike shouted, but the tribal was already well out to sea and swimming farther away.

He emerged from the ocean twenty minutes later, his skin glistening with tiny pearls of water, seaweed clinging to his clothes, sand dripping from the hole in his cap.

'You had me worried sick,' Mike grumbled.

'I thought I would take a bath,' he grinned.

'And what's that you are hiding?'

Eketi brought out his right hand from behind his back. 'Dinner!' he declared, holding up a large fluttering fish.

Mike bought two cans of Coke, Eketi lit a fire, and they shared a tasty meal of roasted fish.

'So how are you liking Chennai, brother?' Mike asked.

'I am loving it!' Eketi gushed. 'I am going mad with all the sounds, colours and lights of this wonderful world.' He took another swig from the Coke can, poked at the dying embers with a stick, and looked at the Nigerian intently. 'You are the nicest and kindest man I have met.'

'We are brothers, my friend, you and I.'

'Can you also help me find a wife?'

'A wife? Of course. Once you do that little job for me, I will have a dozen girls lined up for you to choose from.'

Mike's promise was enough to make Eketi approach the operation to collect money from the jewellery merchant with the pleasurable anticipation of a pig hunt. He was in unusually high spirits as Mike took him to Guindy, in the south-western part of the city.

Munusamy's house was deep inside a residential block and there was a hushed stillness in the area compared to the kinetic bustle of the main streets. A pallid streetlamp cast intriguing shadows on a row of duplex apartments lining both sides of the road.

Mike pointed out Munusamy's house, Number Thirty-Six, which had a carved wooden door. 'I will be waiting for you just around the corner,' he whispered to Eketi and handed him a small envelope. 'Give this to Munusamy. I have explained everything in this note, so you won't have to open your mouth. Best of luck.'

The Nigerian receded into the shadows and Eketi advanced towards Munusamy's door. A servant was expecting him. He led Eketi up a flight of steps and showed him into a drawing room where a balding, middle-aged man was seated on a cream sofa. Mr Munusamy wore a white shirt over a cream-coloured *veshti*. He had a round face dominated by two features: a small rectangular moustache which looked like hair jutting out of his nose, and three horizontal lines of yellow clay on his forehead.

'Welcome, welcome,' he greeted Eketi.

Eketi bowed and handed over the envelope.

Munusamy quickly read Mike's note and looked at the tribal with a crestfallen expression. 'I was looking forward to meeting the great Michael Busari, but it turns out you are just his agent.'

'Give me money,' Eketi said.

'Here it is,' said Munusamy and pulled out a small briefcase which he had neatly concealed behind his legs.

As Eketi bent down to pick up the briefcase, a flashbulb popped in his face with the suddenness of lightning. Almost simultaneously five policemen rushed into the room from various doors and pounced on him.

'You are under arrest,' an Inspector announced.

Before he could comprehend what was happening, he was handcuffed and bundled into a police van.

At the police station, a decrepit-looking building with a shingle roof, he was thrown inside a large cell. He protested his innocence in broken English, and tried to plead with the constables, but they threatened him with sticks. So he curled up on the cement floor and waited for Mike to show up. He was confident his friend would explain everything and have him released from the lock-up before long.

The police station remained a hive of activity all through the night. First to be brought in was a tough-looking hoodlum dressed in a brown leather jacket. Then came a drunk. He swayed into the lock-up and crashed down senseless on the floor. Finally two young boys, no more than sixteen, were dragged inside and mercilessly beaten up by the constables. With each passing hour a sinking dread spread in Eketi's stomach.

Mike didn't turn up even by noon the next day, but a certain Inspector Satya Prakash Pandey from Bihar Police did. He was pot-bellied and constantly chewed betel nut. He had a stern face, with a curled-up moustache, and he gave an impression of fretful impatience, like a wild animal on a leash. The only silver lining was that he spoke Hindi.

'I have come to take you with me to Patna,' he informed Eketi. 'That is where Michael Busari is wanted for murder.'

'Murder?'

'Yes. He swindled a businessman, who committed suicide. Now you, motherfucker, will be our star witness in the court case against Busari.'

'But Mike is a good man.'

'Good man?' the Inspector guffawed. 'Your boss Mr Michael Busari, also known as the Hawk, is wanted in connection with fourteen cases of cheating in seven States. He has defrauded several businessmen with his black dollar and bogus oil-investment swindles. So we laid a trap for him in Chennai. Mr Munusamy was the decoy, and Busari was supposed to be our prize. But instead, we've got you. Are you Nigerian too?'

'No. I am Jiba Korwa from Jharkhand.'

'From Jharkhand? Where in Jharkhand?'

'I . . . I don't remember.'

'You don't remember, eh? Don't worry, this hand of mine has cleared the minds of many hardened gangsters. You are just a greenhorn,' the Inspector smirked.

With his wrists handcuffed, Eketi was driven to the railway station the next afternoon and put on a train to Patna. The only other person in the first-class cabin with him was Inspector Pandey.

The train began its three-day journey to Patna at three twenty-five p.m. and an hour later the Inspector commenced his interrogation. 'OK, sisterfucker, I want to know everything about you,' he said and spat out a stream of blood-red betel-nut juice through the metal bars on the window.

'I told you, I am Jiba Korwa from Jharkhand,' said the tribal.

'And what were you doing in Chennai?'

'I just came to visit.'

Without any warning, the Inspector slapped him with his open palm. Eketi reeled back in pain. 'I told you to tell me the truth, sisterfucker. Once again, where are you from?' the Inspector barked.

'Jharkhand.'

'Which village in Jharkhand?'

'I don't know,' said Eketi and was rewarded with another stinging blow on his cheek.

'I am asking for the last time. Tell me the truth or you will die on this train.'

The grilling continued all through the evening and all through the night. By the middle of the next day, Eketi caved in, unable to withstand the punishment any longer. Sobbing and sniffling, he revealed everything about his journey from Little Andaman, about Ashok, and about his meeting with Busari.

The police officer heard out Eketi patiently. Inserting yet another fresh *paan* into his mouth, he gave a satisfied grunt. 'Finally you have told the truth, motherfucker. They say my hand is like an iron claw; it always manages to extract the facts from the suspect.'

Eketi nursed his cheek. 'Do you like hitting people?'

Pandey shrugged. 'If you don't hit, you don't convict. We are forced to work this way. And then it becomes a bad habit, just like eating betel nut.'

'So you hit people to show your strength?'

'Actually, it is not to prove our strength, but to mask our weakness,' the Inspector said with surprising candour. 'We pick only on the poor and the powerless, because they cannot hit back.'

They did not exchange another word for several hours. As the train thundered through the night, the Inspector reclined in his berth, deep in thought. Eketi sat by the open window, feeling the cold draught on his swollen cheeks like a soothing balm. Suddenly the Inspector tapped him on the shoulder. 'I have decided to do something silly,' he exhaled, and reached for his leather holster.

A bolt of fear shot through Eketi's body. 'Are you . . . are you going to kill me?' he asked, feeling a constriction in his throat.

'That would be too easy.' The Inspector smiled for the first time as he took out a key from the holster.

'Then what?'

'I am going to set you free.'

Eketi looked him in the eye. 'Are you playing a game with me?'

'No, Eketi. This is not a game.' Pandey shook his head slowly. 'This is your life. And it is not very different from mine. Like you, I also feel suffocated at times, working in a job where I meet the scum of society day in and day out. But occasionally I do manage to wipe the tears off a widow's face or put a missing child back into his mother's lap. These are the moments I live for.'

Eketi gazed out of the window. In the near distance his eyes encountered only a whizzing, velvety darkness. But close to the horizon he could see the bright lights of some distant city.

'I have two young sons,' the Inspector continued. 'They think their father is a hero, fighting criminals and killers. But I am just an ordinary man battling the system, mostly losing. I know you are innocent. So releasing you will be a small victory.' He looked at his watch. 'We should now be on the outskirts of Varanasi. I want you to pull this—' he pointed at the emergency chain above his head. 'This will stop the train. Then I want you to get down from the compartment and disappear into the night. I will tell everyone that you escaped while I was sleeping.'

'Why are you doing this?'

'To keep alive your dream. To keep alive my children's dream. If you arrive with me in Patna, you are going to rot in jail for at least five years, pending trial. So run away when you still have the chance.'

'But where will I run to?'

'You cannot do better than Varanasi. People come here to die. I am sending you there to live.' He inserted the key in Eketi's handcuffs and opened them. 'But remember,' he raised a finger, 'ours is a strange and sublime land. You can meet the best people in the world here and the worst. You can experience unparalleled kindness and witness extraordinary cruelty. To survive here, you must change your way of thinking. Don't trust anyone. Don't count on anyone. Here you are entirely on your own.'

'Then maybe I should return to my island,' Eketi mumbled as he massaged his wrists where the handcuffs had cut into the skin.

'That is for you to decide. Life can be ugly. Or it can be

beautiful. It all depends on what you make of it. But whatever you do, stay clear of the police. Not all inspectors are like me.'

'Will you get into trouble for letting me go?'

'The department will probably file yet another case of incompetence and negligence against me. I don't care any longer. I am out of the rat race. But you may just be joining it. Good luck, and don't forget to take your bag.'

As Eketi draped the fake Adidas across his shoulder, Pandey took out some notes from his shirt pocket. 'Take this. It will help you get by for a few days.'

'I will not forget you,' said Eketi, as he accepted the money, his eyes filling with tears.

The Inspector gave him a wan smile and briefly squeezed his hand. 'Now don't just stand there weeping like a donkey, sister-fucker. Yank that damn chain,' he said gruffly, and pulled up a fawn blanket over his head.

Eketi's legs ached. For over two hours he had run non-stop, cutting through dense sugarcane fields and sleepy villages in pursuit of the gleaming lights of the city. Now he was in Chowk, the congested heart of Varanasi, but the twinkling lights had been snuffed out and the bustling streets were empty. An uncanny silence reigned in the area, interrupted only by a stray dog or a car. Beggars slept on pavements underneath shuttered shops. A posse of policemen stood guard in front of an ancient temple.

The only spark of life in the city at this hour was a brightly lit all-night pharmacy. Eketi crept behind a parked jeep and observed the manager drowsing behind a wooden counter, surrounded by glass shelves loaded with boxes and bottles.

A woman arrived and nudged the manager into wakefulness. A couple of minutes later she stepped out of the pharmacy, clutching a brown paper packet, and Eketi had his first glimpse of her face. She was the strangest-looking woman he had ever seen. Almost as tall as Ashok, her eyes were lined with dark kohl, her cheeks were caked in cheap rouge and her lips were painted deep red, but her flat jaw and square chin gave her a manly countenance. She wore a red-and-green sari with an ill-fitting yellow blouse. Her hands were large and hairy. In fact, Eketi could even see a thin line of hair which began from her navel and disappeared into her blouse.

Consumed with curiosity, he began following her. She went through silent back streets littered with rubbish, along dark alleys and cobbled, winding paths, and emerged eventually at the mouth of a crowded, lively street. There were ancient, double-storey houses on both sides of the road, with intricately carved balconies which resonated with music and the tinkling of dancers' ankle bells. On the ground below, women with hard faces and vacant eyes, some only wearing low-cut blouses and petticoats, leaned against shadowy doorways and beckoned passers-by with provocative smiles. There was a corner *paan* shop where a man doled out ready-made triangles of betel leaf, a stall selling bread *pakoras*, and even a store for pre-paid phone cards. The smells of jasmine perfume and fried food mingled in the thick humid air. While the rest of the city was fast asleep, the residents of this street were having a party.

'Welcome to Dal Mandi,' a man wearing a *lungi* and tank top accosted Eketi. 'Would you like to try our goods?' Behind him, a girl in a pink sari giggled. But Eketi took no notice of her, intent only on following the woman who was now walking purposefully towards the far end of the street. The road ended in a T-junction where she turned right into another alley. Eketi turned right too.

Suddenly she whirled around and caught Eketi by his right hand.

'Why are you following me? Do you think I am a prostitute?'

Taken completely by surprise, Eketi struggled to free himself from her grip, which was as strong as a man's. '*Mujhe chhod do!* Leave me!' he cried.

She looked at him closely. 'Who *are* you, you little black devil?'

'First you tell me, *what* are you?'

'What kind of question is that?'

'I mean are you a man or a woman?'

She chuckled. 'This is the question which everyone wants answered. Some men are even prepared to pay to find out.'

'I . . . I don't understand.'

'My name is Dolly. I am the leader of the *hinjras*.'

'*Hinjra?* What's that?'

'You have not heard of eunuchs? Which planet are you from?'

'I honestly don't know about eunuchs.'

'We are the third sex. Between male and female.'

Eketi's eyes opened wide. 'Neither man nor woman. How is that possible?'

'In our country, everything is possible.' Dolly waved her hand. 'But tell me about yourself. Who are you? Where are you from?'

'I am Jiba Korwa from Jharkhand.'

'Jharkhand, eh? I used to have a friend called Mona. She was from Jharkhand too, but not as dark as you. Now she has gone to try her luck in Bombay.'

'Where do you live?'

'Not too far from Dal Mandi.'

'And what is this?' Eketi pointed to the brown packet in her hand.

'Oh this? This is the medicine which I have found with great difficulty. There was only one pharmacy open at this hour. This is for my friend Rekha. Her daughter is extremely sick.'

'What's the matter with her?'

'She has malaria. For ten days she has had a high fever.'

'Malaria? I can cure malaria.'

'You?' She appraised him from head to toe. 'You five-foot joker, you now say you are a doctor?'

'Believe me, I am. A pretty good one, too. On my island I once saved a boy who was going to die of malaria.'

'Island? Now which island is this?'

'*Kujelli!*' Eketi exclaimed and, to cover up his blunder, quickly opened his canvas bag and took out a bunch of dried leaves. 'This plant can cure malaria. If you will take me to your friend, I will treat her daughter.'

'Is that so?' Dolly thought for a moment and then nodded her head. 'OK. No harm in trying you out. Come with me.'

Eketi resumed following her through the twisted by-lanes of the city. They went down a couple of alleys, crossed a stinking open drain, and suddenly Eketi found himself in the enclave of the eunuchs. Even at this time of the night, they were up and about, dressed in saris and *salwar kameez*, with painted faces and outrageous hair-dos. They greeted Dolly and watched Eketi curiously, more friendly than hostile.

The houses here were small and austere, mostly one-room shacks built with brick and cement. Dolly stopped in front of a house with a yellow door. A *hinjra* wearing an orange-and-blue sari with a bunch of jasmine flowers woven into her braid ran out of the door, clutched Dolly and began to weep. 'Tina is going to die. My poor Tina,' she wailed.

Dolly spoke with some of the other eunuchs before turning to Eketi. 'The doctor came to see Tina a little while ago,' she told him. 'He says the girl cannot be saved, the fever has reached her brain. My trip to the dispensary has been useless.' She let go of the medicine packet, which dropped limply to the ground, and smothered her face with her hands.

Eketi stepped forward and pushed open the yellow door.

He entered a small, crowded room. There were pots and pans in one corner, clothes in another. But his eyes were drawn to a mattress on the floor, on which lay a small girl in a frock, surrounded by blankets. She was no older than eight or nine, with a round face and almond-shaped eyes. Frail and thin, she seemed to have been drained of vitality. Her face was pale and there were large red blisters on her neck. Her eyes were closed, but from time to time she mumbled incoherently in her sleep.

Eketi unzipped his canvas bag and got to work. He took out the bunch of dried leaves and asked the girl's mother to grind them into a paste and heat it. Then he mixed the red clay with pig fat and smeared the girl's forehead with horizontal stripes. As Dolly watched sceptically, he applied some yellow clay to the girl's upper lip and rubbed a hot mash of the dried leaves on her stomach. Finally he took out a necklace of bones. 'This is the *chauga-ta*, made of the bones of the great Tomiti. It will heal the body and keep the *eeka* away,' he announced and draped the necklace over the girl's neck.

'Are you some kind of witch doctor?' Dolly asked with a worried look.

'I am only trying to help.'

'Now what should we do?'

'We wait till morning,' he said and yawned. 'I am feeling very sleepy. Is there a place I can lie down?'

'Don't you have your own place?'

'No.'

'I thought so,' Dolly sighed. 'Come, I will take you to my house.'

Her house was the biggest in the area, with two rooms and a tiny kitchen. The painted walls were adorned with framed pictures of gods and goddesses. There was a faded carpet on the floor and even a small folding dining table with metal chairs. A wall clock showed the time as quarter to three. Eketi flopped down on the floor and within minutes was fast asleep.

When he woke up the next morning, Dolly was already up and about. 'You have worked a miracle,' she beamed at him. 'Tina's fever has disappeared. She is feeling much better.'

Tina's mother Rekha came in shortly afterwards and fell at Eketi's feet. 'You are an angel sent from heaven,' she cried, clutching the tribal's hand. 'My daughter and I are forever in debt to you.'

She was followed by another eunuch, who blinked at him coquettishly before extending her arm. 'I have blisters on my forearm. Do you have a remedy for this as well?'

'No, no. I am not a doctor,' Eketi grumbled.

'You must be hungry,' said Dolly. 'I am going to make breakfast.'

Later that day, as Dolly sat at the table chopping vegetables, Eketi sidled up to her. 'My curiosity is killing me.'

'What do you mean?' She arched her eyebrows.

'I am still confused about what you told me last night. How can you be neither man nor woman?'

With a grimace, Dolly dropped her knife, stood up and lifted up her sari. 'See for yourself.'

Eketi gasped in horror. 'Were you . . . were you born this way?'

'No. I was born a man like you, but always felt like a woman trapped inside a man's body. I was the youngest of three brothers and two sisters. My father was a well-to-do clothes merchant in Bareilly. Growing up was sheer torture. My brothers and sisters always taunted me. Even my parents treated me with derision and contempt. They realized I was different but still wanted me to behave like a boy. So the day I turned seventeen, I stole money from my father's shop and ran away to Lucknow, where I met my Guru and got the operation done.'

'What kind of operation?'

'It is excruciating, but they keep you on opium for a number of days, which takes away some of the pain. Then the *nirvana* ceremony is performed.'

'What is that?'

'It means rebirth. A priest cuts off the genitals with a knife. One stroke and my organ was gone.' Dolly made a chopping motion with her hands. Eketi gasped again.

'Once the operation was over, I was deemed to have become a woman. Then my Guru took me under his wing and brought me to Banaras. It was here that I discovered an entire community of eunuchs. I have been living here for seventeen years now. These eunuchs are what I call my family, this is where I belong.'

'So you are actually a man?'

'Originally, yes.'

'Don't you feel strange without your . . . er . . . dick?' Eketi asked hesitatingly.

She laughed. 'You don't need a dick to survive in this country. You need money and brains.'

'And how do you earn money?'

'We sing at weddings and childbirths, housewarmings and other auspicious occasions, and give blessings. People believe that *hinjras* have the power to take ill luck and misfortune from them. I also work occasionally for a bank.'

'What kind of work?'

'Very often people borrow money from the bank but fail to return it. Then the bank asks us *hinjras* to land up at the defaulter's doorstep. We sing bawdy songs and generally create so much nuisance that the man pays up.'

'That sounds like fun! So are you happy being a eunuch?'

'It is not about being happy, Jiba,' she said grimly. 'It is about being free. But enough about me. Tell me, what has brought you from Jharkhand to our Uttar Pradesh?'

'I ran away from my village. I came here to get married.'

'*Wah*, that's a new reason to migrate. And have you found a girl?'

'No,' Eketi smiled shyly, 'but I am looking all the time.'

'Have you decided where you will stay?'

'Can't I stay in this house, with you? You have plenty of room.'

'I don't run a charitable guesthouse,' she said tartly. 'If you stay here, you will have to pay me rent. Have you got any money?'

'Yes, a lot,' he said, and took out the notes given by Inspector Pandey.

Dolly counted them out. 'This is only four hundred. I will treat this as a month's rent.' She leered at him and inserted the notes inside the mysterious confines of her blouse. 'You also need money to eat. I cannot give you free meals every day.'

'Then what should I do?'

'You need to get a job.'

'Will you help me find work?'

'Yes. They are building a new five-star hotel. I'll take you to the construction site tomorrow.'

'Then will you show me a little of your city today?'

'Certainly. Come with me. I'll take you to the *ghats* of Kashi.'

Chowk looked completely different during the day. The area was full of shops selling saris, books and silverware, and roadside eateries selling sweets and *lassi*. The streets swarmed with people. Rickshaws jostled for space with cycles and cows walked alongside cars.

Eketi thought the people on the road were gaping at him, till he realized they were staring at Dolly. Women shrank away in horror as soon as they saw her. Men scowled and gave her a wide berth. Children made fun of her, making lewd catcalls. Some jeered at her by clapping with their palms meeting sideways. She ignored their taunts and guided Eketi through the crowded thoroughfare to an alley which led to a series of terraced stone steps going down to the Ganges, and the tribal had his first view of the *ghats*.

The river gleamed darkly, like molten silver, with little boats bobbing on its surface like dabbling ducks. The embankments were full of pilgrims. Some were sitting under palm-leaf parasols consulting astrologers, some were buying trinkets, and some were taking a dip in the river. Tonsured priests chanted mantras, bearded *sadhus* paid obeisance to the sun and stocky wrestlers honed their bodybuilding skills. The *ghats* stretched all along the riverfront, as far as the eye could see. Thin reeds of smoke hung in the misty air from the funeral pyres burning in the far distance.

'The river unites both pilgrims and mourners,' Dolly said. 'Our city is a celebration of the living as well as the dead.'

'A man told me that people come to this city to die. Why?' Eketi asked.

'Because it is said that if you die in Kashi you go straight to heaven,' replied Dolly.

'So when you die, will you also go straight to heaven?'

'There is no one heaven, Jiba.' She looked benignly at him. 'There are different heavens for different people. We eunuchs even do our cremations secretly.'

A day later, on 1 November, Eketi began his first real job. Dolly took him to what looked like the rim of a huge crater. The construction site inside resembled the ugly bowels of some massive beast. A thin line of women carrying heavy loads on their heads moved across the belly of the beast, and men with pick-axes carved up its entrails. Wooden scaffolds looking like giant swings had been erected all over the site and monster cranes reached for the sky with flickering tongues. The air reeked with the odour of sweat and clanged with the sounds of metal on metal.

Dolly knew the foreman, a man called Babban who had a permanent frown on his face. He took one look at Eketi's rippling muscles and employed him instantly. The tribal was given a shovel and told to join a batch of workers digging a trench.

It was tough going. The shovel kept slipping from Eketi's grip due to perspiration, and yellow dust kept getting in his eyes. The pit was like a furnace and even the soft lumps of soil felt like embers burning his naked feet.

At two o'clock a siren sounded, announcing lunchtime, and Eketi heaved a sigh of relief. The food was just thick rice and watery vegetables, but the brief respite in the shade made it palatable.

The labourers sat in a group and ate their meal quietly. 'Who is the owner of this hotel?' Eketi asked a gaunt-looking man with a permanent stoop squatting next to him. His name was Suraj. His clothes were tattered and dusty and smelt of stale sweat.

'How do I know?' the man shrugged. 'Must be some big *seth*. Why does it matter? We are not going to be living in this hotel.' He peered at Eketi. 'You don't seem to be from here. Have you worked on a construction site before?'

'It's my first time,' Eketi replied.

'I could see that. Don't worry. I have been doing this work for three years and still make mistakes. But look after yourself, otherwise your back will become hunched forever like mine. And don't inhale the dust. It will clog the pores of your body. Sometimes it comes out even in my shit. Look what this work has done to my hands and feet.' Suraj held out both his palms. They were calloused and as rough as coconuts. There were blisters on his feet and the soles had ruptured into rivulets of dried blood.

'Then why do you do this work?' Eketi asked.

'I have five mouths to feed. I need money.'

'And how much money do they pay here?'

'Just enough to get by.'

The siren sounded again and the labourers reluctantly stood

up. All through the afternoon they worked, hauling bricks, loading mud, breaking stones, mixing cement, digging and filling, building the hotel with their bare hands.

When the foreman finally declared the end of the day's work at six in the evening, the defeated men hoisted their pickaxes and shovels to their shoulders, the drooping women picked up their baskets and babies, and lined up before the contractor.

Eketi too collected his wage, consisting of five crisp ten-rupee notes, and began the walk back to Dolly's house.

As he was passing in front of an upmarket shopping centre, his eyes were drawn to a poster adorning the display window of a shop. It showed a magnificent island, piled high with dense green trees and ringed by a turquoise ocean. He stood there for several minutes, and then boldly entered the shop. A young woman was sitting behind a counter doing her nails. A big map of the world was displayed on the wall behind her and a pile of brochures lay at her side. She looked at his dusty clothes and grimy face with frank distaste.

'Yes, what do you want?' she demanded.

'I want to go to the island whose picture is in the window.'

'That is the Andamans,' she sneered.

'Yes, I know. How much does it cost to go there by ship?'

She blew her nails and picked up a brochure with the same photo of the island on the cover. 'We have an organized tour for five days. The total cost for the cheapest package will be nine thousand rupees from Kolkata. Now go, don't waste my time.'

'Can I take one of these?' He indicated the brochure. The girl quickly gave him one, and shooed him out.

'So how did you like the work?' Dolly asked him as soon as he returned.

'I didn't come from my village for this,' Eketi replied, massaging his back. He took out the fifty rupees from his pocket and gave them to Dolly. 'Will you keep this money safely for me?'

'No problem,' said Dolly.

'And can you tell me how many days I will have to work to earn nine thousand?'

Dolly frowned and did a quick calculation. 'One hundred and eighty days. Say six months. Why?'

'I want to visit this island,' he said, holding aloft the tourist brochure like a hunting trophy.

It was the tantalizing promise contained in that glossy sheet of paper which made Eketi forget the ache in his back and the cramp in his legs. After dinner he lay down on the floor, gazing at the picture of the island, feeling the wind rustling through the tall palm trees, hearing the cicadas singing in the dense green jungle, savouring the taste of turtle meat on his tongue.

The next day he was back at the construction site, doing the same work. Soon his hands fell into a rhythm, so that by the end of the week he didn't need to look down at what he was digging. Even though the work became easier, Eketi still hated it and he hated himself for doing it.

His world now revolved between the eunuch's house and the construction site. He had neither the time to explore the rest of the city nor the inclination to get acquainted with the other residents of Dolly's colony. He even put the project of finding a wife on hold. Sunday and Monday, Diwali and New Year meant the same to him – five ten-rupee notes, which he diligently gave Dolly for safekeeping.

Two and a half months passed. As the hotel began rising from the ground, Eketi's hopes also started rising. 'How much money has accumulated by now, do you think, Dolly?' he asked the eunuch one evening.

'A full three thousand,' she replied.

'That means I need just six thousand more for my trip,' he said, surprising her both with the longing in his voice and his newly acquired knowledge of maths.

Dolly gave him a strange look, but didn't say anything. That night, however, she quietly added a thousand rupees from her own purse to the kitty she was keeping on his behalf.

*

Two days later, Eketi was feeding stones into a crusher when all of a sudden there was a loud explosion and a huge cloud of dust rose from a corner of the pit. He rushed towards the scene of the mishap and saw that some bamboo scaffolding had crashed from a considerable height. A worker lay face-down on the ground, covered with dust, his limbs contorted into awkward shapes. Another worker turned him over, and Eketi cried out in anguish. It was Suraj.

Suraj's death led to stoppage of work for two days. So Dolly asked Eketi to accompany her on a mission on behalf of the 'bank people'. Together with four other eunuchs, they proceeded to a crowded market in Bhelupura. Dolly pointed out a shop on the ground floor selling electrical equipment. 'Our target is the owner of this store, Rajneesh Gupta,' she told Eketi. 'I need you to draw him out of the shop, then we will do the rest.'

So Eketi went in and told the mousy-looking owner that there was someone outside waiting to meet him. As soon as a slightly mystified Rajneesh Gupta stepped out of his shop, the *hinjras* pounced on him. Dolly's associates surrounded him and began taunting him, singing and dancing while clapping their hands in unison. Inside that human circle, Dolly stroked Gupta's cheek, tickled him under the armpits, and rained curses on him: 'May your children fail, may your business fail, may your body be infested with insects, may you die a dog's death.' All the other shopkeepers came out to enjoy the fun. They laughed and jeered, and Eketi was surprised to see that it was not the eunuchs they were deriding, but the hapless Gupta.

'Now repay the loan within ten days or we will make another visit.' Dolly jabbed a finger at the owner, before imperiously flicking her plait and calling off her troops.

Eketi couldn't help feel a tinge of pity for Mr Gupta, who remained standing in the middle of the market, red-faced and alone, trying to stifle his sobs.

The next day work resumed inside the pit, but it was no longer the same. The ghost of Suraj haunted the construction site, making the day seem longer, the food blander, the shovel heavier to Eketi. His heart had never been in this work; now even his hands were beginning to revolt.

When he returned home that evening he found the house in complete disarray. The cupboard had been ransacked, there was blood on the floor, and there was no sign of Dolly. It was a tearful Rekha who filled him in. Apparently Rajneesh Gupta had come to the colony that afternoon with three hired goons armed with hockey sticks. They had barged into Dolly's house and beaten her senseless. The eunuch had bled profusely and had required thirty stitches. 'She is now in the district hospital in Kabir Chaura, hanging on to life by a thread.'

'No! No!' the Onge cried and ran out blindly. He had just reached the gates of the hospital when a group of eunuchs trooped out. Four of them held aloft a bamboo stretcher on which lay a body wrapped in a white shroud. They were followed by three other eunuchs, chanting '*Ram Nam Satya Hai*. He didn't need to look at the dead body to know it was Dolly, being taken on her final journey. The death chant rang in his ears with the pealing clarity of hammer hitting metal. The breath went out of his lungs as though someone had punched him in the stomach. He slumped down on the ground like a broken puppet.

He returned from the hospital in a daze and walked with heavy steps to Dolly's house. Entering it, he went straight to the pillaged cupboard and made a desperate search for his savings, only to find every rupee gone. He stood for a while in the room, staring at the dried bloodstains on the floor, imagining the savagery of the afternoon. Then abruptly he picked up his canvas bag and walked out of the colony.

As he crossed Chowk, the air began to resonate with the sound of chanting and the jangling of bells. He looked up at the darkening sky. The sun had set and the *Ganga Aarti*, the evening prayer ceremony, had begun on Dasashwamedh Ghat. But today he felt no temptation to walk down to the river. Dolly had gone to some special heaven for eunuchs. This city was done with her. And he was done with this city.

*

On the outskirts of Varanasi, close to the highway, he came across a stalled truck. It was laden with pilgrims who were going to a place called Magh Mela. The driver, a turbaned Sikh with a long black beard, was trying to repair a puncture. Eketi begged him for a lift and the Sikh relented.

Just before sunrise on 22 January the truck offloaded its human cargo on a concrete bridge overlooking the Ganges, and Eketi found himself in yet another new city.

Dawn was breaking lazily over the holy city of Prayag. The air was cold and bracing. Waves lapped gently at the sandy riverbank. The crimson rays of the embryonic sun tinged the water with rainbow hues. Wooden boats swayed lazily at the river's edge. A smoky haze hung in the atmosphere, clothing the landscape in shades of grey. Flocks of birds rose in the air, smudging the ruddy sky with dark little spots. A sea of coloured banners and saffron pennants fluttered in the wind. In the distance, Naini Bridge rumbled into life as an express train clattered over its metal frame. Akbar's Red Fort dominated the skyline, dwarfing the makeshift buildings and tents which had sprouted all across the temporary township.

This, Eketi learnt, was the Magh Mela, an annual bathing festival. As he stood on the sandy riverbank, a procession of dancers and musicians arrived, preceded by a messenger who carried a turban aloft on a pole. The musicians created a cacophony of gong and drum beats, conch shells and trumpets, heralding the arrival of the Naga *sadhus*. A mighty roar went up as a group of ash-smeared monks ran into the water wearing nothing but marigold garlands, brandishing steel swords and iron tridents and screaming, 'Glory to Mahadev!' Devotees moved away in fright or bowed in reverence the moment the naked Nagas appeared. Eketi stood transfixed as the *sadhus* splashed themselves with water and cartwheeled on the sand. He was fascinated by their long matted hair and fearful red eyes, but most of all he was fascinated by their utter disdain for clothes.

The Nagas were followed by the heads of the various spiritual sects. These saffron-wrapped saints arrived by various means of transport. One came on a spluttering tractor, while another sat on a silver throne in the back of a trailer. Some were borne aloft on leopard-skin rugs in jewelled palanquins, while others came in golden chariots with silk umbrellas, trailed by hundreds of followers singing their praises and chanting *bhajans*.

The converging point for all these groups was *sangam*, that sliver of water which demarcated the meeting point of north and west, where the yellowish-brown currents of the Ganga merged with the bluish-black waters of the Yamuna. The shallow water was crawling with shivering devotees. Men in various stages of undress, displaying all makes of underwear, ladies struggling to protect their modesty while offering prayers with both hands, little boys splashing in the muddy water. Orange marigold flowers bobbed on the water's surface alongside empty Tetra Pak containers and transparent plastic trash. Chants hailing Lord Shiva and Mother Ganges rent the air.

Eketi also took a quick dip in the cold water and then hung around the riverbank, enjoying the free *puris* and *jalebis* being doled out by well-heeled devotees, and generally lazing in the sun. When it became too hot he decided to explore the Mela grounds and walked straight into a makeshift bazaar, reeking of incense and spice. Here women tried on a million coloured glass bangles and purchased copious quantities of vermilion *sindoor*, while little children lay siege to toyshops, begging their fathers to buy them plastic guns and miniature glass animals. Roadside astrologers enticed customers with good-luck charms for everything under the sun. Book stalls did brisk trade with their cheaply printed devotional booklets and lurid posters spread out on the ground, where the old gods and goddesses – Krishna, Lakshmi, Shiva and Durga – jostled for space with new ones – Sachin Tendulkar, Salim Ilyasi, Shabnam Saxena and Shilpa Shetty. A flute vendor kept repeating the same monotonous tune, an indefatigable salesman tried to persuade housewives to try their hand at his seven-in-one aluminium grater, and a glib-talking hawker sold snake oil as a cure for impotence.

The carnival contained several large tents housing attractions for the whole family. Laughter rang out from the Hall of Fun House Mirrors and shrieks from the Freak Show, which promised a man without a stomach and a woman grafted on to a snake's body. There was even a giant wheel, a photo studio and a magic show. But the biggest queue was outside a tent advertised as RANGEELA DISCO DHAMAKA. Men ogled at the ten-foot billboard over the entrance which had cut-outs of two girls in oversized bras and hot pants striking provocative poses. The sound of loud music came from inside the tent.

A ticket vendor sitting inside a booth winked slyly at him. 'Wanna have a look? Only twenty rupees.'

'No,' laughed Eketi. 'Why waste money just to see a woman's breasts?'

He showed much more interest in the archery stall, where customers tried to win teddy bears by using a bow and arrow to puncture balloons pinned to a square board. After observing several failed attempts, he stepped up to the stall owner and handed over a ten-rupee note from the five he still had with him. A group of small children clustered around him and cheered him on. As he took aim, the sinews in his body tensed up. Memories of that last pig hunt on the island came rushing back, touching him with its distant excitement. He released the arrow and it hit the balloon right in the centre of the board. The children whooped and jumped; the owner grimaced and parted with a teddy bear. Eketi handed the toy to a little girl and picked up another arrow. By the time he left the stall, the children had twenty teddy bears to play with and the tearful manager was preparing to close his booth.

Buoyed by his success in archery, Eketi jauntily crossed a gravel road and found himself in a completely different area of the Magh Mela grounds, where the air hummed with the chanting of mantras and the chiming of bells. The *akharas* were here, serving as the temporary headquarters of the various spiritual sects whose leaders competed openly for the attention of the public by employing heavy-duty public-address systems.

It was here that he encountered the Nagas once again. The naked *sadhus* were gathered around a courtyard, sitting on rough charpoys smoking *chillums* or doing physical exercises. In the centre of the courtyard was a mound of ash which they used to daub their bodies with. The *sadhus* retreated to a large white tent after a while and Eketi gingerly stepped into the courtyard. He stripped off his clothes, stuffed them inside his canvas bag and dived into that mound of ash as though it was a tankful of water. Like a buffalo wallowing in the mud, he rolled in the ash, smearing his face, his body and even his hair with grey, luxuriating in the thrill of being naked once again.

As he was about to leave, a Naga *sadhu* emerged from the tent. The tribal crouched on the ground like a cornered animal, but the *sadhu* smiled at him through glazed eyes and offered him a *chillum*. Eketi smiled back and took a deep drag. Even though he had been addicted to *zarda* – chewing tobacco – on the island, he was unprepared for the heady rush of marijuana. It made him feel inexplicably light-headed, as though several small windows had opened up in his brain, making the colours brighter and the sounds sharper. He swayed on his feet and clutched the *sadhu* for support, who grinned at him and shouted '*Alakh Niranjan!*' – 'Glory to the One who can neither be seen nor tainted!' In that instant Eketi became one with the Nagas, and they accepted him as one of their own. Theirs was a house without any distinctions. The ash bleached away all difference, reduced everyone to a uniform shade of grey, and their psychedelic trance brooked no differentiation of class or caste.

Eketi relished being without clothes and roamed the township like a free spirit with licence to paint his body. Living like a Naga *sadhu* carried other advantages as well. Devotees gave him alms, restaurant owners gave him free meals, and the guards at the Hanuman Temple never objected to his sleeping on the covered veranda at night. Within a week, he had learnt to say *alakh niranjan* and offer blessings to devotees, wield a trident and dance around the sacred fire with the other Nagas.

He especially enjoyed smoking the *chillum*. The *ganja* made him forget his pain. It made him forget Dolly and Ashok and Mike, it made him forget about what he would do next, where he would go next. He was content to live simply for the moment.

In this fashion a month went by. Maghi Purnima arrived, the last of the major bathing days before Mahashivratri and the end of the Magh Mela. Eketi was sitting by the riverbank, watching a steady stream of pilgrims take a dip in the *sangam*, when the ground beneath him shook and a massive explosion ripped through the area like a roll of thunder. So strong was the force of the blast that he toppled down. He saw black smoke rising behind him, billowing up into the sky like a whirling cloud. And then shrieks started reverberating in the air. When he got up, there were people lying everywhere, bleeding and screaming. He saw a young boy with his leg blown off, a torso lying headless. The sand was strewn with broken glass, bloodstained clothes, slippers, bracelets and belts. A tea stall made of corrugated iron had been reduced to a smouldering mass of mangled metal. Men and women with blood dripping down their faces were running around with demented looks, desperately calling out the names of their near and dear ones. Fires raged in several places.

The speed of the attack – everything seemed to have happened in the twinkling of an eye – confounded Eketi. Its ferocity overwhelmed him. The Mela had descended into utter chaos. Already a mini stampede was breaking out near the river as the pushing, jostling pilgrims piled on top of each other in their desperation to get out. Police sirens were sounding everywhere. Quickly putting on his red T-shirt and khaki shorts, Eketi followed the hordes sprinting towards the exit. Once he had reached the safety of the main road, he tapped a rickshaw-puller standing by the roadside. 'Which way to the railway station, brother?'

Allahabad railway station bore no sign of the carnage happening in another part of town. Trains came and went. Passengers embarked and disembarked. Porters hustled and bustled. It was business as usual.

Eketi leaned against a cold-water dispenser and wondered which train to take. He had no knowledge of Indian cities, and he had no money. That is when his eyes fell on a thin, clean-shaven man with short black hair sitting on a station bench a short distance away, with a cigarette in his mouth and a grey suitcase nestling between his legs. He gave a start when he realized it was Ashok Rajput.

Eketi could easily have turned around and walked away, but he went up to the welfare officer and folded his hands. 'Hello, Ashok Sahib.'

Ashok looked at him and almost choked. 'You!' he exclaimed.

'Eketi made a big mistake by leaving you,' the tribal said contritely. 'Can you now send me back to my island? I don't want to stay here even one extra day.'

Ashok's initial fluster quickly subsided and Eketi saw the old scornful arrogance return to the welfare officer's face. He threw away his cigarette. 'You worthless black swine. I've spent the last four months desperately searching for you. And you think you can just walk up to me and ask me to send you back? You think I am a bloody travel agent?'

The Onge kneeled down on the ground. 'Eketi begs forgiveness. Now I will do anything you say. Just send me back to Gaubolambe.'

'Then first swear that you will obey my every command.'

'Eketi swears on spirit blood.'

'Good.' Ashok softened. 'On that condition I will take you back to Little Andaman. But not immediately. I still have some business to finish here. Till then you will work as my servant. Understood?'

The Onge nodded.

'What were you doing in Allahabad?' asked Ashok.

'Nothing. I was simply passing time,' said Eketi.

'Did you visit the Magh Mela?'

'Yes. I am coming straight from there.'

'You are lucky to be alive. There was a terrorist attack, one of the biggest. They say at least thirty people were killed in the bomb blast.'

'Were you there too?'

'Yes. I care more about your tribe than you do. I came to the Magh Mela searching for the sacred rock.'

'So did you get it?'

'No,' Ashok said regretfully. 'A thief stole it from Swami Haridas's tent in the mêlée after the bomb blast.'

'Then is it gone for ever?'

'I don't know. I am hoping it will surface when the thief tries to sell it to someone.'

'So where are you going now?'

'To my hometown. To Jaisalmer. That is where you are also going, by the way.'

Their train arrived in Jaisalmer the next morning. The railway station was like a fish market, with a rabble of rickshaw- and taxi-drivers chanting the names of their hotels, touts holding banners advertising all manner of guesthouses, and a mob of commission agents accosting passengers with offers of cut-price camel safaris and free Jeep taxi services, only to be driven back by policemen with sticks.

Ashok blinked in the blazing sun and wiped the perspiration from his brow with a handkerchief. Even though it was the last week of February, dry heat crackled in the air like electricity.

The welfare officer seemed to know everyone in Jaisalmer. '*Pao lagu*, Shekhawatji,' he said to the superintendent at the station. '*Khamma ghani*, Jaggu,' he greeted the owner of a corner cafeteria, who hugged him warmly and offered him a cold drink.

'This is my city,' Ashok wagged a finger at Eketi. 'You try anything funny and I will know in a second. Understand?'

The Onge nodded his head. 'Once Eketi has sworn on spirit blood, he has to keep his promise. An Onge who breaks his promise earns the wrath of the *onkobowkwe*. He dies and becomes an *eeka*, condemned to live below the earth.'

'I am sure you wouldn't want such a terrible fate,' said Ashok. They boarded a battered auto-rickshaw which made a racket as it navigated the narrow streets of the city.

Eketi saw scattered houses, some cows sitting on the side of the road and a woman walking with a pot of water on her head. All of a sudden he shouted, 'Stop!'

'What's the matter?' Ashok asked, clearly annoyed at the interruption.

'Look!' Eketi shrieked, pointing in front of him. Ashok saw a group of three camels lumbering down the road.

'You've never seen them before, but they are perfectly harmless animals.' Ashok laughed and told the driver to continue.

Minutes later they were inside a street market. Rajasthani women in dazzling red-and-orange *odhnis*, their arms loaded with bangles, crowded around clothes shops and fruit vendors while the men sported colourful turbans and impressive handlebar moustaches.

And then, through the haze of heat and dust, a magnificent yellow sandstone fort rose in the distance like a shimmering mirage. With its majestic ramparts, delicately sculpted temple towers and myriad bastions suffused with honey-coloured light, the citadel looked as if it had sprung straight out of some medieval fantasy.

Eketi rubbed his eyes to make sure they were not playing tricks on him. 'What is that?' he asked Ashok in an awestruck voice.

'That is the Jaisalmer Fort. And we are going right inside it.'

The auto-rickshaw protested as it climbed Trikuta Hill, atop which perched the golden fort. As the fort neared, Eketi saw that the bastions were actually half-towers, surrounded by high turrets and joined by thick walls.

They entered the fort complex through a giant gate which led to a cobbled courtyard, from where a maze of narrow lanes led in all directions. The courtyard was full of pavement shops selling colourful quilts, stone artefacts and puppets. A turbaned musician played the *sarangi* while his similarly dressed companion peddled the *manjira*, regaling a flock of foreign tourists who flitted around them, snapping pictures.

As the auto-rickshaw travelled deeper inside, the fort became a city within a city, dotted with magnificent houses. Signboards, banners and electric wires disfigured many of these ancient *havelis*, but the intricacy of the carvings on their latticed façades was nothing less than poetry in stone. The secret, serpentine alleys teemed with activity. Little corner shops sold everything from soap to nails. Roadside fruit-sellers sat with high piles of apples and oranges. Bearded tailors pedalled away at their sewing machines to the bleating of goats. Music blared from roadside restaurants and mingled with chants from the nearby Jain temples. Children flew kites from crumbling rooftops and cows masticated leisurely in the middle of the road.

As they passed a row of painted mud-and-thatch houses, Ashok directed the driver to his ancestral residence, a large, dilapidated double-storeyed *haveli* with latticed windows and a carved wooden door studded with iron spikes. The door was unlocked and they entered an open courtyard.

A lanky boy, around thirteen years of age, dressed in white *kurta* pyjamas, emerged from the veranda. 'Chachu!' he shouted in delighted surprise and ran to Ashok, who embraced him with surprising tenderness.

'How tall have you grown, Rahul!' the welfare officer said.

'You are seeing me after five years, Uncle,' the boy replied.

'Is Bhabhisa home?' Ashok asked.

'Yes. She is in the kitchen. I will call her.'

'No, let me surprise her as well,' Ashok said.

'Who is this fellow with you?' The boy pointed at Eketi.

'This is a servant I picked up from the island. He will work for us now.'

'That is excellent! Lalit, our last servant, ran away last week. But how come he is so black?'

'Didn't you see the photos I sent you? All tribes in the Andaman are like him. But he will be a good worker. Why don't you show him the servants' quarters at the back?' Ashok said and bounded towards the veranda.

The boy looked suspiciously at Eketi. 'Are you an *adamkhor*? A cannibal?'

'What is a cannibal?' Eketi asked.

'Men who eat other men. Uncle says the Andaman Islands are full of cannibal tribes.'

'Only Jarawas are like that. But I've never met one.'

'If you had you wouldn't be standing here today,' the boy laughed. 'My name is Rahul. Come with me.'

He led Eketi through the main door into a side lane which ran parallel to the house. A teenage boy in vest and shorts stood on the pathway with a large Alsatian, which began growling. 'Hey, Rahul, who is this *kalu* with you?' the teenager shouted, tightening the leash on the dog.

'He is our new servant,' Rahul replied.

'Where did you get him from? Africa?'

Rahul did not respond.

'*Jungli! Habshi!*' the boy heckled Eketi as he passed him. The dog strained to break the leash.

'Don't mind Bittu, he is always making fun of people,' Rahul said half apologetically.

The servants' quarters were at the back of the house, two dark, dingy windowless rooms with string beds and coarse blankets, separated by a common toilet. The *haveli* was perched close to the edge of one of the fort's ninety-nine bastions, and immediately behind the servants' quarters was a sandstone parapet where a cow was tethered. It basked in the sun, chewing and flicking its tail occasionally to keep off the flies. Eketi leaned over the parapet and saw the fort wall and below it a steep rocky slope. In the distance the city of Jaisalmer spread like a brown-and-grey tapestry. Square houses with flat roofs lay in haphazard profusion, looking like matchboxes from this height. Close to the horizon he could even make out the sand dunes of the Thar desert, resembling frozen waves. He sniffed the air and was surprised to discover no hint of water near that sea of sand.

Suddenly there was a sharp yelp at his back and he turned around to see the Alsatian lunging at him, its mouth drawn in a tight snarl. 'Bittu! What have you done?' Rahul screamed, but the tribal showed no trace of fear as he gently placed his hand on the mastiff's back. It quietened completely and began licking his hand, emitting low whines of pleasure.

'How did you do that?' Rahul asked in wonder.

'Animals are our friends,' said Eketi. 'It is the *inene* we need to worry about.'

'Who are these *inene*?'

'People like your friend.' He jerked his head at Bittu.

A deep roar pierced the atmosphere just then, making the ground tremble. Eketi looked up and caught two jets streaking across the sky. They banked left and disappeared into the clouds.

'Aeroplane!' the tribal shouted excitedly.

'Not aeroplanes, fighter jets,' Rahul rebuked him gently. 'We have a big air-force base in Jaisalmer. Every day you can see MiG-21s go roaring past. These jets even have bombs.'

'I saw a bomb in Allahabad. It killed thirty people,' said Eketi.

'Only thirty?' Rahul scoffed. 'These jets have bombs which can instantly kill more than a thousand people.'

Another jet went screaming past. 'Is it going to drop a bomb on us?' Eketi asked in alarm.

'No,' Rahul laughed. 'Come now, Mother must be waiting to meet you.'

The drawing room of the *haveli* was a small, rectangular chamber cluttered with antique Shekhawati furniture – carved and decorated settees, padded chairs and low stools. The dhurries on the floor gave off a musty smell of disuse. The mantelpiece was dominated by an old tiger-skin trophy, complete with the preserved head with glass eyes, an artificial cast tongue and teeth bared in an open jaw. The walls were plastered with photographs of a tall, broad-shouldered man with a jutting chin and an impressive, thick moustache that curved upwards at both ends. The room was a shrine to him. He appeared in various poses, mostly with a long rifle in his hands.

'Who is this man?' Eketi asked.

'That is my father,' Rahul said proudly. 'Bravest man in the whole world. You see the tiger skin on the wall? He killed that tiger with his bare hands.'

'I killed a pig once with my bare hands. So where is your father now?'

'In heaven.'

'Oh! How did he die?'

Before Rahul could respond, his mother entered the room, trailed by Ashok. Gulabo was a striking woman in her early thirties with an oval face, an imperious aquiline nose, dark eyes, fine eyebrows and thin lips. The curve of her mouth suggested stiff haughtiness, but her dark eyes hinted at deep sorrows.

She was dressed in a white *kanchi*, a long, loose backless blouse worn over a red pleated skirt. Her head was covered by an orange *odhni*, but her neck and hands were devoid of jewellery. The late-afternoon sunlight filtered through a latticed window, creating filigrees of light and shade on the stuccoed walls. It caught the angular planes of Gulabo's face, severe and unrelenting. This was a woman not to be trifled with.

She sat down on the divan and appraised the tribal. '*Tharo naam kain hai*?'

'Better you speak in Hindi, Bhabhisa,' Ashok advised. 'Tell her your name,' he gestured to Eketi.

'I am Jiba Korwa from Jharkhand,' Eketi parroted.

'But I thought he was from Andaman?' Gulabo lifted her eyebrows.

'He is, Bhabhisa, but no one must know that. That is why I have given him this new name.'

'So what can you do?' Gulabo asked Eketi.

'He will do whatever you say, Bhabhisa,' Ashok interjected, but she cut him short.

'I didn't ask you, Devarsa, I asked him.'

'Whatever you say,' Eketi replied.

She explained his duties rigorously and then waved dismissively at his shorts and T-shirt. 'What are you doing in those ridiculous clothes? From tomorrow you must put on a proper outfit with turban. Then you will at least look like a Rajasthani.'

Eketi's new outfit consisted of a buttoned-up white shirt, high-waisted trousers billowing at the hips and tapering down to the ankles, and a ready-made red turban speckled with orange dots which fitted snugly over his head. He stood in front of the mirror and made a face.

As he picked up a broom, his mind went back to his island. He used to hate the drudgery of housework forced on him by the welfare staff, but the experience of the construction site had transformed him. He now had labourers' hands which couldn't remain idle. So the whole day he worked in the *haveli*, sweeping floors, washing dishes, ironing clothes, making beds. By five o'clock all his chores would be completed and he would then sit down with Rahul in the living room to watch TV. Rahul's main interest was watching movies full of blood and gore, which the tribal found distasteful. On the rare occasions when he got the TV to himself, Eketi engaged in ceaseless channel surfing. He would flick through Doordarshan and HBO, Discovery and National Geographic, taking in the fleeting images from distant worlds. He saw the snow-covered mountains of Switzerland and the wildlife of Africa, the gondolas of Venice and the pyramids of Egypt, but he didn't see what he was desperate to see, a glimpse of his island in the Andamans.

Ashok's family was vegetarian and Gulabo was a good cook. Her dishes had the distinctive flavour of Rajasthan, piquant and zesty. Even though Eketi missed eating pork and fish, slowly he began to relish the staple diet of *dhal, bati* and *churma*. Gulabo added generous helpings of clarified butter to her *missi rotis* and never failed to give Eketi a full glass of buttermilk with every meal. He grew especially fond of her desserts.

Life in the *haveli* followed a set pattern. Rahul spent half the day in school. Ashok spent most of his time inside the house, closeted with Gulabo. And every evening Eketi would sit by the fort wall, one arm draped over the parapet railing, and peer into the gathering darkness, listening to the whispering wind as it blew over the crenellated ramparts of the fort, waiting for Ashok to take him home.

On one particularly warm day in early March, when Rahul was in school and nothing disturbed the drowsy stillness of the torpid afternoon, Eketi was mopping the floor outside Gulabo's room. Ashok was inside with her and Eketi caught snatches of their conversation.

'This tribal is the best servant we have ever had. I've never seen someone work so hard. Can't he stay here for ever?'

'The idiot wants to go back to his island.'

'But I thought you were quitting your job?'

'I am. I don't need it any more. I'm going to get a lot of money.'

'From where?'

'It is a secret.'

'Tell me a little bit more about the tribal.'

'Let's not talk about that tribal. Let's talk about us. You know, Gulabo, that I love you.'

'I know.'

'Then why won't you marry me?'

'First prove your manhood. Your brother killed a man-eating tiger with his bare hands. What have you done?'

'Is my love not enough?'

'For a Rajput woman, honour is more important than love.'

'Don't be so heartless.'

'Don't be such a coward.'

'Is that your final answer?'

'Yes. That is my final answer.'

Ashok emerged from the room a little while later, looking grim-faced. He went out of the house and returned late in the evening. 'You may be headed for your island soon,' he told Eketi. 'I have just found out where the *ingetayi* is.'

'Where?'

'It is now in Delhi, with an industrialist called Vicky Rai. Pack up. That is where we are going tomorrow.'

They arrived at New Delhi railway station early on the morning of 10 March, Ashok with his suitcase, Eketi with his black canvas bag, and took a DTC bus for Mehrauli.

As the bus passed the landmarks of the capital city, Ashok kept up a running commentary for Eketi's benefit. But New Delhi failed to excite the Onge. The Victorian grandeur of Connaught Place, the imposing edifice of India Gate and the majestic presidential complex atop Raisina Hill elicited barely a flicker of interest. As far as Eketi was concerned, the sprawling metropolis was yet another soulless jungle of glass and concrete with the same snarling traffic and discordant sounds that he had become inured to. He pined only for his island.

The bus dropped them in front of the Bhole Nath Temple in Mehrauli. 'This is where I have arranged for our stay,' said Ashok, 'courtesy of Mr Singhania, a very rich businessman who is on the temple's board.'

Eketi was impressed by the temple complex. He was even more impressed by Ashok's suite, which was usually reserved for visiting saints. Spacious and well-furnished, it had marble flooring and a bathroom with gold-plated fittings. Eketi himself was not staying in such luxury. He had been banished to an outhouse, to an empty shack next to the sweeper's quarters. It was just a bare room, without even a bed.

As Eketi put his canvas bag on the floor, the aroma of food drifted in through the open door and made his mouth water. Breakfast was being prepared in the neighbouring *kholi*.

He stepped out of his shack and found himself in a garden. The temple was just stirring to life, but already he could see a fair number of worshippers inside the sanctum sanctorum. A girl was sitting all alone on a wooden bench under a beautiful tree. Even though her back was towards him, she sensed his presence immediately and attempted to get up.

'No, please don't go,' he said hastily.

She sat down again, covering her face with her right palm. Only her black eyes were visible through the finger-wrapped chrysalis of her face.

'Why are you hiding your face?' he asked.

'Because I don't like talking to people.'

He sat down next to her. 'Neither do I.'

There was an awkward silence between them till the girl spoke again. 'Why don't you go away, like the others?'

'Why should I go away?'

'Because I look like this.' She turned towards him suddenly, removing her palm from her face.

Eketi saw that she had pockmarks all over her cheeks and the lower half of her face was disfigured by a harelip. He understood her game instantly. She was trying to frighten him off with her ugliness. 'That's all?' he laughed.

'You are a strange one. What's your name?' she asked.

'They call me by many names. Blackie, cannibal, bastard . . .'

'Why?'

'Because I am different from them.'

'That you are,' she said and lapsed into silence again. Sunlight dappled the garden through the dense foliage of the papaya trees which ringed the edges. A magnificent orange bird fluttered close to the bench. Eketi made a cooing sound from deep within his throat and the bird hopped on to his outstretched hand. He held the bird and gently put it in the girl's lap.

'Is this a trick?' the girl asked.

'No. Birds are our friends.'

'Where are you from?' she asked, releasing the bird.

'I am Jiba Korwa from Jharkhand.'

'Jharkhand? Isn't that the new State? But so far away.'

'I am actually from even further. But that is a long story. What is your name?'

'Champi,' she replied.

'Champi. That's a nice name. What does it mean?'

'I don't really know. It is just a name.'

'Then you should change it to Chilome.'

'Why?'

'In our language, *chilome* means "moon". You are as beautiful as the moon.'

'*Ja, hut,*' Champi said and blushed. After a while she spoke again. 'You know, you're the first outsider who has spoken to me in a year.'

'And you are the first girl I have spoken to since leaving my island.'

'Island? What island?'

'*Kujelli!*' Eketi thumped his head. At the same time a shrill voice came from inside the first outhouse. 'Champi! *Beti*, breakfast is ready!'

'Mother is calling me,' said Champi and stood up. She walked with her right arm outstretched, treading a path which had been seared into her brain through endless repetition. It was only then that Eketi realized that the girl was blind.

Ashok took him to see Vicky Rai's farmhouse after lunch. They went through the Sanjay Gandhi slum, a warren of narrow, dark alleyways containing a conglomeration of small, squalid huts held together by bamboo poles and tattered burlap bags, their roofs an ugly patchwork of tarpaulin, plastic sheets, pieces of metal, old clothes – anything the owners could lay their hands on – and weighed down with rocks as protection against the wind. A group of men wearing *pathan* suits lazed in the open while their women filled pots of water from a municipal tap or chopped vegetables. Naked children caked in dust played with mangy dogs. Piles of rubbish and animal waste littered the ground like dead leaves. The smell of wood smoke and dung cooking fires drifted in the air.

Eketi tugged at Ashok's sleeve. 'Do people really live in these huts?'

Ashok stared at him irritably. 'Of course they do. Have you never been to a slum?'

Eketi shook his head slowly. 'Even birds make better nests on our island.'

Almost directly opposite the slum stood Number Six. Set

behind high metal gates, it was a triple-storey marble mansion, towering over the neighbourhood like a permanent taunt. Behind the mansion the fluted sandstone minaret of the Qutub Minar peeked out, barely a kilometre away.

Crossing the road to take a closer look at the farmhouse, Ashok and Eketi came to the rust-coloured boundary wall, fifteen feet high and topped by barbed wire. 'How will we ever manage to enter this place?' the tribal wondered. 'Even Eketi cannot climb this wall.'

'We will. Don't worry,' Ashok assured him as they passed the main gate, which had at least six guards in police uniforms. They rounded a corner and turned left towards the northern end of the property. They came across a service entrance which appeared to be unguarded. Ashok tried the door, only to find it firmly locked from inside. The barbed-wire-topped boundary wall stretched for another five hundred metres and had no cavities, gaps or fractures which could be exploited. It was only when they were circling the rear boundary that Ashok saw something which made him pause. Tucked inside the cement wall was a small brown metal door, probably some kind of pedestrian entrance. It didn't appear to be in use as the paint had flaked off and the edges were rusted. Ashok tried the rusty metal handle, but the door did not open. In fact, there was so little give that it appeared not only to be locked but also boarded up from the inside. He stepped back and surveyed his surroundings. Behind him was a clump of eucalyptus trees and then a thorny jungle, full of acacia bushes. The brambles made the entire area behind Number Six not only uninhabitable but also virtually inaccessible. 'If only we could get this door to open,' he said wistfully.

'Eketi can open this door by getting inside the boundary wall,' the tribal remarked.

'But how will you get inside the boundary wall?'

'Through this,' Eketi said, tapping the tall eucalyptus tree.

'But the branches of this tree don't extend over the wall. How will you do it?'

'I will show you,' Eketi said and began sliding up the trunk of the eucalyptus tree. Within seconds he had reached the top.

Catching hold of a sturdy branch, he began pulling it down with his weight till it became taut as a slingshot. Then kicking the trunk with his feet, he launched himself like a human arrow at the branches and foliage of a *jamun* tree jutting over the boundary wall. As a horrified Ashok watched, he flew through the air and landed on top of the *jamun* tree. From there it was child's play for him to make his way to the ground. A minute later the rusted metal gate creaked open.

'You know you are mad, don't you?' Ashok shook his head as he entered the door. The tribal grinned, unmindful of the numerous cuts and scratches on his body.

The welfare officer was in a state of mild euphoria as he took his first few steps inside the grounds of Number 6. He couldn't believe that within hours of arriving in Delhi he was actually inside the farmhouse. The sound of flowing water entered his ears, together with the mechanical hum of a lawnmower. He glimpsed a gardener busy shaving the grass on the lawn, barely a hundred feet away, and was about to duck behind a tree when he realized that the natural darkness of the wooded area would make it impossible for anyone on the lawn to detect him. From where he stood, the layout of the entire complex was clearly visible and once the gardener had moved further away he pointed out the main features to Eketi – the three-storey mansion in the distance, the Olympic-sized pool, the gazebo, and the small temple in the right-hand corner of the lawn. 'That is where the *ingetayi* is. I am absolutely certain,' he told Eketi.

'Then let's go and get it,' Eketi said.

'Haven't you learnt anything in the last five months?' Ashok rebuked him. 'Didn't you see the gardener? And there will be twenty other servants and guards in the house. We will be caught in a second.'

'Then let's do it at night, under cover of darkness.'

Ashok indicated the tall electric poles placed at regular intervals on the lawn. 'These are powerful spotlights. I bet you at night they light up this whole area like day.'

'Then how will we do it?'

'Have patience. Something will come to me,' said Ashok.

They spent another fifteen minutes exploring the wooded area, coming across two magnificent peacocks. At the very edge of the wood, near the north-eastern corner, they saw a man-made waterfall. Water cascaded down a few large boulders into a narrow canal which ran alongside a cobbled pathway leading towards the garages and the front gate. Ashok tiptoed towards the garages, which were shuttered, took a good look around and then hurried back to Eketi. 'I've got a plan,' he said excitedly. 'But you must remember the location of these two garages.'

They went out through the same rear gate and walked back to the temple.

Champi was sitting on the wooden bench in the back garden again when Eketi returned. He felt drawn to her like a magnet. As he sat down beside her, Champi smiled. 'Oh, you are back.'

'Do you sit here all the time?' he asked.

'I like it here,' she replied. 'It is quiet. Everyone else prefers the front garden.'

'I didn't know you were blind. Your eyes look just like everyone else's. How did it happen?'

'I was born like this.'

'It must be very hard, not being able to see who you are talking to.'

'I have got used to the blackness now.'

'Maybe Nokai will have a cure for your blindness.'

'Who is Nokai?'

'Our *torale*, medicine man.'

'Really? Can he really make me see?'

'Short of bringing a dead person back to life, he can do anything.'

'Then will you take me to him? To Jharkhand?'

'Actually he doesn't live in Jharkhand. He lives on an island.'

'What is this island you keep talking about?'

Eketi dropped his voice to a whisper. 'I will tell you if you promise to keep it a secret.'

'*Allah kasam*. Promise.' Champi pinched her neck.

'I am not really Jiba Korwa from Jharkhand. I am Eketi Onge from Gaubolambe,' he said conspiratorially.

'Where is that?'

'Little Andaman.'

'And where is that?'

'That is in the middle of the ocean. You get there on a big ship.'

'Then why have you come here?'

'I have come to take back a sacred stone which was stolen from us.'

'And what will you do once you get your sacred stone?'

'I will go back to my island.'

'Oh!' said Champi and fell silent.

'At first I wanted to stay,' Eketi continued. 'I thought I would start a new life here, get a wife. But now I want to go back. The people here behave as if they own the world. And they treat me like I am some kind of animal.'

'I don't think like that,' said Champi.

'That is because you cannot see me. I am not like you people. I am different. And every time someone calls me blackie, something curls inside me. I feel as if I have committed some kind of crime. But the colour of my skin is the colour of my skin. There is nothing I can do about it.'

'I agree. Just as I cannot do anything about my face. It is God's will,' Champi said and slowly raised her right hand. With her index finger, she traced the contours of his face, memorizing every angle, every shallow curve and declension. 'Now I can see you.'

Eketi shivered from her touch and looked into her unseeing eyes. 'Tell me, are you married?'

'What kind of question is that?' Champi giggled. 'Of course not.'

'Neither am I. Will you come with me to my island?'

'And what do you promise me there?'

'Lots of fish and fruit. No one to trouble you. And absolutely no need to work!'

'I would love to visit your island one day, but not now.'

'But why?'

'My family is here. Mother and Munna. How can I leave them?'

'Yes, you are right. I also remember my father and mother a lot.'

'But you must speak to Nokai about me.'

'I will. And if you cannot come with me to Nokai, I will send Nokai to you.'

'What do you mean?'

'Nokai can fly out of his body and go wherever he wants.'

'*Ja Hut!* Now you are sounding just like Aladdin in the TV serial.'

'Honest, I swear on Puluga. Nokai even taught me the trick, but I haven't tried it yet.'

'The things you say!' Champi laughed and made her way back to the house.

Eketi didn't see her again that day, but she remained in his mind, a joyful presence which lent a spring to his step and made him daydream. At night, he lay down on the stone floor of his shack, took out a lump of red clay, mixed it with pig fat and began making delicate designs with his finger on the wall. If Ashok had seen it, he would have recognized it as a wedding pattern.

Four days later, Ashok Rajput paced up and down the marble floor of his guest room. A heady excitement was building inside him, stemming from the latest piece of gossip he had picked up from the neighbourhood tea stall. Vicky Rai was planning to host a big party on 23 March, just over a week from today. This would be his opportunity, he was convinced. All that was required was to give Eketi some elementary electrical training. Slowly but surely, his plan was taking shape.

The same afternoon, two men barged into Eketi's hut at noon. One was in his forties with ginger hair and a scruffy beard, and the other was younger, with an athletic build and spiky black hair. Dressed in nondescript trousers and shirts, they had identical brown jute bags hanging from their shoulders.

'We have heard that you are from Jharkhand, is it true?' the older man asked Eketi.

'Yes,' he replied, feeling a little scared. 'I am Jiba Korwa from Jharkhand.'

'Hello, Comrade Jiba. My name is Comrade Babuli. This is Comrade Uday.'

Eketi nervously fingered his cap.

'Comrade Jiba,' the older man continued, his eyes scanning the room, 'we are from the Maoist Revolutionary Centre – MRC for short – the most progressive revolutionary group in the country. Have you heard of us?'

'No,' said Eketi.

'How can you be from Jharkhand and not know our group? We are the biggest Naxalite organization in the region. And we are fighting to awaken people like you.'

'But I am already awake!'

'Ha! You call this being awake? Your lives are controlled by the imperialist rich. They employ you and pay you a pittance. They grab your land and rape your women. We will change all that.'

'Yes. We are going to destroy this corrupt and hollow bourgeois society and its institutions and replace them with a completely new structure,' the younger man added. 'We are going to create a new India. And we want you to help us.'

'Help you? How?'

'By participating in our armed revolution.'

'So you have come to offer me a job?'

'Comrade Jiba, we are not a government department. We are not offering you a job. We are offering you a lifestyle. A chance to become a hero.'

'And what will I have to do?'

'Become a revolutionary guerrilla. Participate in our people's war. We shall even give you a gun.'

'I don't like guns.' Eketi shook his head. 'They kill people.'

'Comrade Jiba, try to understand,' said Comrade Babuli impatiently. 'Our struggle is to make your life a better one. Tell me, what is the one thing you want most in life?'

'A wife.'

'A wife?' Comrade Uday glared at Eketi as if he had committed heresy. 'Here we are, trying to promote a revolution, and all you can think about is a bloody wife?'

The elder comrade tried to soothe matters. 'It is all right. Comrade Jiba, we understand your needs. We have plenty of girls in our organization. All young revolutionaries. We will find you a wife. All we want from you at this stage is to consider our offer. We will leave behind some literature for you. Have a look, and then one of our associates will contact you. Comrade Uday?' He gestured to his younger colleague.

Comrade Uday delved into his jute bag and handed Eketi a fat bunch of leaflets.

Eketi felt the paper. It was nice and glossy, like the tourist brochure he had picked up from Varanasi, but this one had gory images of severed heads and men in chains.

'I don't like these photos.' He shuddered. 'They will give me bad dreams.'

Comrade Babuli let out a sigh. 'Is there no one around here who believes in our cause? You are the tenth person who has turned us down today. We thought, being from Jharkhand, at least *you* would support us.'

Comrade Uday, however, wasn't prepared to concede defeat. 'Look, you black bastard,' he snapped. 'We can do this the easy way or we can do this the hard way. We just killed a hundred policemen in Gumla District. If you don't cooperate with us, we will go to your village and bump off each and every family member that you have. Am I clear?'

Eketi nodded fearfully.

'So think about our offer. We will contact you again in two weeks' time. OK?'

Eketi nodded again.

'Good. And another word of advice.' Comrade Babuli lowered his voice. 'You better not tell anyone of our visit.'

'Otherwise your family . . .' Comrade Uday made a slashing motion across his neck.

'Red salute,' said Comrade Babuli and raised a clenched fist as he stepped out of the shack.

'*Lal salam*,' said Comrade Uday and made the V sign.

'*Kujelli!*' said Eketi and closed the door. He decided not to tell anyone about these strange visitors.

He continued to meet Champi every day. They would sit on the bench, Eketi would regale her with funny stories about his island and Champi would laugh as she had never laughed before. Most often, however, they would be quiet, sharing an unspoken communion. Their friendship did not need a vocabulary. It grew in between their silences.

On the evening of 20 March Ashok summoned Eketi to his room. 'I have a plan how to get the sacred rock. Now listen carefully. Three days from now, there is going to be a big party at the farmhouse. That is when you will do the job.'

'What will Eketi have to do?'

'I have got you a nice white shirt and black trousers. You wear these new clothes and enter the farmhouse through the back door at around ten o'clock. For an hour or so you just hang around the wooded area, checking that everything is OK. At precisely eleven thirty you walk down to the garages I showed you.'

'Won't they catch me?'

'I doubt it. There will be so many guests, waiters and cooks at the party, no one is likely to notice you, but if someone asks you, you say you are Mr Sharma's driver.'

'Who is Mr Sharma?'

'Doesn't matter. It is a very common surname and there is bound to be some Mr Sharma at the party. Now on the wall between the two garages is the mains switchboard. You will open it and take out the fuse. The electricity for the house will be cut off and the entire place will be in darkness for at least three to four minutes. That is when you run into the garden, go to the temple, make off with the *ingetayi* and get out through the back door again. It's that simple. Do you think you will be able to do it?'

'No. Eketi doesn't know anything about fuses.'

'Don't worry. I will teach you how to do it. Come with me,'

Ashok said and led the way to the rear of the temple. On a side wall was the mains switchboard, housed inside a grey metal panel. Ashok opened the panel door and Eketi saw row upon row of gleaming electrical switches.

'This is what you need to do.' Ashok indicated the first fuse. 'Just grip this white thing here and pull it out.'

Eketi touched it cautiously.

'Don't worry, it won't give you a shock. Now just yank it.'

Eketi pulled the fuse out and all the lights in the temple were suddenly extinguished.

'There you go.' Ashok grinned. He took the fuse from Eketi's hands and plugged it back in, restoring the electricity.

'Can Eketi try again?' the tribal asked and yanked out the fuse a second time. He clapped as the temple was again plunged into darkness, before plugging the fuse back in.

'This is not a game, idiot,' Ashok reprimanded him.

Back in the welfare officer's room, Eketi voiced another doubt. 'You said I have to take out the fuse at eleven thirty. But how will Eketi know when it is eleven thirty? We don't have watches.'

'But I do,' said Ashok and took out a small manual alarm clock from his suitcase. 'This is already set for eleven thirty. When you hear the alarm ring you will know it is time. Keep it with you.'

The tribal pocketed the alarm clock. 'When Eketi is inside the forest, where will you be? In the farmhouse?'

'Right here, in my room, waiting for you to return with the sea-rock,' said Ashok.

'What? You are sending Eketi all alone to the farmhouse?'

'Yes. It is your sacred rock, your initiation ceremony. On this mission you are entirely on your own. If anyone asks you, you don't know me and I don't know you. Promise me that if something goes wrong and you are caught, you will not give my name.'

'Eketi swears on spirit blood,' the tribal said solemnly. 'But will you also promise to take Eketi back to his island after he gets the *ingetayi*?'

'Absolutely. I will personally escort you.'

The tribal paused and fingered his jawbone. 'Can Eketi take someone else with him?'

'Someone else? Who?'

'Champi.'

'Oh, that blind cripple?'

'She is not blind. You people are blind.'

'Can't you see that she is the ugliest girl in this city?'

'She is better than all of you put together. Eketi wants to marry her.'

'Oh really? And do you know what they will call you pair? Mr and Mrs Freak!' Ashok said and began laughing. He restrained himself only when Eketi's eyes began glinting with inexplicable warnings. There was something shadowy and nocturnal about the tribal tonight. Ashok decided to humour him. 'Fine. I will get another ticket for her. Now go and sleep. March 23 is just three days away. And you have work to do.'

The night had a magical, almost dreamlike quality. Eketi lay on the floor, thinking of Champi and his island. He considered the possibility of becoming a *torale* on his return to Gaubolambe. Everything depended on whether Nokai had a cure for Champi's blindness. If the medicine man did not, he would have to find one himself.

All of a sudden he heard scrunching footsteps and became instantly alert. A little while later indistinct raised voices started coming from the neighbouring house. Something seemed to be happening inside Champi's shack.

And then he heard a piercing scream. He knew instantly it was Champi. Like a maddened elephant, he bounded out of the shack and crashed through the rear door of the neighbouring house. The room looked as if it had been lashed by a storm. The mattress had been upturned. He saw Champi's brother Munna sprawled on the floor and Champi's mother lying senseless in one corner. Champi, wearing a green *salwar kameez*, was flailing against a short man dressed in a shimmering cream shirt while a tall, wiry man wearing black trousers watched.

With a terrible roar he launched himself at Champi's

tormentor, grabbed him by the neck and lifted him several feet into the air. He began squeezing the man's neck till his eyeballs started to bulge out of their sockets. The tall man flicked open a Rampuri knife and drew patterns in the air. Eketi flung the short man on to the wooden table, which splintered from the impact, and advanced towards the taller one as though the knife in his hand was a blunt piece of wood. The tall man slashed viciously and a thin line of blood stained the tribal's vest. Yet he continued to advance, unmindful of his injury, his lips curled in a feral snarl. He plucked the knife from the tall man's grasp and opened his mouth wide to reveal his perfect white teeth, which he then sank into the man's left shoulder. It was now the tall man's turn to scream in agony. Meanwhile, gasping and wheezing, the short one got to his feet. He rammed his head into Eketi's back, causing the tribal to lose balance momentarily. But instead of exploiting that little opening, the two men bolted from the hut before Eketi could scramble back to his feet.

Champi was still cowering when Eketi lifted her in his arms and took her out of the shack into the cool night. He sat down on the bench beneath the *gulmohar* tree and made little comforting sounds as Champi clung to him, shaking like a leaf.

'Take me away, Eketi, take me from this place. I want to come with you. I want to marry you. I don't want to stay here any longer,' she sobbed.

'Shhh . . . don't speak.'

'I don't care if Nokai cures my blindness or not. I want to live with you on your island. For ever.'

'I will take you. In two days' time. Till then, wear this.' He untied the black string from his neck containing the jawbone, and fastened it around Champi's neck. 'From now on, Puluga will protect you from any harm.'

'And what about you?'

'Don't worry about me. The *ingetayi* will protect me. I am going to get it soon.'

'From where?'

'A farmhouse belonging to someone called Vicky Rai.'

The Cinderella Project

8 August

I have sent Bhola to Patna to fetch Ram Dulari – my lookalike – and I just can't wait to see her.

9 August

Rosie Mascarenhas announced the news today that *Celebrity House*, a clone of *Big Brother*, has asked me to participate in their next reality show, starting in six months' time. She was insistent that I accept. 'You saw how Shilpa Shetty's career got a new lease of life after she won *Big Brother*. Now she has tea with the Queen of England, meets Prime Ministers and gets Honorary Doctorates. There is even talk of a biopic being made about her.'

'But my career doesn't need a boost,' I said.

'Still, the extra spotlight can do us no harm. Every actress in Bollywood is dying to get on to *Celebrity House*. They are offering it to you on a platter. The script looks pretty good. They want you to have a big cat-fight with another contestant and then walk off in a huff. You'll be out of the house within a week, but the publicity will last for months.'

'But isn't this supposed to be reality TV?' I asked.

'It is,' my publicist said sheepishly. 'But no one will know.'

'Is life not a thousand times too short for us to bore ourselves?' I said and instructed her to turn down the offer.

Reality TV was touted as the great new hope for the digital era. A new genre featuring real people in real situations, laughing real laughs and shedding real tears. But it has fallen prey to the easy temptation of pre-packaged programming, degenerating into a scripted charade controlled by off-screen handlers in which contestants shed fake tears and throw sham tantrums to wring a few drops of interest from the blasé viewers. And why blame the viewers? All entertainment nowadays is prefabricated. Even war. No wonder death has also lost its capacity to move us.

That is why I am waiting for Ram Dulari with bated breath. In a universe in which everything is rigged and predictable, she alone might hold the power to surprise me.

10 August

Ram Dulari arrived today from Patna.

Bhola, who escorted her by train, appeared to be in a daze. He said he had to pinch himself to make sure that he was not with me. Even the watchman downstairs saluted Ram Dulari, mistaking her for me returning from a film shoot.

The resemblance is indeed unsettling. She is slim, a bit less heavy on the hips and exactly the same height as me: five foot four. It felt as if I was staring at myself in the mirror.

I have done only one film in which I had a double role, playing identical twins, but standing in front of Ram Dulari I wondered whether art imitated life or life imitated art. Here we were, Seeta and Geeta, Anju and Manju, Ram and Shyam, together in a single frame. I could hit my identical twin, pull her hair, hold her hand or paint her lips without recourse to special effects.

The poor girl was shaking, whether from exhaustion or fear I didn't know. She had come wearing a ragged green sari – probably the same one in which she had got herself photographed, and her only possession was a battered tan suitcase which would, no doubt, contain similar rags. So I led her to the small empty bedroom next to mine, gave her a couple of my old saris, and told her she would be staying with me. Her eyes grew wide on seeing the opulence of the room and she fell at my feet, sobbing in gratitude.

In the evening she came into my bedroom unannounced, sat down on the carpet and started massaging my legs. I told her this was not necessary, but she was insistent. She rubbed my feet for a full hour and eventually had to be forced to stop, whereupon she started mopping the tiles in my bathroom.

A little while later, when I took dinner to her room I found her sleeping on the floor, curled up in a foetal position. Seeing the childlike innocence of her posture, a strange, indefinable emotion welled up in me, a mixture of tenderness and pity. I sat down beside her on the carpet and gently stroked her hair, transported to the dusty by-lanes of Azamgarh and the dreamy innocence of my own childhood.

I wonder, though, what will I do with her.

12 August

I was still wondering what to do with Ram Dulari when the issue resolved itself. Shanti Bai, my Maharashtrian Brahmin cook for the last three years, has fallen pregnant and suddenly left the job. Ram Dulari has eased into the position immediately. She made me some *kadhi* and *sooji ka halwa* for lunch. I tasted these long-forgotten dishes with relish. Not only was the food yummy, it brought to mind Ma's cooking, the true taste of Uttar Pradesh and Bihar.

Like me, Ram Dulari is a vegetarian. Looks like finding her has been one of my luckiest breaks.

24 August

It's been a fortnight since Ram Dulari came to my flat and she has charmed me completely. It is hard to believe that people like her still exist in the world. Not only is she a great cook, she is also a very hard-working, devoted, honest person who believes in the old-fashioned values of duty and fealty. But her utter naivety and blind trust in everyone are also troubling. This city will gobble her up.

She reminds me so much of my younger sister. I have not been able to do anything for Sapna, but I can at least do something for Ram Dulari. She is an orphan; I will make her my surrogate sister.

26 August

I have thought long and hard about what I can do for Ram Dulari and I have come to a decision. I will transform this gauche village belle into a suave sophisticate. She can never become Shabnam Saxena, but she can at least talk and walk like me. And then I will find a suitable groom for her, give her a lavish wedding.

I know this will be quite a task. She is just an ill-educated villager. But I see in her a certain shy polish. She is a fair-skinned Brahmin, after all, not some vulgar low-caste. With proper grooming, she can be made presentable. Her voice is harsh and grating. With practice, it can be made mellow and refined. She is artless and callow. Through imitation she will become urbane and genteel.

I have also found a perfect name for my mission of transforming an ingénue into a lady.

I will call it the Cinderella Project.

27 August

I called Ram Dulari to my bedroom and told her of my plan. 'I am going to change you into a new person. Look at me. I am offering you the opportunity of becoming just like me. What do you say?'

'But why, *didi*?' she asked. 'How can a servant become like her mistress? It is not right. I am happy as I am.'

'But I am not happy with you as you are.' I made a face. 'If I am your mistress then you have to comply with my wish.'

'*Ji, didi*.' She bowed her head. 'Whatever you command.'

'Good. Then we'll begin tomorrow.'

28 August

The first phase of the transformation began today.

I started with a haircut, snipping away at Ram Dulari's long black tresses, giving her what my Chinese hairstylist Lori would have called an 'easy shoulder-length flippy brunette hairstyle'.

Then I handed her a slinky pink dress, the one I wore in *International Moll*, and told her to go into the bathroom and put it on. It is one of my hottest outfits, with a corset ribbon lace-up front, sexy thigh slits and a handkerchief hemline.

After fifteen minutes, Ram Dulari had still not emerged from the bathroom. So I knocked, entered and nearly died of laughter. She was trying to wear the dress over her blouse and petticoat. It was a struggle to make her understand that the spaghetti straps, low-cut front and exposed back meant she couldn't even wear her bra underneath it.

'Come on, out with your clothes.' I snapped my fingers.

She unfastened her blouse and stopped. I gestured that the bra had to come off too. Her whole frame shook as she unhooked it. Her bra was one of those cheap white shoddy ten-rupee things they sell on the pavement. She tried to cover her bare chest with her hands, but I pushed them down.

Her breasts are big and high and the nipples brown and pointy with small aureoles. I reckon she's a size 36C.

'Now take off your petticoat,' I ordered.

She started crying. 'Please don't ask me to do this, *didi*,' she begged me.

The strangeness of the situation was becoming apparent to me. To an outsider it would have looked like a scene straight out of a lesbian film. I relented. 'OK. Forget it. You don't really need to wear Western clothes.'

Ram Dulari picked up her sari and blouse and ran to her bedroom as if she had just been violated. I could hear her muffled crying.

I knew without any doubt that Ram Dulari is a virgin. This was the first time she had undressed before another person, her natural inhibition overridden only by her unquestioning loyalty to me.

What have I done, wrenching this village maiden from her rural hamlet and bringing her to the evil lights of the city?

But look at it another way. Ram Dulari is virgin territory, a mind not yet awakened, a body not yet touched. She is a *tabula rasa* waiting to be moulded by me in any manner I like. A mother can do this with her daughter – mould her mind and body in her image – but it has to be done painstakingly, over a period of ten to twelve years. The Cinderella Project will try to achieve the same result in just ten months.

Phase One may have been an unmitigated disaster, but all is not yet lost. I simply made a mistake in the sequencing. Before I transform Ram Dulari's body, I need to transform her mind.

30 August

I've started with basic English lessons. Thankfully, since she has been partially educated, I didn't have to begin with R-A-T and C-A-T. I went straight to sentence construction, syntax and grammar.

She is a keen learner, perceptive and intuitive.

'I think you have great potential,' I complimented her. 'Every day, you will sit with me for an hour and do the exercises I tell you. Now say a full sentence in English, anything that comes to your mind.'

'I-liking-learning-English,' she said haltingly, and I clapped in delight.

Phase Two appears to be on track.

14 September

Filmfan says I am vain. To quote that bitch Devyani who interviewed me for the latest issue, 'Shabnam is in love with her own beauty, dazzled by her fair, peach-like complexion.' So what's wrong with that? I am beautiful, I know it, and the world acknowledges it. All this talk about a woman being beautiful from the inside is pure humbug, invented perhaps by some mousy journalist to hide her own ugliness. Ask a plain woman how she feels inside; no inner glow can warm the hearts of dark girls enduring life solely by the promises of Fair and Lovely cream.

23 September

Ram Dulari was able to read a complete short story today. A full three pages. Hooray!

11 October

Box Office takings for my latest multi-starrer, *Hello Partner*, have been disappointing. According to *Trade Guide*, the movie is likely to sink without a trace. I am not entirely unhappy. The film was supposed to be a launch pad for Rabia, yet another untalented star daughter, and the director was an obnoxious jerk who deserved to pay the price for editing out three of my key scenes from the final cut.

The Cinderella Project, on the other hand, is going swimmingly. Ram Dulari has picked up enough English to answer phone calls.

I have a sneaking suspicion that I have a hit on my hands.

25 October

A thick letter arrived today, marked 'Highly Confidential'. Written in childish handwriting, it began, 'My dearest darlin' Shabnam, I reckon a love like ours is as scarce as hen's teeth.'

I laughed so hard, the letter slipped from my hand and went flying out of the window. I didn't even bother to retrieve it.

24 November

I know that a Bollywood actress has to act dumb, especially one who is a sex bomb. Men shouldn't feel intimidated by her brains. But yesterday, in an asinine programme on KTV about celebrity endorsements (I still don't know why Rosie agreed to send me on that show), I violated the golden rule.

The compère, a mousy-looking middle-aged man, tried to attack my campaign for PETA. 'People like you do these campaigns only for cheap publicity without really caring about them or knowing anything about the cause,' he alleged. And then, out of the blue, he asked me, 'Have you heard of Guantanamo Bay?'

'Yes,' I replied. 'It's a military prison somewhere in the US.'

'Wrong. It's at the south-eastern tip of Cuba. This just proves my point. You brainless bimbos of Bollywood have no knowledge of current affairs. All you people care about is fashion and the latest hairstyles.'

Perhaps he was trying to be deliberately provocative, but I couldn't stand his patronizing arrogance. So I laid into him.

'OK, Mister, can you name the film which won the Palm d'Or at this year's Cannes Film Festival?' I countered.

'Er . . . no,' he replied, not expecting a repartee.

'So should I conclude that all compères are smug, self-absorbed idiots who have no knowledge of the arts?'

'That's like comparing apples to oranges,' he protested. 'We make it on the strength of our ability; you have made it only because you have a beautiful face.'

'If that was the case then every *Playboy* centrefold should have made it to Hollywood,' I retorted. 'Cinema does not worship beauty, it worships talent.' And then I proceeded to question him on the philosophy of Martin Heidegger (he had not heard of him), the poetry of Osip Mandelstam (he hadn't heard of him either), the novels of Bernard Malamud (same response) and the films of Ki-duk Kim (ditto). By the end of my grilling the asshole needed a mouse hole to crawl into to prevent further embarrassment.

Rosie was not amused. 'Be prepared, *Stardust* will now

nickname you Dr Shabnam Ph.D.,' she said grimly and shuddered.

Isn't it weird that the ultimate accolade in academia is the ultimate insult in the glamour business?

15 December

I am in Lucknow today, the city where I spent three of the best years of my life. I have come with Annu Sir's musical troupe to give a charity performance to benefit a foundation working for street children.

When I first arrived in Lucknow six years ago I was fresh from Azamgarh, and the capital of Uttar Pradesh seemed to me to be the greatest city in the world. It had wonderful book stores, lovely markets, graceful gardens and, above all, an air of elegance and culture. I fell in love with the *adab* and *tehzeeb* of Lucknow, a welcome change from the rustic rudeness of Azamgarh. The decadent grace of the city has remained a lovely texture in my imagination ever since.

Now when I look at Lucknow, I see it through the prism of my travels around half the world. Compared to Mumbai, Lucknow seems inadequate, a glorified mofussil town full of the squalor and seediness, the clutter and chaos of small-time India. But it will always have a special place in my heart. The city has moulded my life. If Azamgarh was the abattoir of my ambition, Lucknow was the cradle of my dreams. It is here that I learnt to believe in myself, to aspire, to soar.

The Natya Kala Mandir hall was overflowing with people. The moment I was introduced as a daughter of Uttar Pradesh and a product of Lucknow, a great roar erupted from the throng. Screams reverberated around the hall like cannonball blasts. A girl caught hold of my hand and just wouldn't let go, another swooned when she saw me up close. It reminded me of that night in Lucknow when I first saw Madhuri Dixit and was blown away by her ethereal beauty.

Today I was Madhuri Dixit, the cynosure of all eyes. The capacity crowd had come to see me dance, but I was tense and distracted. Throughout the stage show my eyes kept darting to the front rows, searching for a familiar face. My ears strained to hear a familiar voice. Azamgarh, after all, is only 220 kilometres from Lucknow and I was hoping against hope that Babuji or Ma or perhaps Sapna might have heard about my visit and come to see me. But in that sea of faces there was none from my past, and my gaze just encountered the same lascivious grins and lusty eyes that I see at every show from Agra to Amsterdam.

I repaid my debt to the city tonight, and I don't think I shall ever return to it.

31 December

On this last day of the year, Rosie brought me a whole bunch of letters written by some loser called Larry Page. He's been writing me five letters per week since October. What's even more intriguing is that he's American (or at least he claims to be).

The guy is completely off his rocker. He claims that I wrote to him posing as some Sapna Singh and even promised to marry him. Now why a top actress would fall for a goof like him boggles the mind. The poor sod professes his love for me with lines like 'I'd walk through hell in gasoline underwear for you.'

He also tries to give me life lessons. A sample: 'When life gives you lemons . . . make lemonade.' Another gem: 'Life is like a turd sandwich – the more bread you've got, the less shit you have to eat.'

But enough fun and merriment. Rosie is seriously

worried this guy might be a psycho and the next I know I may be running to the High Court to get a restraining order against Mr Larry 'Stalker' Page. So as of today, I've instructed Bahadur to carefully screen all visitors. Anyone looking even remotely like an American is to be denied entry and taken straight to the Andheri police station. I'll also tell Bhola to have a word with DCP Godbole, just in case the sicko has a police record.

Such is the price of fame!

7 January

Ram Dulari has proved to be a most adept pupil. She can now speak English with the glibness of a tour guide. She can wield a knife and fork at the dinner table with the finesse of a dowager. She can pirouette in six-inch pencil heels and eat chop suey with chopsticks.

I had hoped to complete the Cinderella Project in ten months. Ram Dulari has passed with flying colours in just five.

This calls for a celebration.

13 January

Disaster struck me today. As I was getting out of the bathtub after a leisurely bath, I slipped and badly twisted my ankle. Forget walking, now I can't even hobble.

Since this morning Ram Dulari has been applying balm to my swollen left foot and using hot compresses to bring down the swelling. Dr Gupte says it will take at least ten days to heal. Luckily the Guddu Dhanoa film to which I was committed from 10 January has been shelved for the time being, so no cancellations will be necessary. But I will be unable to attend the première of my latest film, *Love in Canada,* which takes place tomorrow at the IMAX theatre.

The producer is Deepak Hirani, my godfather, for whom I have enormous respect, and it will be a huge blow to him to have his leading lady missing from the première line-up. Unfortunately an actress can never be seen in a plaster, otherwise I would have dragged myself to Wadala, come hell or high water.

I was about to call up Deepak Sir to apologize for having to cry off when Bhola stopped me. 'I have an idea, *didi*.'

'What?'

'Why don't we send Ram Dulari to the première?'

'How will that help?'

'I mean we send her in your place, as Shabnam Saxena.'

I gave Bhola the piercing-gaze treatment, the one I use to deal with producers who have a rather liberal interpretation of my no-nudity clause. 'Are you a raving lunatic? How can Ram Dulari become me?'

'Just think, *didi*. She looks just like you. Same height, same build, same skin tone. Once she puts on make-up and your clothes, I bet you no one will be able to tell the difference.'

'But everyone knows she is just a cook.'

'Who knows, *didi*? No one. Ram Dulari never steps out of the house. Even the watchman hasn't seen her.'

He had a point. We had indeed kept Ram Dulari hidden inside the house like a family secret.

'I tell you, *didi*, it is a perfect plan. Ram Dulari will attend the première, but everyone will think you are attending. The crew will be happy. Deepak Sir will be happy, no one will ever know.'

Bhola was persuasive, but I was not convinced. 'How can you be so sure?'

'Because I will go with Ram Dulari, *didi*, be with her throughout. She doesn't have to do much. We'll enter through the rear gate to avoid the fans. She will climb up to the stage to light the lamp and pose with the cast for some photo-ops. Then after watching the film we'll leave again through the rear exit.'

'Supposing someone asks her something?'

'Ram Dulari will not open her mouth. I will spread the word that you have a sore throat. I tell you, *didi*, it's foolproof.'

I still had my doubts. 'But what if it is not? What if she gets caught? What if Salman or Akshay finds out that she is just a lookalike?'

'Then we will pretend it was all a stunt. The movie will get even more publicity. Deepak Sir will certainly not complain.'

It was lunacy, but I was getting caught up in it.

'OK,' I exhaled. 'I'm in. But there is one condition.'

'What?'

'I need to watch the whole thing on video.'

'Done. I'll get you the tape.'

14 January

She was perfect. I couldn't have done it any better. She smiled when she was required to smile, lighted the lamp with just the right touch of reverence, stood stock still for the photographs, didn't flinch from the flashbulbs popping in her face, shook hands with the demureness of a princess and handled the presence of Bollywood stars around her with the sang-froid of a fellow celebrity.

It is a blessing that Ram Dulari has not seen any Hindi films. Any other girl would have started swooning on being within kissing distance of Salman and Akshay. But she wasn't overawed by them. She is herself a star. Created by the Cinderella Project.

Azim Bhai, the stunt director of the movie, was also at the première. I felt like calling him up and telling him that I had pulled off the greatest stunt of them all, and even the cameraman had not been able to spot it!

16 January

Bhola has become a tiger that has tasted blood. He came to me today with another outrageous proposition. B. R. Virmani, the textile magnate, has asked me to become brand ambassador for a new line of jeans being launched by his company. He has offered to pay me five hundred thousand rupees for a five-minute appearance at the opening of a new Liquid Jeans boutique on Friday, just two days from now.

'Virmani's PR man is Rakesh Dattani. I know him very well. He has confided in me that if you don't agree they will offer the deal to Priyanka, your biggest competitor. Now we wouldn't want that, would we?' Bhola said.

'But I can't go. My leg is in plaster.'

'Wrong, *didi*. You *can* go.' He winked and pointed at Ram Dulari.

'This is madness. How the hell do you think Ram Dulari can handle all those fans that will be thronging the store?'

'Simple. We tell Virmani to keep tight security and not to allow any fans to come near her.'

'But doesn't she have to say something when she cuts the ribbon?'

'Yes. Just three lines. Ram Dulari?' He gestured to her.

'So good to be here. I love Liquid Jeans. So will you,' Ram Dulari intoned. Though she stood stiffly like a mannequin, her delivery wasn't bad.

'So this is all a set-up. You two have been conspiring behind my back,' I complained.

'No, *didi*, please don't blame Ram Dulari. I coached her,' Bhola said contritely. 'I made her believe these were your instructions. But if you don't want her to go, she will not go. Your trust is worth much more to us than five lakh rupees.'

I relented. 'Go, we can use this money for Ram Dulari's wedding. But don't forget my videotape.'

18 January

I saw the tape this evening. Ram Dulari was again superb. There were at least three hundred people in that store, mostly college students. She soaked up the adulation, the cheering and the clapping like a circus ringmaster and sashayed up to the podium in her jeans like a catwalk model. I detected a hint of uncertainty when she was asked to speak, a slight quivering, but she didn't stumble. And her voice sounded remarkably like mine. She cut the ribbon like a professional politician and the entire hall burst into deafening applause.

Seeing the mass hysteria Ram Dulari was generating, I had to remind myself that *I* was Shabnam Saxena and she was just an impostor. I was the real deal, she was a fake.

The only mishap occurred as she was leaving, when suddenly a bunch of teenage girls broke through security and descended on her. 'Autograph please, Shabnamji' they clamoured, thrusting autograph books and scraps of paper at her. Ram Dulari froze for a second and the camera captured the look on her face. A cross between baffled and bewildered, like a schoolgirl who doesn't know the answer in an exam. Then Bhola grabbed her by the arm and led her away, trailed by the disappointed cries of my fans.

20 January

'What is autograph, *didi*?' Ram Dulari asked me as I was having lunch.

'It is the last weapon I forgot to put in your armoury,' I conceded.

'Will you teach me how to do autograph?'

So I proceeded to teach her how to sign her name and mine – the waggle on the *S*, the uneven symmetry of the *habna* and the little flourish at the end on the *m*. She caught on very fast and within a day was signing test autographs with such panache that I was tempted to pass on Rosie Mascarenhas's boilerplate replies to her.

'Why do you send me to these functions where I pretend to be you, *didi*?' she asked me as I was about to turn in for the night.

'It is a game, Ram Dulari, just a game,' I replied wearily.

For a second I thought I caught another look on her face, a cross between frustration and resentment, then she smiled at me and walked out of my bedroom.

21 January

My ankle has almost healed. But Dr Gupte says I should not take off the plaster for another three days. Which means that I will also miss the Cine Blitz Awards Night, where I am supposed to receive the award for Best Actress in a Negative Role for my performance in *A Woman's Revenge*.

This time *I* have decided to send Ram Dulari. This will be her ultimate test. If she survives this, she will survive anything.

I will coach her personally in what to say and what to do. Then I will watch it all on TV when the Awards Night is broadcast live.

24 January

I settled down on my bed and switched on the plasma TV. The live coverage had begun and a young lady anchor was showing the activity outside the Andheri Sports Complex as stars pulled up in their cars and posed for the cameras.

Five minutes later my silver E500 Mercedes arrived and Ram Dulari stepped out in a sexy white sari with a sequined border. A very loud roar went up.

I sat on the bed, mesmerized, watching myself preening on the red carpet. I got goosebumps when I waved my hands and thousands of crazed fans began chanting my name. I was blinded by the million flashbulbs which ripped across my eyes as I smiled at the cameras.

Ram Dulari gave a flawless performance once again, not showing any nerves when facing twenty thousand screaming fans. Seeing her receive my award, I felt the same pride in her that Michelangelo must have felt in David, Leonardo da Vinci in Mona Lisa and Nabokov in Lolita. It was the thrill of an artist who sees his creation come to life. But the thrill I received was greater than that of any painter or writer, because my creation was much more than a sterile collection of words or a blotch of colour on a canvas. It was living flesh, not dead marble – thinking, breathing, moving protoplasm. It was imbued with the vitality and fluency of life, which all art aspires to but can never replicate.

'We have seen who is the biggest star of them all,' the anchor said as the camera panned over thousands of fans chanting, 'Shabnam . . . Shabnam.' 'This appears to be the year of Shabnam Saxena, who is looking younger and more beautiful than she has ever looked,' the anchor continued. 'She has already shown her versatility by winning the award for Best Actress in a Negative Role. And she appears set to win many more laurels and conquer many more hearts in the years to come.' The fans went into a frenzy as Ram Dulari signed an autograph on the chest of a teenage boy whose T-shirt proclaimed 'I ♥ Shabbo' and the broadcast went into a momentary freeze-frame.

The Master said, 'Experience, as a desire for experience, does not come off. We must not study ourselves while having an experience.' Watching that freeze frame of mine, I discerned what he meant.

I had suddenly been freed from the mask of celebrity, the mask 'which eats into the face'. For the first time I could watch myself without the psychological baggage of watching myself. I revelled in seeing my popularity from the outside, as it were. It was a strange kind of thrill, like an out-of-body experience without leaving the body.

Tonight Ram Dulari had liberated Shabnam Saxena.

Ram Dulari and Bhola returned at one a.m.

'Well done, Ram Dulari, you didn't miss a step. You were perfect. I am really proud of you,' I beamed at her.

Ram Dulari gazed at me. 'So, *didi*, when are you going to teach me acting?' she asked.

I couldn't believe my ears. Was she out of her mind? I immediately put on my angry-teacher expression, the one I use when dealing with unruly fans.

'Just because you look like me doesn't mean you can act like me, Ram Dulari,' I said in a tone which would have frozen a fire.

'But I can, *didi*. Here, just listen to this,' she said and glibly recited some of my dialogue from *International Moll*.

She must have spent hours watching DVDs of my movies because it was a bravura performance. Her dialogue delivery was flawless. And she put in just the right amount of emotional heft. I had to admit that she could be a bloody good actor. A fist of jealousy squeezed my heart.

'You've had your fun for today. Now go and soak *rajma* for tomorrow's lunch,' I dismissed her.

I glared at Bhola as soon as she had left the room. '*Bas*. Enough. Ram Dulari is not impersonating me any more. I think all this adulation is going to her head.'

'Yes, *didi*,' he admitted sheepishly. 'No more outings for her.'

I felt it was important for Ram Dulari to be reminded of her true station in life. She was simply my cook, and had been transformed into Cinderella at my bidding. And just as Cinderella's fun ended at the stroke of midnight, hers must too.

*

As I write this, I am thinking, what should I do with her? She is a toy I created for my own amusement. But what do you do with a toy once you tire of it? Where do you throw away a thinking, breathing, moving mass of protoplasm?

I tried to remember what Geppetto had done with Pinocchio and that is when it dawned on me that in the original version, Pinocchio had died a gruesome death – hanged for his innumerable faults.

15 February

I was shooting today for Sriram Raghavan's untitled production in Mehboob Studios. But no one seemed to be able to concentrate on work. There was a strange kind of electric tension in the air. I realized that everyone was waiting for the verdict in Vicky Rai's case.

At lunchtime the entire crew gathered in the screening room, where the projector had been hooked up to cable TV. I was in the make-up van and entered the hall to catch Barkha Das grimacing on the big screen. 'We've just received word from inside the courtroom. Vicky Rai has been acquitted for the murder of Ruby Gill,' she announced.

There was stunned silence in the studio. No one could believe the news. For once, even Barkha Das appeared to be lost for words. 'Well, what can I say? This is an absolutely shattering verdict, but not entirely unexpected. For years, India's rich and famous have been able to manipulate the law and get away with murder. Vicky Rai joins that list today. For the common man, it seems, justice is just a dream. It is a sad day not only for the family of Ruby Gill, but for every ordinary Indian.'

I never met Ruby Gill, but for some reason the verdict filled me with a strange sense of sadness, like the kind you experience when you hear about a plane crash in some distant country.

16 February

Jay Chatterjee, of all people, is hosting a party at the Athena Bar to celebrate Vicky Rai's acquittal and has sent me an invitation. How obscene. I don't know what I find more disturbing – the fact that people are gloating over this travesty of justice, or that someone as intelligent and artistic as Jay Chatterjee can be friends with a criminal like Vicky Rai. This was a revelation. Even the Steven Spielberg of Bollywood seems to have feet of clay.

I sent a polite regret, knowing full well that this might harm my prospects of starring in Chatterjee's next film, the one for which he is still searching for the Salim Ilyasi clone. But I have my principles.

Unfortunately I also have my limits. Later in the day when I was doing a photo shoot in Lonavala, a bunch of college students approached me. 'We are sending a petition to the President of India asking for Vicky Rai's re-trial. Our aim is to get ten million signatures on the petition. Will you sign it, Shabnamji?' they asked me.

'No,' I said rather shamefacedly. 'I don't want to get involved in politics.'

'This is not about politics, ma'am,' said an earnest-looking kid. 'It is about justice. It was Ruby today, it could be you or me tomorrow.'

'I sympathize with your cause, but I am unable to lend my name to it,' I said and excused myself. The students went away dejectedly.

I was merely following my secretary Rakeshji's advice – do not get involved in any criticism of the government. It invariably becomes a millstone round your neck and the government can always retaliate. Who wants an income-tax raid or a held-up passport?

In any event, I doubt whether I will ever meet the fate of Ruby Gill. As Barkha said, the rich and famous get away with murder, they don't get murdered themselves.

17 February

I am leaving for a three-week visit to Australia to shoot three song sequences with Hrithik for Mahesh Sir's film *Metro*. This is my first visit to Oz and I am so looking forward to seeing all the places I have heard such a lot about.

Ram Dulari will be all alone in the flat, so I have instructed Bhola to take extra care of the house and of her.

20 February

Sydney must be the greatest city in the world. That first view of the Opera House and Harbour Bridge was magical. Bondi Beach has perhaps more bronzed bodies than any other beach on the planet. And the Australians are great fun-loving people.

I am having a blast.

It is especially funny to see all these Australian girls with blonde hair and blue eyes grinding their hips in tandem with me to a Hindi soundtrack. It has become almost de rigueur in Bollywood to have at least one song with some *firang* white dancers doing *jhatka-matka* at the bidding of our own *desi* brown-skinned actors. In one particular song sequence that we filmed today, the blonde Australian dancers were required to grovel at Hrithik's feet, follow him on all fours, huffing and panting like bitches in heat, and beg him for a kiss.

Is this what is called reverse colonialism?

4 March

A rather interesting episode happened today. A silver-haired man with a craggy face who calls himself Lucio Lombardi met me in my hotel suite. He spoke excellent English and claimed to be the Business Manager of some Arab prince whose name escapes me.

I asked what brought him to Sydney. He said the Prince had seen my pictures and was totally smitten with me. He was prepared to pay me a hundred thousand dollars for one night with him on his birthday on 15 March. I would be flown to London in his private jet, booked into the Dorchester, would spend just one night with the Prince and then be brought back to Mumbai on 16 March.

Mr Lombardi explained all this in the affable tone of a director narrating a script to me. He appeared to be a man with money and connections, but he hadn't reckoned with the temper of an Indian diva.

'I take strong exception to your proposal,' I blasted. 'Who does your prince think I am? Some kind of cheap prostitute?'

I pretended to be offended at Lombardi's crassness, but in reality I wasn't. I know I occupy that indeterminate place in men's consciousness between whore and wife. A wife can be seduced, a whore can be bought. An actress like me can only be propositioned. And that is precisely what Lombardi had done.

The Italian was not prepared to accept no for an answer. He was most persistent, increasing the offer to two hundred thousand dollars, then three, and eventually to half a million dollars, with the added sweetener that fifty per cent would be paid to me immediately, in cash.

As his final ace, he produced a picture of the Prince. My mental image had been of an ugly cripple with venereal disease, but the glossy photo shown me was of a strapping young man dressed in the loose, ankle-length robe which Arab men wear, replete with a checked headdress. He had a long, fair face dominated by a thick brown moustache.

I had to admit that the Prince was handsome (even if it was in an effeminate kind of way) and half a million dollars was serious money. I did my maths. Lombardi was dangling twenty million rupees before me for a one-night stand.

I have nearly sixty million rupees in my bank. But it has taken me three and a half years to get them. Now I was being offered a third of this amount for just one night's work.

And what does 'one night' really mean? It means, essentially, two rounds of sex (even the Prince won't have the staying power for a third). That would translate as twenty-two minutes max. So I would be getting $22,727 per minute. That's $378 per second. Wow! On a per-second basis, probably only Mohammad Ali made more, but then he also got battered and bruised in the boxing ring. I might even enjoy it.

But I still said no.

Lombardi seemed crestfallen. 'You are making a mistake, Miss Saxena, by not accepting this most generous offer. Are you worried about publicity? I assure you, we are most discreet.'

'No,' I said.

'Then is it some outdated morality? Haven't you heard the Italian proverb "Below the navel there is neither religion nor truth"?'

'I am not for sale, Mr Lombardi, and you can tell that to your Prince,' I said and shut the door on him.

Below the navel there may be neither religion nor truth, but behind the forehead there is something called the brain. By refusing the Prince today, I am only increasing his desire. I am confident that by the time his next birthday comes round he will be dying to offer me a million dollars!

Then it shall truly become an 'Indecent Proposal'.

I wonder why we haven't done a Hindi re-make yet.

8 March

How do I even begin to describe the worst day of my life?

I sensed something was wrong the moment I landed at

eight in the evening from Singapore and Bhola did not come to meet me at the airport. Only Kundan was there with the Mercedes.

'Where is Bhola?' I asked the driver.

'I don't know, Madam. I haven't seen him in a week. It was Rakesh Sir who told me to pick you up from the airport.'

Half an hour later, when I reached the flat, I found it in darkness. I switched on the light and gasped. The entire place was in disarray. Sofas had been upturned in the drawing room, my beautiful Waterford crystal vase lay shattered on the floor. The stench of meat emanated from the dining room and I was shocked to see half-finished take-out cartons of chilli chicken and sweet and sour pork lying on the dining table, surrounded by fine threads of chow mein. A pyramid of dirty pots and pans greeted me in the kitchen, with the iron skillet dumped in a corner.

The biggest devastation had been reserved for my bedroom. Sheets had been dragged off the bed and the mattress had been viciously slashed. Drawers had been pulled out and all the *almirahs* were open. There were papers, hair clips and clothes strewn across the carpet. My dressing table had been stripped clean and my entire collection of perfumes and cosmetics was missing. I ran to the adjoining dressing room, which had a floor safe in the walk-in closet. I needn't have bothered. The heavy metal door of the safe had been taken apart with a blow torch and all that was left was a gaping hole. Luckily I keep most of my cash and all my heavy jewellery in a vault at HSBC bank, but I have still lost close to a hundred thousand rupees, some three thousand dollars, five hundred pounds and some euros, an emerald necklace and a Breitling watch. Even more heart-wrenching was the discovery that my entire collection of shoes and handbags had been taken from the closet. My Manolo Blahniks and Christian Louboutins, my Balenciagas and Jimmy Choos, all gone.

As I looked at the carnage in the dressing room, the sickening realization hit me like a blow to the stomach that robbers had entered the flat, ransacked it in a frenzy, taken everything of value, eaten a leisurely Chinese dinner, and killed Bhola and Ram Dulari.

I stood there, enveloped by the cold silence of the house, trying to gather enough courage to wrench open the bathroom door and discover two bruised and bloated bodies floating in a crimson tub. My tub!

I couldn't do it. So I returned to the bedroom and picked up the phone on the bedside table to call the police. That's when I discovered a handwritten message taped to the handset. 'Before you call the police,' it said in vaguely familiar handwriting, 'have a look at the videotape in the bottom right-hand drawer of your dressing table.'

I rushed to the dressing table and opened the bottom right-hand drawer. There was a VHS tape lying there, black, without any cover or label. Its very anonymity made it seem faintly menacing.

For some reason the robbers had not taken any of the electronic equipment in the flat. My entertainment unit with the plasma TV, the music system and the DVD player was still intact. With trembling hands I put the tape into the video player and switched on the TV. I half expected to see Ram Dulari's dead body floating in a bathtub, but what I saw was entirely unexpected. There was a bathtub all right, but the only person floating in it was me, and I was completely naked.

The twenty-minute video showed me soaking in the bath, playing with the shower head, spraying the foam bubbles from my body, doing the kinds of things a lonely girl does in the bathroom.

I was horrified that a camera had captured these images of me. But what troubled me even more was the fact that the images were from my own bathroom.

I opened the bathroom door and peeped inside. There

were no bodies in the marble bathtub. There was just an eerie silence, broken only by the metronomic drips of water leaking from the tap. I looked up at the recessed lights in the ceiling. At first glance they all looked the same, but in the centre one immediately above the tub I could make out the liquid glisten of a camera lens.

I went back to the bedroom and examined the note once again. In a flash I recognized the handwriting. It was Bhola's. He had tried to disguise it, but the slanting ts were a dead giveaway.

The set-up was becoming clear to me. Bhola had installed cameras in my bedroom and bathroom, had been secretly taping me for close to nine months and made God knows how many tapes. Taking advantage of my absence, he had looted the house, ransacked it to make it look as if it was the handiwork of robbers, and was now threatening that if I went to the police he would make the tape public.

This man, who used to call me his sister, had now become a blackmailer. And he had chosen his target well. No one could understand my predicament better than me. A sex bomb's appeal lies in keeping the sex hidden. Just as a woman in lingerie is considered sexier than a nude, when titillation descends into porn the mystique ends. The entire Indian film industry is based on the concept of chaste titillation. You can show a bit of cleavage here, a flash of thigh there, but never the whole shebang. Bollywood actresses can be sexy, but must at all times be decent.

I knew that if this tape was exposed, it could destroy my reputation, send my career into a tailspin from which it might be impossible to recover. I knew I couldn't go to the police.

I tried calling Bhola on his mobile, but failed to get through. 'The subscriber you have dialled is no longer available,' said a pre-recorded message. Bhola had probably already acquired a new mobile. For all I knew he might not even be in India.

How can I have made such a big mistake, keeping a treacherous snake as my assistant secretary? But there's no point crying over spilled milk. As the Master says, never yield to remorse, but tell yourself that remorse would simply mean adding to the first act of stupidity a second.

There's just one question dancing in my mind. What has Bhola done to poor Ram Dulari?

12 March

It has been four days since Ram Dulari was kidnapped. I think she is dead. I can feel it in my bones. She has been killed by Bhola, her body chopped into little pieces, dumped in a sack, weighed with a heavy stone and dropped into the ocean, where she probably rests with the fish.

As the police will tell you, there is a designated time frame for the recovery of missing persons. The moment you pass that point, the chances of finding the hostage alive recede drastically. I pity parents who continue to hope for the return of their kidnapped child after months or even years.

Life is all about cutting your losses and moving on. Like I have.

Ram Dulari R.I.P. Bhola R.I.H. (That's Rot in Hell. Eventually.)

13 March

Producer 'Jugs' Luthra, better known as the soft-porn king of Bollywood, met me today. A fleshy, corpulent man who wheezes when he speaks, he has nevertheless made four hits in a row. 'So, Shabnam, can we begin shooting from 15 April?' he asked in his breathless voice.

'Shooting for what?'

'For my film, *Sexy Number One.*'

'Luthra Sahib, I told you six months ago that I cannot do your film. I was not comfortable with all those kissing and bathing scenes you wanted.'

'But then you changed your mind. I have already paid you fifty lakhs in advance. In cash, too.'

'Fifty lakhs in advance?'

'Yes. Your secretary Bhola conveyed your acceptance to me last month and said you needed the money immediately. He even gave me dates in April and May. The production goes to the floor in a month's time. I will ask Jatin to discuss the costumes with you. They will be a bit skimpy, as you know, but then the script demands some skin. I assure you, I will have all your shots filmed very aesthetically.'

My head started spinning. Bhola had taken five million on my behalf and got me involved in a sleazy B-movie? 'I am sorry, there must be some confusion. I never authorized Bhola to agree to your project. And my dates are always arranged by Rakeshji, not Bhola.'

'What are you saying, Shabnam? You have even signed the contract, on the basis of which I released the advance.'

'Contract?'

'Yes, here it is.' He opened his briefcase and handed me a typewritten document. It was my standard contract, with the no-nudity clause prominently missing. At the bottom of the document was my signature and the date – 17 February, the day I was leaving for Australia.

I looked at the signature. I had never signed such a contract, but the signature seemed genuine. And that's when it struck me. Bhola must have got Ram Dulari to sign it. If she could give perfect autographs, she could also forge my signature on a contract.

'Look, Mr Luthra, I am definitely not doing your film,' I said firmly.

The producer became angry. 'Then I shall sue you for breach of contract,' he wheezed.

'I am sure we can resolve this amicably. I am prepared to return your money if you are prepared to tear up this contract. And as a goodwill gesture, I will make a two-minute guest appearance in your film for free.'

He thought about it. 'I agree, but only on one condition. That you return my money by tomorrow. The entire fifty *peti*. In cash.'

'I promise. I will go to the bank first thing in the morning.'

I heaved a sigh of relief at getting out of this risqué contract. I didn't expect Jugs to agree so readily. But he knows he can find plenty of girls willing to do roles in *chhote kapde* – itsy-bitsy clothes – the euphemism for censor-approved nudity – for one-tenth my signing fee. The film industry is full of teenage girls ready to expose themselves at a minute's notice. They will put on any costume the producer gives them, do a pole dance that would put a Las Vegas strip joint to shame, and agree to crawl around on all fours in flesh-coloured panties.

14 March

The bank manager, a nice suited gentleman, welcomed me with noticeably less warmth than on earlier occasions. I asked him to withdraw fifty lakhs in cash from my account. He smiled frostily and said the bank wouldn't be able to give me such a large overdraft.

'Overdraft? Why do I need an overdraft when I have so much money in the bank?'

'You are forgetting, Shabnamji, that on 16 February you came here and withdrew every penny from your account, even cashing in your fixed deposits. You said you were transferring to another bank.'

'But . . . but I couldn't have done that. I haven't visited the bank in months.'

'You came personally with your secretary, Mr Bhola Srivastava. Don't you remember we sat in this very room and I explained to you how you would lose interest on the fixed deposits? You signed all the forms and collected the cash. Then you went to the vault and withdrew all your belongings.'

Every word the bank manager said was like a hammer blow on my brain. Six crore rupees, gone. All my heavy gold jewellery, gone. My 24-carat Dubai gold coins, gone. My platinum pendant, gone. My voice, gone.

'I . . . I . . . I don't know how . . . how this . . . h-happened.'

The manager gave me the compassionate look which people give those who are in imminent danger of being sent to a mental institution.

I returned to the flat in a daze, told Rakeshji to cancel all my engagements for the day, and slumped down on the bed.

I wondered how many other producers Bhola has given dates to and taken money from. I looked around at the furniture that I have managed to put back in place. How soon before I get an eviction notice and everything is auctioned to pay off my creditors?

Life, at its core, is war. I cannot be a silent spectator to my own financial ruin, to the systematic destruction of my career. I will go to the police and tell them everything about Bhola. How he had defrauded me, robbed me, forced Ram Dulari to impersonate me and then probably killed her.

I will deal with the tape when it becomes public. It will embarrass me, certainly, but it won't destroy me. And whatever doesn't destroy me only makes me stronger.

I have decided to pay a visit to DCP Godbole, but only on 18 March. I will not allow Bhola's perfidy to spoil my birthday.

17 March

I turn twenty-three today. All day producers and directors have been calling me up to wish me well. Bouquets have been arriving by the dozen; the whole house reeks of roses and lilies.

Rosie Mascarenhas tells me she has been flooded with cards from my fans. At the last count nearly thirty thousand had arrived, breaking all previous postal records.

Deepak Sir is hosting a birthday bash for me at the Sheraton this evening.

Even in the midst of all this festivity, my mind is tinged with sadness. Because no one will call to wish me Happy Birthday from Azamgarh. In my first year in Mumbai, I waited by the phone from morning till night on 17 March, hoping against hope for a call from Babuji and Ma, but it never came. My family has cut me off so completely that they probably don't even remember it's my birthday.

18 March

This evening a delivery arrived from DHL. I opened it up to discover a small packet, all neatly wrapped and ribboned.

I tore open the gold paper and received a shock. Because nestling in my hand was another videotape, black, without a cover or label. There was a small Post-it note attached to the bottom of the tape. 'Belated Happy Birthday. If you are still thinking of going to the police, see this,' it said in Bhola's slanting handwriting.

I inserted the tape into the video player, expecting to see the next instalment of 'Adventures of a Lonely Girl', but what appeared on the screen sent a jolt of electricity down my spine.

The tape showed me performing various sex acts on a

man. The man's face was never shown, but from his wheatish skin tone and the paunch of his hairy belly I knew without doubt that it was Bhola. The footage was graphic. Its explicitness numbed me. My bath tape looked like a Disney film by comparison.

The tape made a few things clear to me. One, that Ram Dulari was very much alive. And two, that she was a willing accomplice in all of Bhola's crimes. How a coy virgin had metamorphosed into a raging nymphomaniac was still a mystery to me, but her betrayal stung me more than Bhola's.

Bhola and Ram Dulari, what a team they made. They were a modern-day Bonnie and Clyde, a real-life Bunty and Babli, running riot, painting the town red, swindling, fucking, faking their way through to sixty million bucks. And leaving me to pay their bills.

For a long time I simply sat on the bed, paralysed. If you gaze for long enough into an abyss, the abyss gazes back at you. Then I began considering my options. The bath tape had nailed me, but this one had Ram Dulari in the lead role. I couldn't be held accountable for the actions of my doppelgänger. If I went to the police and Bhola released this tape, what was the worst that could happen? Going by recent examples, the tape would travel around the world as an internet video clip and rest eventually in cyberspace heaven, a permanent archive to refresh and relieve porn addicts.

I began thinking of Pamela Anderson and Paris Hilton. I thought of all the acres of free publicity, record box-office receipts. I would become the most famous Indian actress in the world, grab the number-one spot with just this one sleazy hit. And then, of course, I would conveniently blame it all on Ram Dulari!

No, no, no. It was all wrong. What was I thinking? This is India. Here exposing your belly button is seen as indecent exposure. Here a woman in a bikini leads to street protests. And how would I ever prove that it was the 'fake' me on tape? Especially after the release of the 'original' bath tape.

I should think police case. Think magistrate. Think jail. Think riots by the Society for Moral Regeneration. Think my effigies being burnt, my movie posters being shredded. Think being shunned by the film industry. Think the end of my career.

Shit!

Think, dammit. Just Think. THINK.

20 March

The call I have been waiting four years for came today.

At precisely nine twenty p.m. the telephone rang and a jaded operator asked me if I was Shabnam Saxena. 'Yes, this is Shabnam Saxena,' I said.

'Please speak, your caller is on line,' she droned, completely oblivious to the fact that she had just spoken to one of India's biggest celebrities.

'*Beti*, this is Ma speaking. I am calling from a PCO.' I heard my mother's thin voice and my heart leapt into my mouth.

The line was very bad, but I sensed instantly that this was not a call to wish me Happy Birthday. It was a cry for help.

Ma was imploring me to return immediately to Azamgarh. 'There has been a big tragedy,' she said. 'Your father is in hospital, fighting for his life. I cannot say anything on the phone. Just come, my daughter. Just come.'

'Yes, Ma,' I said, fighting back the tears. 'I am coming.'

21 March

I have returned to Azamgarh, the town of my birth. I flew from Mumbai to Varanasi and then hired a taxi to take me the final ninety kilometres. Lest I be recognized and mobbed, I put on a *burqa* over my jeans.

Lucknow changed a lot in three years, but Azamgarh has remained unchanged even after seven. It is the same congested cesspool dotted with dilapidated houses and decaying slums. The roads are full of potholes. Rubbish lies piled up at every street corner. Roadside drains overflow with sewer water. Cows roam the roads freely. Posters of politicians with plastic smiles and folded hands decorate every empty space.

Kurmitola, where our ancestral house stands, has become a claustrophobic monstrosity. Its narrow streets used to teem with rickshaws and cycles, but now they buzz with the sounds of car horns, three-wheeler klaxons and screeching tyres. Pigeons flutter from the balconies of spectacularly ruined houses. Battered hoardings display garish film posters and advertisements for sex clinics. Dexterous craftsmen in tatty clothes work in decrepit shops. Wrinkled men smoke ancient hookahs on filthy pavements, looking like derelict reminders of a forgotten past.

I had no difficulty in locating my house, at the edge of a field used by children for games of cricket and *gulli danda*. I knocked on the weather-beaten door and Ma opened it. She looked older and greyer than I had ever seen her. We embraced, shed a few tears, then she made me sit on a creaky charpoy in the octagonal courtyard where Sapna and I used to play hopscotch and told me the reason for calling me to Azamgarh.

Two days ago, Sapna was abducted while returning from college. She was taken to a small house in Sarai Meer, a notorious locality just outside the city, known for its gangsters. There her abductor tried to rape her, but Sapna somehow managed to get hold of the gangster's gun and shot him dead.

She returned home within hours of her abduction, but

Babuji had a heart attack on receiving the news. Now he is in hospital and Sapna is hiding in the house, terrified that the police might come any minute to take her away for murder. In desperation, Ma has turned to me as a last resort.

I gripped Ma's hand as she narrated these events, her voice breaking.

'Your sister came back trembling like a leaf,' she continued. 'I couldn't look into her eyes, so full of pain. Lawlessness has increased so much in this city that no girl is safe. Well, what can you expect when the Home Minister of the State is himself a known criminal? Your Babuji will still not admit it, but I say to you, *beti*, you did the right thing by going away to Bombay. I only wish you had taken your little sister with you. Then we wouldn't have had to see this day.'

'Between right and wrong there is accident, Ma, which is neither right nor wrong, over which we have no control.'

'You are right, *beti*. Whatever is destined will come to pass.'

'Where is Sapna?' I asked.

'She is hiding in the luggage room and refuses to come out. The poor girl has not eaten in forty-eight hours. Perhaps you can make her listen.'

I remembered the luggage room was the gloomiest room in the house. It was windowless and the air inside was dark and lifeless, radiating the musty smell of dust and mouldy wood. It was the perfect hiding spot when Sapna and I used to play hide and seek, but neither of us could bear staying in that creepy room longer than ten minutes. Now Sapna had been holed up there for two full days.

I ran up the steps to the luggage room and knocked on the battered wooden door, its paint peeling in strips away from the wood. 'It is me, Sapna. Open up.'

There was a brief silence, and then Sapna opened the door and fell into my embrace. She looked haggard and gaunt, with dark circles under her eyes. She draped her arms around me and hugged me tightly, her fingers digging into my spine, searching for the familiar indentations of childhood in the terrain of my back. Then she broke down and cried, her frail body racked by sobs. Her tears flowed freely till she had none left. I stroked her head and silently shared her grief.

At my urging, Sapna finally ate a meal. Then we left for the hospital to see Babuji, Sapna also dressed in a black *burqa* like me.

The room in the ICU was dim and quiet. My elder sister Sarita was there, sitting on a chair with the same harassed look on her face as when I had last seen her, the look of an unhappily married woman with three unruly children. She embraced me more warmly than I expected. We were never that close, but perhaps my fame had bridged the gap.

Babuji lay on a metal bed with a green sheet, breathing through a tube. He has shrunk since I last saw him. Old age has defined the furrows on his face and the veins on his hands; illness has deepened them. His hair has thinned out, leaving bald patches on the scalp. He groaned occasionally in his sleep.

I have done many such scenes in movies – the dutiful daughter at the father's deathbed – but I had almost forgotten the antiseptic smell of a real hospital. The steady blip of the heart monitor resonated in the room like a radio signal in outer space. I listened to the pneumatic hiss and whoosh of the ventilator, saw the green digital surge of the EKG and felt a tiny wave of relief.

A bespectacled doctor in a white coat entered the room and checked the chart attached to the bed.

'Is he making progress, Doc?' I asked him.

The doctor was clearly surprised at being asked a question in English by a woman in a *burqa*. 'Yes. He is making a good recovery. But we need to monitor him closely for the next three days.'

'Please give him the best care possible. Money is no object.'

I felt funny saying this, because money clearly is an object. I am neck deep in debt without a penny in the bank. But when you are grappling with something as elemental as murder, concerns about money begin to seem inconsequential.

As soon as the doctor left, I caught hold of Sapna's hand. 'Babuji will be fine. Now take me to Sarai Meer. To the house where that man took you.'

She wrenched her hand away. 'No, *didi*. I cannot bear to return to that place.'

'But you have to, Sapna,' I implored her. 'I have to remove all evidence of your visit to that house.'

'I cannot see that man again, not even his dead body.'

'I promise you, I will take just ten minutes.'

After much cajoling, Sapna agreed to take me to Sarai Meer. As our auto-rickshaw passed the familiar landmarks of my childhood and youth, memories of another age came flooding back to me. I remembered stolen afternoons spent sucking sweetened crushed ice from the hawker in front of the Inter College, bunking from school to see *Hum Aapke Hain Kaun* at the Delight Cinema, window-shopping expeditions to Asif Ganj, the spicy *chaat* of Nathu Sweets on MG Road.

Sapna asked the driver to stop outside the main market in Sarai Meer. From there we proceeded to our destination on foot.

This was a predominantly Muslim area, but there weren't many *burqa*-clad women walking about. Most of the houses were run-down shanties. Clothes fluttered from rickety balconies and cable-TV wires looped from every roof. I peered into the cavernous grocery shops and the bright pharmacies, the tiny video-rental shops and the PCOs that had sprouted in the locality like a crop of mushrooms. The aroma of freshly cooked meat drifted from smoky food stalls.

Sapna clung to me like a drowning girl holding on to a wooden plank. I could sense her desperation from the way her nails gouged my skin and I knew that my little sister had lost her innocence. For her, the familiar world of Azamgarh had suddenly become foreign and evil, and I was her only refuge.

What Bhola had done to me was nothing compared to what had happened to her. I had paid the price of fame, but she had paid the price of puberty, of simply being a woman in a town full of lecherous men.

As Ma said, no girl was safe in this city. Even a three-year-old could be raped and mutilated by the perverts who roamed the streets with abandon. I railed against these bastards who had denied my sister even the feminine happiness of visiting a market.

Sapna stopped at the mouth of a long alley framing the green dome and lone minaret of a mosque in the far distance, and glanced furtively left and right. The piercing cry of an *azaan* suddenly rent the air, calling the faithful to prayer, and a flock of pigeons rose into the grey sky from their perch on the minaret's railing. A stream of bearded worshippers began making their way towards the mosque.

We waited till the crowd had thinned; then Sapna led me along the cobbled alley to a single-storey house with a nondescript door. The door was unlocked and we entered into a courtyard with a dying guava tree in the centre. Crossing the courtyard, we came to another door with a metal latch. Sapna covered her face with her hands as I gently pushed it open. A swarm of flies and the stench of rotting flesh assailed me.

I stepped into a small room which contained a ceiling fan, a wooden four-poster bed with a green cover, a desk, on which rested an earthen pot for water and an unopened bottle of Triple X rum, and a wooden cupboard. There were no calendars on the bare walls, no photographs or personal belongings of any kind. It was a room without memory, an impersonal place of assignation.

The man lay face-down on the stone floor, dressed in white *kurta* pyjamas. He was tall and heavy set and very dead. Next to his body was a pistol in a matt-black finish.

Seeing a dead body up close can be quite unnerving, especially one that has begun to rot. I flipped open my veil, clenched my nose and picked up the gun. It was a Beretta 3032 Tomcat, compact and lightweight. 'Is this the gun you shot him with?'

Sapna nodded and shivered. 'He said he knew I was your sister. He kept saying, "No one can get Shabnam, but at least I can say I got Shabnam's sister." A sob escaped her lips and I grasped her hand once again. I, too, was guilty by association, complicit in the bastard's crime.

'I need to see his face,' I said.

'I don't,' wailed Sapna.

'Come on, help me.' I grabbed the man by his waist and tried to turn him over. He was like a large, inert boulder and I had to pin my leg against his hip and push with all my might before I succeeded in tipping him over on to his back.

Bile filled my mouth as soon as I saw his bloated body. The stomach had distended like a helium balloon and his hands and feet were as stiff as cement. Some kind of fluid had leaked from his mouth, nose, eyes and ears and congealed into a sticky mucous-like substance. His skin had turned a waxy greenish-blue. His face was almost unrecognizable because of the grotesque bloating and the eyes had sunk into the skull. All I could make out was that he had a large, clean-shaven face, disfigured with numerous pockmarks, perhaps the residuum of a childhood disease. His left ear had a deep cut, as though someone had slashed it with a knife. And in the middle of his forehead was a small disc-like hole where the bullet had gone in. There was surprisingly little blood.

'Any idea who this fellow is?' I asked Sapna, breathing through my mouth.

'No, *didi*. I'd never seen him before. He just grabbed me from behind as I was walking out of college and pushed me into a taxi. At least twenty students must have seen me being abducted, but no one dared to raise an alarm.'

'Did anyone see you when he brought you here?'

'I don't know. He bound and gagged me. I think I must have been unconscious when he brought me to this house.'

'Was there a . . . struggle?'

'Yes. He asked me to undress. When I refused he lunged at me, caught hold of my *kameez* and tore it in half. That's when I glimpsed his gun lying underneath the pillow and grabbed it. He charged at me like a mad bull and the gun went off. I swear, *didi*, I didn't mean to kill him. I only wanted to get away from him.'

'Didn't neighbours hear the gun shot?'

'They must have, but gun shots are so common in Sarai Meer, nobody pays any attention to them.'

'Then how did you go home in a torn *kameez*?'

'I took one of his *kurtas* from the cupboard, ran to the main road and took an auto-rickshaw home.'

I pictured the scene in my mind, then went to the cupboard and opened it. It contained a couple of shirts and pairs of trousers on thin metal hangers. All the shelves were empty, but when I peered deeper, I discovered a black canvas bag stuffed into the inner recesses of the bottom shelf. I pulled it out and unzipped it. It was full of stacks of crisp new hundred-rupee notes.

Sapna's eyes widened on seeing the cash. 'Oh *didi*, how much do you think there is?'

'I don't know. But at least seven or eight lakhs,' I said. 'Let's find out who this bastard is.' I rummaged through the dead man's *kurta* pockets and came up with a tattered black leather wallet and a clunky blue Nokia mobile. The wallet contained 3,325 rupees and a few coins, but not a scrap of paper which could identify him. I turned to the mobile. It was dead too. It probably needed recharging.

'OK, let me start removing evidence of our visit,' I said, and for the next half-hour proceeded to wipe every inch of the room with a handkerchief to make sure no fingerprints were left anywhere. I cleaned the pistol as well and put it into the canvas bag. When I lifted the bag, I found it was really quite heavy.

'What are you doing, *didi*?' Sapna cried. 'You are stealing money.'

'We need it more than he does,' I said, dropping the dead man's wallet into the bag.

We closed the door to the room as before, wiped the metal latch clean, crossed the courtyard and stepped into the alley once again. No sooner had I stepped into the street than a bearded man in a grey *pathan* suit pointed his grubby finger at me. 'Isn't she Shabnam Saxena?' he asked his similarly dressed companion, who gaped at me with his mouth open.

'Yes. It is Shabnam. SHABNAM IS HERE!' he screamed at the top of his voice.

'Shit!' I swore softly as I realized that I had forgotten to pull down the veil over my face. People were beginning to stare at me, even with my face now covered. I grabbed Sapna's arm and half ran, half walked to the mouth of the alley, lugging the heavy bag with me. Luckily an empty auto-rickshaw was passing by and I jumped into it, pulling Sapna in as the startled driver almost overturned. 'Take us to Kurmitola. Quick. I'll pay you five hundred rupees.'

The driver did another double-take and gunned his glorified scooter as though it was a James Bond vehicle.

We counted the money this evening. It is ten lakh rupees. I handed over the loot to Ma. She needs it more than I do. But Sapna was still inconsolable. 'Now I have got you involved as well, *didi*. The police will catch you,' she wailed. She clung to me like a daughter as we slept in Babuji's bedroom, but when I got up later to get a glass of water I found her missing. I discovered her in the bathroom, sitting on the wet floor, trying to slash her wrists with Babuji's shaving blade.

'What are you doing, Sapna?' I screamed and snatched the blade from her trembling fingers. Her whole body shook as if she was in the grip of a violent chill. I helped her back to the bed, and lay down with her, pulling the heavy woollen blanket over us completely, smothering both the cold and my sobs.

It was inside that blanket's dark cocoon, as I listened to my little sister's muffled heartbeats, that I had my first real epiphany. With startling clarity, the impermanence of life, the transience of fame and the true meaning of family were revealed to me. I saw the starkness of Sapna's predicament and the source of her poignant anxiety, and I decided in that instant that come what may, I would protect my sister. Even if it meant taking the rap for murder.

At the same time, I remembered Barkha Das's words – how the rich and famous manipulate the law and get away with murder – and wished I had an ace up my sleeve which could trump all our troubles, an ally in high places. Someone who could get the body disposed off and get the whole thing hushed up. And that's when it struck me, I know such a man. He is a part-time producer, occasional murderer and full-time philanderer. More importantly, he is the son of the Home Minister of Uttar Pradesh, who controls the entire police force of the State. And his name is Vicky Rai.

22 March

I called him up on my mobile. Luckily his number wasn't engaged.

'Is that really you, Shabnam? I hope my Caller ID is not playing tricks on me.'

'Vicky, I need your help.'

'So you want the National Award, after all?'

'No. It is much more serious than that.'

'Really? Have you murdered someone? Just joking. Ha!'

'I cannot talk on the phone. I need to see you.'

'Well I've been dying to see you for a very long time.'

'Can I come today?'

'Today? No, today is a bad day. Why don't you come tomorrow? Come straight to Number Six.'

'Number Six?'

'Yeah. That's my farmhouse in Mehrauli. Every taxi-driver in Delhi knows the address. Tomorrow night I am throwing the biggest party on earth. Celebrating my acquittal.'

'I need to see you privately. Not at a party.'

'We will meet in private, darling, but after the party.'

'But you must promise that you will help me.'

'Of course, I promise. Anything you want. But my help comes at a price.'

'I am willing to pay it.'

'This isn't just about your starring in *Plan B*.'

'I know what you are talking about, Vicky.'

'Good. Then I'll see you tomorrow, 23 March at eight p.m. at Number Six.'

'See you.'

'One more thing, Shabnam.'

'What?'

'Wear something sexy, OK?'

So this is it. The die has been cast. I refused to sleep with a prince, but I have just agreed to sleep with a murderer. Sisterly love has extracted the ultimate price. And I shall pay it willingly.

I took out the dead man's Beretta, pressed the release

button and ejected the magazine. I have handled enough guns in films to know them inside-out. There are six cartridges left. I reinserted the magazine and carefully put the pistol inside my handbag.

I am going to a murderer's house; the least I can do is go with back-up. My own Plan B.

EVIDENCE

'There are no facts, only interpretations.'

Friedrich Nietzsche, *Daybreak*

14

Restoration

MOHAN KUMAR looks at his watch and inserts a hand in the pocket of his *kurta,* feeling the cold metal of the pistol. It is a timely reminder of the mission he is here to undertake.

It has been over an hour since he entered the gates of Number Six. The strong police presence outside the farmhouse had surprised him. But luckily there was no screening through a door-frame metal-detector for those arriving with their invitation cards.

Vicky Rai had greeted him in his usual pompous manner. 'Hello, Kumar – or should I address you as Gandhi Baba? Glad you could make it.' The hostility between them hung in the air like fog. For a brief moment he had flirted with the idea of shooting Vicky Rai then and there, but his hands had suddenly turned clammy and his heart had started palpitating alarmingly, and he had quietly slunk away into the garden.

His mind has been playing tricks on him all evening, strengthening his resolve one moment and breaking it the next. He swings between confidence and despair. And matters are not helped by the strangers who keep distracting him. They waylay him every few minutes, either to compliment him on his exploits as Gandhi Baba or to seek a favour. 'You deserved the Nobel Peace Prize, Gandhi Baba,' says one. 'Would you agree to address the World Leadership Conclave next July?' requests another. He smiles at them, while inside him the anxiety is growing. He wants to end it, quickly.

To take his mind off the issue of murder, he tries to focus on the mechanics of the act. The party is much bigger than he expected – there must be at least four hundred people on the sprawling lawns of Number Six, another hundred inside the house – and he will have to shoot Vicky Rai in full view of all the guests. This does not faze him. On the contrary, he relishes the prospect of a public execution. It will be an apt lesson for all future Vicky Rais. He touches the butt of the Walther PPK again and senses its power seep into his hand.

He moves towards the gazebo, hoping to locate a suitable vantage spot. The swimming pool is bathed in light, its cool blue water shimmering like glass under the bright spotlights. A girl in a blue bikini suddenly dives into the pool, splashing him with water. As he brushes the drops from his *khadi* vest, a flashbulb pops in his face, blinding him momentarily. He loses his footing and is about to fall into the pool when someone catches his arm and steadies him. For a few seconds he sees only blackness. When his vision clears he blinks at his benefactor. It is a bearded waiter in a red-and-black outfit. 'Thank you,' he mumbles, feeling flustered. He will have to be more careful, he reminds himself.

There are a good number of people around the pool, sipping wine and swaying to the music. They are all under twenty-five, and he feels old and out of place. He is about to turn away when a statuesque blonde girl in a body-hugging dress approaches him, strutting like a model on a catwalk. 'Ghandi Baba, how lovely to see you,' she drawls, pirouetting seductively in front of him. He can smell liquor on her breath. 'I'm Lisa. I'm in India for a photo shoot on the Kama Sutra. I could teach you some interesting positions.' She laughs and tries to kiss him.

'Ram, Ram,' he says and steps back hurriedly. In the process he collides with a waiter heading for the bar with six bottles of whisky on a tray. The tray falls from the waiter's hands and the bottles tumble to the paved stone floor and shatter. The air begins to reek of alcohol. So pungent are the fumes that he begins to feel dizzy. He stumbles away from the pool, feeling nauseous and strangely light-headed. He lurches down the lawn, moving further and further away from the crowd.

Before he knows it, he is deep inside a wooded area, where the lights of the garden do not reach. The moon is a giant white disc hanging above the treetops, its chalky light the only illumination in the forested gloom. He hears the steady gurgle of a waterfall some distance away, but closer to him the only sound is that of his own laboured breathing. He is wheezing slightly from all the running. Something is happening inside his brain, some kind of chemical reaction. His mind has become a kaleidoscope of shifting thoughts and images. Old suppressed memories are rising up, a fog is lifting, but only partially.

His foot crunches on something. First there is a creak and the snap of a breaking twig, and then he hears a faint hissing sound. He looks down to find a snake on the ground, and from the shape of its large head he knows instantly that it is a cobra. It is poised just above his right leg, its slippery tongue flickering in and out. He freezes and the blood stops coursing through his veins.

The snake rears its head, preparing to strike. *I am going to die*, he thinks. Just then he hears another twig break and suddenly a hand grips the head of the snake and lifts it off the ground. The cobra writhes for a while till it is flung far away.

'Who . . . who are you?' he asks, trying to peer into the silvery darkness.

A shadow shifts and a strange young man steps forward. He is dressed in a white shirt and black trousers, with a red Gap cap on his head and a black bag draped over his shoulder. His skin is so black that he merges with the darkness, but the whites of his eyes shine like torches. 'I am Jiba Korwa from Jharkhand,' he says.

'What are you doing here?'

'Waiting.'

'Thank you. You saved my life.'

'And who are you?'

'I am Mohan . . . Mohandas . . . Karam . . . Kumar. No, no –

that is not right . . . Let me say it again. I – am – Mohan Kumar. Yes. And I hate snakes.'

'I have removed the snake, but you are still fearful.'

'How can you tell?'

'I can smell your fear. Is it because of the shadow?'

'What shadow?'

'The shadow that dogs you like the moon. The *embekte*.'

'*Embekte*? What is that?'

'There are two spirits in every man – *eeka* and *embekte*. When a man dies of natural causes, like an illness, he becomes an *eeka* and goes to live below the earth. But when a man dies suddenly, such as if he is killed, then the other spirit *embekte* comes out and tries to find a new body. It takes temporary shelter in whichever living body it can find. This is what you people call a ghost. And a ghost has taken hold of your body.'

'Oh my God, so you can actually see it?'

'No, I cannot see it. I can only see its shadow. Is it a good spirit or a bad one?'

'A very bad one. It makes me do all kinds of weird things. Can you . . . can you do something about it?'

'I could.'

'The doctors say I have DID, but I know it is really a case of possession. I need an exorcist, not a psychotherapist. Do you know how to take a spirit out?'

'Yes. I am half a *torale*. I can get rid of the shadow.'

'Then do so. I want my life back. In return I'll give you whatever you want.'

'Can you give me some money?'

'How much?'

'Two times nine thousand.'

'That's eighteen thousand. That's a lot of money. What do you want it for?'

'To buy tickets to go back to my village.'

'Let's do a deal. If you can cure me, the money is yours.'

'Then lie down.'

'Here, on the ground?'

'Yes. And take off your shirt. I need to put some red clay on your chest and face.'

'Now that you've saved my life, how can I refuse your instructions?' He strips off his *kurta* and vest and lies down on the hard ground, unmindful of the ants which are crawling over his legs and the twigs digging into his back.

The tribal unzips his black canvas bag and takes out a lump of red clay, which he mixes with pig fat. He then draws a fine herringbone design on Mohan Kumar's chest and daubs a few horizontal lines on his face.

'What are you doing?' Mohan worries.

'I am summoning the spirits, who will draw away the *embekte*. Now close your eyes and don't speak.'

The tribal takes out a charm necklace made of bones and drapes it around Mohan's neck. Then, putting his left hand on Kumar's head, and holding a small white bone in his right, he begins chanting, swaying back and forth in a circular motion, faster and faster.

Mohan feels an excruciating pain, as though a corkscrew is being twisted inside his brain. He groans in agony, feeling his skin being peeled off. And then he passes out.

When he opens his eyes, the tribal is still sitting by his side, gazing at him intently.

'Is it done?' Mohan asks.

'Yes. I took the *embekte* out of your body.'

Mohan presses his temples and finds that the pain has gone. He feels cleansed, whole. He sits up and begins putting on his clothes. 'You have done something which no one else could do. That spirit was causing me a lot of trouble, even though it was that of a very famous man.'

'Man?'

'Yes, the spirit which possessed me was that of Mohandas Karamchand Gandhi. Surely you have heard of Mahatma Gandhi?'

'No, you are mistaken. It was not a man who possessed you, it was a woman.'

'Woman? How do you know?'

'I talked to it. It was very stubborn.'

'What was her name?'

'Ruby Gill.'

'Ruby Gill!' Mohan exclaims. He feels the bulk of the pistol in his *kurta* pocket and becomes thoughtful. 'So all along it was Ruby Gill leading me on, pretending to be Mahatma Gandhi . . . It's beginning to make sense now.'

The tribal tugs at his sleeve. 'Will you give me the money?'

'Yes, yes, of course.' He opens a black leather wallet and takes out a wad of thousand-rupee notes. 'You asked for eighteen; I am giving you twenty. This can buy you a ticket even to London!'

The tribal accepts the money and bows in gratitude. 'You are very kind.'

Mohan Kumar scrubs his face with a handkerchief, removing traces of the red clay. Standing up, he dusts his *dhoti*. 'This is the last time I am wearing this silly dress.'

He steps out from the thicket on to the lawn and looks at his watch. It is a quarter past eleven. The party appears to be in full swing. There are at least half a dozen girls in the pool and the bar area is thronged with guests. He strides quickly towards the gazebo.

'Do you have Chivas?' he asks the bartender, who nods. 'Then give me a large Scotch, neat.'

He gulps down the whisky in one shot, wipes his mouth with the sleeve of his *kurta* and asks for a refill. Spotting the CEO of Rai Textile Mill, he pats him jovially on the back. 'So, Raha, how are things?'

Raha turns around, adjusts his steel-rimmed glasses, and is surprised to see Mohan Kumar. 'I didn't expect to see you at this party, Mr Kumar,' he says coldly.

'Let bygones be bygones, Raha. I was suffering from a medical disorder, but I am fully cured now. In fact, I will explain it all to Vicky. Have you seen him?'

'He has just gone inside the house with Shabnam Saxena.'

Mohan drains his second glass and starts walking towards the house. The blonde model who had tried to kiss him is standing in the way, sipping what looks like a strawberry daiquiri. 'Ooh, Ghandi Baba, you are back,' she coos.

He smiles at her. 'Yes, I am back. And I am keen for some experiments in untruth. When do you want to begin?'

She comes within kissing distance of him. 'How about right now?'

'I need to sort out a few issues first. But good things come to those who wait.' He winks and pinches her bottom.

She squeals.

Acquisition

'HOWDY! I'm Rick Myers,' I introduced myself, feeling as uncomfortable in the Armani suit I had bought from Connaught Place as an elephant in underpants.

The host, dressed in an equally smart dark suit and purple tie, clasped me in a bear hug as though he was my long-lost brother. I got worried he might start fingering the Glock in the inside pocket of my jacket. 'Welcome to Number Six,' he said. 'Lizzie told me you were coming.' Squinting at me, he tapped his chin. 'Haven't we met somewhere, Mr Myers?'

I had recognized him immediately from the scar running down the left side of his face. He was the hombre who had fired me from the call centre. 'I doubt it,' I said. 'I got this name just yesterday.'

'Yesterday? What do you mean?'

I corrected myself. 'I mean I arrived in your country just yesterday. So the chances of us having met are slim to none, and slim just got up and left.'

'I really like your sense of humour, Mr Myers. I am in the same line as you – film production. Perhaps we can do business together.' He pointed to the man standing next to him. 'Let me introduce you to my father, Mr Jagannath Rai, Home Minister of Uttar Pradesh.'

The pop was a heavy-set, hairy man, with a round face and a

thick, curled-up moustache. He folded his hands in greeting, looking greasy as fried lard.

I stepped into the garden and was awestruck at how huge and beautiful the farmhouse was. The three-storey house was made entirely of marble, there was a lawn the size of three baseball pitches, a swimming pool as big as Lake Waco, a temple, and a gazebo lit up like the fourth of July. Far in the distance I could even make out a jungle. The place was bigger than the Governor's mansion in Austin, but I couldn't figure out why it was called a farmhouse. I could see neither any animals nor any farmers on the property.

There were more people on the lawn than you could shake a stick at. And they all looked like big guns in their expensive threads. Music played from large loudspeakers. Waiters hovered around with all kinds of goodies. I remembered Lizzie's warning and decided to check first if any of those Al Qaeda dudes were snooping around. I peered into the forest, looked behind all the trees and that's when I saw a man in a blue suit sneaking across the lawn, close to the boundary wall, with a packet in his hands. Suddenly I felt like a real FBI officer. I began following him, like Mel Gibson tracked those baddies in *Lethal Weapon*. I was hoping to confront him with my gun, when he entered the little temple in the corner of the lawn. I saw him fold his hands and bow his head before the Indian gods. It seemed he had only come to offer prayers.

Disappointed, I decided to get a drink and began moving towards the gazebo where the bar was set up. Near the pool a bunch of journalists armed with cameras and flash guns were hanging around, snapping pictures of some pretty young things who were posing like film stars on the red carpet. I immediately started searching for Shabnam. A lanky man with a camera in one hand and a twitch in one eye goggled at me. 'Excuse me, are you Michael J. Fox?'

'No,' I said. 'I'm Rick Myers, Hollywood producer.'

The moment I said this, the girls were all over me. They began peppering me with questions.

'Are you making a film in India?'

'Can you please get me a role?'

'Will you take me with you to Hollywood?'

The last time I was surrounded by so many girls was in Third Grade when they were all taking a good look at my willie. Mizz Henrietta Loretta had given us a new kind of exam called an IQ test and I foolishly bet Betsy Walton that I would score more than her. We were both pretty much bottom of the class but I thought I was smarter than her. As it turned out, I did score as high as 48 on that test, but she still beat me by getting a 50. So I had to take off my shorts in front of the whole class in what still remains the most embarrassing experience of my life.

Even as I was trying to figure out how to get rid of all these crazy chicks, I heard a ruckus at the bar. A waiter had dropped a whole tray of drinks and a tall man wearing an Indian dress was having a hissy fit, staggering around like a blind horse in a pumpkin patch. Ten seconds later I saw him running across the lawn like a scalded dog.

A young girl, who looked like her belly button wasn't dry yet, tapped me on the arm. 'Do you know any Hollywood stars?' she pouted.

'Yeah,' I replied. 'Arnie Schwarzenegger is my best buddy.'

She almost swooned. Another girl kissed me on the cheek without any warning and whispered, 'Can I meet you in your hotel room?'

I hadn't even put on my deodorant spray, yet these girls were becoming hornier than four-balled tomcats. So I excused myself and headed straight for the house, hoping to find Shabnam there. I walked through a door into a large round hall which had marble flooring smoother than a baby's ass. The sofas had been pushed into the corners and there were large windows on either side of the room, one opening on to the lawn and the other on to the driveway. There were plenty of people in the hall, talking and drinking at a wooden bar stacked with bottles. I looked around for Shabnam, but she wasn't there. So I went back into the garden and picked a quiet spot far from those batty girls.

Around eleven o'clock there was a sudden buzz on the lawn and everyone started moving towards the house. 'What's happening?' I asked a waiter. 'They say Shabnam Saxena is here,' he replied, and quick as a hiccup I was back in the hall. Five minutes later, in walked the woman of my dreams, looking even more beautiful than her photograph. She was wearing a tight-fitting dress and carried a moccasin handbag. I could smell her perfume from fifty feet away.

Shabnam took an empty sofa and Vicky Rai sat down beside her. From the way Shabnam cringed when his hand grazed her arm, I knew she didn't fancy him. I felt like drawing my Glock and blowing out his brains. They spoke in low voices and I saw Shabnam shake her head several times. A waiter with a thick black beard brought in a trayful of drinks. Shabnam took an orange juice; Vicky Rai asked for tequila. I hovered near them, hoping to catch Shabnam's eye. Fifteen minutes passed by, but Vicky Rai didn't budge from the sofa. Just when I was beginning to wonder if his backside was coated with superglue, his pop came in and told him to get up. 'Iqbal Mian has come. He wants to meet you.' Vicky made a face and stood up reluctantly. Sensing my opportunity, I plonked myself on the sofa faster than the Undertaker does a choke slam on his opponent.

Shabnam looked at me like a warehouse inspector checking out new merchandise. I extended my hand. 'Hi! I'm Rick Myers, Hollywood producer. I've been fixin' to meet you for ages, Shabnam. Just saw your film *Love in Canada* on the telly.'

She shook my hand warmly. 'What are you doing in India, Mr Myers?'

'Believe it or not, I came just to see you.'

'To offer me a role in an American film?'

'Yeah.'

'What's it going to be called?'

'Er . . . I was thinking of *Love in Waco*.'

She smiled. I inched closer to her on the sofa and dropped my voice to a whisper. 'Listen, Shabnam, I know you are in a whole lot of trouble.'

She became more nervous than a fly in a glue pot. 'What do you mean?'

'I mean I know all about Sapna.'

The moment I said 'Sapna' she crumpled; the fight went out of her body like gas from a hot-air balloon.

'How did you find out?'

'A PI by the name of Mr Gupta tipped me off. I tell you, that guy is smarter than a tree full of owls.'

'I am indeed in great difficulty,' she said, wringing her hands. 'I came to Vicky Rai for help from his father. But he asks a high price.'

'I wouldn't go partners on a butcher's knife with him,' I said. 'He's more slippery than a pig on ice.'

'Then what should I do?'

'Take my help. I'm the guy for you.'

'What can a Hollywood producer do to help me?'

I took a quick look around and then leaned closer. 'I'm not really a Hollywood producer. I'm a forklift operator at Walmart. But I've been drafted into the FBI's Witness Protection Programme.'

She raised her eyebrows. 'And why exactly would the FBI offer you such a programme?'

'Coz I closed the contract on some real scumbags over in Pakistan. The FBI gave me fifteen million dollars as a reward and the President wrote me a very nice letter.'

Shabnam flicked her fingers across her face. 'Come on now, you're just pulling my leg.'

'You don't believe me? You want to see proof?'

She nodded and I took out the letter from the President from my suit pocket.

She read it and looked at me. 'But this is addressed to Larry Page.' She frowned. 'Now where have I heard that name?'

'Larry Page used to be my real name. But now the FBI have given me this new name – Rick Myers. I still haven't cottoned on to it.'

Shabnam wasn't even listening to me. She snapped her fingers.

'Larry Page . . . You're the American who has been writing me all those letters, aren't you?'

'Yeah. That's me,' I said and looked her in the eye. 'I'm madly in love with you!'

That went down like a pregnant pole-vaulter. Shabnam got up from the sofa faster than a striped-assed ape and wagged a finger at me. 'Please keep away from me, Mr Page. I want nothing to do with you.'

She turned her back on me and began talking to a tall dude with a black beard.

I felt as mad as a one-legged man at a butt-kicking contest.

16

Sacrifice

'HELLO, TRIPURARI?'

'Yes, Bhaiyyaji. Where are you calling from? Aren't you supposed to be at Vicky's party?'

'Yes, yes. I am calling from Number Six. Tell me, have you been in touch with Mukhtar?'

'Mukhtar? No, Bhaiyyaji. I haven't spoken to him for over two weeks. What's the matter? You sound tense.'

'I gave Mukhtar a job a week ago, on 17 March. Did he come to get money from you, by any chance?'

'No, Bhaiyyaji. And what is this job you gave Mukhtar? You never mentioned anything to me.'

'I'll tell you later. For the moment, try and find him for me. Ask him to give me a call. I've been trying to call him for the past three days but it looks like his mobile is switched off.'

'He must be lying drunk somewhere with a girl.'

'Wherever he is, just find him for me, OK? And then let me know.'

'I will, Bhaiyyaji.'

(*Disconnect.*)

Revenge

THE RICH may live very differently from the poor, but they don't die differently. A bullet does not discriminate between a king and a pauper, a tycoon and his worker. Standing in front of the wrought-iron gates of Number Six, looking at the glittering lights of the farmhouse, watching expensive imported cars enter the elegant driveway, I envy the conceit of the gun. One bullet is all it will take to end Vicky Rai's pomp and show. One bullet and *khallas*!

I see policemen with walkie-talkies standing behind a barricade and quicken my steps. There is a big crowd of curious onlookers on the road, straining to catch a glimpse of the celebrity guests. There is a rumour going around that Shabnam Saxena is expected any minute.

I turn left into the side lane and lurk by the service entrance, waiting for Ritu to come out. Compared to the hustle and bustle on the main road, the side lane is peaceful and quiet, though it is full of parked cars.

At five to eleven the metal gate creaks ajar and Ritu emerges, clad in a red *salwar kameez* and lugging a blue bag. Her injuries have still not healed fully, and her eyes are red and swollen. It seems she has been crying. We embrace silently. I take the precaution of keeping my left hand hidden inside the Benetton jacket I am wearing.

'Let's go, Munna.' She clutches my arm and begins to pull me towards the main road when I gently stop her.

'I have to tell you something, Ritu.'

'Whatever you have to say, you can tell me at the railway station. We don't have time to lose.'

'I am not going to the railway station.'

'What?'

'That is what I came to tell you. I am not going to Mumbai.'

'Why?'

'Let's go inside the farmhouse and I will tell you.'

She gives me a baffled look and retraces her steps to the service gate. She peeks in furtively before pushing it open and pulling me inside.

I see a manicured lawn in the distance with people laughing and chatting. There is even a swimming pool in which some girls are frolicking. Waiters in red-and-black uniforms hover around a gazebo.

Ritu propels me behind a huge *jamun* tree, its leafy foliage acting as a natural screen from the people on the lawn. Further to our right is a makeshift tent where the cooks are busy cooking.

'You'd better have a good explanation, Munna, for this about-face. You have no idea of the risk I took in sneaking out of the house,' she upbraids me. 'If Vicky finds out, he will kill me.'

I am prepared for her outburst. 'I know, Ritu. I have come to liberate you from fear.'

'What do you mean?'

'You will find out soon enough.'

'You have started speaking in riddles again. Tell me clearly why you are refusing to come to Mumbai. Is something wrong?'

'Everything is wrong, Ritu.' I look down at my feet, unable to look her in the eye. 'I have found another girl. I am going to marry her.'

She gives me a stricken look. 'Why are you saying this, Munna? Don't I have enough troubles already?'

'Every word of what I am saying is true.'

'So now you tell me that you don't love me any more?'

'Yes.' I nod and launch into my parting monologue. '*Bole toh*, love is a real bitch. It shows people like us dreams which can never become real. Perhaps the poor shouldn't even be allowed the right to love. I now realize that you were right, our love is a prohibited one. We can run away from here, but we cannot run away from that reality. So forget that you ever met me, Ritu. From this moment, erase me from your life for ever.'

She listens to me quietly and when I have finished, flashes me an accusing look. 'So this is it, eh? You think I can just erase you from my life like a teacher erases chalk marks from a blackboard? As if nothing has happened between us?' She draws closer to me. 'Do you know, Munna, why love is considered the greatest gift? Because it makes two people into one. They become joined in body and soul. I have become you and you have become me. And now I know you better than you know yourself. I can say from the bottom of my heart that what you are telling me is not true.'

I try to evade her eyes again. 'You and I can never be one. There is too big a chasm between us.'

'You are still lying. Look into my eyes, Munna, and swear on my life that you don't love me,' she says with sudden vehemence. When I don't reply she pulls my left hand from inside my jacket. In the process the plaster on my wrist gets exposed.

'What is this?' She immediately becomes concerned. 'How did you get hurt?'

'It is nothing . . . I fell down,' I dissemble, but Ritu remains unconvinced. Her hands fly to my face, looking for hidden injuries, and her fingers graze the bandage at the back of my head.

'Ahhhh!' I cry out in pain.

'Oh my God, what have they done to you?' she cries.

'Believe me, it is not serious. There is nothing to worry about.'

'It was my brother, wasn't it?' she asks. 'He wasn't content with hitting me. He had to do this to you as well. Now I understand why you came to break off with me.' I detect a hardening in her voice. Her sorrow is giving way to anger.

'Don't jump to conclusions, Ritu. I honestly don't know who they were.'

'But I know very well. And I will never forgive my brother for hurting you. Now no power on earth can keep me away from you,' she declares and I see a new look in her eyes, a look of utter fearlessness. 'Come with me, Munna. In front of this entire assembly I will announce that I am going to marry you.'

'And you think everyone will applaud you for marrying a sweeper's son? This is not a film, Ritu, this is life. And life does not have happy endings like films do.'

'But this is *my* life. And from today I will live it on my terms. I refuse to be cowed by two criminals who claim to be my father and brother.'

'Then let us make a pact here and now. Promise me that you won't do anything rash. And I promise to take you from here as soon as my injuries have healed.'

'I will wait for that day, Munna.'

A light wind begins blowing across the lawn. It ruffles Ritu's hair, pushing a few dark strands over her face. At that moment I feel as if standing in front of me is an angel who has come down from heaven to bless me and touch my sordid life with her purity and innocence. And I know that, try as I might, I cannot live without her. But perhaps I can die for her.

I sense a commotion on the lawn. 'Oh, it looks like Shabnam Saxena has arrived,' says Ritu.

'Can I see her?'

'Don't be silly. You must leave before someone spots you. Take good care of yourself, Munna. I love you.' She gives me a quick kiss on the lips and walks back towards the house. I creep deeper into the gloom and take out the gun. I need to feel its power once again, to stiffen my resolve to kill Vicky Rai.

'If I were you, I wouldn't use that gun,' a voice speaks up behind me.

I am so startled, the gun drops from my hand.

A tall man with a straggly black beard steps forward. He is dressed in off-white *kurta* pyjamas and has a fawn-coloured shawl draped over his shoulders.

'Don't worry, my dear fellow, I am not a policeman. But I

couldn't help overhearing your conversation with the lovely Ritu.'

I hastily pick up the gun and put it back into my jacket pocket.

'I have never heard such moving dialogue in my life,' he continues, fingering his straggly beard. 'You are a born actor. Let me take another look at you. Can you move a little into the light? Yes, that's perfect. Oh my God, you are magnificent. I have finally found my hero.'

'Who are you?'

'I am Jay Chatterjee, the film director. And I have decided to cast you as the hero in my next film, without any screen test. For the heroine's role I was thinking of Shabnam Saxena, but she will look too old against you. Now I think I will have to discover a new heroine as well.'

'Shabnam Saxena? Hero? What are you talking about? Is this one of those candid-camera pranks?'

'Jay Chatterjee does not believe in pranks,' the man says sternly. 'Get ready for instant stardom. Your life is made. But you will need a new name.'

'Why?'

'A name like Munna won't take you far in our industry. From today, you shall be known as . . . Chirag. The Lamp. I love it!' He takes out his wallet and extracts some notes. 'Here's twenty thousand. Consider this your signing amount, Chirag.'

I accept the money with trembling hands. 'I . . . I still find all this hard to believe.'

'This is what life is all about. You never know what's round the corner.'

'But I am just a sweeper's son.'

'So what? Johnny Walker was a bus conductor. Raaj Kumar was a sub-inspector. Mehmood was a driver. When Lady Luck knocks, she only sees a door. She doesn't see who's behind it.'

Jay Chatterjee notes down my mobile number and strolls back to the lawn, his fingers playing an imaginary piano. I remain standing under the tree for a long time, shivering with excitement.

My brain begins dreaming up new scenarios for me. I see myself in Mumbai, sitting with Ritu in a Mercedes, surrounded by thousands of screaming fans, mostly girls. They beg for my autograph and profess their undying love as the police charge them with *lathis*. I step out of the car and raise my hand. The policemen back off. 'Chirag! Chirag! Chirag!' a loud chant goes up and fifteen rockets scream into the sky all at once.

I open my eyes and discover that I am still in Delhi. But there are real rockets shooting over my head.

Are they for Vicky Rai, or for me? What do you say? *Kya bole?*

18

Redemption

EKETI CROUCHED behind a *kadam* tree and waited for the alarm to ring. The forested area was quiet, but the sound of laughter drifted across the brightly lit lawn. He had no sense of how much time had passed, but he was patient. A lot had happened since he had entered the farmhouse through that rear gate. He had killed a snake and successfully performed a ritual exorcism, something which even the great Nokai would have been proud of. And best of all, now he didn't need to depend on Ashok to return to his island. He had enough money to buy tickets for himself and Champi.

Thinking of Champi brought a smile to his face and an ache to his heart. He was waiting to rush back to her with the sacred rock. Tomorrow they would travel to Kolkata to board the ship for Little Andaman, where they would receive a hero's welcome. He patted the canvas bag by his side. It was his only remaining link to the island. The clay, the bones, the pellets all brought to his mind the scents and sensations of Gaubolambe, which loomed larger in his imagination with every passing day.

Suddenly little beeps began emanating from the canvas bag. Eketi stood up with a start and switched off the alarm. He dusted down his black trousers, slung the bag over his shoulder and set off on his mission.

He reached the cobbled pathway that led to the garages and

paused. In the middle of the path a small tent had been erected, inside which an army of cooks was busy frying, peeling and chopping. Large aluminium pots simmered on gas stoves. A perspiring man in a vest was bent over a clay *tandoor*, spearing freshly made *rotis* with a long metal skewer.

Eketi skirted the tent from the rear and proceeded down the path. He reached the garages without any difficulty. There was an empty plastic chair and immediately above it, embedded in the wall between the two garages, was a metal cabinet, painted blue. He was about to open the cabinet door when a hand fell on his shoulder. 'Hold it!' a stern voice boomed behind him.

He whirled around to find a dark man dressed in a white shirt and grey trousers glaring at him. There was a hockey stick in his right hand.

'Who are you?' the man demanded brusquely.

'I am Mr Sharma's driver,' he replied, swallowing hard.

'Then what are you doing traipsing around here? All the drivers are supposed to eat in the outside tent. Go over there.' He pointed towards the gate.

'Yes,' he said and half ran, half walked towards the gate. Rounding the corner, he leaned against the wall, his body still limp with shock.

He saw that he had reached the front driveway, where a row of cars was lined up, but none of the drivers was around. They were all having dinner inside a tent erected just behind the left entrance gate. The deathly silence in the portico was a sharp contrast to the music and laughter emanating from the garden at the back.

Hiding behind a marble column, Eketi peeked back at the cobbled pathway. The man in the grey trousers was now sitting on the plastic chair directly below the switchboard, wiping his neck with a handkerchief, the hockey stick leaning against his left leg. He did not appear to be a regular guard, but it was evident that he was stationed there specifically to ensure that no one tampered with the switchboard. Eketi wondered what to do. Should he go back to the Bhole Nath Temple and ask Ashok? Should he just make a dash for the *ingetayi*, light or no light? A whizzing sound came from above and he looked up to see a great green flower burst in the sky. The fireworks had started on the rear lawn.

He edged inside the portico and came across an open casement window. Peeping in, he saw a large hall full of people talking and drinking. The bass whine of a speaker suddenly split the air and a tall man wearing a dark suit and purple tie walked towards a mike positioned just behind the open window. The man turned to face the crowd, tapped the mike a couple of times and began speaking. 'Friends, we are gathered here today to celebrate my acquittal,' Eketi heard him say. 'All along I maintained my innocence. I am glad the court also recognized it. I am thankful to all of you whose support kept me afloat through those dark days and nights when I didn't know whether I would be spending the rest of my life in a dingy cell. So this is to say thank you. But the person I need to thank the most is my father, the one man responsible for making me what I am today. Dad, can you please come up here and say a few words?'

An older, heavy-set man, wearing white *kurta* pyjamas, walked up to the mike and embraced the man in the suit, who clung to him as if it was their last meeting. Eketi even detected a tear coursing down the suited man's cheek. Then the older man began speaking.

'It is always a mistake to give a politician a mike,' he said and there was mild tittering. 'But I am standing here today not as the Home Minister of Uttar Pradesh but as a father. And nothing gives a father greater happiness than to see his children prosper and flourish. Nothing pains a father more than to see his son being implicated in a totally fabricated case. I am glad that the long dark night is over and my son can now live like a free man. This is a victory for all those who have faith in the judiciary and in justice. To my son I wish a very long life. May Lord Shiva bless all of you.'

There were murmurs of approval from the people in the room. A cracker burst loudly and the sky was lit up by a brilliant orange pumpkin.

Eketi went back to his vantage point against the wall. He peeked at the garages again, hoping that the man in the grey trousers might have gone. But he was still there, except now he was standing up and looking left and right, as if checking that the coast was clear. As Eketi watched, the man turned towards the switchboard, opened the cabinet and fiddled briefly. Instantly, darkness descended over the entire farmhouse.

The tribal quivered with excitement. This was his cue. He raced down the cobbled pathway soundlessly and ran on to the lawn, which was also in pitch darkness. He was halfway across the grounds when his foot struck a wooden table and he went sprawling on to the grass. A loud bang came from inside the house, as though an engine had backfired, and he sensed a dark figure rush out on to the lawn. Eketi's left leg was hurting badly, but ignoring the pain he bounded the last few steps to the temple, his eyes accustomed by now to the darkness. Dropping his canvas bag to the floor, he began feeling his way around the walls, which had recessed alcoves containing idols of various deities. It took him half a minute to locate the one with the *ingetayi*. He touched it, felt its smooth surface, the markings on top, and his fingers began throbbing on their own. All else became a blur as he picked up the sea-rock. It lifted off its base easily. Slipping it into the canvas bag, he swung the bag across his shoulder and began running down the lawn, his heart singing. He was going home. To Champi. To Gaubolambe.

He had almost reached the edge of the wood when the lights came back on. 'Stop!' someone shouted behind him. He turned around and saw a constable with a raised baton speeding across the lawn towards him.

He tried to make a dash for the safety of the thicket, but at that very moment his injured left leg gave up on him. He fell down in a heap and within seconds the cop was upon him.

'What have you just done, bastard?' the constable wheezed, breathing deeply.

'Nothing,' said Eketi, his face distorted with pain.

'Give me your bag,' the constable said, whacking him on the legs with his *lathi*.

With a startled cry, Eketi let go of the bag. The constable lifted it and was surprised by its weight. 'What have you got inside? Let's take a look,' he muttered as he unzipped the bag. One by one he started taking out its contents – the small lumps of red and white clay, the pouch of pig fat, the bone necklace, and finally the sacred rock. 'Oh, this looks like a *shivling*! Where did you steal it from?' Before Eketi could reply, the constable groped in the bag one final time. His fingers touched something hard and metallic and his eyebrows rose as he drew out a silver-coloured gun. It was a locally made improvised revolver, a *katta*.

'And what is this, motherfucker?'

'I don't know. That is not mine,' Eketi replied, completely taken aback.

'Then how come it is inside your bag?'

'I don't know how it got there.'

'Don't worry, we will find out,' said the constable as he took out a pair of handcuffs. 'Come on, blackie, you are under arrest.'

Evacuation

24 March

I have been arrested. For murdering Vicky Rai.

These aren't the opening lines of a film script or a novel. I am writing them sitting on a wobbly bench inside the record room of Mehrauli police station, where I have been detained along with five other suspects. It is a large room, full of files piled high on metal shelves fifteen feet tall. Cobwebs festoon every corner and an ancient fan hangs from the wooden ceiling. The room has the musty smell of a library intermingled with the fetid stench of a morgue. The occasional gust of air blowing in from the small window with an iron grille is therefore a relief. I can hear the faint pitter-patter of raindrops. It has been raining steadily for the past two hours.

I had made a fashionably late entrance at the party, arriving at the farmhouse just after eleven. The lawn was packed with people. It seemed the Who's Who of Delhi had come to celebrate Vicky's acquittal. Jagannath Rai was there too, with an army of hangers-on in starched white *kurta* pyjamas. I was sickened by this vulgar display of political muscle, this affront to justice. But I was even more sickened by Vicky Rai. Having seen him up close – the scaly scar running down his left cheek, the way spit dribbled out of his mouth when he became excited – I felt disgusted at my decision to seek his help. I was going to pay a very high price indeed for saving my sister.

And then I met the weirdest American in the whole world. He was cute, with a strong resemblance to Michael J. Fox; he was rich, having just received fifteen million dollars; and he was madly in love with me. But he turned out to be the psycho Rosie had warned me about. So I got rid of Mr Larry Page, a.k.a. Rick Myers, faster than he could say 'Howdy'.

At the stroke of midnight fireworks began in the garden and speeches began in the marble drawing room. Vicky Rai and his father spoke as if they were members of a mutual admiration society. Their corny panegyrics made me cringe. Then Vicky went to the bar and began mixing a drink. That is when the lights went out and the entire house was plunged into darkness. Living in Mumbai, I had almost forgotten the power cuts which used to plague Azamgarh. But somehow the lights going off at Number Six did not seem to fit the pattern of an unscheduled load-shedding. It smacked more of deliberate mischief.

'*Arrey*, what happened?' I exclaimed.

'Switch on the generator,' someone shouted.

And then a shot rang out. 'Noooooo!' Jagannath Rai screamed. Another cracker burst outside, but it was so loud it seemed as if it had burst inside the room, almost shattering my eardrums.

There was complete confusion and pandemonium for the three minutes or so that the house remained in pitch darkness. Then the lights came on, blinding my eyes with their sudden dazzle. The first thing I saw was Vicky Rai's body, slumped below the window, next to the bar. Blood had seeped into his white shirt, turning it crimson. I heard another high-pitched scream and realized it was mine. At that moment ten police constables barged into the hall, led by an Inspector with a curled-up moustache.

'Freeze! Nobody move,' the Inspector bawled, as though this was an episode of *C.I.D.* He saw Vicky Rai's body and bent down to examine it. He felt the wrist and lifted the eyelids. 'He is finished,' he pronounced, before fixing his gaze on the guests in the room. 'I know one of you has done it. So I have cordoned off the entire farmhouse. Now the police will check each and every one of you. No one will be allowed to leave Number Six till our search is over. Preetam Singh, begin frisking the guests.'

I heard this and my hands started turning cold. The American was standing close to me and became the first guest to be searched. A constable asked him to spread his arms and legs. He stood grinning like a scarecrow while the policeman patted him down, and shockingly a sleek black Glock equipped with a silencer emerged from inside his suit. 'What is this?' the constable cried as he dangled the pistol from his index finger.

'Well, dip me in shit and call me stinky!' Larry exclaimed. 'I have no idea how that gun got there. I don't even know how to fire that damn thing.'

'Take him in for questioning,' the Inspector directed the constable and turned his attention to me. 'Shabnamji, if you don't mind, I need to check your purse.' Before I could mouth a suitable protest, he snatched the moccasin bag from my hand. Snapping it open, he sifted through it with the dexterity of a Customs officer. Out came the Beretta. 'Oh! You have a gun too?' he said in the surprised tone of a priest discovering a nun in a brothel.

I detected a sly gleam in the Inspector's eyes as he examined the gun. 'Can I ask you, Miss Shabnam, why you brought this gun to the party?'

'I carry it for self-protection,' I replied icily, hoping he couldn't hear the thudding of my heart as clearly as I could.

He ejected the magazine, examined it and then smelt it.

'Hmmm . . . one bullet has been fired. Are you sure you didn't use it on Vicky Rai?'

'Of course not,' I snapped, adopting the contemptuous tone I use to put down underlings who try to get fresh with me.

'Still, you will have to come to the police station. Meeta –' he gestured to a frumpy-looking lady constable, 'take her away.'

As Meeta was leading me out, I came across Mr Mohan Kumar, now more famous as Gandhi Baba, appearing to have an epileptic fit. He was foaming at the lips and trying desperately to eject something from his mouth. A constable stood next to him with a gleaming Walther PPK, which appeared to have come out of his *kurta* pocket. I wondered how the apostle of non-violence would explain what he was doing with a gun inside the farmhouse. What new version of *gandhigiri* was he trying out?

It seemed that Mr Jagannath Rai was having similar difficulties. 'I am telling you, this is a licensed Webley & Scott which I have been keeping with me for the last twenty years,' he was explaining to a constable who was busy reading the markings on a grey revolver with a wooden butt. Finding that his plea was falling on deaf ears, Jagannath Rai turned to the Inspector. 'Someone has killed my only son. Instead of trying to catch the murderer, you are trying to blame me, the father? I am the Home Minister of Uttar Pradesh. I will have all of you arrested.'

'Look, Mr Rai.' The Inspector glowered at him. 'This is not Uttar Pradesh, where you can do as you please. This is Delhi and here you will do as we please. Every person who has a gun on these premises is a murder suspect. And that includes you. Preetam Singh, take him into custody.'

We were all herded into a blue van with wire-mesh windows and taken to the Mehrauli police station. The record room was the dingiest room in the police station, but it was still better than a lock-up. It was here that I met the two remaining suspects, easily the most intriguing of the lot. One was a short-statured tribal from Jharkhand, with the blackest skin I have ever seen. He took no notice of me, but sat alone on the floor, and appeared to be pining for some girl called Champi. He kept asking every passing constable for news of her. The policemen swore at him and made threatening gestures.

The other suspect was a lanky youth called Munna Mobile with long, curly hair. He was handsome in a rakish kind of way, reminding me of Salim Ilyasi, but there was also a disconcerting cockiness about him. He told me he was out in the garden when the lights went out. But he couldn't explain satisfactorily what he was doing in the garden with a Chinese Black Star pistol in his pocket.

A stream of constables kept entering the record room. They pretended to examine the files but I knew they were interested mainly in ogling me, the biggest celebrity to grace their crummy police station.

Mohan Kumar, a.k.a.Gandhi Baba, wandered around the room like a lost boy before sitting down beside me. He leered at me in an odd way. 'So, Shabnam, have you finally decided to appear in *Plan B*?'

He sounded so eerily like Vicky Rai that I almost jumped out of my skin. The guy really creeped me out.

I shifted immediately to the next bench, where Larry Page sat brooding. The Master's words came to me: 'Of all men's miseries the bitterest is this: to know so much and to have control over nothing.' For the first time I realized what a prisoner on death row was up against. How powerless he must feel against the might of the State. As the uncouth constables undressed me mentally, a lump of fear formed in my throat. I was convinced that sooner or later they would discover the body in Azamgarh, find out that the gun recovered from me was used to kill him and charge me with murder. I would be at the mercy of these lusty-eyed cops, who were already salivating at the prospect of interrogating me. I would certainly be stripped and quite possibly raped.

And even if I managed to survive the murder rap, I wouldn't be able to avoid bankruptcy. This morning I discovered that Bhola has taken money not only from Jugs Luthra, but from at least four other producers.

Jagannath Rai was standing in a corner, busy speaking to his lawyer. But I knew that I didn't need a lawyer; I needed an escape artist.

In the face of my rapidly shrinking options, I reappraised the American sitting next to me. He claimed to be a humble forklift operator, but after the recovery of that Glock from him my hunch was that he was an undercover agent. To earn a reward of fifteen million dollars and get a commendation letter from the US President, he must be the smartest FBI operative in the business, yet he put on a brilliant act of appearing to be dumb, aping those bumbling detectives of film and fiction. He could be my ticket to safety and sanctuary.

I sidled up to him. 'Larry, you said you were in some kind of Witness Protection Programme. Do you think I might be able to join you?'

He almost fell off the bench. 'Say that again?'

'I was thinking, could I come with you to the States?'

'Now you're reading my mail. I'll find out right now,' he trilled and punched a number on his mobile phone.

Within ten minutes he had an answer. 'I've spoken to Lizzie, the CIA Station Chief. She told me she'll pull some strings and get you included in the Witness Protection Programme. She's already working, as we speak, to get us out of here. A USAF Boeing 757 is standing by to fly us to the States. But there is one hitch.'

'What?'

'Lizzie said you can enter the programme only as my lawfully wedded wife.' He fell to his knees and clasped his hands. 'Tell me, Shabnam, will you marry me?'

I gazed at his lovesick face and stood up from the

bench. I walked towards the grille window and looked out. The rain had stopped, but a pale mist hung in the air. The earth was awakening, its fertility rejuvenated. It smelt of mud and grass, fresh and new. The night had ended and the sun was beginning to peek over the horizon, heralding a brand-new day. It touched me with its simple promise and my decision was made.

'Yes.' I let out a deep breath. 'I will marry you, Larry.'

'You've made me happier than a pig in sunshine,' he said, swooning with joy. 'So will you leave films for me?'

I smiled. 'For you, I will even leave the country.' I liked this man. In time I might even come to love him.

Larry did a little jig, then stopped, as if remembering something. 'Lizzie said there was one other thing.'

'What now?'

'You cannot remain Shabnam. Everyone in the Witness Protection Programme has to acquire a whole new ID. You gotta pick a new name and Lizzie will get you a new passport in a jiffy.'

I thought about that new name. Something neat and simple, yet one that would mark a complete break from my *filmi* past. A name that would be the exact opposite of Shabnam Saxena. And it came to me in a flash. 'I've got my new name.' I snapped my fingers.

'What is it? Tell me, tell me,' Larry clamoured.

'Ram Dulari,' I said triumphantly.

SOLUTION

'If you want to live in the city you have to think ahead three turns, and look behind a lie to see the truth and then behind that truth to see the lie.'

Vikram Chandra, *Sacred Games*

20

The Bare Truth

Arun Advani's column, 27 March

MURDER, SEX AND AUDIOTAPE

There was a time when solving murders was easy. They fell into predictable patterns of cause and effect; were slotted into neat categories of motive like *jar, joru* or *jameen*. Money, woman or land.

Nowadays you have serial killers, sex maniacs, junkies and psychopaths stalking our streets. Sick people who kill just for fun. And the graph is rising constantly. A violent crime is committed in India every three minutes, a murder every sixteen. Worse, of the ninety murder cases recorded every day, the vast majority never get solved.

Luckily, the murder of Vivek 'Vicky' Rai will not meet this fate. Because true to the promise I made earlier in this column, I have solved the case, uncovered the bare truth.

I must confess, though, that in this exposé there has been some divine providence at work. People tend to think that the main tools which we investigative journalists use are hidden microphones and miniaturized recording devices. But that is not true. The biggest resource we have is not a piece of electronic equipment; it is the support and cooperation of members of the public. They are the ones who provide the anonymous tip-off which becomes the lead in a murder case. They are the ones whose observant eyes and alert ears often result in the seizure of a suspect. It is the vigilance and diligence of a concerned citizen which has helped me blow the lid on India's most high-profile murder case.

Yesterday morning a thick packet arrived at my flat. It was yellow, nondescript, with just a typewritten label giving my name and address. When I tore it open, I discovered eight audio tapes nestling inside the bubble wrap. I spent the whole of yesterday and most of last night listening to and transcribing the tapes.

The entire transcript will be published in tomorrow's edition of this newspaper. Reserve your copy now, because the evidence on what I have named the 'Jagannath Rai Tapes' is nothing short of explosive.

There were six suspects in Vicky Rai's murder, but only one murderer. As I write this, the ballistics report has yet to come. But there is no need for it now. I can announce the name of the murderer: it is Mukhtar Ansari, a well-known contract killer whose main base of operations is Uttar Pradesh. And the man who gave the contract is none other than Jagannath Rai, the Home Minister of Uttar Pradesh. Vicky Rai's dad.

The Jagannath Rai Tapes are not just a chronicle of a father reaching his nadir. They also document the depths to which our polity has descended. They lay bare the cynical machinations and brazen wheeler-dealing which oil the creaking wheels of democracy in our most populous State. They expose the sordid mess in Uttar Pradesh, which the probing beam of investigative reporting has either not reached or has warped into the pallid light of yellow journalism. The message of the tapes is a bleak one. There are no heroes in shining armour. We are all naked in the hammam. But the buck stops with us, citizens and voters. It is our apathy and indifference that has led to the criminalization of politics and allowed mafia dons like Jagannath Rai to win elections, become MLAs and ministers, and convert the entire State into their fiefdom, where they can break the law with impunity. The Home Minister's involvement in Vicky Rai's death is only the tip of the iceberg. For a fuller record of his murderous (and amorous) activities, readers will have to wait till tomorrow.

Extrapolating from the tapes, I shall now put forward a hypothesis of what really happened on the fateful night of 23 March. Jagannath Rai had decided to get rid of his wayward son to secure the support of his wayward flock of MLAs and become Chief Minister. He gave the contract to his trusted hitman, Mukhtar Ansari. The plan was simple. Jagannath Rai left the service entrance of Vicky Rai's farmhouse unlocked, which enabled Mukhtar Ansari to come in undetected. He had the farmhouse lights switched off at precisely five minutes past midnight. Mukhtar finished off his work in that instant and raced out through the service door before the police swooped down and sealed the exits.

I can only speculate over what the six suspects were doing in Vicky Rai's farmhouse with guns in their possession. But I can say this with complete certainty: they did not kill Vicky Rai. The killer – Mukhtar Ansari – is out there, at large. He needs to be caught before he kills again.

To the Good Samaritan who sent me the tapes, I say 'Thank You'. To Jagannath Rai, I say 'Good Riddance'. The publication of the transcript should signal the termination of both his political and criminal career. It should mark the end of a sorry chapter in the history of the State which has the largest proportion of elected representatives in our Parliament.

It is my fervent hope that the publication of the Jagannath Rai Tapes becomes a clarion call to our leaders and to all citizens of our country. Let us resolve to cleanse the political system of criminal elements and ensure that law-breakers do not become law-makers. That is the only way to safeguard and strengthen our democracy. That is the only way to ensure a future worthy of our children.

21

Breaking News

Aired 28 March – 10:07

THIS IS A RUSH TRANSCRIPT. THIS COPY MAY NOT BE IN ITS FINAL FORM AND MAY BE UPDATED.

BARKHA DAS: The publication of the Jagannath Rai Tapes by Arun Advani has come like a bombshell. Politicians in Lucknow, whose names are featured in the explicit transcripts, are scurrying for cover . . . In a day of fast-moving developments, Jagannath Rai, the Home Minister of Uttar Pradesh, was arrested for the murders of Vicky Rai, Pradeep Dubey, Lakhan Thakur, Navneet Brar and Rukhsana Afsar, and the abduction of Gopal Mani Tripathi's son . . . We have our Lucknow correspondent, Anant Rastogi, standing by. Anant, what's the latest?

ANANT RASTOGI: Barkhaji, it looks like the end of the road for Jagannath Rai. For twenty years he has kept the State in his iron grip, conducting a reign of terror and oppression, but finally the law has caught up with him. I think the People's Welfare Party is now paying the price of keeping criminals like him in its fold.

BARKHA DAS: But Jagannath Rai is claiming that all these cases are fabricated, that there is no evidence, and that this is a conspiracy by the Chief Minister.

ANANT RASTOGI: He cannot deny the evidence on the tapes. Now his voice has been confirmed by experts. The Chief Minister has, therefore, moved swiftly to limit the damage.

BARKHA DAS: Very true, Anant. In fact, a short while ago we managed to speak to the Chief Minister himself. This is what he had to say:

CHIEF MINISTER OF UTTAR PRADESH: My party, the People's Welfare Party, is deeply disturbed at the charges laid against Jagannath Rai. If they are proved to be true then he deserves the severest punishment. Jagannath Rai has not only been removed as Home Minister, he has also been stripped of his membership of the PWP. The entry of criminals into politics is an unfortunate reality and every political party is equally guilty. I take this opportunity to call for soul-searching by all political parties. As a first step to cleanse public life, my party, the PWP, has taken a decision that henceforth no legislator with a criminal record will be made a minister.

BARKHA DAS: Well, those are welcome words from the Chief Minister and we hope other political parties will follow suit. Meanwhile, full-scale efforts are underway to track down Mukhtar Ansari, the contract killer hired by Jagannath Rai. A Special Task Force of police is believed to have obtained some vital clues in the case. We shall keep you posted on the latest developments. For now, this is Barkha Das signing off for ITN Live.

Breaking News

Aired 28 March – 14:35

THIS IS A RUSH TRANSCRIPT. THIS COPY MAY NOT BE IN ITS FINAL FORM AND MAY BE UPDATED.

BARKHA DAS: There have been dramatic developments in the Vicky Rai murder case. Police have reported a breakthrough in their hunt for Mukhtar Ansari. His badly decomposed body was discovered earlier today in a house in Sarai Meer on the outskirts of Azamgarh. Forensic experts have confirmed that he died of a gunshot wound, and that his body had been lying in the house for at least a week. If this is correct, there is no way Mukhtar Ansari could have been in Vicky Rai's farm-house on 23 March. So who killed Vicky Rai? To answer this question, I now have the Police Commissioner of Delhi, Mr K. D. Sahay, joining us via videolink. Thank you, Sir, for talking to us. I believe you have some news in the Vicky Rai murder case?

K. D. SAHAY: Well, Barkha, first of all I want to caution your viewers that they should not believe all that they read in the papers. The great investigative journalist Arun Advani's famous hypothesis has been exposed as a fabric of lies.

BARKHA DAS: With due respect, Arun Advani couldn't have known about Mukhtar Ansari's murder. But have you got any more leads, Sir?

K. D. SAHAY: Leads? We've cracked the case! I am in a position to tell your viewers who killed Vicky Rai. You see, we had six suspects who were all found to be carrying guns on the night of the murder. And we managed to recover the bullet, which passed through Vicky Rai's body and got lodged in the wooden bar. The final ballistics report which came in yesterday showed that Vicky Rai was killed by a .32 bore bullet. And the gun which matched the bullet was recovered from Jiba Korwa, a tribal from Jharkhand. He was carrying a locally made improvised revolver of .32 bore, popularly called a *katta*, and that has been conclusively proven to be the murder weapon. Jiba Korwa was seen lurking near the mains switchboard. It was he who first switched off the lights, then ran into the hall and shot Vicky Rai.

BARKHA DAS: And what is Jiba Korwa's explanation for being in the farmhouse that night?

K. D. SAHAY: He gave us a cock-and-bull story – pardon the expression – that he had come to the farmhouse to steal a *shivling* which belonged to his tribe, but Vicky Rai never had this *shivling* in the first place. Our contacts with police in other States have revealed that Korwa has a criminal record a mile long. He is wanted for fraud in Tamil Nadu and murder in Bihar. But the real breakthrough came when we searched Korwa's quarters and recovered a considerable amount of Naxalite literature. We believe he is one of the ringleaders of the Maoist Revolutionary Centre, an outlawed Naxalite group responsible for killing over one hundred policemen in Jharkhand alone.

BARKHA DAS: But why would the Naxalites target someone like Vicky Rai?

K. D. SAHAY: Because Vicky was investing in the Special Economic Zone project in Jharkhand. The Naxalites had been sending him death threats. Finally they got him. But we have also got the murderer – Naxalite leader Jiba Korwa.

BARKHA DAS: Thank you, Mr Commissioner, and congratulations on solving this case. That was Police Commissioner K .D. Sahay. So it looks like the final chapter in the Vicky Rai murder case has been written. Or has it? This is Barkha Das, reporting for ITN Live.

Breaking News

Aired 31 March – 13:21

THIS IS A RUSH TRANSCRIPT. THIS COPY MAY NOT BE IN ITS FINAL FORM AND MAY BE UPDATED.

BARKHA DAS: In a sensational development, well-known actress Shabnam Saxena and her secretary Bhola Srivastava were arrested today in an apartment in Khar, Mumbai, for the murder of Mukhtar Ansari. Several incriminating tapes were also recovered from the couple's possession. We have our Mumbai correspondent Rakesh Vaidya standing by. Rakesh, what do you have for us?

RAKESH VAIDYA: Well, Barkha, after Sanjay Dutt's conviction in the 1993 Mumbai serial blasts case, this is easily the biggest scandal to hit the Indian film world. The industry is still in shock. Producers who had paid millions to Shabnam are keeping their fingers crossed.

BARKHA DAS: Do the police have any idea what might have prompted such a prominent actress to do such a thing?

RAKESH VAIDYA: Well, the police are working on several leads right now, Barkha. What I have learnt is that Shabnam was having a love affair with her secretary, Bhola Srivastava, who had made several rather graphic tapes of her. These tapes somehow fell into the hands of Mukhtar Ansari, who began blackmailing her. So Shabnam went to Azamgarh to pay off Mukhtar and retrieve the tapes. We don't know what really happened in Azamgarh, but there are witnesses who saw her leaving the house where Mukhtar Ansari's body was subsequently found. As you know, she was also one of the suspects in Vicky Rai's murder, but had been allowed to go after ballistics confirmed that the gun found in her possession was not the murder weapon. Now the police have conclusive proof that the same gun was used to kill Mukhtar Ansari. The tapes have also been recovered from Bhola Srivastava's flat, so it all seems to fit in.

BARKHA DAS: Do we have any word from Shabnam at all? How is she responding to these allegations?

RAKESH VAIDYA: Well, Barkha, the bizarre thing is that Shabnam Saxena is now claiming she is not Shabnam Saxena at all, but some girl called Ram Dulari from a village in Bihar. She says she has never been to Azamgarh in her life and was only Shabnam's stunt double. Obviously no one is buying this outlandish theory. It looks to me as if she is going to go for an insanity plea. I can say this—

BARKHA DAS: One second, Rakesh, I have just been handed a note which says that a short while ago police shot dead Jiba Korwa, the notorious Naxalite leader, as he was attempting to escape from the Mehrauli police station lock-up. The Maoist Revolutionary Centre has condemned the police action and vowed to take revenge. But coming back to the Shabnam Saxena saga, Rakesh, it seems to be getting curiouser and curiouser.

RAKESH VAIDYA: Absolutely, Barkha. At this point only one thing is clear. We will not be seeing any new Shabnam Saxena releases for a long time. No pun intended. (*Laughter.*)

BARKHA DAS: Thanks, Rakesh. Well, just a reminder of our top story. Shabnam Saxena and her secretary and lover Bhola Srivastava are in jail for the murder of dreaded gangster Mukhtar Ansari. We don't know how this will turn out in the end, but it has all the hallmarks of a blockbuster. We will continue to keep you updated on this fast-developing story as more reports come in. And don't forget to tune in to our 'Insight' special at 19:00 hours. Tonight we focus on Bollywood's links to crime. This is Barkha Das signing off for ITN Live.

24

The Bare Truth

Arun Advani's column, 1 April

J'ACCUSE!

Dear Madame President,

As a concerned citizen of this great democratic country, I am compelled to write this letter to you. You are the highest constitutional functionary in the land. On you rests the mantle of upholding the Constitution. I felt it my duty, therefore, to remind you that the 'Right to Life and Liberty' guaranteed by Article 21 of our Constitution was denied yesterday to an Indian citizen by the name of Jiba Korwa.

Jiba Korwa who? you might ask. According to the police, he was a dreaded terrorist belonging to the outlawed Maoist Revolutionary Centre, who was shot dead yesterday afternoon by Sub-Inspector Vijay Yadav as he attempted to escape from the Mehrauli police station lock-up, where he was being detained in connection with the murder of industrialist Vicky Rai. Ballistics evidence had already proved conclusively that the bullet which killed Vicky Rai was fired from the gun which was discovered in Korwa's possession on the night of the murder. Apparently, before he was killed Korwa even signed a confession statement. His death, therefore, marks a neat, tidy ending. As I write this, the police must be patting themselves on the back for having solved this high-profile murder case without having to toil at the courts. A few gallantry medals are probably being doled out to the valiant Inspector Vijay Yadav and his team, who shot dead the feared Naxalite and made our capital a safer, more secure place. The media has already moved on to other stories. Who is interested in the life of a wretched Naxalite from some dusty village in Jharkhand anyway? And the death of a terrorist has become so banal and commonplace that we do not linger over it for more than a few moments, before moving on to much more interesting things, like the shenanigans of Shabnam Saxena or the gossip behind the latest Cabinet reshuffle.

To paraphrase Shakespeare, I come to bury Jiba, not to praise him. But what if I were to tell you, Madame President, that the man the police killed was not Jiba Korwa at all? That far from being a Naxalite terrorist, he was the custodian of an almost extinct heritage, one of the last of the planet's first humans? There, I think I am finally getting your attention.

Jiba Korwa's real name was Eketi. He was not from Jharkhand, but from an island called Little Andaman in the Bay of Bengal. He belonged to the Onge tribe, a Negrito race of primitive hunter-gatherers which still uses bows and arrows. At the last count, there were ninety-seven Onge left. Thanks to Sub-Inspector Vijay Yadav, now there are only ninety-six.

How do I know all this? you might ask, Madame President. You see, I met Eketi the day before he was killed. At three p.m. on 30 March, I presented myself at the Mehrauli police station and produced an ID which identified me as Akhilesh Mishra, Joint Director in the Intelligence Bureau looking after Internal Security, with special oversight for the Naxalite Cell. Inspector Rajbir Singh, the Station House Officer, saluted me smartly and took me to the lock-up where Jiba Korwa was being held.

It was a small, claustrophobic space, ten feet by eight feet, with mouldy walls, a cracked stone floor and a small grilled window framing a sliver of blue sky. It contained a metal bed with a torn and tattered mattress, an earthen pot for water, and a filthy plastic bucket. The day was unusually warm and the heat in the cell was almost suffocating. But more than by the heat, my senses were assailed by a fetid, cloying smell, the odour of neglect. 'The bastard refuses to wear clothes, doesn't bathe, and they don't use a deodorant where he comes from, Sir,' Inspector Singh offered by way of explanation.

The prisoner was lying curled up in a foetal position on the ground, underneath the window, with his back towards us, so I couldn't see his face. His skin was very dark, the colour of polished ebony, and he had close-cropped, peppercorn hair. He was naked save for a red loincloth, which appeared to have been fashioned from the remains of a T-shirt. He seemed oblivious to our presence and didn't wake up even when the Inspector prodded him with his cane.

'Get up, you bastard!' the Inspector commanded and kicked him in the back three or four times. I winced. But the blows didn't seem to register on the prisoner at all. He remained in his curled-up position, as if in a catatonic trance.

'You don't need to get physical,' I said to the Inspector and gently patted the prisoner on the shoulder.

It was like a magic formula. The prisoner reacted instantly, turning around and sitting up with alacrity. He was quite short, just under five feet, but it was a shock to see how young he was. He had a chiselled, oval face, with high cheekbones and full lips. There was not an ounce of extra fat on his body. He had the lean, toned physique of a prizefighter, but I could see clearly the welt marks where the police had whipped him. His teeth were even and dazzling white, but it was his eyes which had me riveted. Clear white, with small black irises, they seemed to ooze an elemental force. They bore into me like twin points of a laser, unsettling me. Dressed in my crisp white shirt and brown corduroy trousers, I felt exposed, naked and vulnerable in his presence.

It was only then that I noticed he was chained by his leg to the bed and there were manacles on his hands. 'This is for our protection, Sir, this chap is very dangerous, one of the ringleaders of the Naxalites,' the Inspector added, and walked out, leaving me alone with the prisoner.

I did not introduce myself. I simply took his hand in mine, looked into his eyes and said, 'I know you are not a Naxalite. I know you did not kill Vicky Rai.'

He appraised me with frank curiosity.

'Tell me your story, and I promise to get you out of here,' I assured him.

He was shy and reticent at first, but under my gentle prodding, opened up to me. What he didn't tell the police, despite three days of continuous torture, he told me in three hours, simply because I treated him as a fellow human being. He spoke in simple Hindi, but once he began his story, there was no stopping him. It was a cathartic outpouring of all the pent-up emotion bubbling inside him ever since he landed on the shores of our peninsula six months ago. He spoke of the people he had met and the experiences he had had. He spoke of his dreams and his desires, his hurts and humiliations, his hopelessness and helplessness. Above all, he spoke of his yearning for his island and his love for a blind, deformed girl called Champi, better known as the Face of Bhopal.

Did you know, Madame President, that the word 'Onge' means 'Man'? Eketi was a true man, the last of a vanishing breed.

He had ventured knowingly into what his tribe calls the land of the *kwentale*, or foreigners. For a brief while he was blinded by the glare of our civilization, entranced by the alluring traps of modernity, but very soon he saw through the artificial glitter of our lives to glimpse the darkness which festers in our cities and in our hearts. He was horrified by the elaborate cruelty we perpetrate on each other in the name of war and religion. He was shocked by the way we treat our women as sex objects and violate them to satisfy our lust. Within six months he had seen enough. He wanted to return to his island, to his own primitive way of life where want exists but war doesn't, where disease exists, but depravity doesn't.

He was an unlikely prophet, a memento mori who held up a mirror to our faces, but we did not heed him. He tried to correct us; we tried to corrupt him. He extended a hand of friendship; we chained him and manacled him. He sought our understanding; we killed him. His death serves as a précis of our culture, a withering indictment of all that is wrong with us. This is the bare truth, Madame President, and it is terrifying.

Even more terrifying is the fact that he had nothing to do with Vicky Rai's murder. Eketi had come to mainland India on a quest, having taken a vow to recover an ancient stone, shaped like a phallus, which had been protecting his tribe for centuries but which had fallen prey to the greed of an Indian welfare officer posted on Little Andaman. Another welfare officer called Ashok Rajput offered to help the tribe recover the sacred stone and smuggled Eketi to our shores. The quest for the *ingetayi* took Eketi from Kolkata to Chennai, to the *ghats* of Varanasi and the Magh Mela in Allahabad, then to the desert sands of Jaisalmer and finally to our capital city. The sacred rock was last seen in possession of the now disgraced guru Swami Haridas in Allahabad. That is where it was stolen by Ashok Rajput, who, unknown to Eketi, had his own agenda.

You see, Madame President, Ashok Rajput was the brother of Kishore Rajput, the forest ranger working in the wildlife sanctuary in Rajasthan who was eliminated twelve years ago because he would have implicated Vicky Rai in the killing of the two black bucks. Ashok Rajput was in love with his brother's wife, a fiery woman called Gulabo, but the widow had made a condition before she would agree to marry him – that he must first avenge his brother's death and kill Vicky Rai. You probably know more about these Rajasthani women, Madame President, but I know something about revenge. It does not have an expiry date.

So Ashok Rajput spun Eketi a yarn that the *ingetayi* was now in Vicky Rai's farmhouse and brought him to Delhi. Eketi stayed in the Bhole Nath Temple in Mehrauli, close to the farmhouse. While the tribal befriended the blind Champi, Ashok Rajput made his plan. On the night of the murder, he entered the farmhouse well before Eketi did, through an unused rear door. He came in wearing a blue suit, planted the *shivling* in the small temple in Vicky Rai's garden, and then merged with the other guests. Eketi was instructed to come in at ten o'clock, switch off the mains just after midnight, run to the temple, take the sacred rock and quickly dash out of the farmhouse through the same rear gate. The lights were switched off at exactly five minutes past midnight. That is when Ashok Rajput shot Vicky Rai at point-blank range. Then he rushed out of the hall, stole into the temple which Eketi had already reached and deposited the murder weapon in the tribal's open canvas bag. When Eketi retrieved the sacred rock from the temple and put it in his canvas bag, he inadvertently also took the gun. Ashok Rajput was hoping that Eketi would manage to smuggle the murder weapon out of the farmhouse, but the tribal was nabbed by the police and subsequently framed for murder.

The police tortured Eketi for three days, but he adamantly refused to squeal on Rajput, sticking to a code of honour that we abandoned long ago.

Yesterday, according to police accounts, Eketi ripped out his manacles, broke open the chain, used his teeth to bite through the iron bars of his window and slithered out of it. Sub Inspector Yadav, who happened to be standing behind the police station, saw Eketi escaping and challenged him to stop. The tribal charged at him, forcing Yadav to shoot him dead.

I wonder, Madame President, if you saw the pictures they put out of Inspector Yadav and his team grinning over the tribal's bloated body. Eketi's face is twisted at an absurd angle, showing the impossibility of his escape. There is a grimace frozen on his face, mocking the scales of justice.

In a way we are all responsible for Eketi's death, complicit in the act through our conspiracy of silence and our tolerance of injustice. There is an epidemic of apathy in our country which will result in the deaths of many more Eketis, unless we do something to restore the moral fabric of our society.

But this letter is becoming far too long, Madame President, and it is time to conclude it.

I accuse retired welfare officer S. K. Banerjee of stealing the sacred rock from the Onge, which compelled Eketi to undertake a hazardous journey to mainland India, where he eventually met his death.

I accuse Sub Inspector Vijay Singh Yadav of torturing and killing Eketi, in complete contravention of the laws of the land and without due process. This police officer has a history of sadistic behaviour, which has resulted in several custodial deaths over the years. It is time that we divested him of his uniform and put him on trial for murder.

I accuse Police Commissioner K. D. Sahay of being complicit in Eketi's death by failing to ensure his safety in the police lock-up and accepting his 'signed' confession when Eketi didn't even know how to write.

I accuse Inspector Rajbir Singh of falsely implicating Eketi as a Naxalite without verifying his antecedents. One does not expect inspectors to be amateur anthropologists, but surely anyone with common sense will know that there are no jet-black *adivasis* in Jharkhand with negro-style peppercorn hair.

I accuse the crime-scene experts of not exerting due diligence and failing to establish the connection between Eketi and Ashok Rajput.

Finally, I accuse Ashok Rajput of murdering Vicky Rai and framing an innocent tribal.

In making these accusations I am aware that I am opening myself to libel. I also freely admit to having transgressed the law by impersonating a government officer. I expose myself to these risks voluntarily, in the interest of serving the ends of justice.

Let the police come and arrest me. I am waiting. But my voice will not be stilled. Come what may, I shall continue to dare to tell the bare truth.

With my deepest respect, Madame President,
Your fellow citizen and loyal Indian,
Arun Advani.

25
Breaking News

Aired 2 April – 15:37

THIS IS A RUSH TRANSCRIPT. THIS COPY MAY NOT BE IN ITS FINAL FORM AND MAY BE UPDATED.

BARKHA DAS: On 13 January 1898, writer Emile Zola's famous incendiary open letter to the President of France blew the lid off the Dreyfus Affair and caused 'one of the great commotions of history'. Investigative journalist Arun Advani's 2,402-word open letter to the President of India – an impassioned defence of the tribal Eketi, who was wrongly killed for the murder of Vicky Rai – has similarly electrified the nation. The government has been compelled to swing into action. Sub Inspector Vijay Yadav has been arrested and charged with the murder of Eketi Onge. Inspector Rajbir Singh and Police Commissioner K. D. Sahay have both been suspended. A nationwide manhunt has been launched for Ashok Rajput. We have our crime correspondent Jatin Mahajan standing by in front of Mehrauli police station. Let's turn to him for the latest. Jatin, we are hearing reports of commotion outside the police station. What's happening?

JATIN MAHAJAN: It is unbelievable, Barkha. We are witnessing extraordinary scenes. The entire population of the Sanjay Gandhi slum, it seems, has come out on to the streets and surrounded the police station. Slogans are being raised against the police and Sub Inspector Vijay Yadav.

BARKHA DAS: Who is leading the demonstrators, Jatin?

JATIN MAHAJAN: It is Munna Mobile, who, you will recall, was himself a suspect in the Vicky Rai murder case. A large number of students have also joined the slum-dwellers. There is considerable anger at the death of Eketi. Arun Advani's latest piece has really galvanized the public. People are saying that they have had enough. They will not tolerate police brutality and high-handedness any longer. They will not have one kind of justice for the rich and another for the poor.

BARKHA DAS: Absolutely, Jatin. In fact, responding to the public sentiment, the government has already announced that a whole host of high-profile cases in which the rich and famous had been let off are now going to be re-opened. A commission is being set up to look at reforms of the police and of the entire system of collecting evidence.

JATIN MAHAJAN: Also don't forget, Barkha, the government has announced another look at the entire compensation package for the victims of the Bhopal Gas Tragedy.

BARKHA DAS: Yes, Eketi's death has also focused the spotlight on Champi Bhopali, the Face of Bhopal. The tribal was in love with her and had promised to cure her blindness. How has his death affected her, Jatin?

JATIN MAHAJAN: Well, Barkha, Champi refuses to believe that Eketi is dead. She claims he visits her every night and talks to her.

BARKHA DAS: Isn't it one of the great ironies of our time that all these years when Champi Bhopali was highlighting the plight of the victims denied compensation in the Bhopal Gas Tragedy, no one thought about her own plight, Jatin?

JATIN MAHAJAN: Precisely, Barkha. All of us remember her as the Face of Bhopal, but none of us thought of doing anything for that face. Only now, following the public outcry over Eketi's murder, have a whole host of individuals and NGOs stepped forward to help her. Sufficient funds have been collected for her plastic surgery. There is even talk of a retinal eye transplant which might restore her vision. So in death Eketi may have done more for her than we, the living, were ever going to do.

BARKHA DAS: Well, Eketi's death has clearly been a much-needed wake-up call for all of us. Are we looking at the dawn of a new India? This is the question I will be posing in *Burning Issue* immediately after the nine o'clock news. Do join me for that panel discussion. This is Barkha Das reporting for ITN Live.

26

Sting Operation

'Welcome, welcome, Singhania. Come and have some sweets. Today is one of the greatest days of my life. Second only to the day I became Chief Minister.'

'I know, Netaji. I just heard the news on the radio. '

'Yes. Jagannath Rai has been formally charged with the murders of Pradeep Dubey, Lakhan Thakur and Navneet Brar and with the abduction of Gopal Mani Tripathi's son. We couldn't pin the Rukhsana Afsar suicide on him, but it doesn't matter. With Tripurari Sharan turning approver, we have enough to hang Jagannath. Now all the party MLAs who joined him are in hot water. I am demanding two crores from each of them before I agree to take them back. They have to pay a price for their foolishness.'

'So your Chief Minister's chair is safe till the next elections.'

'Why only till the next elections? Haven't you seen the opinion poll in the *Daily News*? My decision to get rid of all tainted ministers has boosted my approval ratings to 67 per cent. High Command has now given me a totally free hand. I think another term is a sure shot.'

'Jagannath Rai's downfall has been very swift indeed.'

'That bastard thought he was being very clever, getting all his dirty work done by Mukhtar. But these twopenny gangsters can never beat us professional politicians. The idiot believed that just because he was Home Minister he was above the law. He didn't have a clue that I had been having his phone tapped for the last three years. And people can be so indiscreet on the phone.'

'Is that why you never discuss business with me on the phone?'

'One can never be too careful, Singhania. Though no one would dare tap the Chief Minister's phone. (*Laughs.*)

'So was it you who sent the tapes to Advani?'

'Who else, Singhania? Use a snake to kill a snake. Advani promptly published the tapes, finishing Jagannath's political career and eliminating the biggest threat to my post. It's a pity Mukhtar wasn't allowed to kill Vicky Rai. That would have been the icing on the cake. Why did Shabnam Saxena do something so idiotic?'

'I have no time for Shabnam Saxena. My biggest headache is Ashok Rajput.'

'Ashok Rajput? That fellow who murdered Vicky Rai? What's your connection to him?'

'He is the son of Vinay Rajput, who was my father's masseuse. You know we are originally from Rajasthan. I grew up with Kishore and Ashok in Jaisalmer. When Kishore died, I helped Ashok get that job in the Tribal Welfare Department.'

'Is it true, this story about him wanting to marry his brother's widow?'

'Yes, Netaji. Gulabo was always a bit weird. It was at her urging that Ashok decided to kill Vicky Rai.'

'Aha! So Rajput has already confessed his crime to you.'

'Yes, he has. He told me this was his second attempt. About six years ago he managed to enter the farmhouse with a gun, but his nerve failed him at the last minute. This time round he decided to take advantage of that tribal Eketi. I actually saw Ashok at the party, dressed in a snazzy blue suit. I found it strange that he had been invited to

Number Six, but even I couldn't have guessed that he had gained entry to kill Vicky Rai. Now, since 24 March he has been holed up at my Meerut guesthouse. He thought he had got away with murder when the police arrested Eketi, but that Arun Advani is too clever. How he ferrets out information is simply amazing.'

'What are you going to do about Rajput?'

'I have been advising him to go to the police and make a clean breast of it. But he is still hoping for a miracle and has asked me to give you a message.'

'What is that?'

'Ashok Rajput is willing to give you this stunning *shivling* (*sound of unwrapping*), if you can somehow save him from the gallows.'

'*Arrey*, isn't this the *shivling* that the tribal was trying to steal on the night of the murder?'

(*Laughs.*) 'No, Netaji. Ashok Rajput had a replica made by a sculptor in Jaisalmer and planted it in the temple in Vicky Rai's garden. What you are seeing is the genuine article, which he stole from Swami Haridas in Allahabad.'

'*Wah!* What a magnificent piece. So smooth, and what are all these strange letters on it?'

'According to Onge legend, these were engraved by the first man. Chief Minister Sahib, this *shivling* is the rarest and most ancient antique in the country. It's priceless.'

'I want it, Singhania, and in return I will try to save your friend. Because I know he is innocent.'

'And on what basis are you saying this, Netaji?'

'On the basis of what Delhi Police Commissioner K. D. Sahay told me in confidence. KD and I are old friends. You see, the police discovered another spent .32 bore cartridge in the garden of Vicky's farmhouse.'

'But Rajput fired only once.'

'Exactly. So there was another person who fired a bullet at Vicky Rai that night.'

'It makes sense . . . I thought I heard another gunshot immediately after the first one, but others said it was a cracker burst.'

'It was this second gunshot that actually killed Vicky Rai. The bullet passed cleanly through his body and landed in the garden.'

'But then the police should have found another gun!'

'That is where the problem lies! KD says the police sealed the premises immediately after the first gunshot. So the murderer couldn't have managed to escape. Then they went over the farmhouse with a toothcomb. They frisked each and every person present at Number Six. Checked every vehicle that was parked inside and on the road. But they did not discover any other gun, apart from the six recovered from the six suspects. So they went for the only option available to them. They pinned the murder on Eketi, and suppressed all evidence of the second bullet and the seventh gun.'

'Oh my God! Then who is the real killer?'

'Singhania, you have wealth, but you don't have brains. Now I will tell you who really killed Vicky Rai.'

'Who, Netaji?'

'It was Jagannath's daughter, Ritu.'

'Ritu Rai? But how? And how do you know this?'

'This was revealed to me by my new best friend, Tripurari Sharan. But before I tell you his theory, I have to tell you a little story. I have a man who occasionally works for me called Chhotu Lochan.'

'Oh, that notorious gangster?'

'What can I do? Politics demands both money and muscle. Even Chief Ministers have to keep some pet dogs. Just as Jagannath had Mukhtar, I have Lochan. I have used him for a few operations. '

'Go on, this is getting interesting.'

'Lochan told me that on 20 January he kidnapped a child from Noida, the seven-year-old son of an industrialist who owns four factories. Ransom was set at seventy-five lakhs. The father delivered the money on 26 January, Republic Day. It was put in a black attaché case and left inside a dustbin in an alley behind the Goenka School in Mehrauli. Lochan's man Brijesh was to collect it, but Brijesh's mobile phone was stolen by Munna Mobile. So when Lochan relayed the pick-up location, Munna heard it and made off with the briefcase.'

'Don't tell me! That two-bit mobile-phone thief got away with seventy-five lakhs?'

'Yes. It was with all that money that he befriended Ritu Rai, started a love affair.'

'Then what happened?'

'What always happens. Lochan tracked down Munna Mobile eventually. The tentacles of these people extend everywhere. So he sent in three of his goons, who beat Munna up badly, even broke his fingers, and took back the briefcase.'

'How sad! That is what I don't like about gangsters. The way they resort to violence. I abhor violence. '

'Anyway, the twist in the tale is that Munna never told Ritu about the briefcase, but Ritu told her family about wanting to marry Munna. Both Vicky and Jagannath were completely opposed to it. Tripurari says there were daily show-downs between brother and sister. So when she discovered what had been done to Munna, she thought that Vicky Rai had sent in the goons to teach Munna a lesson, and flew into a rage. Ritu is adept at handling guns. Did you know she is the State air-pistol champion? So on the night of the party, she, too, was in the hall with a gun. It was she who got the fuse taken out of the mains switchboard at a pre-determined time. As soon as the lights went out, she shot her brother with a .32-bore pistol and then hid the murder weapon in some private nook of the house, which the police have not been able to figure out till now.'

'Amazing! So Ritu has got off scot-free?'

'Hasn't she suffered enough, being Jagannath's daughter? Now she is marrying Munna, who, in turn, is getting a hero's role in some film. So it looks like there will be one happy ending at least.'

'Then what should I tell Ashok Rajput?'

'Tell him to stay put while I work out a strategy. And thank him for the *shivling*. It will have pride of place in this house from today.'

'It is supposed to be the ultimate good-luck charm.'

'I can feel the positive vibrations already. Through the blessings of Lord Shiva, I will now remain Chief Minister for the rest of my life.'

'Now, if you have time, Netaji, can I discuss the Badaun Cement Plant with you?'

'I have time to discuss even the textile mill project. The whole State is yours, Singhania. Now that Jagannath is out of the way, we will enjoy the fruits together.'

(*Laughter.*)

CONFESSION

'Nothing in the world is harder than speaking the truth.'

Fyodor Mikhailovich Dostoevsky,
Crime and Punishment

27

The Truth

I COULD TELL you the name I gave the police, but you wouldn't recognize it. A better clue might be the outfit I was wearing. It was a red waistcoat with brass buttons, worn over a white shirt and complemented by pleated black trousers and patent leather shoes. Don't forget those shoes.

No one really took any notice of me. I was deemed to be one of those faceless service people who unobtrusively keep a big party going. I could just as easily have been one of the hordes who fill the streets when there is a big political rally or religious procession, that blur of colour when the TV camera pans over the stands in a cricket match, or in the anonymous queue which forms in front of polling booths during elections.

You want me to be more specific? OK, I was the bearded waiter at the party. I was standing next to Vicky Rai when the lights went out. And I shot him at point-blank range.

If this comes as a shock to you, I apologize. There is something gruesome about murder, about the forcible ending of a life, which doesn't sit well with our conscience and our criminal-justice system. 'Thou shalt not kill' is a biblical injunction, after all. But there are occasions when murder is not only justified, it is necessary. And I am not referring here to legally sanctioned murder: the State executing a terrorist or an enemy soldier killed in war. I am talking about murder as a ritual of righteousness. In the Mahabharata, Arjuna had a duty as a Kshatriya warrior to fight the evil Kauravas on the battlefield of Kurukshetra. I am also a warrior, fighting a righteous war against the forces of evil in society. In killing Vicky Rai I simply did my duty, upheld my *dharma*.

Please believe me, I had no personal score to settle with Vicky Rai. I am not related to any of the six homeless people he mowed down as a teenager. I had never set eyes on Kishore Rajput, the forest ranger whom he got killed. Ruby Gill was neither my colleague, nor my sister, nor my lover. I didn't know her, never met her.

I presume my action will be seen as vigilante justice. The act of a citizen who takes the law into his own hands when the actions of established authorities are insufficient.

And the actions of established authorities clearly were insufficient. Vicky Rai broke one law after another and received one acquittal after another. The final straw came when he was even exonerated of the murder of Ruby Gill.

Our great epics tell us that when evil becomes all-pervasive, God comes down to restore goodness. With all due respect, that's nonsense. No one comes down from heaven to sort out the mess on earth. You have to clean up the shit yourselves. You have to take off your shoes, hitch up your trousers and wade into the sodden muddy pit.

That is what I did. My conscience left me no other choice.

The middle class is supposed to act as the conscience of the nation, an ethical beacon guarding against the excesses of the upper class and the defeatism of the underclass. It is the middle class which challenges the status quo, which brought about the great revolutions of the world – in France, China and Russia, in Mexico, Algeria and Vietnam. But not in India. Our middle class believes firmly in the preservation of the status quo. Unconcerned with the declining standards in public life, apathetic about the plight of the poor, it indulges in rampant consumerism. We have become a nation of voyeurs, hooked on inane soap operas about scheming mothers-in-law and suffering housewives, feeding on the carcass of others' misfortunes, salivating at the break-up of a celebrity marriage, mesmerized by flickering TV images of politicians caught accepting bribes on camera.

I have nothing against voyeurs. I admit, in my younger days even I was tempted occasionally to peep into my neighbour's house, hoping to catch a glimpse of his young daughter taking a bath. But what if instead you catch your neighbour choking his middle-aged wife to death? What do you do then? Do you slink into your bed like a half-guilty thief or do you rush into the neighbour's house and put a stop to the crime?

This was the dilemma I faced when I listened to the tapes of Vicky Rai's conversations. You see, I had been tapping his phone for the past two years, just as the Chief Minister was tapping Jagannath Rai's phone.

When I first began the phone tap, I had no idea what I was getting into. It seemed like a harmless way to ferret out information and it was easy. India is an eavesdropper's paradise. Nobody is bothered about infringement of civil liberties, privacy rights and data protection. All you need is some electronic equipment which can be bought off the shelf from any shop in Palika Bazaar and some connections in the phone department and you are all set for some freelance tapping. I currently have seven intercepts running all the way from Jammu to Jabalpur.

For two years I listened to Vicky Rai's voice on a daily basis. I listened to the favours being exchanged, the bribes being paid, the frauds being perpetrated, the girls being seduced. I heard ear-numbing accounts of how laws were broken and subverted, how evidence was falsified, how justice was trampled upon, raped, pillaged and sold to the highest bidder. Every infraction was like a band of iron squeezing my heart. Every injustice was like a nail being driven into my body.

And then, on 17 March, I heard a conversation which set me on fire. I will play you a small clip from that tape. Listen carefully.

> 'Hello, Vicky baba, recognize me?'
> 'Is it Mukhtar?'

'Yes, Vicky baba. I am sorry to call you so late, but—'

'What's the matter? You sound very worried.'

'You remember, Vicky baba, how we used to play together in Lucknow? You would sit on my back and I would race to the *peepul* tree and then you would say "Take me to—" '

'I am sure you haven't called me at one o'clock in the morning to reminisce about my childhood. Come to the point, Mukhtar. Are you in some kind of trouble again?'

'No, Vicky baba, *you* are in trouble.'

'What do you mean?'

'Boss called me to his house an hour ago.'

'So? Who did Dad want bumped off this time?'

'You, Vicky baba. He gave me a contract to kill you.'

'Have you gone mad?'

'No, Vicky baba. I swear on my dead father. This is exactly what Boss asked me to do.'

(*Long pause.*)

'I still don't believe this.'

'I couldn't either. I have seen you grow up in front of my eyes, Vicky baba. How can I take your life?'

'When did Dad tell you to carry out the hit?'

'On 23 March. When you are going to have some big party at Number Six.'

'I see.'

(*Long pause.*)

'I don't know what's happened to Boss. He is not the man he used to be. This fight for the Chief Minister's chair has warped his brain.'

'Mukhtar, will you do a job for me?'

'*Hukum*, Vicky baba.'

'I want you to kill Mr Jagannath Rai. On the same day, at the same place. I will pay you one hundred times what Dad would have paid you. Will you accept my contract?'

'Vicky baba, how can—'

'I will send you ten lakhs right away, and the balance on

completing the job. You don't need to do any more hits after this one. Do we have a deal?'

'I don't know what to say, Vicky baba.'

'It will be your easiest hit, Mukhtar. I will keep the service entrance unlocked. You come in through there with your gun. I will be at the bar in the big hall and I will ensure that Dad is in the other corner, next to the bay window which opens on to the driveway. At exactly five minutes past midnight I will get my trusted servant Shankar to switch off the mains. Fireworks will already be going on at the time. You finish off your work as soon as the lights blow and race out through the service gate. Can anything be simpler?'

(*Long pause*.)

'Do we have a deal, Mukhtar?'

'Yes, Boss.'

'Good. Then I suggest you disappear for a while. Do not take any calls from Dad.'

'Yes, Boss. I will hole out in Sarai Meer, and then come to Number Six only on the twenty-third.'

'Fine. I will have your advance sent to Azamgarh.'

'*Meherbani. Khuda hafiz.*'

(*Disconnect*.)

Something snapped in my brain when I heard this tape. How long can you see what is happening around you and remain unaffected by it? How long can you pretend you are not a citizen of this country, not a thinking, feeling man? And I said to myself, 'Enough is enough.' I decided to kill Vicky Rai, mete out my own justice to him. If the corrupt father was going to die, then so would the depraved son.

To kill a man you need three things. A powerful motive, strong nerves and a good gun. I was motivated and steady, all I required was a reliable gun. I went for a country-made pistol, a compact semi-automatic .32 fabricated in Bamhaur; cheap, dependable and completely untraceable. Then I paid a visit to Akram Bhai, a wizened old cobbler who owns a small shop behind Jama Masjid, specializing in custom-made footwear. He made me a pair of patent-leather shoes which, once you lifted the insole, contained a hollow compartment in the heel big enough to secrete a wad of cash. Or a bar of gold. Or a compact gun.

So on 23 March, I, too, was in Number Six with a pistol in my pocket. Getting inside the farmhouse was child's play. I slipped in through the unlocked service gate wearing a fake beard and the red-and-black uniform of the waiters from Elite Tent House, who, I knew from an earlier intercept, were doing the catering at the party. I picked up a tray and hung around the garden, watching the guests laughing and the booze flowing. It was a typical Delhi party of the rich, with the usual air-kissing and pointless hugging, the ritual exchange of business cards and the predatory circling of women flaunting their bodies.

Just before midnight, a fireworks display began. Rockets screamed, crackers burst, bombs exploded in celebration of Vicky Rai's acquittal. At the stroke of midnight I moved from the lawn into the big hall. I saw Vicky Rai making a speech in front of a mike. Then he asked his father to speak and went to the bar on the far side of the hall. As he began mixing a drink, I edged closer to him. The room was chock-full of people, including the film star Shabnam Saxena, and it would have been impossible to shoot him and not be caught. My muscles tightened and a knot formed in the pit of my stomach. I waited for the lights to go out. At precisely 12.05 a.m. they did and I whipped out my gun. A shot rang out and Jagannath Rai screamed. Thinking that Mukhtar had done his job, in that very instant I shot Vicky Rai at point-blank range. He was standing directly in front of the open window and my bullet must have passed clean through him. Coincidentally, another loud cracker bomb burst at that very second and camouflaged the sound of my gunshot.

Shooting a man is the easy part. The tough part is keeping your nerves in control after the act. My hands began shaking and my heart started hammering so violently I thought I was going to have a coronary. The gun almost slipped out of my grasp. With trembling fingers I took off my left shoe, lifted the insole and deposited the pistol in the hollow compartment. I had just about managed to retie my shoelace when the lights came back on and the police rushed in. They asked for my name and address. I showed them a fake ID identifying me as a waiter. They frisked me from neck to ankle and didn't find anything. They let me go.

Would I have done things differently if I had known that Mukhtar Ansari was not going to keep his appointment? I don't know. It was only when the lights came on and I saw Jagannath Rai very much alive that I realized something had gone wrong. Now, of course, it is clear that it was Ashok Rajput who fired the first bullet, also a .32 calibre from a locally made improvised revolver. It narrowly missed Vicky and got lodged in the wooden bar. Vicky Rai was actually killed by the second bullet – my bullet. If the police had searched the premises thoroughly they would have discovered a spent .32 cartridge in the garden outside.

I hope you see the irony – Vicky Rai was acquitted in the Ruby Gill murder case because the police said the two bullets were fired from two different guns, but Ashok Rajput has been arrested because this time the police are loath to accept the two-gun theory! If only he had not confessed, a smart lawyer might have been able to get him off.

Many years ago I saw a film – I forget its name. It was one of those arty movies in which people don't speak much and the camera pans slowly, settling on minute details of everyday life, such as an empty swing creaking back and forth for two minutes. The film was about a village full of poor people being exploited by a feudal landlord. Most of the film is a blur to me now, but I still remember its last scene. It showed a small boy throwing a stone at the *zamindar*'s mansion, breaking a window. I was too young then to understand what that stone meant. Now I do. Great revolutions begin with a tiny spark.

I have lit that spark. A revolution is now underway. Youths like Munna Mobile are the foot soldiers of this revolution. They are vociferously demanding their rights. They will no longer tolerate injustice silently.

Just as every revolution has a hero, it also has some collateral damage. I feel a tinge of regret for Ashok Rajput. I genuinely mourn Eketi's death. I did try to help him, but it was a case of too little, too late. His death will forever remain on my conscience, a cross that I have to bear. But his sacrifice was not in vain. Vicky Rai is dead. Jagannath Rai is as good as dead. Justice has been done. Henceforth the criminal rich will no longer be able to sleep easily. They know now that retribution can return to haunt them at any time.

I suppose I can take some pride in carrying out the perfect murder. No one has any inkling about what I have done – neither my wife, nor my colleagues at the newspaper. I still go to the office at the usual time and stay late. I share a meal with the other reporters during the lunch hour, laugh at their corny jokes, join in their silly discussions on politics and promotions. Their petty gossiping and shallow concerns nauseate me. Their smugness and complacency amaze me. Am I the only one with a sense of what it means to be a committed investigative journalist? Am I the only man with a mission?

I know I plough a lonely furrow. But I shall soldier on. Because there is still a lot of filth out there. I am still listening to phone conversations which make my blood boil and start a buzzing in my brain.

And even murder can become addictive.

Acknowledgements

This was a difficult book to write, and not just because it was my second one. The very ambition of the novel – to tell the interlocking stories of six disparate lives in a tightly schematic space – made it a daunting enterprise. That I was able to reach this page owes a lot to the generous support of my friends and colleagues and the patience of my family – my wife Aparna, to whom this book is dedicated, and my sons Aditya and Varun.

Jane Lawson, my editor on *Q & A*, and Peter Buckman, my agent, were early and enthusiastic supporters of the concept and encouraged me to go on. Thereafter it was my new editor Rochelle Venables (Jane having happily pushed off on maternity leave) and the team at Transworld who shepherded the project with admirable vigour and commitment. I must thank Kate Samano, in particular, for her meticulous copyediting.

Even though Eketi is an entirely fictional character, my research on the Onge tribe was aided greatly by Madhusree Mukerjee's lucid book *The Land of the Naked People: Encounters with Stone Age Islanders* (Penguin India, 2003). Vishvajit Pandya's ethnographical inquiry into Andamanese rituals and customs (*Above the Forest*, OUP, 1993) and Badal Kumar Basu's study *The Onge* (Seagull Books, 1990) were also useful sources of information. For those wishing to explore this subject further, I would wholeheartedly recommend George Weber's website (www.andaman.org), a veritable treasure trove of information on the tribes of the Andaman.

I am indebted to my colleagues Navdeep Suri and J. S. Parmar for many valuable suggestions. I also wish to place on record my thanks to Damon Galgut, Chris Copass, Avinash Mohnany, Manoj Malaviya, Sarvagya Ram Mishra, Captain Subhash Gouniyal, R. K. Rathi, Lopa Banerjee, Uma Dhyani, Rati Bhan Tripathi, Vakil Ramdas and Roland Galahargue. Google, as always, was an invaluable tool.

Finally, I must record my gratitude to the wonderful people of South Africa, the fertile ground where this novel took shape on weekends and holidays.